The Third Grace

The Three Graces, by James Pradier, 1831

A Novel

The Third Grace

By Deb Elkink

GREENBRIER BOOK COMPANY, NEW BERN, NC

The Third Grace

Greenbrier Book Company
P.O. Box 12721
New Bern, NC 28561
Visit our Website at www.greenbrierbooks.com

The characters and events in this book are fictitious. Any similarity to real persons, living or dead, is coincidental and not intended by the author.

Most scripture quotations are taken from the Holy Bible, New International Version®. NIV®. Copyright © 1973, 1978, 1984 by International Bible Society. Used by permission of Zondervan Publishing House.

Cover design by Anton Khodakovsky

Cover photograph by Jeff Ruane

ISBN: 978-1-937573-00-3

First Print Edition

To all my lost sisters wandering alone
out of earshot—His voice still calls.

Acknowledgments

Thank you, my dear family—**Gerrit,** for giving me the rural life and funding trips to France; **Tyler,** for your literacy; **Meghan,** for your confidence; and **Challis,** for your unflagging encouragement. You cheered me on till the cows came home.

I'd also like to thank **Elma Eidse Neufeld,** for passing on to me Mennonite taste buds and faith; **Lorenda Harder,** for exclaiming approvingly during long-distance readings; **Derrick Neufeld** and **Bruce Hindmarsh,** for in different ways introducing me to the world of academia; **Grant Richison,** for holding out to me the Word of life; *mes amies françaises* **Christelle, Flo, Hélène,** and **Alix,** for linguistic and cultural guidance; countless friends (a handful of whom read an early draft), for nipping at my heels until the finished product was delivered; and of course **Ron and Janet Benrey** of Greenbrier Book Company, for affording this late-blooming novelist the joy of publication.

Man has always lost his way.
He has been a tramp ever since Eden;
but he always knew, or thought he knew,
what he was looking for.
—G.K. Chesterton, *What's Wrong with the World*

Be mindful, goddess! of thy promise made;
Must sad Ulysses ever be delay'd?
Around their lord my sad companions mourn,
Each breast beats homeward, anxious to return.
—Homer, *Odyssey*

One

Light from the floor lamp winked at Aglaia through the garnet wine as her guest swirled the glass upward—winked as though it shared Aglaia's secret, just waiting for her to ask her question again. But she held back. She was pacing herself…

She studied the profile of Dr. Lou Chapman, the critical eye and the nose thrust aggressively into the bouquet of the vintage. She shifted on the sofa and reached for her goblet to mimic Lou's actions, careful not to slosh her own wine over the rim. She didn't want to appear gauche; it was awkward enough trying to draw out from Lou the information she needed to prevail in her search.

Maybe she shouldn't have asked the professor up following the theater tonight after all, she thought. Work had been demanding of late, and this afternoon's traffic brutal in the drenching rain. She'd arrived back at her apartment with no time to slouch into relaxation—just a few minutes to pin her hair into a messy nest and slip on the sapphire chemise that now lay against her skin, silky as a French boy's whisper.

"Nice legs," Lou said.

Aglaia crossed them instinctively but caught herself before saying thanks, realizing just in time that the compliment was intended for the wine. Feeling foolish, she straightened her back and feigned a worldly, knowing air.

Lou picked up the bottle, tilted it towards the light, and read the label through the bottom half of trendy spectacles. "Where did you purchase it?"

"At Santé on East Sixth Avenue," Aglaia said with a shrug, as though she stopped in at the posh Denver cellar regularly on her way home from work rather than just the once—last week for a tasting with her wine appreciation class. But Aglaia wondered if she'd ever truly appreciate wine. This bottle of imported pinot noir had cost her dearly but it was worth the money to gain Lou's confidence and, besides, Aglaia's growing collection of corks in the green bowl on the coffee table proved she was recovering from her habit of temperance.

With eyes closed Lou sampled the wine, swished, sucked air in past pursed lips. "Subdued, earthy with a subtle berry, long finish. Excellent choice."

Aglaia couldn't detect earth or berry, but she was glad now she hadn't caved in to her first impulse to grab a domestic merlot at half the price.

"A toast to your enduring success in the arts," Lou said, wine stem raised, "even if it is in the private sector instead of the university, where talent like yours belongs."

Glasses clinked; the two women sipped.

Aglaia swallowed the astringent and watched Lou's eyebrows, the most animated part of her face. They signaled her mood, usually dipping downward at the outer edges in world-weariness but arching now in approval. Lou's slate-cold eyes themselves were flat, two dimensional, and gave nothing away.

Aglaia angled her glass and looked into its blood-red interior. Wine was a symbol of communion, she thought, and she was using it with carnal deliberation to seal this relationship that had so much to offer her. As she lifted the glass to her lips again, she hoped her own silhouette projected an image of glamor. Alcohol had been taboo in the home of her youth. In her current lapsed state, the mere thought of consuming it was intoxicating in itself—

and emboldening. She was about to pose her question again when Lou spoke up.

"The costumes in tonight's performance were remarkable, but your Phantom stole the show."

"Not *my* Phantom exactly," Aglaia said.

"Don't be coy. You're obviously an accomplished artisan and you deserve to be discovered."

Heat rushed to Aglaia's cheeks but she knew she'd earned the praise. Her boss at Incognito Costume Shop wouldn't let another employee touch the feature pieces contracted for the production, and they'd shown well on stage tonight.

Earlier this evening the curtains had closed to robust applause, but Aglaia waited until the last scalloped hem and tip of a feathered cap disappeared into the wings before joining in with the rest of the audience. When she recognized a critic from the *Denver Post* dashing backstage for an interview with the cast, she knew for certain that the name of Aglaia Klassen, up-and-coming costume designer, would appear again in the weekend reviews; her creations had worked their usual opening night magic. Indeed, Aglaia herself had been transported in her imagination to the play's setting of the world-famous opera house in Paris.

Paris! It was the city of her dreams where, in just three days' time, she'd finally be walking in the flesh. Aglaia took another sip to sober her elation over the imminent business trip, particularly regarding her plans for how she'd spend her free time there. Of course this would include a whirlwind tour of the city sights but other, admittedly idealistic, aspirations were at the forefront of her mind and had been all evening.

After the play, as Lou had driven through the city to take her home, Aglaia barely heard her scholarly assessment of the musical score because she was caught up in her thoughts of international travel. When Aglaia did speak, it was to articulate the undercurrent running though her subconscious for most of the performance—for most of her life, it seemed. That was when she'd casually brought the subject up with Lou.

"I wonder how someone can just disappear in Paris."

Lou, slowing to make the turn onto Aglaia's street, had said, "I suppose you're talking about the masked villain spiriting the fair maiden away to his lair beneath the Opéra Garnier."

"No, I mean nowadays, in real life. How would someone find a missing person in Paris?"

"That's hardly the first question that comes to mind in critiquing *The Phantom of the Opera*," Lou had said, and she coughed out a laugh as if expecting an analysis of the play's Faustian implications or something as cerebral. Aglaia's own interests were much more intuitive, and she'd let the matter drop as Lou pulled into the space facing the apartment block, armed the car lock, and followed her up the steps while pontificating on the literary elements of the script.

Lou had remarked on Aglaia's use of the Greek mask of tragedy as a pattern for the Phantom's own disguise—a clever adaptation—and her mirroring of Hellenistic fashion in the simplicity of the heroine's robe, guessing correctly that Aglaia's inspiration had come from the Greek style of the Opéra's architecture.

But all the while, right up to the time Lou had opened the wine, Aglaia was reviewing and reframing her question—her *quest*—regarding Paris. Lou, a sociologist at Platte River University and a jetsetter, was versed in things European, and Aglaia could use an expert at this point. Her Internet surveillance over the past month had turned up nothing very helpful.

Now Lou plucked a cat hair from the arm of the loveseat and Aglaia regretted not having vacuumed more thoroughly—Lou probably had a cleaning lady. Before the other woman could resume her intellectualized thread of the discussion on the evening's entertainment, and at the risk of sounding fixated, Aglaia ventured a third query.

"So, Lou, if you were looking for someone in Paris, where would you start?"

This time Lou heard her, though she frowned. It clearly wasn't her topic of choice. "Well, maybe I'd launch an investigation through the *préfecture* or contact the American embassy. Sightseers must go missing now and then. Or," she gibed, "are you afraid of getting lost yourself when you're over there, all alone in the big, bad city?"

Aglaia ignored her sarcasm. "It's not a tourist issue."

"You're referring to a resident?" Lou asked with her eyebrow cocked. "The telephone book then, I suppose."

The local phone book, of course. Aglaia would start with that notion as soon as she got to Paris. It might be a long shot, but she had this one chance for disclosure and she wasn't going to let it slip away. She knew now how she would begin her on-site manhunt and felt herself unwinding for the first time all night.

But then the apartment buzzer rasped.

She didn't expect anyone. Before she could answer it, the door was bumped open by her elderly mother. Tina Klassen, cheeks perpetually rouged by prairie wind and high blood pressure, was caught midsentence as though continuing an interrupted dialogue, her Low German accent still discernible.

"… and your father is in such a hurry to get home, Mary Grace. When harvest is wet like this and so late, you know how tense he is."

She pronounced it "tanse" and, more out of habit than necessity, threw a *Plautdietsch* word into her ramble here and there— about the rain rotting the crops on the *Laundt* and about how Henry was waiting in the *Trock* outside. The tongue of the Klassen heritage was still spoken in many rural Mennonite households, but it was just partially understood and strictly avoided by Aglaia herself. She hoped Lou didn't catch Tina's flat, sticky words and the use of her old name, which Mom still hadn't given up after all these years—or wouldn't give up.

Maybe it was just as well. Tina wasn't able to pronounce "Aglaia" correctly either, no matter how many times she was reminded that it rhymed with "I'll pay ya."

Tina pushed farther into the apartment. "Your father needed to pick up a tractor part none of the local dealerships had, and I don't like it when he drives alone so long and so far. I only have a minute, dear. I brought you some fresh-baked *Zwieback*."

Aglaia was trying to lose a few pounds before the trip but—

oh!—those rolls smelled delicious. The aroma disarmed her; she knew she should be hustling Tina out the door but couldn't find her words.

"Did you get my parcel?" her mother asked, not yet noticing Lou sitting on Aglaia's couch. "I didn't know I was coming to town or I would have waited to bring it along and saved the postage. But I wanted to be sure it got to you before you left on your trip."

In fact, when Aglaia received the package yesterday after work, she immediately began to tear at the brown paper, piqued about what her mother might be sending, until she saw the two-word title on the spine glaring through torn edges: *Holy Bible*. Annoyance at her mother's intrusiveness soured her then and rose again now like acid in the back of her throat. Tina knew Aglaia was disinterested in religion—and that was an understatement.

Before Aglaia could shut the closet door, her mother spotted the packet amongst the shoes in the shadow of the coats and reached down for it. "Why, it's right here," she said. "Didn't you read the note to call me?" Aglaia hadn't gotten that far in her unwrapping, and she recoiled as Tina shoved the bundle at her. Then her mother glanced up, for the first time seeing Lou in the living room. "Oh, my," Tina said, tightening the knot on her kerchief, "I didn't know you had company."

Tina seemed to have shriveled even since the last time she and Henry made the two-hundred-mile pilgrimage to Denver— a city, a state, a lifetime away from their Nebraska farm. Aglaia looked down on her though she wasn't tall herself. She looked as far down on Mom as she looked up at Lou. Tina's jacket didn't hide the dowdy housedress and her shoes were muddy. Aglaia was sorry again that she ever gave her mother a key to the apartment. Resigned, she made introductions.

"It's a pleasure to meet you." Lou arose and offered a manicured hand. "Do come in," she said, as if she were the hostess. Aglaia didn't blame Lou for wanting to compensate for her own uncomfortable silence.

But Tina, a teetotaler, now eyed up the wine glasses and Aglaia could almost hear her judgmental thoughts about her daughter's rejection of long-held Klassen values. Aglaia couldn't risk letting Tina make further comment in Lou's presence and took hold of her mother's arm to steer her towards the outer hallway.

"Isn't that Dad honking outside? You have a long drive home tonight." That was true; they wouldn't get back until well after midnight. "I'll walk you down."

"No, no. I need to explain." Tina, flustered, ripped the butcher's paper fully off the cumbersome black leather book, exposing it to Lou's purview. "I found this when I was digging around under the basement stairs. I haven't opened that trunk since the summer the French boy came to stay with us. You remember?"

Did she remember? It was all Aglaia could do to keep her memories under wraps.

Tina was opening the Bible now to the dedication page. "It says, 'Presented to François Vivier from the Klassens.' I thought to myself, that boy must have meant to take this home with him, since he carried it to church every Sunday he was with us, and to every Wednesday prayer meeting."

Horrified, Aglaia opened her mouth to protest, but no sound emerged. This was worse than she first imagined—worse than her mother simply sending her a Bible for reasons of maternal concern over her spiritual state. Tina was trotting out the one aspect of Aglaia's life she'd been trying to hide, especially from Lou. Not only was this a Bible that linked her to a personal religion, but also the very Bible owned by the person who'd totally reformed her religion.

"He wrote notes into the margins, starting right here in Genesis," Tina said. She pointed to a finely penciled script but, thankfully, didn't read the misquotation aloud: *In the beginning, the gods created.* Tina went on, "It was too small for me to make out without my reading glasses there in the basement, and Henry was about to leave for town so I had to rush if I wanted to get it into the mail. Can you see what it says?" Tina held the book out at arm's length for a moment before giving up. "Anyway, I decided that, since you were going to Paris, you should pack it into your suitcase and take it to him."

Aglaia bit down hard to stop herself from exclaiming and kept her face turned towards her mom so that the other woman wouldn't discern her mortification. She heard Lou say under her breath, "Ah, hence the questions," and was immobilized by her mother's proposition—in fact, by her own resolution—to find François, which sounded completely ridiculous when spoken aloud.

"Mom, I have no idea where he lives," she said, but in her heart she wanted to shout, *If only I knew where he lived!*

Tina responded, "He said he was going back to that famous school. What was it called?"

"The Sorbonne, but that was years ago." Aglaia kept her voice curt, not wanting to give Lou—who was openly eavesdropping— any reason to suppose she'd put up with the nonsense of taking a Bible along to France. "Who knows what's happened to him since? It'd be impossible to find him."

Aglaia doubted her mother would yield to the argument. Once she got a bone in her teeth, she was stubborn. Aglaia wouldn't mention that looking for François had been her daydream all along. Hoping her own voice didn't reveal her desire, she quickly added, "Besides, I'm in Paris for only a few days." Only a few days allotted to explore the world's most elegant city, an impossible few days to run an old heartthrob to ground.

Tina's wrinkles deepened as her forehead puckered. True to her nature, she persisted, "I just know he'd want this precious *Büak.*"

As if François would care about that Bible, Aglaia thought.

Tina fiddled with the cover, thumbing the gilded edges that on her own Bible had long ago lost their shine. A museum postcard slipped from between the pages to the floor, image facing up, immediately recognizable to Aglaia. She hadn't seen the postcard for fifteen years and she stared at it, transfixed all over again by the sculpture of the three nude women. Helpless, she plummeted into the memory of that first viewing like a pebble into the pond behind the barn, once again sitting with her family around the table with François on the warm May night he came to them—seated close to him, touched by his breath.

Tarrying together, the three marble nudes stand silken in the light, immortal young sisters polished with the ages—arm encircling waist, head on shoulder. Mary Grace is intoxicated with them, captured on one of the many glossy cards he brought to show off Paris to his American host family. She doesn't pay attention to his descriptions of the Eiffel Tower or the bridges, but only to the timbre of his voice, the poetry weaving through his hesitant English.

He turns to her for a moment and says, "They have your name, non? Les Trois Grâces—*Mary Grace.*"

Her brother grins and kicks her under the table but she ignores him. She's consumed with the statues and with François's fingertips tracing the two-dimensional outline, caressing the nymphen forms as though they're warm and living flesh. She's disconcerted because her own womanhood is so new. Does he mean to excite her?

Lou stepped forward to pick up the card before Aglaia shook her reverie.

Tina squinted at it. "I hope that French *Jung* didn't take such a picture into church with him."

"Perhaps he was using it as a bookmark," Lou said. She turned the card over and Aglaia saw it was blank except for the museum information printed on the back. "Pradier, 1790-1832. *Les Trois Grâces*—the Three Graces," Lou read aloud. "Your François appreciated the female form, I see—good taste."

Aglaia attempted to change the course of conversation. "Mom, it's too bad I didn't know you were coming tonight or I'd have gotten you and Dad tickets for the play." Not that they ever attended the stage.

But Lou, looking at the photo again, continued in spite of Aglaia's red herring. "Pradier sculpted in the neo-classical style and used the ancient Greek myths as subject material. The Three Graces, companions of Aphrodite, were very popular, and you can see that Pradier included their signature themes of fertility, beauty, and hospitality in this work. Note the way he utilized plants and jewels to get his idea across." She stretched her arm out so that mother and daughter could see what she meant, but Aglaia knew Lou's point would be lost on Tina. "The mythology of Greece made its imprint throughout history along many avenues," Lou said. "For example, the plot of *The Phantom of the Opera* may well have had its origins in the story of Europa, the beautiful maiden who was stolen away by Zeus disguised as a bull."

Tina scrunched her face in confusion.

As for Aglaia, she'd first heard the Greek tale whispered into her eager young ear by François's impassioned young lips, and then read it again in *Bulfinch's Mythology*, a text she discovered in twelfth grade on the shelves of the school library after her curiosity about the gods had been aroused. Her reading matter since her childhood days might surprise and even disturb Tina if she understood its content; it was nothing like the holy pap Aglaia was brought up on. But Tina's disapproval wasn't her concern at the moment, for Lou—satisfied with her examination of the postcard—was now craning towards the Bible as though she wanted to get a good close look at it next.

"Mom, I'll take that," Aglaia said. She reached for the book.

Tina handed it off to her readily. "Then you *will* return it to the boy? I knew you'd agree that it's just meant to be."

Aglaia intended only to get it out of sight—out of Lou's sight, especially. The thought of delivering it was preposterous. But she zipped it into the front pouch of her suitcase, packed and ready on the entry table. There was time enough to deal with it later, after she got rid of her mother and recouped her image with Lou, who probably thought she was totally incompetent about now.

Two

Lou's nose itched with a suppressed sneeze. She should have taken her antihistamine before coming to Aglaia's apartment but hadn't guessed the girl owned a mangy cat. From her spot on the couch, Lou watched her hostess lock the door behind Tina's ample posterior and then detour into the kitchen.

Overall she was amused with the evening's events—with the onstage showcasing of Aglaia's outstanding costumes, her nervous hospitality in bringing Lou home, her crippling embarrassment over Tina and the Bible, and her ambiguity regarding the mysterious French boy. This last point was evidently the reason for her pestering inquisition about how to locate someone in Paris. Aglaia Klassen was more complex than Lou had previously detected and worth investigation, if for that reason alone.

But Lou had other reasons for grooming Aglaia, and she waited impatiently for her young recruit to return to the dialogue. She mustn't rush the girl, she reminded herself. The mood was almost right for Lou to bring up her idea of employment, and a bit more dallying should ease Aglaia's tension, soften her guard, and allow the topic to spring up naturally.

Aglaia deliberated in front of the open refrigerator, taking deep, slow breaths to regain her self-possession after the interference of her mother. She rinsed a cluster of seedless grapes and patted a dampened hand over her face.

Aglaia sizzled with humiliation. Tina had terrible timing, dragging the stink of the barnyard back into her life just as she was making headway into civility and shirking emotions she'd been smothering since leaving the farm so long ago.

That had taken some doing—setting aside the meaning of rural family to consort with urban strangers, pretending she preferred the noise of traffic to the solitary whistle of the wind, even walking past a church without reading the week's sermon title. Now she bristled against her mother's intermittent reminders of what life used to be like.

Desperation tonight had made her jam the Bible into her bag as if she were going to take it along to the airport on Sunday, but she did it only to shut her mother up—and not only because of her lack of refinement when it came to consumption of alcohol. If allowed, her mom would have gone on about the writing in the Bible, and Aglaia had already glimpsed a second notation unseen by Tina, shocking words that leapt off the page: *Naked and we felt no shame.* She gouged the hull out of a strawberry, fearing what else François might have written.

Aglaia had not held a Bible in her hands since the morning after her high-school graduation, out by the burning barrel so early that the screen door hadn't yet clapped shut behind her father on his way to milk the Holstein. The memory drew her in.

"Presented to Mary Grace Klassen from Dad and Mom," the front page reads, her father's compact penmanship filling in the blanks. The front cover curls up at one corner, bonded leather letting loose, the ribbon marker fraying. Years of her own childish notes fill the margins, the latest thread all in purple ink from the youth group's study of the main themes. "Chaos to cosmos to covenant," she's written on the first page. "Freedom from slavery... Possessing the land... Judgment and mercy... Praises..." It took the full summer before twelfth grade to get through to Revelation, and she's hardly looked at those words in the year since.

She douses the book along with yesterday's trash in diesel fuel from the green jerry can to be sure of a good, hot burn, then strikes a match and tucks it in through the jagged hole near the bottom. In minutes her crime of sacrilege is spent—dust to dust, ashes to ashes, the Word cremated.

Aglaia blinked back to the present. What must Lou think of her—all manure, no demure? She tipped her chin down towards the kettle on the counter to check the smoky liner around her prairie-sky eyes, her delicate nose bulging comically. She fingered her ragged blonde bangs into place and then carried the fruit-and-cheese plate into the other room, suddenly unsure of her calculated composure.

"Oh no, I wouldn't want to ruin the finish of the wine—with cheddar of all things," Lou said, waving away the plate, and Aglaia criticized herself for another *faux pas*. As she stood undecided about whether to set it down anyway or take it back to the kitchen, she could see Lou was appraising her from head to heel. "Before tonight I'd never have guessed you were raised in the country," Lou said, "and by such conservative church folk at that."

"You can't pick your family, as they say," Aglaia said in self-defense, keeping the plate after all and reclaiming her place on the couch. Her eyes focused on the postcard, now lying on the coffee table. Maybe she could minimize the damage done by Tina's intrusion. "My mother's old school—just plain old, for that matter," she said. "In fact, people often mistake her for my grandmother."

Lou didn't blink, as if waiting for more information. Aglaia tried again. "My father won't be able to keep farming much longer. It's all he can do to harvest the crop and get seed back into the soil again, never mind the livestock he used to keep. Not a profitable enterprise." Farming was a dicey occupation undertaken less for the money than for the lifestyle—if that's how one chose to live. The identity of the farm girl was one Aglaia consciously rejected when she took up her new life in the city. There was no compromise, no choice but to make a clean break of it, and no going back. "Besides," she added for good measure, hoping her tone of finality would satisfy Lou so they could move on, "my family history is water under the bridge."

"Don't be so quick to dismiss your genealogy," Lou said. "We're all just products of our environment, Aglaia—you of yours and I of mine. And Tina of hers, after all."

She topped off her wine glass and splashed a bit more into Aglaia's. "We must embrace the influences of our past and make peace with them to truly become complete and free women within our individual selves. Only then will we contribute positively to the narrative of the larger community." Aglaia supposed Lou used the same delivery style in her lectures at the university—chin raised, tone pompous. She was being patronized but ignored the insult; Lou *was* a patron, after all. In the months since they met, she'd already asked Aglaia to two university functions—three counting the one coming up in a couple of weeks.

Lou continued, "Take your mother as an example. She's intriguing. What's her background?"

That was a loaded question! How could Aglaia even begin to explain her parents' ancestral roots as strangers in a strange land, in but not of the world, perpetually seeking asylum?

Every honorable Mennonite home instructed its children on the events of the displaced pacifistic denomination, begun by Swiss and Dutch Anabaptists in the late 1400s and taking to the road under persecution. By the seventeenth century, one group had already made its way to Pennsylvania, but Aglaia's great-great-great-grandparents had been born in Prussia, and their children on the steppes of southern Russia.

The Empress Catherine was to this day lauded for her gift of religious freedom—Aglaia had three cousins named after the tsarina—but, with the threat of militant nationalism, another wave of migration washed her forebears onto the shores of North America in 1874. Trains and boats and wagons carried them far inland, where they tamed the wilds and lived in huge families, settlements swelling and fanning westward.

Her parents were born, married, and still lived in an isolated community in southwestern Nebraska—Tiege, a village that kept its Mennonite flavor longer than some. The Klassens were not from the stricter nonconformist sects that insisted women wear head coverings in and out of church—though a couple of Ohio relatives had married into bonnets—yet Aglaia survived without a television until she was thirteen years old. Her parents still didn't own a computer.

How could Aglaia even begin to encapsulate her background for Lou?

"Well," she began, "since Dad was the first-born son, he ended up with the homestead."

"I didn't ask about your father," Lou interrupted with a sniff, chastising her. "Tell me, were you close to Tina as a girl? She's your matrix. Her story becomes yours."

Close to her mother? She didn't think about that any more, about the closeness when the family was whole. Lou's words swept her back to the vegetable garden on a warm morning, when the new potatoes were the size of marbles and the bright green feathers of dill tickled her pudgy arms.

"Mary Grace, hold the plant before you pull the pea off, like this," *Mom instructs, placing work-reddened hands over her own small, soft ones and helping her pinch a pod off the vine. "That's a good job, dear. We'll make a fine* Supp *for lunch." Mother and child pad their way back to the house over the turned-up earth between the even rows, and Mary Grace reaches up to hold onto the edge of the basket. They sing the chorus she's learning for her part in the Sunday school recital: "There shall be showers of blessing: This is the promise of love..."*

Lou touched her knee. "You're antagonistic about discussing your relationship."

"Antagonistic? No, it's just that there hasn't been much of a relationship to discuss since I left." Aglaia nibbled on a slice of apple.

She recollected her own haste to get away then and wished she could escape the conversation now. "Leaving was natural for me to do. All country kids head for the big city the minute they're released from school, you know."

"Do you carry guilt over that?"

"Not at all," she said too quickly.

"Guilt is the domain of the church," Lou said. "Women like Tina have forgotten the essentially feminine nature of goodness, of god-ness. True spirituality is not paternalistic but puts us beyond the pejorative grasp of hegemonic teachings."

"I'm sure my mom hasn't questioned her faith to that degree." Tina wouldn't even know what "pejorative" or "hegemonic" meant. Aglaia wasn't sure she knew herself.

"She's quaint," Lou said. "I've spent a great deal of time, as you know, studying women from ancient traditions. We all speak in different voices but there is a unity among us, a strong bond that, once acknowledged, brings solidarity. This is how we articulate our message."

Aglaia wondered what message that would be. She considered quizzing Lou about her own mother, but hesitated. She wasn't quick enough to turn the topic, could hardly turn her own mind from that poignant image of her mom in the garden.

"Let's explore your inner response to Tina." Lou sat forward, her nostrils flaring as though she'd caught a scent. "Why do you reject her truth?"

"You think I should believe what she believes?" If only Lou knew the extent of her mother's religious practices, or of her own keen involvement as a girl.

"Of course not. Belief isn't synonymous with acceptance. One must respectfully allow others to hold to their own truths. Just let her be who she is, Aglaia."

"She didn't strike you as, well, backward?" Aglaia's conscience twitched over criticizing her own flesh and blood out loud. Lou was right—she couldn't escape the omnipresence of that built-in, handed-down, bred-in-the-bone guilt.

"Not everyone attains the same level of gentility. Our responsibility is to build ourselves up on the corpus of our own aptitudes and on one another's, to learn from our mistakes rather than fall by them. Your mother holds power over you, Aglaia. You need to reclaim your autonomy." Lou reclined and directed a piercing gaze over her uplifted goblet.

Aglaia didn't know what she was expected to say. She looked away and swallowed thickly, realizing how parched she was. It was as if she couldn't get enough to drink these days, though she carried a water bottle with her everywhere. Tonight the wine didn't quench her thirst, either—didn't quell her memories.

"Speaking of women's empowerment, this postcard is almost iconic," Lou said. She picked the card up and Aglaia fought back a grimace, annoyed that she hadn't slipped it under the plate before it caught Lou's eye again. "Pradier's rendition of the Three Graces from Greek mythology represents quintessential womanhood. You must view the sculpture when you're in Paris. You're intending to tour the Louvre, aren't you?"

Aglaia nodded. "Of course." Pradier's work was to be her first stop, with the sculptures in room thirty-two of the Richelieu wing. She'd spend the good part of a day in the palace museum, with the Three Graces as her focus. She'd already mapped out her course using the Louvre's website to find several pieces picturing the trio, which included painting and drawing, carving and fresco.

Aglaia may not have had that postcard in hand for the past fifteen years, but nothing could curtail the growth of her interest in the underlying subject matter all this time. That insidious interest germinated by François sprouted quickly and grew persistently over months and years, like a vine curling itself into her thoughts and habits. Even her decorating tastes were affected. She let her glance skip over her apartment—over the potted palm by the window, the curtains of fine linen, and the walls painted Aegean blue and lined at the top with a stenciled border in Greek key motif. It was a stage set for her imagination.

So she certainly intended to visit the Louvre, along with other top tourist sites—as many as she could squeeze in around her probably futile search for François. Weeks ago she started flipping through travel guides for opening times and subway maps, anticipating the exotic solitude of visiting France unaccompanied. It reminded her of how she'd come to this state and this city as a young adult, a lone explorer in unknown surroundings looking for her future. A familiar pang wrenched her stomach—of anxiety, or maybe hope.

Lou, who was still studying the card, commented, "I see you have a poster over your bed that belongs in the same category." When had Lou looked into her bedroom? "Botticelli's *Allegory of Spring*, painted in the late fifteenth century," Lou said.

Greek mythology was one thing, but Aglaia didn't know all that much about art history. She couldn't boast of having seen the original painting in—where was it?— Florence. She'd never been to Italy, never been out of the States, for that matter. But she'd pored over color plates of the great works of art in her boss's office library, studying the field-squash hat of Dürer's *Erasmus* and the white honeycombed collar on Rembrandt's *Scholar* or, even better, the crisp folds of Caravaggio's *Narcissus*.

So, when she saw the Botticelli poster at a trade show, she begged it from the vendor while he was tearing down his display. It wasn't the first souvenir of the Three Graces she'd collected over the years. She found the small brass replica of the statue grouping at a second-hand store, and bought online the glass bowl etched with the Graces' forms that held her handful of wine corks. But the poster was her latest addition.

"The transparent gowns were a pattern for me when I designed the fairy costumes for a production of *A Midsummer Night's Dream*," Aglaia said. The gauzy, billowing garments lent a surreal quality to the play that was noticed by the press.

"Did you take into account Botticelli's underlying point—the authorial intent behind his painting?" Lou asked. "Some experts interpret *Allegory* to mean that the instinctual passions of the physical realm break the barrier between heaven and earth, raising sexual love to a spiritual sphere." Lou licked her middle finger and, watching Aglaia's discomfiture, ran it around the rim of the glass until the crystal began to ring. It unnerved Aglaia.

"I seem to recall hearing about the three goddesses guarding the entrance to the heavens or something," Aglaia said. Seem to recall, indeed! She hadn't rid her mind of the images of those three women since François first began to tell her their stories. But she was cautious about admitting anything Lou might use against her to pull out other information she wasn't yet ready to share.

"Guarding, or tempting perhaps," Lou suggested as though titillated by the thought of the threesome luring unwitting passersby to sample their charms. "I can imagine them gathered before the throne of Zeus, their father—that randy god of Mount Olympus— as the hordes of the heavens regaled one another with tales of their meddling in the lives of the humans below. Can't you envision it, Aglaia?"

"Well, they were only myths, after all," she answered, but her own fantasizing was richer than she let on.

"Don't underrate the power of oral story, even if it isn't in the written form of your particular religion," Lou said. "The adventures of superheroes of old, recounted from generation to generation and present in every civilization, adequately explicated the origins of the world and the nature of humanity for the people of that day. And the fanciful details of the lives of the gods hold real lessons for us today. In fact," Lou continued, "I'm presenting a series on feminine deification in my women's studies course for the summer interim session. You'd find the material stimulating. Why not call in sick tomorrow and attend my class?"

"Oh, I couldn't." Aglaia was genuinely sorry. "I'm tying up loose ends in the studio before I leave."

Aglaia hadn't missed a day of work since being hired on at Incognito a decade ago, not counting a bout of the 'flu and some car trouble one winter morning. Diligence earned her steady promotions as well as her current distinction, the ambassadorial trip to France. Her boss trusted her. That's why he appointed her as supervisor and go-between when the CEO at head office in Montreal—who made the preliminary contact with the costume museum in Paris—tossed this crust down to its Denver branch. Finally she had her chance to visit Paris—her chance to find François! Now was not the time to jeopardize her job.

But Lou's next words did just that.

Three

"Aglaia, have you ever considered the academic life? Our university theater department is advertising for a wardrobe consultant. It's an entry-level position, to be sure, but it could eventually lead to some lecturing possibilities."

Aglaia, startled at the unexpected turn in conversation, slopped her wine after all, and the cool liquid seeped through to her knee. She moved her glass to hide the stain and composed herself before answering.

This idea of a job at Platte River University must be what Lou had been hinting at for several weeks now, Aglaia thought—actually, ever since they first met. Had Lou heard the rumors about financial difficulties at the costume shop? What with the layoffs forced on some of Incognito's staff, Aglaia couldn't envision a better opportunity than working for PRU to bolster her vocational reputation and replace lost employment, if it came to that. Being hired by the upscale metropolitan institute would give her prestige, job security, and even a sense of identity she seemed to have misplaced along the way somewhere. She could hardly believe her luck.

"I may not have the credentials to work for a university," Aglaia hedged, her heart hammering in her chest. She wanted to abandon decorum and bounce up from her seat, to let the grin inside her find its way to her mouth and her eyes, but this was the time for austerity. She used to hate snobs but now found herself wanting to become one. At this point she needed to be circumspect. Just maybe her work record and the recent press attention would outweigh her lack of formal education.

Aglaia had never even completed her bachelor's degree in fine arts. She ran out of money after her first few semesters, her parents not offering any of the life insurance payment to help with tuition. After that, in those first years in the city when she was just fighting to survive, she couldn't afford to take even the odd community college class that might catch her eye—hand-dyed batik or ethnic embroidery. But since beginning work at Incognito, Aglaia had fully accessed the annual budget for professional development. She enrolled in fashion design workshops and textile seminars and millinery sessions, and then even won a scholarship to last summer's intensive two-week course in stage costume construction at the technical institute. It was a mish-mash of accredited and informal classes, but most of what she'd learned came from one-on-one tutelage by her boss.

So she was flattered by Lou's suggestion. Considering the woman's faculty position and her age—she was in her mid-forties, a dozen years Aglaia's senior—Lou was well ahead of her in the career track and in life experience. Aglaia aspired to someday have Lou's imperturbable grace and sophistication.

"You underestimate your potential," Lou said. "I saw it immediately when we met at the health club in the spring. Who else sews her own workout clothes?"

"You're too kind," Aglaia said. She straightened her dress strap, self-conscious. She'd noticed Lou's attire at the women's gym, as well—all top-of-the-line athletic wear with prominent brand identification. Of course, she recalled spotting Lou several years before they officially met at the club, back when Aglaia still stopped in for lunch at the campus cafeteria on occasion to rub shoulders with real students. No longer in her twenties, she didn't blend in as well any more. But it was back then that she first admired Lou from afar, not speculating they might someday be friends.

Outside of the gym, she never saw Lou in anything but designer clothes—usually dark neutrals with vertical stripes that gave her even more height. Aglaia herself approached dressing differently. She preferred the originality of her own handmade clothes and often incorporated vintage fabric or bits of antique beadwork in her sewing. She dressed to state her opinion, choosing a grey plaid shirt if constrained to visit her parents' farm or a vivid turquoise knit when brainstorming for a new costume at work. Lou, on the other hand, always exuded crisp classiness. At the moment, she lounged back on the upholstery in a studied elegance of pearls and paisley and smart leather heels. Her precise bob framed the hollow cheeks, every brunette hair keeping its place so that her earrings hardly showed.

"Your period pieces in the dramatic productions I've seen so far have been impressive," Lou said. "You must do a fair bit of investigation before you start sketching."

"I erase a lot," Aglaia said, reluctant to take all the credit for her designs, "but my boss does keep a great reference library for us at work. He points me to the right books, and he's a stickler for details." Just today Ebenezer MacAdam had vetoed the use of polyester thread on a pair of cotton bloomers. According to him, even illusion was worth authenticity, his whimsical costumes reflecting what was true about reality—Little Red Riding Hood's innocence shown in a cape woven of pure lamb's wool or the wickedness of the villain in fur from a real wolf. "Eb always says art is only an imitation of life."

Interest sharpened the countenance of the professor, quick as usual to discuss anything philosophical. "That's not very pragmatic," she said. "I think imitation is an art in itself, and that audiences expect deception as part of the game."

"In the theater, of course," Aglaia stipulated, but she was struck by her own duplicity when it came to everyday life, careful as she was to project just the right image.

Lou rubbed at an invisible spot on her glass. "Well, judging by your product, your form of realism works for you. The talk around the university is that you're a rising star. The dean of the drama department apparently reads the critics' picks in the entertainment section of the city paper. So," Lou smiled at Aglaia as if anticipating the effect of her next words. "I've taken the liberty of recommending you for possible placement as the new wardrobe consultant. You'll be hearing from the university soon."

Aglaia inhaled her wine in surprise and, gulping for air, excused herself to get a drink of water.

Lou was gratified by Aglaia's reaction, interpreting it as exhilaration over the possibility of a job at PRU. The girl's loyalty might be bought after all, she thought. Her catechizing of Aglaia was proceeding as intended, and she would be very valuable in helping to shake up the university administration that kept Lou imprisoned in academic mediocrity. Lou had known it the moment she first spotted Aglaia, sweating on the gym's stationary bike and chatting familiarly with Dr. Dayna Yates—newly appointed associate dean of PRU's department of sociology at the tender age of thirty-five, and the person who effectively held in her hands the future of Dr. Chapman, Ph.D.

Lou's move west to Colorado seven years ago had been motivated by the hope of securing her success in academia. True, Denver was inferior to the cosmopolitan New York City in almost every respect, but here she'd become a big fish in a small pond with access to those in authority, and she was a virtuoso at networking.

From the outset, it was the pursuit of tenure that had lured her from her former, dead-end posting. Platte River University recognized her proficiency in cultural studies and she accepted their offer of a tenure-track position in the faculty of social sciences—her chance at full validity as a scholar. She strategized her plan, buffering herself with a wall of professional peers—senior colleagues, department heads, and point persons within the political structure at PRU. To situate herself in the hierarchy and carve out her own area of interest, she developed a socio-anthropological program cementing the departments of art and social science through women's studies. She could boast of a sound body of work appearing in top-tier journals in her field, she carried a respectable class load, and she regularly presented papers at conferences. She even volunteered as chair of several visible committees. Everything was ticking along nicely.

But then Yates came on board—hired, Lou surmised sourly, mainly for fundraising skills that brought to the university multiple large research grants from the federal government. She was fast-tracked by the administration, and Lou's own prospects for academic security began to dissipate. Then simultaneously several journals rejected Lou's latest papers without even asking her to resubmit, and the members of her tenure committee—now prejudiced by Dayna Yates—started criticizing the adequacy of her research. She was being shut out.

Lou ground the heel of her red-soled Louboutin into Aglaia's living room carpet, fuming as she thought about her failure to stop the snubbing.

In order to get tenure, she needed to gain some sort of social capital, and she had an inkling that she'd found it in the most unlikely person of Aglaia Klassen. She conceptualized her opportunity that day at the gym when she saw Dayna—who usually wouldn't give Lou the time of day—chatting up the cute blonde on the stationary bike beside her. Lou maneuvered an introduction to Aglaia and the girl jumped at her overture. Over coffee the next day, Aglaia told her about her renewed acquaintance with Dayna, whom she'd met years ago and not seen again until recently. The two younger women seemed to get along famously, and Dayna even asked Aglaia to her home for a back-yard barbeque that was attended as well by the provost of the university. Lou had not been invited. However, she hoped a three-way friendship would soon remedy her status.

The fortuitous reunion of school chums would further work in Lou's favor if Aglaia succumbed to Lou's employment scheme, which was truly inspired if she had to say so herself. She'd exaggerated when she insinuated that, as wardrobe consultant, Aglaia might deliver a classroom lesson or two; no unaccredited teacher took the lecturn at PRU. But in Lou's economy, exaggerations didn't really equate with lies.

Lou drained the last drop from her glass but Aglaia, whom she heard closing a cupboard door in the kitchen and turning on a tap, hadn't offered to open a second bottle. Never mind, Lou thought; they'd be sharing many more evenings like this if Aglaia accepted her proposal. She was growing fond of the girl and wanted to spend more time with her. Despite Lou's coolness—her clinical inquiry about Tina, for example—she was anything but unaffected by Aglaia's ingenuous charm.

But all the talk of mother-daughter relations earlier tonight did nothing to curb Lou's ongoing disquietude in her personal life, which she traced back to the day she lost all respect for her own mother—the day her father left. Lou reviewed again that last morning in her childhood before theirs became a "broken home." It might suggest how she could breech Aglaia's rigid exterior. She didn't have much other experience of family to reference.

In retrospect Lou didn't think that her mother and father had been arguing with any more vehemence than usual, but on that morning in her first week of grade school the housekeeper pushed her out the door with gentle urgency. Lou still heard her parents' verbal slashing and the way it faded as she trailed along the sidewalk behind her older sister, watching the kick-flip of the navy pleats on the back of Linda's uniform.

Within a few years, Lou recognized her father's signature on the child support checks more readily than his picture in her baby album. She never blamed him. He was weak and Mother's moods—of explosion and then disengagement—were impossible for her husband or daughters to bear. Mother would rage until the three of them rose to her goading, and then she'd beat them into submission with her club of silence.

The abuse should have drawn her closer to her sister, she supposed, but each dealt with the pain in her own way. While Lou pursued her career in education, Linda jettisoned her future and got married to a boring accountant who, at least, was able to afford the mortgage on their bungalow.

Now, between driving kids to sports events and running a home business, Linda spent all her spare time at the hospice where Mother was contained, helping the nuns spoon mashed banana between her gums and change her diaper. It was the easy way out for Linda, Lou supposed, and once again she thanked her stars that she'd managed to gain independence through self-determination, just as her father had done in leaving her mother. Long ago, Lou left Mother, too.

Aglaia was tipsy. Her wine glass was now empty and she had a drowsy, after-bath feeling as she slumped on the sofa. She checked her watch. She didn't actually want Lou to leave, or at least didn't want Lou to know she wanted her to leave. But the other woman rose to her feet, smoothed out her skirt, and stepped towards the hallway. She approached the table and rested one hand on the outer pouch of the suitcase, then worked at the zipper.

"Are you looking for something?" Aglaia stammered, instantly sober.

"No, just curious about this Bible. You know my penchant for cultural investigation, and biblical literature is, after all, the foundation of Western values." Lou removed the book and Aglaia was astonished at her audacity. Lou continued, "More than that, the devotional interaction we see between the reader and the text is based on an almost magical view of reality. It's fascinating."

Aglaia found her feet and almost shouted, "That's private!"

Lou's brows shot upward. She ignored Aglaia's outstretched hand. "Private? I should think it's the most public writing of all time. The world's bestseller, isn't that what they say?" She weighed the book in her hand, her thumb slipping into place ready to open it. "In fact, your theologians have very publicly discussed angels and heads of pins for centuries now, although recent literary scholarship has brought to light issues worthy of more serious debate."

"Then you must have several versions of it in your own book-shelves." Aglaia sounded petulant to her own ears. She didn't want Lou misunderstanding; she had no desire to support any theologians. She just wanted that Bible shut and safely stowed away before Lou discovered the subject of the writing in the margins.

"I have one or two copies, although my area is more generally anthropological than theological. What version is this?" To Aglaia's relief, Lou kept the cover closed and read the spine, then moved back to the couch and sat again. Maybe she wouldn't open it after all. Lou said, "You should use the King James Version instead for its literary worth. It was first printed in 1611 and heavily influenced subsequent English vocabulary and literature. Of course, the value of biblical myth to society goes far beyond linguistics. The stories in these pages, if properly informed by content from every religion and reinterpreted within the contemporary milieu, speak of the metaphysical yearning of all humanity for the divine."

A faint ringing emanated from the suede bag at Lou's feet. Aglaia was thankful for the interruption, only in part because it forestalled the danger of Lou opening the Bible. Something in her rebelled at the professor's instructive tone and vocabulary, but she couldn't let that show now—not after the job offer Lou had just dangled before her. When Lou set the Bible down to answer her phone, Aglaia took her seat, slid the book off the coffee table, and clamped it to her lap with both hands.

Her own wariness of the Bible went beyond Lou's dry, academic dismissal. After all, hadn't she read it in the fervor of her youth for sheer joy—read it in her room every morning under crumpled bed sheets, submerged in the poetry and the prophecy, memorizing lines that sang in her heart?

It wasn't just the stories, either, of Daniel in the lions' den or the good Samaritan. Gullible as she was, she'd known back then with such certainty that this was God's true Word to her, God speaking directly from His own heart to hers.

And the gullibility didn't stop with just her reading. In spite of her shyness, she was always ready back then to impart her convictions to anyone who'd listen. It was natural to talk to François about it, too—in the beginning at least. She thought of the first time she and her older brother took him to their youth group.

"You can follow along in the English," she says, and opens François's brand-new Bible to the Psalms for him.

He tilts his head at her, his smile mischievous. "You will sit close to me and help, non?" And he moves his leg so that his knee brushes hers.

Joel snorts. "Nice going, Sis. Your sucking up in French class pays off at last. Lucky you didn't take German after all."

François ignores the brotherly bantering but she's embarrassed, and even more so as he looks over at her own Bible every now and then throughout the reading. There's no hiding the verses she underlined at a different time in a different frame of mind, and François smirks as Pastor Reimer reads aloud other verses on the facing page, and he presses his leg closer to hers: As the deer pants for streams of water, so my soul pants for you… All night long I flood my bed with weeping and drench my couch with tears… You turned my wailing into dancing and clothed me with joy. This is new magic to her, the magic of words that shield implication beneath connotation. François's silent reading of the words, his flickering glance and half-smile, give her goose bumps.

From that first Wednesday on, they followed the same routine. He'd find a seat in the basement of the rural church and toss his backpack onto the bench beside him, waiting for her until she pulled away from Naomi and the other adolescent girls all swooning over his dark eyes and swarthy skin, all envying her and considering her honored, blessed among women.

The first full-length sermon François heard on a Sunday morning was about Paul and the riot in Ephesus. She saw him circle the name of Artemis in his Bible during the service. Later around the dinner table, as Tina spooned out *Sauerkraut* and pork ribs simmered with prunes, so succulent and tangy that Aglaia's mouth watered before she lifted fork to lips, Henry asked François if he'd enjoyed the morning's message.

The Artemis he knew was the Greek goddess of the hunt, François told them, keen to relate. Artemis was one of many, many children of Zeus, and a half-sister to the Three Graces he'd shown them on the postcard. According to the tale, he said, Artemis was once bathing naked in a valley stream while her sentinels, the Graces, hung her clothes on the limb of an olive tree. When a passing hunter hid in the grove and spied on Artemis, she turned him into a stag for his indecency and he was killed by his own hounds. With just a short story, François managed to combine sexuality and violence and mythology into one horrendous affront to the Klassen family's day of rest.

It was the first and only time he ventured to give his opinion on such matters openly, no doubt because of the wordless feedback he received from Henry and Tina and even from Joel—a message of censure in their posture and reproof in their eyes that even his foreign sensibilities could detect. But it was just the inauguration of his clandestine storytelling to Aglaia, which soon dried up her interest in other reading, sucking away all her attention and blotting out her former absorption in the Scriptures. By the time François left the farm, she'd heard dozens of tales from ancient Greece recounting the intricate dealings between the gods, the demi-gods, and humanity. By the time Aglaia left the farm, she was ready and willing to put away such childish things as Bible lessons, and the chimeras of mythology became a means to feed her creative imagination for real-life, productive work, far away from pews and preachers.

If only she could rid herself of the other, unwelcome, relentless memories that brought such arid loneliness—a loneliness Aglaia now had hopes of ending, if she could at long last unearth François Vivier.

Lou was still talking on her phone but she was almost ready to hang up, Aglaia could tell by the shortness in her voice. She had only a moment before Lou would turn back to her and so, following her hunch, she stole a quick peek at the book of Acts in François's Bible. Yes, there it was—the name *Artemis* circled. Aglaia folded down the corner of the page and shut the book again as Lou finished off with the student who'd managed to get her cell number and dared to call this late in the evening.

"That's correct, your first assignment is due on Monday. But I'm thinking of giving a week's extension to the class, so don't worry about it," Lou said. She disconnected, tapped her gel nails on the hard shell of the phone in contemplation, and then blindsided Aglaia with the dreaded question.

"So, who is this François anyway?"

Aglaia swallowed. "Just an exchange student we had at the farm one summer." Did she sound cavalier enough?

"Your first lover?"

Aglaia almost choked on a grape. "I was only seventeen!"

"Seventeen is old enough. I met my 'true love' about that age, then suffered through the short but intense hell of marriage and divorce for my bother," she said. "Come now, Aglaia, give me a few details. Ever since we met I've assumed you're subject to some unrequited love, since I haven't observed any men in your life."

"I'm not presently dating."

"That's a standard line for evading confidences. Why are you not presently dating? You're certainly a beauty—sultry mouth, come-hither eyes." Lou assessed her frankly, even drawing her finger along the line of Aglaia's jawbone though she turned her face away at the touch. "Don't tell me the men aren't looking."

"*I'm* not looking."

"I won't pry further, then. But at least tell me how you intend to find your elusive French boyfriend after all this time to fulfill your mother's great commission." She motioned towards Aglaia's whitened knuckles gripping the Bible.

"Oh no, I won't be taking this along on my trip!"

"Tina won't ask you about it? You gave your word, you know. Or at least you insinuated it."

"I'll explain it all to her when I return."

But what would Aglaia explain, exactly, since her mother believed it was possible to find François? That she didn't have enough room in her luggage? That the book was too heavy to tow around Paris? Her mother would see right through her excuses and bring up the whole argument again about how Aglaia had forsaken the faith of her fathers, had surely lost her salvation in the process of finding herself. If she brought the Bible back undelivered, Mom would insist on scrutinizing it for some clue—an address, per-haps—and the threat that François had written something more incriminating than Aglaia had read thus far was too great a gamble.

Lou eventually got up to leave. She tugged her navy trench coat off a hanger in the hall closet and donned it, buttoning up against the rain splattering the window. She took the few steps back into the sitting area and bent down. "You won't mind if I borrow this postcard of the Three Graces for tomorrow's lecture? It's particu-larly applicable and the photo is so clear." She pocketed it before Aglaia could object.

Ebenezer MacAdam, general manager of Incognito Costume Shop and Aglaia's boss, lay snug in his bed on the rainy Thursday night, with the wife of his youth tucked in beside him. He removed his reading glasses, clicked off the lamp, and felt Iona's feet shift closer, their coolness transferring to him beneath the feathertick.

"Be my guest," Eb said, meaning it, and she plastered them up against his legs, making him shiver. It had been part of their bed-time ritual for nearly forty-five years, and was cherished by him because of it.

"Ian rang today," Iona said, yawning.

Their son was a computer programmer and data administrator for a shipping firm out of Honolulu. He didn't telephone often and Eb missed him, too.

"Everything okay?"

Iona sighed. "The twins have the sniffles."

They hadn't seen their eight-year-old grandchildren in more than two years. Now, with Britney at her age expecting another bairn in a few months, Ian was justifying holding off coming home for another Christmas.

"He sounded grouchy," Iona said, "I worry about him."

"Poor lad has a restless heart," Eb said.

Iona murmured assent, but Eb knew her maternal sorrow

encompassed more than a wandering son. Their own second child had been a precious baby girl, stillborn. Eb took some of the blame for his wife's sadness, having poured his own grief into his work so that he neglected both Iona and Ian until it was almost too late.

Father reconciled with son before Ian went off to university, but years of emotional absence left its scars. And Eb's marriage suffered as well, but dear Iona loyally loved her husband through it all. Now in their late sixties and with a significant wedding anniversary coming up, it was time for a second honeymoon, Eb thought. What better place than Hawaii's beaches? If only he could get away from his job—his besetting sin. And he was working to that end.

Ebenezer came to North America as a young man eager to earn his living with the needle, and started in Montreal before Incognito sent him down to the fledgling U.S. office.

He preferred the entrepreneurial attitude here, and was soon manager of a thriving storefront, eventually expanding the Colorado branch of the individual sales-and-rentals business to include stage productions, films, and festivals. Headquarters was impressed but, with fears of a slowing economy, now threatened to close the Denver site and move essential staff up to Canada.

Under duress, Eb had already offered severance packages to two older members of the team. It was Aglaia he was most concerned for.

"I wonder how her Shakespearian designs were received by the audience tonight," Eb mused aloud. But Iona was already sleeping, he judged by the even breathing from her side of the bed. He kept his next thoughts to himself as he repositioned his legs to warm Iona's feet more completely.

Aglaia was almost like a daughter to him. He saw a divine spark of creativity in her love of costume making—there was something spiritual about her—but she was restless, too, just like Ian. Perhaps Eb could have prevented the rift in his own family; perhaps even now there was something he could do to at least bring solace to the lass.

Eb was a man who believed in prayer, especially when he had

heavy thoughts. *Bless these children of yours*, he appealed simply and silently into the dome of the firmament beyond his window. *There's naught that I can do to change them—and if I tried, I'd only bungle it anyway. And while you're about it, Father, change me, too.* Then like a child himself, Eb slipped from meditation into sleep.

Four

Late afternoon light streamed in through the workroom window of Incognito. Aglaia had tossed and turned all last night after Lou left, her alarm finally startling her out of fitfulness and into a day of intense activity, now abating as she sat alone. She was still manually occupied but free to ruminate.

Aglaia suspected she cried when she slept because her lashes were crystallized when she awakened some mornings and because her pillow had stains. And she knew she dreamed because she came up through them sometimes, resurfacing into consciousness, her eyes scraping open as she reached into the bedside drawer for her bottle of drops.

She used to love to recount her dreams at the breakfast table before the country school bus flashed its lights at the end of their driveway, Joel offering far-flung interpretations and her father shaking his head and muttering, "Vain imaginings." They were hilarious, cheerful dreams of cherubs flying backwards through a rain forest or choirs singing hymns to conjoined twins—uncomplicated dreams that made her laugh at the silliness.

But when François came with his stories of far-away and long-ago Greece, her slumber absorbed the distorted character of Mor-

44

pheus (god of dreams), who was son of Hypnos (god of sleep), who was son of Nyx (goddess of night). Her dreams became jumbled nightmares of Scripture and myth, of creation by Uranus and resurrection by Adonis and salvation by endless appeasement of the gods. It was then Aglaia stopped sharing dream details with her family, though throughout the day she treasured the inky residue of feelings they left behind.

These days, though Aglaia was still subject to the tyranny of Morpheus whenever she forgot her herbal sleep aid, there was no occasion for morning analysis. In the first place, although her job was creative, it wasn't always conducive to woolgathering, especially the past weeks with her international project demanding such close attention. Besides, she refused to ponder remnants of nightmares any longer, and she could call up full-blown daydreams whenever she wanted a little romance—reminiscences *she* picked and chose. During waking hours she managed her imagination intentionally, or tried to, categorizing her memories as neatly as she arranged the color-coded thread rack at work, with pleasurable thoughts as close at hand as her buttonhole twist.

This morning at work, her head aching from too much wine in her apartment with Lou, Aglaia had finished the paperwork necessary for smooth importation procedures at the French border. So she was free to complete the remaining stitches in solitude, as everyone but her boss had left for the weekend. She heard him in the next room, his bass voice chanting out a low-key refrain, and she caught a few words: "My soul doth thirst… deep unto deep doth call." Likely they were from the Scottish psalter, the out-of-print hymnal he was fond of paging through, with its worn fabric cover, its lyrics written in crabbed lettering.

Ebenezer MacAdam was a gnome of a man with a brogue as thick as the butter on his lunch scones, a generous man with nothing of the Scrooge about him despite his unwieldy name. Aglaia calculated that Eb must be past retirement age, but his energy was steadfast. He closed the shop by himself every evening, and, by the time she arrived the next morning, he was paging through bills or oiling the machines, teacup at his elbow, a measuring tape around his collar like a loosened necktie. Eb drove to work in a classic tartan-red MGB that he'd restored and continued to maintain himself, usually with the top down and at the mercy of the elements until the frost was too sharp. He pushed his luck well into the winter and came in some mornings with ice coating his whiskers.

On Aglaia's worktable, a stray beam of sunlight played on metallic threads in the garment rumpled in a heap before her. She plugged the buds of her iPod into her ears to listen to the muted crooning of a male vocalist with a guitar rather than Eb's sentiments, and lifted the heavy gown onto her lap to pick at the bodice.

The rest of the costume was completed—petticoat and stays and beaver-trimmed cape. Representative of relations between Europe and North America, it was a replica of an outfit worn by a minor historical figure—a Parisian lady in the entourage of a governor visiting New France in the eighteenth century. Researchers at Incognito's headquarters authenticated the particulars of its style and sent Eb's office both a small oil portrait of the lady and documentation in the form of a letter home to her daughter—endorsements the Paris museum required, of course. This was the most advanced dressmaking commission Aglaia had yet undertaken and she was given some latitude in executing it.

Aglaia stroked the bisque brocade embossed with *fleurs de lys*, which she'd specially ordered from France a year ago for the ensemble. She alone designed and cut and stitched the creation from the beginning, ignoring offers of help from the teen volunteering at Incognito as part of his student work program. Aglaia owned the project from the beginning, and even now the texture and the weight of the cloth in her hand brought a deep tranquility.

From the time she was a child playing with colorful scraps that fell to the floor, listening to the drone and punch of Mom's antiquated Singer machine, she'd hankered to sew. She learned the smell of the flax beneath linen, savored the variance between silk and wool. She had a habit still of chewing a strand each time she laid out a length of yard goods, ready for the shears. She made a sacrament of touching and sniffing and tasting—a sensual adulation.

Aglaia recalled the first dress she made for herself from start to finish, using a size eight Vogue pattern and indigo challis speckled with wildflowers.

The spell of the cloth binds her, winds itself through her imagination as she determines the straight of grain and matches up the print and struts in her mind in front of the panel of 4-H adjudicators. But today she has a different critic in view. She is engrossed when Joel enters the basement laundry room.

"You'd rather sit at the sewing machine than eat?" he asks. "Mom called you twice." But the sundress is completed so she tries it on for the family—for François—after supper.

"When in heaven's name will you ever wear that?" her father asks. His idea of high fashion is a sturdy twill shirt for the cattle sale at the auction ring. But his eyes sparkle at her.

"Henry, don't discourage her," Mom says. "It's lovely, Mary Grace. Maybe you'll wear it to the church picnic next week."

Her mind fast-forwarded to the picnic where, in the shade of an apple tree, she unfastened the top button when everyone but François crowded around the potluck table.

"You are beautiful, mon enchanteresse," he says, and then spins for her the tale of a great weaving competition called by Athena, the goddess of household arts and crafts, against Arachne, the mortal daughter of a famous dyer of purple wool.

"I image you there at that contest, my little Mary Grace." His mouth is close to her ear and she hears him over the noisy picnickers loading their plates and calling out to them to get something to eat before it's all gone. And she imagines, with his coaxing, being at that contest, imagines being one of the assisting Graces fixing the warp threads onto the loom before the great virgin goddess, passing the weft shuttle back and forth in a frenzy through the tapestry, tying off the ends in a race against time. When Arachne won, François says, the vengeful Athena turned her into a spider to spin a cobweb for eternity.

François touches her hand but she pulls away, fearful someone might see—and maybe Joel has, for he's the closest to them and he's glowering over his potato salad now. François winks at her. Has he

been teasing, just playing with her all along? No one winks nowa-
days, she thinks, at least not the local boys who know nothing about
flirting.

But her spoonful of jelly salad tastes like ambrosia.

Aglaia chose her needle from the stash of gold-plated "be-
tweens" Eb supplied; she knotted the thread, then caught a loose
edge within a fine seam allowance threatening to fray. Only a man-
nequin would ever wear this costume. Even so, the idea of unfinished seams vexed Aglaia. The piece must be perfect when she
handed it over to the curator of the world-renowned collection
at the Musée de l'Histoire du Costume. As Lou said, this was her
chance to promote herself on an international scale. *Le Parisien*
had already printed an advertisement of the upcoming exhibition.

Aglaia didn't turn her nose up at public acknowledgement here
at home, either. She glanced at the line of frames that hung on her
wall—occupational qualifications and certifications, competition
placements, a merit award. Granted, no postsecondary diploma
hung in the lineup. But Lou's unveiling last night of her recom-
mendation of Aglaia for a position in theater costuming at the
university took some of the sting out of her lack of academic credentials. The job would give her standing within the arts community—proof to herself that she'd broken free from the straitjacket
of her agricultural past. If she could up her profile as a seasoned
urban artist, maybe she'd finally feel like one. She was tired of living on the run—running from emotions and definitions she never
asked for. Running from the farm.

But Aglaia didn't want to think about what a job offer might
mean to her current situation—her employment at Incognito and
Eb's selfless provision towards her professional reputation. She
wouldn't think about that just yet.

Aglaia readjusted the halogen lamp and looked at her reflection bent over the mass of creamy skirts piling up about her like
cumulous clouds. She recalled the time she spent in front of her
vanity mirror when she first moved to the city, practicing an air of
aloof detachment. She'd tell herself stories full of scandal or com-
edy or pathos to see if she could maintain the reserve. But here in

the cloister of her sewing room, the contentment was almost real.

This hour of creation gratified Aglaia most, when conception had grown from sketch into near fruition and she could allow her mind to meander as her hands manufactured. Lately she'd become adept at conjuring scenarios of lingering with François at outdoor cafés, strolling with him along the Champs Élysées, or window-shopping in the Marais. The girls at work had more than once commented on her other-worldly abstraction, and last week she missed a lunch break entirely, shut up in her studio with a new bolt of charmeuse.

They called that fabric her latest fling—not that she ever talked to them about her real social life, which was in fact devoid of men. No, all her romance was relegated to the vault of her thoughts, where she could keep a close eye on it and steer clear of further pain. She knew her lack of confidence with men stemmed from confusion about what she had to offer—about who she was. She'd lost a piece of herself when François left.

So Aglaia was grateful for a career that rewarded imagination and gave her definition. It was no one else's concern, least of all her coworkers', what actually occupied her mind, whether designs for a new costume or amorous cogitations. But the truth was that she'd been undergoing a decrease in control over the ebb and flow of her thoughts lately, hounded by unbidden—forbidden—memories, as though her emotional seams were coming undone. Maybe it was the stress of the Paris deadline. The danger had less to do with the time she wasted immersed in daydreaming than with the choice of the dream—that is, with the dream that chose her. Her repertoire was vast but certain doors should be kept shut, she believed. Everyone had recollections they locked up. It was called forgetting, wasn't it? Removing from sight, putting away as far as east was from west.

That bloody Bible, then, became a problem. She avoided reading it last night after Lou left, in spite of her curiosity over François's notations. She was just too tired. It held a summer's worth of memories but she wasn't yet up to the task of unraveling them. In fact, she was slightly peeved at the opportunity.

Aglaia took a sip from her Evian bottle and turned up the volume of the CD—she'd always been partial to the guitar—so that Eb's voice was totally blocked out.

She didn't hum, but she pierced her needle in and out, keeping time with the musical beat. Marking rhythm was as close as she got to singing these days, after years of painful discord, although she sensed deep within her heart a melody, as though someone were sweeping across the broken strings to stir the dormant chords again.

"Chantez—sing!" François calls out to the youth group as he strums some generic tune that somehow fits the evangelical chorus he couldn't have learned in France. Tousled hair falls over his forehead in waves and his eyes are closed as he feels his way into the song, his thick lashes fluttering slightly. Will he suddenly open those eyes and catch all the girls gaping?

At last the church teens have someone who can play a guitar. The off-tune piano's been rolled back under the stairs but Naomi says she doesn't mind giving up the job as accompanist. Now, because of François, even the guys join in on the refrain.

"I don't know how he does it," Joel says later when the two of them walk out to the truck ahead of the others. Joel's riding boots kick up dust that hangs in the hot evening air before it sifts back onto the brome and kosha weed growing on the side of the parking lot.

"Does what?" Mary Grace hasn't spent much time alone with her brother lately and doesn't like the absence, though she's instigated some of it. But she misses the after-hours chats in his bedroom or hers, long after their parents are asleep. Summers are busier for him now that he's graduated and is expected to do a grown man's work in the fields, but for the first summer in a couple of years she wishes they were kids again. More to the point, with François around she and Joel aren't sole companions anymore and, truth be told, she wouldn't mind a hike with her brother out to the poplar bluff in the hills like old times, carrying a bag of peanut butter sandwiches and a jar of creamy milk.

"Wins everyone over like that," Joel answers, "and he's only been here for a couple of weeks. I should have listened to Mom and Dad,

and thought longer before arranging for a student exchange. I mean, when will I ever go to Paris in return anyway?"

He sounds envious of François. Joel's never been popular, mostly because of his slight birth defect, but Mary Grace has repeatedly assured him that no one even notices the thin scar on his upper lip anymore, largely hidden by his sparse and tidy moustache. His pronunciation is flawless now, but his classmates haven't forgotten that he was excused every Thursday afternoon through sixth grade for speech therapy sessions.

"Well, François is pretty cool," she admits. She must have hit a nerve because Joel is silent. "Didn't he get you an invitation to that party last Friday?" she asks. "I mean, that group never invited you to anything before."

It wasn't Joel's crowd until François showed up. Somehow, in the short time he's been here, François's gotten in good with the new principal's niece, who's visiting for the summer before going off to college. Dayna's a wild child, from what Mary Grace can tell—rumors of the party she threw haven't died down yet. But the girl's hospitality didn't extend to mere high-school kids, and Mary Grace is still pouting that she couldn't go, couldn't watch out for François. He smelled like perfume when he came home.

Her brother looks back at the kids hanging around the church steps. He plants his booted foot on the bumper of the truck and crosses his arms over his knee.

"Yeah, the party," he says with a frown. "Not really my thing, Sis. I'm glad you didn't go. I don't think François Vivier is all he seems to be." And he pats her arm in the brotherly way that always makes her feel so safe, but François walks up and she doesn't want to feel safe right now.

Aglaia tugged herself back to the moment, stitching too aggressively on her costume on a Friday afternoon at work, incensed all over again at being high-jacked by her daydreams into psychological territory she feared. She had a few questions to ask François if she found him again. *When* she found him again, she corrected herself.

Five

Over at the university, Dr. Lou Chapman's feet pinched in her new pumps as she stood on the podium and lectured her classroom of sophomore women, three token males garrisoned in the back corner. She gestured towards the overhead screen and wished she had her art slides in electronic format. Maybe she'd allocate that job to her teaching assistant, she thought, who was a lazy worker and needed to pick up on his responsibilities.

"This painting of the Annunciation depicts what theologians have sometimes called the 'seminal conception,' " she said. "We see the messenger angel Gabriel before the kneeling Mary in a typical example of the Renaissance domination of masculinity over femininity. Can anyone identify the symbolism of the artist?"

No one offered a comment. Lou continued, "The white lily indicates his belief in Mary's virginal purity, and the descending dove of the Spirit is the instrument by which the girl is about to be impregnated."

One of the young men made a lewd comment and the other two sniggered. Lou presumed they were engineering students enrolled in her course as an elective, more to socialize than to learn. Their tomfoolery elicited the reaction of several girls sitting close to them, who either grinned along or rolled their eyes.

Lou perused the audience. Most of her pupils were consumed with taking notes, recording her monologue word for word. Perhaps that irritated her more than the rowdiness of the few boys who signed up each semester for her courses. That is, the girls these days blindly worshipped her pedagogic authority even when it came to the balderdash behind religious art, not entertaining an original thought but taking everything she said as gospel. It was a paradox: She deserved their full attention, but in their ignorance they didn't even understand what they were idolizing.

In contrast to their immaturity, Aglaia was almost erudite despite her quirky upbringing and her deficiency in formal education. She was, after all, several years older than any of the undergrads and fairly well read, though she retained a naïveté that Lou found beguiling. She turned back to the painting.

"If you could read Latin, you would know that the letters issuing from the mouth of the angel proclaim, 'Hail, thou that art highly favored, the Lord is with thee.' The words themselves were able to 'enflesh,' as it were, the Word of God."

A tentative hand was raised. "What is Mary reading?"

"Excellent question. She's studying the hallowed Scriptures, humbling herself before the literature of her fathers," Lou said, wondering how many of them caught her sardonic intent. "In point of fact, as a lowly female in that day she wouldn't have been able to read at all. But the artist's imagery is obvious—Mary is the conduit between the written and the spoken message, and as a result of her submission brings forth the Son of God into our world." She paused and then in qualification emphasized, "But keep in mind that this biblical myth of incarnation is preceded by, and resonates with, the equally valid tales of earlier cultures."

At that, a couple of students squirmed in their desks, likely preparing to blurt out some Sunday school verse to prove the Bible's eclipsing pre-eminence. That should provoke discussion. Ah yes, one girl was collecting herself.

"Are you saying the Bible is just fiction?"

"What do you think?" Lou asked.

The student prevaricated. "Well, I know some people who believe it's true."

"But truth isn't the antithesis of fiction, is it?" Lou asked, playing the devil's advocate. "Fiction isn't a lie, but rather a form of truth. Jesus Himself told parables—hypothetical stories meant to illustrate a profound reality."

This simple argument always stumped the Bible thumpers, fewer in number now than even a decade ago. A pity, as the religious pupils always brought up the most contentious issues and always fell the hardest when given correct thinking skills. Her goal in the classroom was dissonance, and controversy her subversive teaching tool.

Lou allowed her logic to register before continuing. "So Christian writings parallel other philosophical literature. For example, we all know every fable carries a moral. 'The Tortoise and the Hare' by Aesop teaches us that slow and steady wins the race. This sounds remarkably like the biblical injunction to run the race of faith with perseverance to the finish line, doesn't it?"

Blank stares faced Lou. Her patent rejection of the Bible as a unique source of truth was lost on them. She tried again.

"Take another of the Greek fables, 'The Ant and the Grasshopper,' identical in theme to the command in the book of Proverbs that says, 'Go to the ant, you sluggard; consider its ways and be wise.' These virtues, whether told through Aesop or the Bible, all hold our society in good stead. All were situated as well in the mythology of foregoing and ensuing civilizations."

Lou doubted her students were catching the concept. If they were unfamiliar with Greek fables, there was little use in her alluding to lofty literary tragedies like *Agamemnon*, so she forwarded through several screens and stopped at the enlargement of Aglaia's postcard. The nudity perked up the backbenchers. Men were so predictable. "Mary subjected herself to the rule and words of Gabriel," she continued, "but in our course material we will explore alternative expressions of response to male prerogative."

Lou thought how necessary it was to provide her students with an example of church-sanctioned art like the Van der Weyden

painting of Mary so they could grasp the monumental and demor-
alizing effect of patriarchy. Greek society provided a proper foil.

"You see on the screen a sculpture portraying the *Charites*,
commonly known as the Three Graces. These goddesses presided
over the banquet, the dance, and all the arts. They attended the
most regal deities and garbed them in magnificent apparel."

No wonder seamstress Aglaia was taken with them, Lou
thought.

"They granted talents to mortals. Perhaps you've read Spenser,
who said about them, 'These three on men all gracious gifts bestow.' Homer wrote about them as well, in both the *Iliad* and the
Odyssey, as you'll no doubt know, having completed your assigned
readings." She noted panic in some of her students, who madly
paged through their papers. Of course, the syllabus didn't schedule
that reading until next week, but she liked to keep them on their
toes. "The influence of Grecian narrative upon our world cannot
be overstated."

Lou picked up her pointer and directed its shadow over the
photo from Aglaia's postcard. "Pradier's carving is merely one
depiction of the Graces—a favorite theme in European art. The
stance of the subjects shows them in communion with one another, a leisurely camaraderie at odds with the stiff, hierarchical
formality we saw between Mary and Gabriel. The Graces help us
understand the freedom that the pre-Christian ancients—those
happy pagans—celebrated in conjunction with womanhood. Refer
to my article, 'Women and Myth: The Enunciation of the Feminine
in the Rhetoric of the Sages.' "

To the rustling of the handout, Lou considered how well received the title had been by the editor of a journal in which the
piece was published last year, and how she'd hoped in vain that
this paper would be the one to put her over the top with the tenure committee. The class probably didn't appreciate her word play
between "enunciation" and the "Annunciation" of Gabriel just discussed, but it hadn't been lost on Aglaia when she read the article.
Despite her abysmal lack of schooling, Aglaia was sharp. She had
clarity of eye, a directness of gaze, that was more than intellectual

and almost moral in nature, perhaps as the legendary Eve might have had before her fall into sin. Aglaia, too, must be hiding something shameful. Everyone does, Lou was sure.

One student who sat in the front row was trying to make eye contact with Lou, flicking her hair with a pen. She looked vaguely familiar. What was her name—Winona? Willow? She was another example of the trite stereotype increasingly evident around the university in the past several years despite the establishment of feminism in the general and scholarly populace. Too much makeup, white t-shirt stretched tightly enough to show off the vibrant print of her padded bra. In the formative days of the women's movement when Lou was just pubescent, her older sister had dropped out of the elite Manhattan prep school to burn her own bra in the streets, to Lou's envy. Later on in university, and thanks to a girlfriend, Lou got caught up herself in a street demonstration parading for gender rights. Soon she decided the publicity of activism wouldn't suit her academic image and she now kept her preferences concealed for the most part, unless it was to her professional or personal advantage to associate with any particular cause.

Lou went on with her lecture. She related the dying of the gods to the corresponding seasonal death of the crops and vegetation, and supported the thesis that the redemptive rituals performed to assure vitality were based upon the female reproductive cycle. One could see a reflection of this abundant fertility in the first of Pradier's Graces—Thalia, if she recalled the name correctly—who clutched a garland of flowers and encircled her sisters with it. Religious ceremony was cosmic and magical, she told them, with an angry deity requiring conciliatory sacrifice from terrorized humanity or from one another.

Lou stifled a yawn and decided her lecture needed more peppy illustration—for herself as well as her students. She flipped through her support material and exhibited another painting with a colorful story behind it.

"*The Return of Persephone* by the Victorian Frederic Leighton captures the idea. Hades, the god of the underworld whose land is named after him, desired Persephone. While she was picking flowers in a field with other maidens, he burst forth from a crevice in the ground and"—she inserted a suggestive inflection—"*plucked* her like a bloom herself. He carried her off and the abduction grieved her mother, goddess of the harvest, who appealed to Zeus. He decided Persephone must return to the land of the living to restore its verdancy, but unfortunately Persephone had eaten a pomegranate, the food of the dead. This required her to revisit the underworld throughout the year, and since then the seasons of growth wax and wane with her presence and absence." Lou finished the lecture with a final comment: "Even the ancients attributed to woman the power to influence her environs."

The class ended and the hall emptied as she gathered her papers together, ready to head back to her office on the east side of the social sciences wing. In front of her, seven or eight girls swarmed the few males leaving the room, vying for favor. So much for feminine autonomy!

Minutes later Lou was in her office, shutting down her computer and tidying her desktop in preparation for a meeting with Dr. Oliver Upton, head of the theater department and co-author of her recent paper promoting women's studies through the arts. He was one of her few academic proponents and a conspirator with her in a venture Platte River University might not officially approve, as it wasn't strictly educational even though it would be advantageous to the institution.

Months ago, before the media got hold of the news about the movie to be shot on location in Denver and area by a subsidiary of one of the big Hollywood studios, Oliver nosed it out through his film studio contacts.

It was a prequel to *The Life and Times of Buffalo Bill*, a western starring Brad Pitt, which had made enough profit to warrant the film company's return to the area for a second serving.

From what she'd read about the first movie—Lou hadn't bothered to see it herself, though all of her students raved about it—*Buffalo Bill* wasn't just a "duster" reeking of testosterone. The director shone favorable light upon frontier women of the Wild West, such as Annie Oakley and Calamity Jane, and Lou had even referred in her classes to the film as an object lesson for early suffrage.

With his information about a prequel coming to town, Oliver directly approached Lou, conjecturing correctly that she'd be interested in his idea, as they'd pooled information to their mutual benefit at other times. Lou and Oliver clarified their prospects and agreed to work together for ostensibly altruistic ends, although Lou figured Oliver was as interested in his advancement as she was in hers. He wanted a piece of the movie action for his own monetary reward hidden under the banner of publicly funded arts (she'd leave the ethics of that for him to defend). Lou, on the other hand, wanted primarily to secure her university tenure, which offered its own compensations.

So Lou and Oliver had waited for the movie company to call for bids by local trades in the Denver area, including costumers, and the announcement was made a fortnight ago. Incognito was certain to be the main competitor of PRU's theater department, but Lou was bound and determined for the name of Platte River University instead to appear in the credit roll of the film. And she, Dr. Lou Chapman, wanted to be known as the one to snag the competition's head designer—none other than Aglaia Klassen, highly visible emerging artist and personal friend of the tenure committee's Dayna Yates, associate head of sociology. If Aglaia were to accept the job Lou was arranging for her and thus disable the competition, Dayna might look more highly upon Lou's value to the school and validate her for the effective amalgamation of the arts and sociology departments.

To top it off, there was always the possibility that Aglaia might be privy to Incognito's bid for the costuming contract, but Lou was treading carefully when soliciting information from her new little friend, who could very well balk if she surmised that Lou was using her as a drawing card. Lou might be able to leak the right numbers through Oliver and ensure that the contract would be granted to the university—not that they would admit to using insider information. Either way, whether through access to Incognito's bid or only that company's handicap in losing Aglaia, Lou's influence in procuring a movie deal that gave continent-wide publicity to the school was sure to be recompensed and result in her tenureship by PRU. It was a brilliant plot.

Lou heard a knock on the half-opened door and called, "Come in, Oliver." But it was a student instead who stuck her head into the office—the attentive girl from the front row of her lecture.

"Can I talk to you for a minute, Dr. Chapman?"

Lou rose to intercept her. "I'm expecting someone for an appointment momentarily," she said, just as she saw Oliver Upton plowing down the hallway towards them. "It shouldn't be long. Why not wait out here for me?" Lou motioned her colleague in and closed the door on the student with a thud as Oliver took a chair.

"How's your progress with that young designer?" he demanded, getting right to down to business. He crossed one leg over the other and jiggled his foot. "You know I want the guarantee that she'll be on my team before I submit the bid to RoundUp Studios. The sooner, the better."

"I'm massaging her," Lou replied. She felt the time pressure herself.

"Closing date's coming up. They're not cutting us much slack, but since they're bringing the bulk of the wardrobe and their own costume supervisor with them, I suppose they think of us merely as back-up support." Oliver retied his shoelace and smoothed his sock. "But I'm just not confident that we have anyone currently on staff who can handle the artistic demands, especially since we'll have to depend on student input for much of the labor. It's a managerial nightmare, if I ever imagined one."

"I think she'll bite, Oliver. I've inferred to Aglaia that you'll give her a lecturing position in the arts program."

"That's outrageous. My M.A. students, who are clamoring for teaching time themselves, would riot—to say nothing of the stage designers we hire on contract for only a season or a particular production. It would be viewed as nepotism, pure and simple."

"Yes, of course," Lou said, thinking that nepotism was nothing new in their profession. "But I wanted to sweeten the pot, even if it's with an empty promise. At any rate, you do have the school's authority to hire her away from the competitor and that's—"

"Wait a minute," Oliver cut her off. He rubbed his pointy beard between thumb and forefinger. "Your suggestion of Aglaia as a lecturer has given me an idea. I might be able to call in a few favors after all and facilitate a special honor that should grease the wheels of our plan."

Lou admired the craftiness of Oliver's mind as he outlined his idea and concluded. "I'll let you know if I make any headway. In the meanwhile," he said, rising from his chair to leave, "speed your end of the process up, Lou."

Oliver's supercilious manner befitted his seniority but irritated her. She didn't comment and Oliver said, "Now, I see you're keeping the university chancellor's granddaughter waiting in the hall, so I'll let you go."

Chancellor Wadsworth's granddaughter? Lou castigated herself for failing to recognize the student, and this time she ushered her into her office with deference.

"Dr. Chapman, I've been reading your book about women regaining power." Her obsequious flattery left Lou unmoved; she expected to be read. But she assumed false appreciation and tried to recall if they'd ever met.

"How can I help you?"

"Well, um, you might not remember me from winter semester, but I had a, like, session with you here in the office."

At that Lou examined her more closely. Funny she couldn't recall the meeting, particularly in light of the girl's connections. There'd been so many encounters in this office, with so many girls who needed "consoling," that she sometimes got them mixed up.

"Certainly, Ms. Wadsworth." She guessed that the girl went by the chancellor's last name.

"Whitney," the girl reminded her. "Could we maybe talk? If you have, like, a few minutes?"

"I always have time for a student." In truth Lou was impatient to get back to her condo; she had a lot to do in the next few days. But she was always mindful to keep her options open when it came to potential alliances, and a plum like this didn't fall into her lap every day.

"It's about the quiz last week. I've got it here," Whitney said, rifling around in her book bag. "I was so busy with my poetry assignment that I didn't have time to study."

"I don't review marks given on examinations, and I can't start making exceptions now. But given your obvious aptitude," Lou exaggerated, "you might bring up your grade by writing an extra paper for me."

"I can do that. What topic should it be on?"

Lou was thoughtful, wanting to set the tone for future interactions. "Perhaps you could merge women's issues with your predilection for verse by focusing on the lyrical style developed by the Greek poet Sappho, who was exiled from her beloved island of Lesbos." Lou withdrew a key from her desk drawer and swiveled her chair to face the wall of streak-free glass-fronted bookshelves. "You strike me as a reliable person, Whitney. I'll lend you a resource that might start the juices flowing, and then we can meet to discuss the subject further." Lou often found Sappho stimulating to more than the intellect of her students.

"Thanks, Dr. Chapman."

"Call me Lou," she said. The girl smiled at the floor. "Let's set a date, then," Lou said as she consulted her electronic calendar. "I'm clearing my schedule for next week and am unavailable, but we can meet in the week following."

As Whitney left, Lou pondered the state of young women these days. Something about them always got to her, maybe their vulnerability or their awe. She wasn't fooled into thinking that Whitney was intrinsically different, although her family tree set her apart. But all these girls began to look the same, all voiced the same shallow thoughts with a cloying dedication to quoting her out of context. She admitted some personal benefit from the relationships she cultivated—a consciousness that she was making a difference, having a small influence on lives in a fashion lecturing and publishing could never quite accomplish. An emotional impact.

Of course, Whitney Wadsworth's lineage changed the scenario

slightly, and their interaction might go well beyond the one-on-one mentorship that was Lou's signature. Chancellor Wadsworth was merely a figurehead in the structure of the university, but one could never foretell all the repercussions of bridge building when it came to social contacts. She'd keep Whitney as the ace up her sleeve.

Lou had no close acquaintances in her own age group, just academic associates and those she met at conferences. The classroom had become her social pool. She'd tutored countless girls exactly like Whitney Wadsworth, insecure and transparent—needy girls who molded themselves beneath her supervision in compliance, so eager to please for the moment, for the grade. Clay she could remake in her own image.

Perhaps that was another reason for her attraction to Aglaia, Lou thought, returning to her best prospect for success in the issue of tenure as she walked out to her car in the parking lot. Aglaia, older and slightly wiser, was a fascinating proselyte who didn't throw herself at Lou. There was an enigma about her, a recalcitrance even. Introspective with a bittersweet melancholy about her, Aglaia needed someone to rescue her from the banality of her life. Lou hadn't quite figured out what got Aglaia's blood up, but she was enjoying chipping away the exterior to expose the heart that beat beneath.

Six

Aglaia bit off the end of the knotted thread after her last stitch on the costume despite the proximity of her scissors lying within arm's reach on her office worktable. She'd been role-playing her arrival—how to catch the train to Paris from Charles de Gaulle airport, how to ask in French for directions to her hotel. And, of course, how to find a guy in Paris! This trip was a coming-of-age thing for her, and Paris was the ultimate escape into glamor.

Even aside from her hopes to look up François, she needed a diversion from the humdrum of her life.

There! She admitted the city wasn't all she hoped for back when she was fresh off the farm, dazzled with the lights and a long way from gravel roads. When she first moved, it was enough just to hop a bus to a mall full of name-brand jeans she could never find in the Sears catalogue. That catalogue was the best shopping she got before she acquired her license, if Dad or Joel wouldn't drive her the ninety miles into Sterling or—even better—all the way to Denver.

The village of Tiege, population 392, was where the paved road began, three miles from the Klassens' gate. It offered only a small general store that sold wilted lettuce, stale candy, and pails of udder balm. The village's chief attractions were the post office, church, and K-12 school—oh, and the service center for tires and fuel.

Her intentions even then, when she first moved, were farther reaching than the shopping mall. Once she'd found an apartment and part-time work doing alterations at a local menswear store, she enrolled in her first university courses and thought her future was set. She got to know a small group of fellow students but, when the cash ran out and she had to get a full-time job, she dropped out of the loop. Aglaia was lucky to find employment at Eb's shop ten years ago, and she never left. Now this position Lou talked about might offer her another step up.

So, all in all, the move to the city had been good for her, a springboard to bigger things. She was ready for the challenge of international travel, and this week in Paris would nourish the inner woman, as Lou might say. Sometimes Aglaia doubted there was anything alive in there, other than her art and her memories and her hopes to one day meet François again.

Until recently, she'd held that daydreaming was creative—a lubricant to her design process, the oil of imagination. But lately she felt as though she were drying up and her voice becoming muted—her own physical voice if not her interior dialogue. People were asking her more often to speak up because they couldn't quite make out what she was saying.

It wasn't timorousness; she was daring enough. It was as if she were being shuttered, closed up within her own skin, calcifying from the outside inward like a hardening mask at the aesthetician's. Would she even bleed anymore if she pricked herself?

Aglaia rolled the needle between her fingers, thread tickling the palm of her right hand. It was an idiotic notion, but she couldn't recall the last time she'd jabbed herself. She squeezed the tip of her left thumb till it was a dull red and poked at it with the needle. Too thick.

She pushed harder against the resistance of the toughened skin until, with a slight release of pressure and a sting, the needle slid past the barrier. A crimson bead welled up; she was ridiculously relieved. Maybe it was the relief that made her drop her guard for a minute, so that a fragment of prose snuck into her mind: *The Lord* said, *"What have you done? Listen! Your brother's blood cries out to me from the ground."*

Aglaia shook the words from her head, along with the picture of the preacher waggling his finger at the congregation—at her—as he held his Bible high above their heads and admonished them against the sins of Cain. Years of memorizing Scripture had left the shrapnel of rogue verses to trouble her, the Word never returning void, always hitting its mark. Only other thoughts could displace them, so she deliberately remembered a different scene from that summer—something disassociated from the Bible.

They're skeet shooting.

"Pull!" Joel calls to her, and the clay pigeon gyrates crazily above the field in front of them. A shot rings out, and a chip flies from the saucer.

"Pull!" François this time. He blasts the skeet, which explodes into shards. With each shot Mary Grace flinches, the sound an assault to her ears.

François ignores her, consumed with this new task, and Mary Grace observes him with an intensity she grants herself only when she knows no one else is watching. They're a quarter of a mile from the house out on the prairie, and she squats on her haunches behind the two young men, poised to release the catch on their verbal commands, poised to recoil. François has tossed his shirt to the ground and his torso gleams with sweat and bulges with muscles newly acquired by riding, shoveling grain, lifting bales. His profile shows the strong line of his clenched jaw. He cradles his shotgun between arm and ribcage and rakes his hand through his hair, pushing it off his forehead. Then he reaches for the jug, gulps greedily, and flashes her a smile.

"Pull!" Joel yells.

The precious fabric was still draped over Aglaia's knees, her thumb was bleeding, and she was stunned at her own carelessness. She had no time to deal with stains on the costume! She sucked on her thumb, the metallic taste reminding her of rusty well water, and then bound it with a scrap of muslin tied into a clumsy knot.

Aglaia scraped her stool back from the workbench and let the folds fall out of the gown and hung it up for steaming. She knew the source of her problem well enough. It was the farm. It plagued her—the memories of that summer, the religious confusion, the unfulfilled prophecy of what her life was meant to be. Mom and Dad tried to reconcile with her after she left Nebraska for Denver, haranguing her to at least see a pastor for counseling, but she stopped answering their phone calls until they let her be. The internal stress wasn't so easily diverted. She thought running from it would give her space but it shadowed her and accompanied her, just outside of her direct line of sight, and she wouldn't look at the issue squarely as if it had the power—like Medusa's writhing locks—to turn her to stone.

She had no intention of going to a shrink but she'd end up there if she didn't watch out.

Aglaia heard a file drawer close in an adjoining office and realized that her boss was still on the job, waiting for her to be done so he could lock the shop and enjoy his weekend off. She was anxious to get home, too, and go over her last-minute list so she could officially close up her suitcase.

Aglaia plugged in the steamer and topped up the water level. While it heated, she shuffled through some drawings for a future project waiting on her desk. For the first time she detected that her sketches of the models resembled the statues on the postcard pilfered by Lou—heads poised, mouths closed, eyes glazed and blind. The difference was in how dressed her fashion figures were compared to the smooth nakedness of the Graces wearing only the sunlight filtering onto them from an outside source. Her work was about covering up, not uncovering. It wasn't quite the take her boss had on their occupation, though. She recollected a conversation that took place near the beginning of her training.

"Lass," Eb had said, "you want to behold the eyes of your customers."

"Why's that?" She'd gotten used to his meaningful observations after the first couple of months working the retail counter out front, filling orders for Halloween costumes from drop-ins off the street before she'd been allowed to even pick up her drafting pencil and prove how much she was learning by watching Eb. The work at the beginning seemed so simple, a matter of flicking through the rotary card files for "Merlin" or "Rapunzel" and notifying the stock boy to bag the item.

"The eyes are the window to the soul," he answered. "You can find out what costumes they really need."

"But the customers tell me that," she argued.

He laughed at her, a rumbling chortle that shook his belly and blew his sandy moustache out from his mouth like a curtain in the breeze. How could she take offence? Eb's laughter was never a put-down. She heard he once dressed an octogenarian as Little Bo Peep and a burly biker in a sailor suit—and both came back the next year for more. His inventory was loaded with literary and fairytale characters, hardly anything dark or oppressing—fairies and mermaids and unicorns, the Little Gingerbread Man and the Steadfast Tin Soldier. Even his witches had a sweetness about them.

"Look deeply, Aglaia. Most of the time they just think they know. Use that inquisitive mind of yours to expose the true personality trying to get out. That's what costuming is all about—not hiding under a false identity but exposing the true one."

That was advice from years ago she was still learning to apply in her job and, at the same time, still trying to avoid applying personally.

The steamer hissed and she lifted it off its hook, the hose a hot snake, and she was back on the farm again.

"Get it away from me!" François recoils from the garter snake like a girl, and she can't help but laugh at Joel's prank, surprised as she is by François's reaction.

"It won't bite," she reassures him.

Joel grins. "In fact, we grill these and eat 'em for snacks."

Maybe François buys that one—his lips sour with disgust but even then look kissable.

And later, perhaps to redeem himself for his weak fright, he tells her the story of Asclepius, god of healing who not only saved lives but also brought back the dead, and of his descendent Hippocrates, whose snake-entwined rod became the symbol of rebirth.

So she tells him about Moses, who set up a pole with a bronze snake fixed on it to heal his followers bitten by vipers of judgment, to heal those grumblers who detested the lifesaving manna that was sweet as wafers with honey, as cakes baked with oil. And when they gazed upon that pole-borne snake in submission to the Great Physician, they lived.

But François stares at her, incredulous, as if to ask, "Who would believe such a story?"

The fabric let go of its wrinkles and she allowed it to cool before she folded it in layers of tissue paper and packed it into the traveling box, just the right size to fit in the plane's overhead bin. She hitched it up by its sturdy handle; it wasn't too heavy and felt secure in her grip—like the little overnight bag she used for pajama parties as a girl.

"Where are you going with that valise, ma petite?" *He's leaning against the weathered wood of the house as though waiting for her, the brim of his baseball cap pulled low and a piece of grass between his teeth in a parody of the country boy.*

"It's Naomi's birthday, so I'm spending the night at her place."

He scowls at that. Why would it bug him? "You are best of friends, non?"

"Have been for years, François." Is it that he'll miss her for the evening? Mary Grace could hope.

"You tell each other secrets, then?"

"We talk all about you," she teases. He turns from her without another word and she's hurt.

When she tells Naomi about François's reaction, her girlfriend quickly changes the subject, and soon after that she's gone off to the city, leaving Mary Grace stuck in the sticks. But she doesn't pine too long because François is around to keep her company. Oh, what company!

Aglaia set the package back on the table and sat down again to rub her temples. The chaotic flood of thoughts was going to drown her if she didn't find some way to contain them and sort out their meaning. There was a pattern she couldn't put her finger on.

This latest resurgence was in all likelihood due to the stupid idea of her mother's to take that Bible back to François. Aglaia's own decision to look for him might be slightly far-fetched, especially after all this time, and slightly frightening. But upon meeting him, to push a Bible on him like some soapbox fanatic earning brownie points with God—now that was just downright humiliating.

However, on second thought, maybe packing the Bible along to Paris wasn't such a bad idea after all. It would give Aglaia a pretext—should she actually find François—for tracking him down in the first place. If he wasn't glad to see her, she could smooth it over by telling him that she'd been sent by Tina, who implored her to make the delivery, and what could he do then but thank her? Aglaia might still look the fool, but she could blame it on her doddering mother.

Maybe the delivery wasn't impossible. Maybe, with luck, she *could* track him down and—as an added bonus—get that Bible off her hands and out of her sight. The one action would have the double effect of putting to rest the question of François and faith, and giving her some peace about the whole affair. At the very least, taking the book along with her wouldn't do any harm.

Aglaia stood up and switched off her tabletop lamp. As she pivoted to reach for the costume box, her ankle turned and she stumbled against the chair, sending it clattering.

Seven

Searing pain ripped through Aglaia's ankle and she sprawled on the floor, unable for a moment to stand up.

Eb scurried into the room. "Are you hurt, lass?"

In spite of the pain, Aglaia let out a short giggle when she saw him. Over his usual sweater and slacks, Eb wore a burlap monk's robe with attached cowl and scapular, conjured up for the annual Renaissance fair, just past. The robe suited her boss, whose blue-grey eyes, misty as a crystal ball, were topped with a set of bushy brows once gold, now silver—a backward alchemy. He stooped to help her stand.

"Can you put any weight on the foot?"

"I'm okay," she said, but he led her to the couch in his office, raised her foot onto a cushion, and tapped a tablet from a white bottle. Then he served her a cup of tea and a cookie.

"Good to keep a tin of shortbread at hand for emergencies like this," he said, helping himself to one. "My dear wife disapproves because of my diabetes, but I just say to her, 'It's only a body, Iona.'"

"I'm so sorry to put you out," she said. He was fussing over her.

"No, no—it's not a bother. I can see it's swelling. You bide here and I'll trot off to the grocer's next door and fetch a bag of frozen peas for you." He bustled out, still wearing the mediaeval attire.

Aglaia nestled back into the quilt. Who kept a quilt in his office? Perhaps Eb's wife crafted it by hand back in the old country, piecing the plaid and paisley blocks, outlining each thistle blossom with fine stitches. Aglaia's ankle throbbed, so she concentrated on her surroundings instead.

The whole of the room was a tumultuous clutter. The desk was loaded with files, fabric samples, patterns, and books—so many books! They spilled from the ceiling-to-floor shelving and piled up in drifts in the corners, beside the settee, behind the door. It was a madman's library. Aglaia never ceased to be amazed at how Eb MacAdam could so quickly answer her queries with a quote or put his hand on the very volume she needed for a design. She often saw him in here alone, lost in a story world, engrossed in *Pilgrim's Progress* while reaching for *Gulliver's Travels*.

There was some order he alone could decipher. Illustrated manuals of contemporary and historical costumes of the world were mixed in with theological tomes and novels—the Brothers Grimm snuggled up to Dostoyevsky, Thomas Aquinas visiting Narnia. Four full sets of encyclopedias, bound in various colors, were seeded now among *Arabian Nights* and *Knights of the Round Table* and *Dark Night of the Soul*—the wheat and tares together.

She set down her tea and eased a green-jacketed copy of Hesiod's *Theogony* from the closest, teetering column of books. She opened it to the first page and familiar names leapt out at her: Cronos, Hebe, Oceanus. They hadn't always been known to her. She remembered the first time she saw them in print, in an illustrated children's book of mythology that François found in the foreign language section of the bookstore in town and bought, just for her.

"It's in French. Maybe you'd like to practice?" François's English is improving daily, becoming more natural.

"I can't read these words, François."

"But I'll help you," he promises, "as you're helping me with my learning." So she flounders her way through the first few lines and François fills in background information about the primordial god who swallowed his children whole upon birth. They admire the draw-

ings of Poseidon and voluptuous Demeter and, of course, the picture of the Three Graces that accentuates the details of their sexuality.

Reading romantic prose with François behind the haystacks, with the sun setting in the west, while munching carrots tugged from garden soil is her idea of a perfect summer evening. But it gets better.

As the stars come out in the growing blackness above and a chill falls like dew on her skin, François removes his denim jacket and places it around her shoulders, letting his arm linger. Mary Grace stiffens and he hugs her closer, outlining the constellations with his finger in the sky. He tells her how the boastful vanity of Cassiopeia led to her daughter Andromeda's being stripped naked and chained to the ragged cliffs as a sacrifice to a hideous sea monster.

Then, pointing over there, he relates the adventure of Zeus, in the form of an eagle, snatching the most comely youth Ganymede and transforming him into the constellation of Aquarius, the Water Carrier. And can she see the stringed lyre of the grieving young Orpheus, who lost his lover to death and whose dirge echoes for all time? Yes— there, with its crowning star, Vega.

Mary Grace hears Joel calling and she makes François run with her all the way back to the house, forgetting the children's book outside to get ruined by the elements. She prefers François's verbal edition better anyway.

"You've finished your biscuit," Eb said, re-entering the office.

He had the robe slung over his arm now; perhaps a child on the street had pointed the monk's garb out to his amused parents, or Eb found suddenly that he was still wearing it at the store till as he fumbled for his wallet in his pants pocket. While he hung it on the coat rack, Aglaia swapped the book of myths she held for *The Count of Monte Cristo*; she didn't want Eb to notice the moodiness she knew would be dimming her eyes.

"Oh, you've found one of my favorites." He motioned to Dumas's book on her lap. "Nothing like a story to take you out of yourself." He pressed the pack of peas against her ankle with gentle pressure.

"I've always wanted to ask you something, Eb," she said, thinking fast and blinking away that last memory. "About your fiction. I understand the encyclopedias and the picture books for costume ideas, but why do you have all these novels with no illustrations at all?"

He was frowning over the swelling ankle, maybe concerned it was a bad enough sprain to interfere with travel. He served himself a cup of tea and answered her question.

"In this case, a picture is not worth a thousand words. Illustrations are useful tools, but they change over time and with different artists. Compare an early drawing of Peter Pan by this artist," he said, grunting as he stretched for a 1915 edition, "with one based on the movie release forty years later."

She inspected the pages in the two books Eb opened for her. "I get it. It's like the Pinocchio costume I designed as my first major assignment from you. You made me study a lot of pictures first."

"And you ended up with a style distinctive from all of them," Eb said, nodding, "even more recognizable to our clients—a longer nose on the mask, limbs more obviously jointed, the addition of marionette strings. A caricature, almost."

"But you liked the costume I came up with."

"I'm not criticizing you, lass, but simply noting that your own expression was yet another *interpretation* of what the writer had in mind to begin with, several versions back. Looking at other artists' pictures is a good way for a baby designer to start off." He stirred his tea and sipped. "But I find going to the source—the original story, that is—much more reliable when I desire exact *representation* for our designs."

The ibuprofen was kicking in now, and Aglaia flexed her ankle as Eb continued.

"I view the costume as a three-dimensional re-creation of the two-dimensional page," Eb said. "You see what I'm getting at? The words of a story themselves, in turn, only illustrate a larger idea underneath—the principle of an inanimate, wooden puppet becoming a flesh-and-blood boy, for example." He warmed to his analogy. "So the seed of the writer's internal truth sprouts into the tree of the word, which produces the fruit—that is, the illustration of the costume."

A relaxed silence fell on them as they drank their tea. Aglaia speculated upon the difference between the two characters they were discussing, Pinocchio and Peter Pan—one who wanted to be a real boy through and through, and one who aspired to never growing up. Conversations with Eb often took such a contemplative turn; it seemed her boss, as usual, was discussing a subject that went beyond costume design. Was he giving her some covert message now? He was prone to wax numinous on theological issues. At times it made her nervous that he might break out into a religious furor like some televangelist, but he never did.

Eb mentioned not long ago that she might soon have a stronger role at Incognito, letting him take a back seat and even finally retire. Perhaps today he was using a teachable moment to pass on more of his own wisdom surreptitiously—not that he ever hid his convictions. Rather, he administered them to his staff like Eucharist wafers, in tidbits over lunch break or through a memo commending them for their good effort on behalf of the company. He talked about "transcendence" and "resonance" and "vestiges, the thumbprint of the Creator." Very mystical.

"What is the chief end of man, after all?" he asked her now, out of the blue. Did he expect her to answer? She munched on another cookie. "We're all longing for that one true love, that great romance," he said. She knew he wasn't talking about Iona, whose photo commanded the only clear spot on his walnut desk. Eb saw the direction of her glance and grinned. "No, I mean the search for purpose and significance. Now, temporally speaking, I'd like to think the purpose of my costumes has been to reveal the real in this masked and disguised generation. But on a grander scale, I myself am being unmasked and my failures laid open to my own view. So many of my years I spent fearing to be discovered for the fraud I really am. Yet here it is the autumn of my life and I stand naked, as it were, before a Judge more kindly than myself."

He held his tongue until she felt compelled to say something.

"Everybody wants to put on a good face, though."

"That's it, lass. We call it 'civility' or some such nonsense. We want to ignore the big questions. As an old friend tells us," and here he placed his hand on a time-worn book by Dante, "we all wake one day, midway the path of life, to find ourselves in a dark wood where the right way is wholly lost and gone. Perhaps trying to look good is the first step homeward."

She brushed crumbs off the blanket, wordless under Eb's scrutiny and under the condemning words written in Italy a thousand years ago. She'd encountered Dante's writing for the first time right here in her boss's office. At home in her growing-up years, the Klassen family subscribed only to *Our Daily Bread*; they didn't own a library card and most of her secular reading was confined to school texts. Otherwise, she chose her books by their cover, like most kids, and she never chose Dante. When she left home, her newly stimulated hunger for reading took her further back than the Christian classics of Europe.

"But come, it's getting late. We must get you home." Eb collected the teacups and plate. "Why not leave your car parked here overnight and let me drive you? I'll have one of the staff take it over to your place in the morning, unless you feel you can't go to Paris after all."

"Oh no, Eb. It's my left ankle. I can still drive." She pulled herself to her feet and took a few tentative steps. There was no way she'd let a little fall threaten her chance to see François. "I promise I'll consult a doctor if this ankle doesn't feel better by tomorrow afternoon, and I have a visitor coming to stay overnight who'll keep watch over me. Besides," she quipped, "your car's trunk isn't roomy enough for our French lady's baggage."

Eb retrieved the documents from the office safe and picked up the costume box to carry them out to Aglaia's car for her. But he stopped abruptly before closing the door. "You need a cane," he said, and disappeared into the stock room, re-emerging with a tall, crooked rod. The tips of his moustache were twitching. "Moses' staff. But don't go beating on any rocks demanding water or there'll be hell to pay."

Aglaia gone, Eb shook the droplets off his car cover and folded it into the boot of his '62 MGB. He'd bought the Roadster for a song several years ago. It was in a horrid state then, but now its reconditioned interior—black leather with red piping—was as supple and smooth as when it left Abingdon, he'd wager. Most of his labor was hidden under the bonnet but there was much yet to accomplish, and he'd love more time to tinker. It was just as well that Aglaia didn't accept his offer of a ride home, he thought as he eyed the grey sky and shifted into reverse. The lass would likely have gotten drenched, adding insult to the injury of her swollen ankle.

Eb worried about more than Aglaia's physical health. He saw in her a twistedness not confined to her ankle, a digression in the soul he found was not uncommon in creative dispositions. It was there when she first came to Incognito but he couldn't explain its specific source, though he knew it involved her imagination, and he had compassion for her suffering.

This imagination of Aglaia's helped make their business productive, and Eb was indebted to her sheer ingenuity in costume design, which he'd been fostering all along. He saw the Creator in Aglaia's creativity. In the whole sphere of the universe, only man had the conscious impulse of art, Eb thought—no animal painted a portrait, no vegetable drafted a blueprint, no mineral narrated a story. The exercise of art, like worship, was a human response.

But Eb discerned in Aglaia an unnatural, occult curiosity. Maybe it was her reading, he thought as he reflected on her interest in his collection. "You are what you eat," the saying went, but Eb believed one was what one *read*, and feeding the imagination with the wrong sustenance was worse than reaching for a bag of crisps instead of a carrot stick. What a person borrowed from the library bookshelves was as telling as what she loaded into her grocery trolley.

Eb didn't know with certainty Aglaia's tastes in reading, but he picked up cues from how she approached her design—for example, the calculated way she studied illustrations of Hermès's winged sandals and of the Sirens' feathers before designing her most recent archangel. On occasion she made off-hand references to Greek mythological deities and creatures when researching ideas, and often speckled her rough costume sketches with doodles of snakes and stars and symbols. Eb held scruples against vetoing her line of inquiry; she might see his concern as censure rather than guidance. But every season brought more of the degenerating influence of mythology to her work and she seemed to be devolving, using her craft as an incantation to call up the gods of fantasy, or perhaps exploiting the gods to feed her craft. Maybe the lass thought she was specializing in her field.

Eb downshifted behind a cube van, caught in its fumes for a block. Inner-city traffic was heavy these days with all the construction.

Of course, Eb thought, mythology as story was an art itself. Even savages saw something behind the constellations of the sky or the stones of the ground, behind a tree or a pod or an elephant tusk, their barbarous souls stirred to seek truth by means of beauty—though they always ended up carving a face into it and bowing the knee before it.

Humanity ever found it natural to worship, straining for a peek of the divine behind the physical realm and finding, in the case of the pagans, "a mere filth and litter of spawning gods," as old Chesterton put it. The mythology of ancient cultures, and even the fables and folktales Eb himself found so illustrative—both Olympus's Zeus and Pinocchio's Geppetto—began as imaginative explanation but failed to satisfy longings only true deity could fulfill.

The words of Saint Augustine ricocheted down the millennia to Eb: "We love those things by which we are carried along for the sake of that towards which we are carried." It was natural to love our creativity, he thought, patting the restored dashboard of his MGB with affection, but the whole goal of driving was to get oneself home. The whole goal of art was to convey the concept it carried—the object or idea being portrayed. The moment one idolized the method, one lost the message. Eb was inclined to think that Aglaia was catching a ride on the myths without knowing where they were taking her. There was a difference between using art to get to a destination, and clinging to art for the sake of the art. What was Aglaia's destination?

Eb himself, in bitterness over the death of his wee daughter, had wasted years running in circles to escape facing a loving God. *Father,* he muttered now, always only a breath away from prayer, *I hate to see Aglaia bound in some fatalistic cycle, going 'round and 'round as on a fairground carousel she can't dismount. Give her the eyes to focus on you waiting in the sidelines to take her homeward.*

A drop hit Eb's nose and another his cheek. He was just blocks away from Iona's cooking and he was hungry. Dear Iona fed him so faithfully! Maybe they should splurge and go out to dinner one night soon. If his career hopes came to fruition, before long he'd be treating her to the freshest pineapple she'd ever tasted.

Eight

Aglaia hobbled out of her kitchen through the sliding doors to the third-story patio on Saturday morning with her favorite pottery mug in hand. The best thing about her apartment was the view of Mount Evans from her deck. She sat in the cool dawn with her left foot resting on the other patio chair. The snow-tipped Rockies glistened blue with ghostly transparency, floating on a bed of cloud. A distant thought sang into her mind like a hymn: *I lift up my eyes to the hills—where does my help come from?*

Aglaia blinked away the words brought up by the sight of creation in its grandeur. Why couldn't she enjoy the beauty of nature without the ever-present voice within pointing her to something beyond?

The first time she'd seen the mountains was the year she was six. Her father had bolted a borrowed camper onto the back of the half-ton, and the four of them rattled over gravel roads and turned west onto the highway. How had Mom convinced Dad to leave the farm on such a sunny day, with hay to mow? The oscillation and the availability of Joel's shoulder conspired to send her back to sleep, and hours later her lids fluttered open just as they rounded the curve of a lake—opened upon the broken reflection of the mountains on the watery surface, their jagged peaks pointing down as though heaven had fallen into earth.

On the balcony, Aglaia covered her knees against the chilly breeze and wished for socks but was too lazy to move. She cupped her hands around the steaming coffee mug. On early mornings like this as a girl she used to catch her mother at the kitchen table with her elbows on the oilcloth reading, or resting her head on her forearms in prayer. Dad would come in from the chores and join Mom, the two of them murmuring in *Plautdietsch* while she peeped through the stairway banister and strained in vain to catch a secret before she'd burst in on them for a hug.

"What are you doing up at this hour?" he asks, then lifts her up into his lap and rubs his nose into her neck, making her giggle. "Soon you'll be too big to sit on my lap," he threatens. But Daddy's always ready to hug her when the work is done. He slides the Bible over— not the old German Bible anymore but the English one, so she and Joel can understand it—and reads the morning's passage aloud, her nose tickly with the hay dust on his sleeve.

"On the morning of the third day there was thunder and lightning, with a thick cloud over the mountain." His voice is rumbly. "And the whole mountain trembled violently." The mountain of her father quakes beneath her and hugs her closer. "The Lord descended to the top of Mount Sinai and called Moses to the top of the mountain. So Moses went up. And God spoke all these words..."

Aglaia assumed her parents still followed the morning devotional ritual, even with the house empty of offspring now and so many chores waiting for him. But did her father miss the touch of his daughter?

She thought about yesterday and the enveloping security of Eb's office. She didn't know two men as different as her father was from her boss. Dad let her know he loved her long after he stopped cuddling her, when she grew breasts; it was an awkward time, her puberty. And he still gave in to Tina's insistence and called Aglaia occasionally, though he hated using the telephone for anything other than agricultural dealings—to order diesel fuel, perhaps, or ask how the neighbor was making out with his new-fangled baler.

But he found words themselves extravagant. Dad was a meat-and-potatoes man in more than his diet.

Her dignified boss, on the other hand, was profoundly communicative, with every utterance full of connotation, often cryptic but always meaningful—always accompanied with a glint of his eye, a challenge to dig deeper, to come closer. But closer to what?

Recently Eb embroiled her in a discussion regarding names. He said that each costume, like any artist's painting, was incomplete until it was christened. "Take my name, for example," he said. "It originated when the Israelites subdued the giant Philistines. Samuel set up a megalithic monument—a 'standing stone'—and called it Ebenezer, meaning 'Thus far has the Lord helped us.' "

But she was reticent to talk about given names since she'd so thoroughly rejected her own, and so Eb turned back to the costume. "Agonize over the choice," he coached her when she'd been ready to settle for the generic "Bunch of Grapes" for her purple padded fabrication. "An artist must name her piece deliberately, imputing meaning, *knowing* that creation. Call him out, Aglaia." She'd opted for "Dionysus" and earned a cluck and a rueful smile from her boss.

Yes, Eb was full of bonhomie. Good will radiated from him, but it was accompanied by another quality—astuteness, maybe, or a sharp awareness short of cunning. A person wanted to sidle up next to him even though dressmaker headpins often bristled from his sleeve if he'd been helping one of the seamstresses with her work. A person wanted to hug him, but didn't.

Aglaia returned to the kitchen to refill her mug. Her cat stretched on the couch and yawned, his elfin tongue curling around a lazy "Meow" before he bounded over to rub against Aglaia's housecoat.

She picked him up and he climbed to her shoulder and arranged himself around her neck like a fur collar, his purring idling against her ear as she opened a fishy can of breakfast for him. The tabby was a barn cat, picked up at the ASPCA shelter last fall after her former cat lost his four-year battle against city traffic. She'd never buy one of those snooty Siamese or Himalayan breeds, and not just because of the price.

"Here you go, Zephyr," she said as he sprang to the floor.

What Eb had said about names was true, she thought; they told a lot about a person and even about a pet. The farm crawled with cats when she was young but for some reason the Klassen family never labeled them "Fluffy" or "Snowball," instead talking about them in general terms like "the mama cat" or "that mean tri-color" or "the stray." Dad liked them around to keep down the rodent population, and Mom always made sure, in the coldest part of winter, to set table scraps outside by the step.

On occasion one cat or another made a mad dash into the kitchen, and Joel would always smuggle it into the basement for a quick snuggle.

Aglaia dubbed each of her cats "Zephyr" now—all three cats in turn that she'd owned since they formally named the first one on that perilous summer day in the hayloft.

Mary Grace hunts for the boys for an hour. She calls their names into the machine shop and the bunkhouse, and spies out the pasture but finds Joel's horse unsaddled, unridden, standing against the backdrop of the thunderheads with its mane blowing. As the storm breaks the hot sky open, she thinks of the loft and scales the splintery ladder with the ease of her tomboy days. She doesn't hear François picking on his guitar until she's halfway up the barn wall. She hoists herself through the wooden doorframe into the loft and catches sight of Joel grabbing at the fleeing tomcat.

"He goes like the wind!" Joel complains.

She hasn't climbed that ladder for over a year, and when she finds them there, it strikes her again what a haven the place is— the musty perfume of the bales, the daylight jabbing ghostly fingers through gaps in the shingles.

François is smoking something that smells sweeter than the hay.

"What are you doing?" She's aghast that Joel hasn't put a stop to it, if only because Dad's been adamant about their never *lighting matches in this firetrap. But more, she's thrilled at the danger of what she's walked into. She looks from François to Joel, and gets the impression the two have had words about it and François has won.*

But she doesn't leave the barn—she doesn't run to tattle. How can she? François's charcoal eyes smile away her indignation.

"You've come here to sing with me?" François asks as he strums a chord. "Or maybe to smoke with me?" He winks at her again. "Joel won't try, but you will, non?"

He takes the joint from his lips and raises it to hers, daring her while Joel watches with distress in his eyes. She remembers the pact she made with her brother, but she takes the slightest puff anyway and starts coughing. She's never even smoked a cigarette, never mind a joint. Joel grits his teeth but François smiles, and so she takes a second draw—this time deeper. She knows she should leave now, but hail as hard as Pharaoh's heart begins a staccato on the barn roof.

The tomcat reappears to skulk near François, curls up against him without invitation, then snags at Joel when he reaches to pet him. "Let's name him Zephyr," François says, "for the west wind."

François makes her feel like a Zephyr, nervous and needy and naughty all at once.

Aglaia never touched drugs again—even an accidental buzz from her premeditated use of wine unsettled her. She pulled a pair of socks from the dryer, crushed ice for her ankle, and returned to the balcony to go through her must-do list, mentally ticking off items: flight confirmed, walking shoes and passport packed, lasagna ready for the oven.

Blast Naomi's timing, insisting on a visit the evening before her European departure. The medical appointment had been made months before Aglaia's airline ticket was booked and Naomi couldn't afford a hotel room, but it annoyed Aglaia all the same. It wasn't completely untimely, Aglaia admitted to herself; Naomi had agreed to take Zephyr back with her for the week and drop him off at Mom and Dad's, a couple of miles up the road from her place. She seemed eager to please since getting back in touch with Aglaia after years of estrangement.

They'd been so close as girls. Naomi was less than a year older than she but a grade ahead in school. Her mother died of cancer when Naomi was in junior high; after that she often dismounted the bus with Aglaia to hang around till it was time to beg a ride home to help her father fix supper for her younger siblings. Naomi blended into the Klassen household as though born to it. She always came up with fun things for them to do—bike to the scene of a prairie fire, build a fort with Joel. There wasn't a sniff of competition between the girls in those days, not even over report cards. Naomi didn't mind that Aglaia always aced her classes. She'd just say, "You deserve it for all the studying you do."

They were also of one mind in things spiritual. As freckled, braid-sporting youngsters, as prim preteens, through the pimple stage and out the other end to unsullied womanhood, they worshipped together on the hard wooden benches every Sunday, raising their voices in harmony to praise the Lord.

They sang their girlish duets at weddings and funerals, exhorting the congregation to rejoice at marital bonding and rejoice at earthly parting—as though they had experience in these areas themselves!

They witnessed through the testimony of music for the multicultural festival at the fairgrounds, and all the housewives with bags of *Portselkje* to sell—committed to furthering the Mennonite way of life first through the stomach—would nod in appreciation as they passed the girls on their way to the fritter booth. Naomi and Aglaia even cut a recording of sorts entitled "Sisterly Songs of Sweetness," on sale in the church basement for $5.95.

It was unconscionable, Aglaia thought now, letting kids make such certain declaration. But immediately and almost audibly she was chastised by the Psalmist, who sang to God: *From the lips of children and infants you have ordained praise.* She banished the verse from her conscience, telling herself that people had always worshipped something—blindly, fatalistically. What gave the God of the Jews alone the right to demand all praise? He was as inconstant in giving her happiness as some trident-wielding sea-god dredged up from the wishful thinking of ancient Greeks. What was wrong with her parents—with that whole community—for encouraging empty hope, as though God were that simple and just waiting for a word of adoration to bring Him glory?

Furthermore, what was wrong with Naomi for still buying into it? But then she'd always followed authority, sheep-like. Such a good and contented girl, never on the cusp of sin, never tempted—except, perhaps, to overindulge at the table.

Unless she counted Naomi's uncharacteristic impulsiveness right at the end of their teenage friendship. Perhaps Naomi's desertion when she just up and moved away might be classified as a sin. It was Aglaia's first significant loss in that summer of loss, when she was left to navigate her last year of school alone. Within that year, that very autumn, Naomi married her high-school beau but, by the time Mr. and Mrs. Byron Enns moved back out to the country with their blossoming family, Aglaia was long gone. Over the years she saw Naomi now and then, when she couldn't avoid going home for Christmas or some such occasion, but she'd been able to shun most contact.

Naomi began to pester her in spring about getting together for a coffee, after the birth of her sixth child, probably in an attempt at temporary emancipation from the bawling hordes at home. Her insistence on re-establishing a friendship best left dead might have another cause: Perhaps Naomi had been sent by Tina and Henry. They were seeing more of each other lately, Aglaia heard, Naomi running a cake over for Dad's birthday or helping Mom with mending now that her eyesight was going. It was a conspiracy, an attempt to bring Aglaia back into the fold, she suspected.

So she surprised herself by agreeing to that first meeting a few months ago. She gave Naomi directions to the Starbucks on Larimer, half wishing she'd get lost. In fact, in the end the get-together had *not* bored Aglaia. Naomi nursed her baby under the cover of a blanket, then made a cozy intimacy for the three of them as she rearranged the napkins on the table in front of the coffee shop fireplace while Aglaia collected the lattes and biscotti from the barista at the espresso machine. Naomi even smelled soothing when Aglaia bent over her to put the cups down—like sheets hung in the sunlight.

Aglaia was curious, at the time, about her own positive responsiveness towards the homey comfort, as if she missed the domesticity of farm and family more than she admitted. Most of her friends were of a different ilk altogether—working girls she met over drinks, who valued their independence and talked about the beaches at all-inclusive resorts in Cancun or the availability of men at their favorite clubs in the city. Then there was Lou, of course—but was she really a friend or was theirs another work-related association? Aglaia wasn't sure.

She turned the ice pack over on her ankle, which was numb but less swollen, and resumed her consideration of the issue of friendship. Now, Dayna Yates had been a surprise. They'd never formally met back in their teens, as Dayna was closer to Joel in age. But Aglaia hadn't forgotten the striking city visitor who cut such a wide swath as a teen in the village. She recognized her the day they met at the gym, when Dayna took her place on the stationary bike beside her and initiated the conversation

"Aglaia is an unusual name," Dayna had said after introductions, "but I met someone with your surname once in a small town in Nebraska—a Joel Klassen. Any relation?"

She nodded. "He was my brother."

"What a coincidence," Dayna said, pausing to select the program on her bicycle. "He died, didn't he?"

Not many people asked such a question so directly, and it took Aglaia's breath away to hear it aloud. But Dayna looked Aglaia square in the face without apology or embarrassment and went on. "He was the nicest guy I met in Tiege. He once said something about wanting a girlfriend just like his sister."

That was Joel, all right.

"But you didn't know him well. I mean, you were only around for that one summer, weren't you?" Aglaia asked

"Yeah—party season. That was quite the vacation," Dayna said, pumping hard now on her bike so that the small towel hanging from her handlebar swung back and forth. "Joel asked me to that church club of his once, but I was too high and mighty then to risk my reputation." She chirped out a laugh of self-derision. "I'd never known any guy to be so respectful of girls—opening doors for us and standing when we entered the room. He sure took some ribbing over that, didn't he?"

"But you invited him to one of your parties," Aglaia said. She recalled Joel coming home early that night, leaving François to his mischief—whatever that was. "You were kind to include him."

"I was a snot." Dayna laughed outright at herself now. "I was only thinking that he was of legal drinking age and would chip in for the keg. I never invited him again. Do you know that night he never even drank one beer? He sat alone and nursed a cola. When a fight broke out over some girl, he tried to give her a ride home but she was pretty far gone by then. Way too happy." Dayna shook her head. "Thankfully we all grow up eventually."

At that, Aglaia pedaled faster. Joel never got the chance to grow up. Dayna must have understood; she changed the subject.

Since her reunion with Dayna at the gym, Aglaia thought, even before Lou came into the mix, their relationship took the same pattern. Dayna would approach a question head on—just put it out there and accept the response, along with any blame she herself might bear. But she wasn't afraid to place blame, either, as was evident when the subject of Lou Chapman came up a few days ago.

"Why do you spend time with that woman?" Dayna had asked. "She's full of herself and she's a user."

Aglaia was taken aback by Dayna's criticism. "Isn't there some sort of loyalty you academics have for each other?" she asked.

"Only when it's earned," Dayna said, shaking her head. "Lou's literary theory is flawed, she lacks a consistent hermeneutic, and she employs a moderated esotericism as the authoritative subtext informing the academy. Her revisionist presuppositions interfere with proper scholarship." Aglaia thought Dayna noticed her lack of comprehension about this time because she dropped the lingo and explained, "I'm no proponent of religion, Aglaia—even if I do send our daughter to Sunday school. But Lou makes a point of emphatically denying the impact of Christian civilization on society. I find it absurd that she distorts the historical record like that—it can't hold water and it ends up bringing aspersion on our discipline as a whole. We don't need that kind of bias. Besides," she added, "it's well known around the university that Lou oversteps her bounds with the students and even uses their research in her journal articles without crediting their work. It's just not right."

Aglaia hadn't welcomed the information; it didn't line up with her perception of Lou's standing at PRU. Touchy subjects like Christianity and ethics seldom came up in her talking with Lou— at least, that was, before the unfortunate appearance of Tina in her apartment Thursday night. She and Lou tended to concentrate on the more neutral area of the arts, but now Aglaia hoped her decision about whether to pursue employment with the university wouldn't become be a matter of morality. She'd worked too hard at evading controversy to bungle it at this point, when she was so close to achieving success.

The kitchen phone rang. Aglaia limped over to pick it up, then headed to the living room couch. Who'd call at 8:45 on a Saturday morning?

"I knew you'd be awake. You can take the girl out of the country but you can't take the country out of the girl, eh?"

"Good morning, Naomi."

"I'm trying out this new cell phone Byron bought me. He made me take it in case I break down along the way, but I think it's actually so he can get hold of me when he can't find the formula for the baby. I weaned him last week—the baby, that is, not Byron!" Her laugh was a gurgle. "I'm calling to make sure that we're still on for tonight. Can I pick anything up for you?"

"Would you mind stopping by a bakery to get a baguette for supper? Oh, and I need some toothpaste. I won't be leaving the apartment today." Aglaia explained her injury and Naomi offered to drive her to the airport the next morning before departing for home. That way, Aglaia could save airport parking fees and have help with her luggage. Naomi hung up after promising to be there by six.

Aglaia, restive, tapped a rhythm with her good foot against the leg of the coffee table. She wasn't used to sitting still. The television held no interest for her and she could almost recite her guidebook to Paris word for word already. Hitting the gym one last time before she squeezed into her new jeans was out of the question—her ankle had to stay elevated. It was going to be a long day.

From her spot on the couch she could see the suitcase and

there was no excuse left for avoiding that Bible—François's Bible with those two dangerous phrases handwritten by him into the margins of Genesis. Since she'd decided to take it along with her to Paris, she couldn't very well hand it over to him unexamined— even if the thought of opening that book rang alarm bells in her mind. She should at least take a look at it, and she'd just make sure to ignore the text itself.

Nine

With Zephyr warming her lap, Aglaia opened the Bible for the first time since it came in the mail three days ago.

She'd been right in her suspicions. François had written notes into the margins beginning at the first chapter of the first book. In formal lettering, he'd transcribed themes beside each book's title, as she had done in her Bible at the same time, following Pastor Reimer's spidery outline on the chalkboard in the church basement: *Exodus, thirst in the desert; Deuteronomy, rock of salvation; John, light shining in darkness; Philippians, joy!* But below these careful words copied on the onionskin pages were bits of scrawled commentary, some of it in French—François's personal notations.

Beside the story of Noah and the flood, for example, he'd written *arc-en-ciel*. As he made that note, was he imagining his first sighting of a prairie rainbow, stretching unbroken from horizon to horizon without the interruption of buildings or light standards? She remembered the two of them lying on their backs in the damp summer grass, his quick gasp, his quiet awe.

"You know how the rainbow came to be, don't you?" he asks.

That's a straightforward question for a girl raised by parents who read the great stories of the Bible to her at bedtime.

But as she opens her mouth to answer that it's God's memento of promise, he interrupts her to tell how Iris, the cupbearer of the gods, lifted the waters of the oceans up into the clouds to connect heaven and earth, dressed in a rainbow woven by the Three Graces.

He sighs. She hasn't ever heard a boy sigh for the sake of beauty, and the radiance of his rainbow shines inside her, too, so that she doesn't correct him.

And again, here, where the nomads trod the ceaseless desert seeking the Promised Land, he'd written *singing sand*. He was thinking, she was sure, of the two of them standing on the crest of the dune out in the east pasture, catching the faint, far-away tinkling of the wind-blown sand, like bells or the call of a pan flute, wafting at the edge of their hearing. A few pages later he'd written *windmill*. What could he have meant but their drive to the north quarter that blistering day to put minerals out for the cows?

Mary Grace describes the mechanism to him. "So the wind turns the blades and rotates the gear to drive the rod attached to the plunger in the cylinder, which sucks the water through the sand point up the pipe, bringing it to the surface from below the dune," she says, proud she doesn't need Joel to prompt her.

She's glad to be alone with François for once, out from under Joel's protective eye. He can be smothering sometimes. Dad's been too busy to notice her moods lately and, thankfully, Mom hasn't yet figured out that François can make her spine tingle.

François's eyes follow the pointing of her finger from the top of the windmill down the wooden structure to the large metal trough, where the dribble from the spout makes ripples on the surface of the water, cool and inviting.

"On y va!" he blurts. He bolts from the truck's cab and yanks his t-shirt over his head and kicks the tennis shoes free from his feet despite her shouted warning to watch out for cactus. He startles the cows gathering around the blue salt blocks, and they scatter upon his whoops as he jumps, waist deep, into the icy pool.

She pursues him too closely and he slaps a handful of water up over her. Shrieking, she retaliates, and soon they're wet to the bone with their teeth chattering in spite of the sun.

Aglaia flipped over half an inch of pages to Esther, where his unruly hand had circled *beautiful young virgins* and *harem* and *concubines*. Aglaia squinted to make out the letters of his comment: Had he written "Mary Grace" here? No, it said *J'adore les Grâces américaines.* She read it again, to be sure.

He loved the American *Graces*—plural? Aglaia leaned her head back on the couch, confounded. There was no denying that François had been a healthy, red-blooded young man. He must have been eyeing up all the girls in Tiege, and there were some cute ones. But somehow, back then, she convinced herself she was his sole focus. A niggling jealousy gave her a slight cramp in her belly all these years later. Just reading the disturbing sentence brought back teenage insecurities, but this was still early in the Bible, early in the summer. Perhaps he'd written it before anything got started between the two of them.

She turned a couple hundred pages till she came to Song of Songs—a book that captivated her long before she met François Vivier, introduced at a sleep-over with other girls whose mothers, like hers, checked through school backpacks to ensure that no romance novels entered their homes. They missed the sexiest one, right under their noses in their own Holy Bibles! Now it appeared that François, as well, found the poems of interest.

Aglaia saw she was correct in her assumption that she'd discover something informative in this book of love; François was a lover, and Song of Songs would have appealed to him. He'd underlined many verses: *How beautiful you are, my darling! Oh, how beautiful!... You have stolen my heart with one glance from your eyes... Love burns like a blazing fire, like a mighty flame.* In the margins François had written *Aphrodite, déesse de l'amour*, the phrase likely meaning "goddess of love" in English. Aglaia knew all about her, this patron of courtesans—manifestation of the planet called Venus, the evening star—who maddened men with amorous passion as dusk fell. In the aphrodisiac of her own imagination, Aglaia pictured her now, adorned by her handmaiden Graces in twinkling jewelry forged in a furnace worked by the great Cyclopes.

She went on to read more of Solomon's words: *You are a garden locked up, my sister, my bride; you are a spring enclosed, a sealed fountain.* Here François had written *at the spring.* Aglaia's mind flashed back and she closed her eyes to savor again her very first kiss.

Under the close cover of the night, with his palm coupling hers, they drift down to the spring-fed pond behind the barn where the prairie grass grows like wool and scratches her legs. The aspens, roots drinking deeply of the sweet, scarce water, tremble above them like guardians of her innocence, and the buffalo-berry bushes sigh in the breeze.

The moon-washed water, embossed with circles of insects alighting, reflects their two forms tilted towards one another, shoulders touching. She quivers, taut with anticipation. He hasn't held her hand until tonight, hasn't stroked her hair or touched her face. Now his breath is hot on her cheek as she turns to see his longing eyes.

"Graceful Mary Grace," he whispers, and then his lips press on hers—on her virgin lips—and that's all. But it's enough for her.

Aglaia frittered the Saturday away between the sofa and her bed, leafing through the Bible, honing in on his faded lettering in Luke and then skipping back to Kings or Micah, reading at random and envisioning the scenes behind François's comments. In other words, she spent the day at the farm with him. It made a confusing collage in her mind. Perhaps if she began at the front and progressed through the whole thing chronologically, she'd sort out the mayhem of memories that have for years now flitted around her imagination like impish sprites, shadows glimpsed and never laid hold of.

By late afternoon Aglaia's ankle was almost normal, and supper was ready when Naomi rang to be let in. Her childhood friend deposited an overnight bag on the floor before wrapping Aglaia in a matronly hug. Her back had the soft folds of a more mature woman and her hair was over-processed, nothing like the lustrous tresses she kept as a girl, but her dimples were as deep as ever, her hazel eyes as quick to light up with cheer.

"You've lost weight again," Naomi said. "Scrawny thing. How do you ever plan to catch a man?"

Aglaia opened her mouth to retort but Naomi went on. "I have good news from the doctor." Aglaia had forgotten that Naomi was expecting some test results at her follow-up appointment today. "He says the biopsy showed no cancer after all."

She clapped her hands in delight, her mouth open in a wide grin as though bringing news Aglaia must have been waiting in agony to hear. Naomi had never been as pretty as Aglaia, a fact she freely admitted as a teen. But she still wore joy on her face like a makeup.

"Congratulations," Aglaia said with false optimism, cautious about celebrating. Naomi's mother had died young and her own longevity was doubtful; her hope seemed ill founded. But Naomi was always so full of hope.

"Tell me all about your trip," Naomi urged after she gave Aglaia an unasked-for update on her children's progress in school and how she was thinking that maybe she should take them all out of class and teach them at home for a few years. "Your mother filled me in last week about how you had to rush your passport application through to get it approved in time. What have you sewn?" she asked. "Let me see it all!"

Aglaia protested that her bag was already packed, that she hardly had time to make anything new, but Naomi opened the suitcase and used the couch for her display rack as she spread the pieces out, one by one. She admired the khaki jacket, the sateen skirt printed with papyrus, and the hemp knit top. Aglaia's little black dress made of silk velvet burnout, set off with cobalt-blue enameled Japanese buttons purchased at an estate sale, almost sent her into convulsions.

"Fabulous! With that neckline, you'll have the Frenchmen drooling."

Aglaia wanted only one of them to drool, but she didn't mention this to Naomi. "I can't imagine I'll need anything so fancy, but it packs well," she said. Naomi remarked on the obvious attributes of the clothing, such as color and sheen of the fabric, but of course she couldn't appreciate the less visible quality behind the handiwork—the anchoring stitches holding seams to lining, the initials embroidered into a cuff. Aglaia smoothed out the white blouse collar of the shirt that went with her charcoal worsted blazer and pencil skirt. "I'll wear this suit for the day I meet with the museum people."

Aglaia expected to live in her jeans most of the time she was in Paris, but she recalled the memo from head office about arrangements for media coverage at the gallery. Montreal viewed the delivery of the costume as a great photo opportunity encouraging francophonic relations, not to mention the international advertising it afforded for Incognito. Her boss, however, was disgusted over the antics of headquarters to pander to the expectations of the snobs in France, but Eb knew what side his bread was buttered on, he said, so he didn't air his opinions to his employers. Had it been left up to him, he'd have forgone personal delivery and simply sent the costume overseas by FedEx. He couldn't be bothered with the fanfare but acted relieved by Aglaia's interest in jumping through these hoops.

Eb's Canadian overseers had been hounding him lately, and not just about the Paris enterprise. Eb was a deferential manager who didn't enjoy—or employ—micromanagement. As she repacked her bag, Aglaia wondered what was up. It might have something to do with that movie he mentioned a few weeks ago. Incognito Denver occasionally contracted out its designs and labor for cinematographic projects, but most were local shoots that Eb supervised himself—happy enough to support the popular literature of the people in this increasingly illiterate world, as he said. The current movie, whatever it was, involved a larger film company from California, earning the special attention of the CEO in Montreal. When she returned, Aglaia would have to ask Eb about the movie and their role in it.

Meanwhile, Aglaia concentrated on Paris, and she was committed to doing Eb proud. The assignment confirmed her worth within the company. Her boss thought she was up to it, so she'd swallow her qualms and rise to the challenge. She had no idea about comportment in such grand circles, but she'd have to wing it. If only she had Lou's self-assurance!

Dinner with Naomi started out well. Aglaia served a crisp Cae-
sar salad and garlic bread alongside the bubbling lasagna, which
was cheesy and spiced with nutmeg. But when Naomi insisted on
praying before the meal, Aglaia thought it was a good thing she
hadn't opened the bottle of wine she'd picked up to have on hand.
Something twigged in her memory about Naomi not touching alcohol these days for religious reasons, though that hadn't always
been the case. The unopened bottle sat on the counter. It was a red
from the Napa that had attracted Aglaia because of its label bearing a sketch of the Three Graces, and named after one of them—
Euphrosyne—which was fitting in light of that Grace's personality
as the embodiment of mirth and merriment. Well, she'd save the
merriment for more appreciative company, she thought.

As the meal progressed, Aglaia realized afresh why she didn't
want to get too close to her old friend. The woman was too self-
righteous.

"Isn't it terrific how God has brought us back into one another's lives?" Naomi's question was predictable, the subject of God's
goodness being the evangelical fallback to any lagging conversation.

Aglaia replied tartly, "It seems to me *you're* the one that's
brought us back together." If you can call this together, she thought,
a forced evening between the city mouse and the country mouse.

"Friendship is worth a bit of work, Mary Grace."

There! On top of it all, Naomi persisted in calling her by the
old name, left behind for a reason.

Throughout Aglaia's childhood as Mary Grace, she'd heard the
family stories about her namesake, *Taunte* Maria—that venerable
missionary to the lost who forged inroads into the jungles of Bo-
livia with the voice of an angel, with songs that spanned the gap
of misunderstanding between God and her transfixed listeners in
loincloths. The elders at Aglaia's church held Maria in high esteem.
Her great-aunt had passed along to her the gift of song, they surmised; would she someday follow in her footsteps? These were big
shoes to fill and Aglaia had *wanted* to fill them as a girl, until it
dawned on her that she'd be trading the farm for even more re-

moteness—the isolation of the sanctified. As for her middle name, it was ludicrous. She'd always felt graceless, never more than as a teenager going through her clumsy stage. What had her parents been thinking? Altogether, "Mary Grace" was such a mouthful. There was no diminutive for it, no nickname.

The whole congregation called her rebellious when she refused to attend choir any longer, that last year at home when she was so alone. She was probably depressed.

She officially changed her name down at the vital statistics registry office as soon as she moved to Denver. The bureaucrat who processed her application stank of onions and leaned too close when he pressed her fingertips into the printing pad and rolled them, one by one, over the form as though she were a common criminal. It took months before every document was changed—birth certificate, driver's license—but finally she was Mary Grace no longer. She'd purged herself, every official piece of ID now bearing her chosen name. The old was gone, the new had come! Until, that is, her mother mailed her a church bulletin with a prayer request for Mary Grace who was wandering as a prodigal in the wicked city, or she bumped into a schoolmate who failed to recall the day of reckoning—the day of Joel's funeral—when in her heart Aglaia put to death her old nature.

"For dust you are and to dust you will return," the preacher says.

She hunkers on the front pew, staring at the floor between her shoes and blocking out the singing around her—"Rock of ages, cleft for me"—and the drone of the pastor with his promises of resurrection, this so-called hope held out to Henry and Tina and Mary Grace. But when he says that God is gracious in this hideous act of His sovereignty, she can keep silent no longer.

She pushes away from the hard bench and faces the other mourners and presses her back against that casket holding the stone-cold dead, the stench of the flowers nauseating her.

"I am Aglaia," she exclaims, the name leaping to her lips from some subconscious cavern for the first time, each word of the sentence deliberate and spoken loudly enough to disturb the fat Grossmama dozing in the back row.

Tina plucks at her sleeve, hisses at her to settle down.

"Don't call me Mary Grace anymore," she growls to the congregation. A pronouncement foams in her soul and forms on her tongue like a creed, and she fairly shouts it: "There is no grace!"

Her father stands then, his own rare tears dropping onto her hair as he takes her out to weep in privacy.

" 'Aglaia,' " Naomi said.

Aglaia regained her sense of time.

"I'm sorry, I meant to call you 'Aglaia,' though for the life of me I can't get used to that name."

"It's okay. I go by either," she fibbed, "now that I've recovered from my identity crisis." Even as she said this, she knew it took more than an official name change to earn the graciousness and elegance she longed for.

"Have you?"

"Have I what?"

"Recovered." Naomi chased her salad around the plate with her fork. "You're so self-sufficient here in your own apartment with your hoity-toity job taking you to exotic places. But for a while tonight it's been like old times with you, sitting together and sharing, until your eyes go hollow and you zone out for a while."

Nowtheyweregettingdowntotherealmotivationbehind Naomi's visit, Aglaia thought—to harass her into the kinship they once had. "It will never be like old times," she said. She half wished she were wrong.

"I know people change, sometimes out of self-defense." Naomi stuck a leafy forkful into her mouth and talked around it. "It's just that you're so pent up. Where did all the spit and vinegar go?"

"People *do* change, Naomi. They leave certain things behind them."

"Like their family?"

Offended, Aglaia rose from the table, laying her napkin across her chair, and put the kettle on. Her family involvement was none of Naomi's business.

But Naomi was never one for tact and wouldn't let it go. "Don't you ever miss the farm, your parents? Don't you miss me?"

Aglaia's fist clenched around the kettle's handle. She willed herself to relax before turning back to Naomi.

"Do I miss you? Why, you're here right now," she said with unnatural lightness, seething inside. Was Naomi completely devoid of subtlety, of the ability to respect boundaries? What was it with these women in her life?

"But *you're* not really here, are you?" A spark ignited Naomi's eyes and one corner of her mouth curled up and she asked, "Don't you ever just want to bust out and sing?"

She lunged to her feet then, threw her head back melodramatically, and opened her mouth like a baby bird for its sustenance. In that instant Aglaia knew what was coming, recognized the deep intake of breath and the posture they used to assume when they practiced out behind the spring, filling the skies with their melodious cries where no one but heaven could hear.

Sure enough, with operatic intensity Naomi began to belt out the clearest, craziest soprano Aglaia had heard since their youthful excesses.

"Come, thou fount of every blessing, tune my heart to sing thy grace…"

"Stop it," Aglaia hushed.

"Streams of mercy never ceasing, call for songs of loudest praise."

"The neighbors will call the police, Naomi!"

But there was no stemming the flow once she got going. She cascaded all over the treble clef, grasping Aglaia's hands and swinging her into a drunken jive in disregard of the ankle.

Naomi towed Aglaia out through the open patio door onto the deck, her frizz bouncing all around her flushed cheeks as she howled. Her musical laughter was so infectious that, near the end of the song, Aglaia started to weaken and almost joined in on the last line herself.

Panting, Naomi stood facing Aglaia in the duskiness of the overcast evening. A car door slammed in the parking lot three stories below and Aglaia heard the clapping of one set of hands. She and Naomi popped their heads over the railing to determine their audience. Lou, dressed in a crisp navy pantsuit, stood in front of her burnished BMW.

Aglaia withdrew from the deck's edge. Lou must have seen and heard the whole thing, and now Naomi bowed to Lou in burlesque exaggeration. "A friend of yours?" she asked. "Let's invite her up."

"No, I'll go down and find out what she wants," Aglaia objected, averse to allowing both women into the same room at the same time, feng shui to meet rustic homestead. But Naomi was already yelling at Lou to join them, assuring Aglaia that the interruption wouldn't be an inconvenience at all and that she was dying to meet any of her chic acquaintances. By the time Aglaia slid the glass door closed behind her, Naomi was halfway down the hallway cheering Lou up the steps as though she were a long-lost buddy.

Ten

Lou Chapman mounted the stairs of the apartment block, the private smells of the commoner curling out from under closed doors to assault her—cigarette smoke, fried fish, burnt sugar. The dumpling who'd been wailing and flailing on the balcony beckoned her in, introduced herself as Aglaia's best friend, and offered to take the folder out of her hands, even pulling at it.

"Thank you, but I'll give it to her myself," Lou said, and snatched it back.

Her snub went unremarked by Naomi, who set about clearing the table of dirty dishes like a maid while Aglaia apprised Lou about the injury to her ankle. The news pleased Lou; she wasn't one for gratuitous pain, but the injury might work into her strategy very well. She decided to say nothing about that strategy just yet.

Aglaia's fine hair was blown about and her eyes shone with an unconscious freshness that now and again disarmed Lou. Despite Aglaia's studied indifference—the languid stance, the tilt of her head and how she crossed her arms and waited a cautious breath before answering—she couldn't hide a liveliness that leaked out when her guard was down, Lou thought.

"I didn't think I'd see you until I got back from France," Aglaia said.

"I'm full of surprises. I can stay just a moment, but I wanted to drop off reading material for your trip—a few pieces I've written." Lou was being modest. The half-dozen articles published in prestigious journals over the past couple of years represented the meat of her doctoral work and translated well into her pending monograph—though, of course, she'd written or co-authored scores of articles over the span of her career. Despite her recent publishing setback, she was convinced of the soundness of her research and the contribution it made to the sociological literature.

Aglaia skimmed the first page of a paper relating to Greek mythology and art. "You shouldn't have gone to such a bother."

"I had them in my computer files," Lou said. Educating Aglaia would take more effort than printing out a few articles, which at any rate wouldn't be fully comprehended by the girl, but it was a starting point. Aglaia had been receptive so far.

Naomi wiped her hands on a dishtowel and peered over Aglaia's shoulder with her nose wrinkled, no doubt scandalized by the illustrations of Aphrodite and her cohort.

"What interest have you in art?" Lou asked her. The answer was evident in Naomi's lack of fashion sense and Lou didn't care that she put the woman on the spot. That was what teachers did.

"Art? Well, I haven't taken any college classes on it, if that's what you mean. Nothing like this stuff." She paused, then added, brightening, "But I began collecting plates a few years ago."

Lou was puzzled. "Photographic plates from art books?"

"No, I mean dinner plates."

"Oh, porcelain plates?" Lou asked, her curiosity piqued. Her own mother had inherited a fine collection, the value of which Lou came to appreciate only as an adult. Not that she'd laid her eyes on them in years.

"I don't know about porcelain. My kids got me started. They bought the first one at the drugstore as a birthday gift—it was decorated with peonies—and now I have about ten of them, all colors and sizes."

How predictably lowbrow, Lou thought, smothering a snicker. The priceless set of antique Limoges plates of her memory, each individually hand painted and rimmed in gold, used to be displayed on the dining room wall above the wainscoting in the 6,000-square-foot house in New York, before the divorce. The plates didn't all survive Mother's temper. Had her sister salvaged any when she packed up for the house sale, kneeling alone in front of cardboard boxes and wearing stained sweats with her hair drawn back in a severe ponytail? Pity how Linda had let herself go. Lou shut the intrusive picture out of her mind and focused on the woman before her.

Naomi was not unattractive, she thought, just a bit bovine with her wide-set eyes and short, straight lashes. Her blouse strained over her bosom and the elasticized waistband accentuated the thickness of her torso, yet there was something generous about her that implied succor. Perhaps she was the perfect person to shed more light on their mutual acquaintance, Aglaia Klassen.

"What is it that you do in life?" Lou didn't veil her condescension but doubted Naomi would pick up on it.

The woman launched into an animated account while Aglaia stood away from them and kept her gaze averted, busying herself with the packet of articles but not reading them, Lou noted. Disassociating, perhaps?

"Byron and I grow grain and keep livestock, same as most everyone in the area. We live too far from the village for me to work outside of the home and, anyway, I have a full-time job with the kids, believe you me." Naomi spoke with no chagrin and sprinkled many of her sentences with a merry laugh. "Seeding and harvest are pretty busy for me, though our two older sons help out a lot. They're fourteen and thirteen. Then we've got four younger ones."

Lou thought her eyes must be glazing over. This talk of agriculture and children was unbearable, and now Naomi grabbed her purse from the counter. "I have family photos, if you'd like to see the kids."

"No, thank you," Lou declined with alacrity. Naomi froze for an instant at the rebuff and then replaced her purse, still smiling but now fingering the silver cross of her necklace. The woman went on with her trite monologue. "I also have a huge garden and put up lots of peas and tomatoes and beans," Naomi said. "It helps make ends meet."

"Lou knows all about farming, don't you, Lou?" Aglaia's interjection, delivered in a derisive tone abnormal for her, proved she was listening in after all.

"Really?" Naomi asked.

"Yes, she tells me she grows herbs in her window box." Lou heard Aglaia's passive-aggressive scorn as the first indication of any real alliance she felt with Naomi. Apparently her friend didn't pick up on Aglaia's sarcastic tone.

"Parsley?" Naomi asked. "Dill? I have a great *Borscht* recipe, if you'd like it, Lou."

"I don't cook much," Lou responded. The woman truly was vacuous, she thought. "I cultivate herbs such as tarragon and rosemary for flavored vinegars, and grow many for their healing properties, to stimulate my chakras and energize my aura. I grow calendula, shiso, and lemongrass for hot infusions—"

"She means tea," Aglaia interposed. Lou was amused by Aglaia's compulsion to interpret her to Naomi, and she questioned how close the women truly were.

"So you two have known each other for a long time?" she asked.

Aglaia, sulking, shoveled the papers back into the manila folder, but Naomi answered amiably, "Forever. We were delivered by the same doctor, went to the same country school. I even married her second cousin."

"You're shirttail relatives, then." Not surprising, Lou thought. She'd learned enough by now to deduce the communal atmosphere under which Aglaia had been raised.

"Practically everyone around Tiege is related," Naomi confirmed. "Byron was the best I could do after I was jilted by Joel Klassen, her brother, when I was nine."

Lou noticed that Aglaia was chewing on her thumbnail.

"You must have a lot of stories to tell on her, then," Lou said, trying to coax out an anecdote or two. This was the first she'd heard about a brother; she thought Aglaia was an only child. "Sneaking a drink from Daddy's liquor cabinet," she suggested, "or meeting the boys in the bushes behind the school?"

"No liquor cabinet," Aglaia said.

"Well, in our church youth group—" Naomi began with a conspiratorial grin, but Aglaia broke in. "We went our separate ways before there was much time for that, didn't we?" Aglaia frowned a warning at Naomi as she kicked away from the table and headed for the kitchen counter. "Decaf, anyone?" She pulled three mugs from the cupboard with such force Lou thought they'd chip.

"Continue," Lou said to Naomi, ignoring the interruption. "Aglaia promotes herself as the model of piety." Tight-lipped Aglaia had intimated no such thing and Lou didn't anticipate great revelations from Naomi, but she found the tension delicious.

However, Naomi was at last picking up on Aglaia's distress and looked from Lou to Aglaia and back again.

"We've been out of touch for years and just reconnected," Aglaia said.

Was she defending Naomi or distancing herself from the woman? Lou surmised there was more here than two girlfriends getting reacquainted, but she didn't have time to explore that now.

"I'd better run along and let you get on with your visit, I suppose," she said. "I need to stop at the mall before it closes, and you two will need your beauty sleep." She wished Aglaia *bon voyage* in what she knew was a flawless accent, and gave her an impetuous peck on the cheek. Aglaia cringed and looked sullen at Lou's parting shot: "Naomi, do ask Aglaia all about the special book delivery she's making in Paris." She bet Aglaia hadn't gotten around to that topic yet. It should cause a dither. Too bad she wasn't able to stay and listen in to the trouble her words would stir up.

Lou let herself out of the apartment and was still smirking when she slid into the leather driver's seat and touched up her lipstick in the rearview mirror. What a contrast between her polished reflection and the dowdy Naomi Enns, but more than looks differentiated them. She'd encountered many women like Naomi in past years—research subjects or relatives of students or just the great

unwashed. Insipid, slavish things trapped in a web of negative relationships by domineering men or poverty or religion. Granted,
Lou thought as she blotted her lips, Naomi didn't appear to be un-
happy. That was the irony—these women were unaware of their
own misery.

But fun as it was to provoke a little dissension between Naomi
and Aglaia, Lou's greater concern lay with the woeful state of education regarding gender rights, most women not understanding
their own power. They, like Naomi, were blind to the incredible
influences that shaped their culture and determined their destiny
because they wouldn't speak up and change their situation, pas-
sively accepting the hand dealt to them by their circumstances and
history.

Considering how Aglaia squirmed tonight, she was evidently
not at ease with her past—a healthy sign of her growing self-aware-
ness. The sooner she made a complete break with the inhibiting
traditions of her background, the better. Narrow-minded friends
like Naomi bog a woman down. Aglaia needed to get away from
that one—needed protection, almost. She merited much higher
company.

Well, Lou thought as she wheeled out of the parking lot, she'd
do everything in her power to remedy Aglaia's plight.

Eleven

Aglaia's temples throbbed as she dead-bolted the door after Lou, never so relieved as now to see her go. Her apprehension about Lou meeting Naomi had been fully warranted, and she blamed herself for not following her first inclination to intercept Lou before she made it up the apartment steps in the first place.

"What was that all about?" Naomi asked. "What did she mean about the special delivery? And what's up with her magical voodoo herb talk and the papers she gave you? You don't actually read that stuff, do you?"

Aglaia ignored the questions she least wanted to answer. "The articles are helpful in defining artistic expression in my costuming."

"Right, your sewing."

Aglaia closed her eyes for a moment against Naomi's breeziness that managed to make her career sound like a hobby, a pastime to keep her occupied until she got married or found her real calling. Naomi might be excused for not realizing the acclamation Aglaia was receiving in her profession by arts reviewers, but didn't she at least recall how hard Aglaia worked as a teen making their matching skirts for church duets? Or the outfits she put together for the two of them to tell the story of King Solomon to the five year olds in the Vacation Bible School class they co-taught one week that summer?

"*Magnifique!*" *François blurts as he comes upon her pirouetting in her new costume.*

"It's nothing." She knows she's blushing. The Queen of Sheba's skimpy chiffon scarves don't cover an undergarment as insubstantial as her bikini.

"Nothing?" He touches the filmy fabric and then runs his palm over her back. "Something from heaven, I think."

The warmth rushes past her face down her neck to her chest, her breasts. Mary Grace sucks in a cooling breath. To distract him from ogling her body, she finds herself babbling, describing the royal caravan of Sheba—its camels carrying a treasure-load of spices and gold and jewels bound for the wisest man in the world as a gift from the queen for all his answers to all her questions.

"A pot-de-vin?" he asks her. "A bribe?" She thinks it's more of a peace offering but François continues, "Do you know about Hera, the queen of heaven, and her pot-de-vin?"

The prospect of another of his stories drives the biblical account out of her mind. He draws her down to sit on the floor next to him and tells her about Hera, the goddess of marriage, who was tricked into wet-nursing the orphaned baby Heracles; when she discovered the hoax, she jerked him from her breast so that her milk flowed out into the sky to form the Milky Way.

Hera, François tells her, was a powerful and angry deity who meddled in the affairs of men and seduced the gods to get her own way. The Three Graces were favorite companions of hers, yet she found them dispensable—a kind of currency for her own pleasure, as his tale goes on to prove.

"Zeus was the greatest of kings—like your Solomon, perhaps," François proposes, and Mary Grace disagrees but doesn't interrupt his story to say so.

Hera was Zeus's sister, constrained to marry him because of his unbrotherly lust for her, and she was filled with malice over the requirement. In revenge against him, she plotted to put her husband-

brother, Zeus, into a deep sleep and solicited the soporific help of
Hypnos in return for the favors of one of the Graces. Hypnos, greedy
to possess his own goddess, inspected the trio with lecherous intent.

"Which of the three did Hera give to Hypnos?" he asks in his
creamy voice, his hand reaching again for her body "The Grace of
croissance, *the Grace of* beauté, *or the Grace of* bonheur?"

Growth. Beauty. Happiness. Which one did Zeus prefer?

"So what is it about Lou's articles that help your deep artistic expression, exactly?" Naomi hadn't let the subject drop during Aglaia's mental absence. How long had she been waiting for a
response?

"The reading Lou provides is a free education," Aglaia replied.
"She's an expert in her field, you know. Art takes many forms as it
communicates truth, which is the sum experience of culture from
the prehistoric times to our era."

"Truth is the sum… ?"

Aglaia couldn't expect her to get it. "My work is the same as
any poem or painting. It's an outward and visible reflection of inward and emotional beliefs." She heard her own accommodation, a
blending of Eb's sacramental vocabulary and François's pantheistic
elaborations and Lou's high-and-mighty philosophy. It sickened
her slightly. "Besides, I love to sew and I'm good at it."

"I'm good at cooking meals for the branding crew," Naomi said
in a lighter, teasing tone now. "Does that qualify as art? Or what
about my artistic expression of wiping a drippy nose?"

"People often trivialize what they don't understand," Aglaia answered. The strike at Naomi's intellect hit the mark and the woman
shut her mouth and flinched as if in pain. Aglaia tried to diminish
her insult, which sounded too much like something Lou might say.
"It's just that you haven't got a complete picture of me and my life.
You weren't watching when I scraped my way up, barely keeping
body and soul together." How could Naomi have seen? Her head
was already in a diaper pail when eighteen-year-old Aglaia was
struggling to pay her rent by taking in piecework alterations in her
first, dingy basement suite, hemming trousers late into the night
before cramming for exams that never paid off. "I was dying to fin-

ish my schooling, but Dad never could find it in his heart to lend me tuition. Every cent went into keeping that farm afloat."

"That's not fair, Aglaia. You know he did his best, given the circumstances."

"He's never valued learning and Mom doesn't, either. They bury themselves in their grunt work. I'm lucky to have found Lou, who's a real friend," she said, in spite of her earlier questioning about the nature of their affiliation. "She's taken me under her wing and introduced me to some very important people. She's a complex person, sophisticated and intelligent."

"Since when have those been the qualities of a friend?" Naomi countered, as if she could read Aglaia's doubt. Naomi went on, ruthless. "I don't mean to sound judgmental, but Lou isn't your type. I don't trust her."

"She probably doesn't trust you."

Naomi added more sugar to her cup, clinking her spoon against the pottery. "You were embarrassed by me in front of Lou."

"I wasn't embarrassed," she said, her objection weak.

"You were sticking up for me. Pitying me, even."

"It's not you, Naomi. Rural life just isn't my context anymore."

"So what is your *context*?"

This had to stop, Aglaia thought. "I don't want to get into an argument when I'm boarding a plane early tomorrow for my first trip to Europe."

Naomi was quiet for a minute and fiddled with the spoon in her hand, likely sorry for her churlish words, as Aglaia reprimanded herself for her poor deportment as a hostess.

"Well, anyway, tell me about this mysterious delivery Lou mentioned," Naomi said.

They had to discuss something, Aglaia thought. At least this subject shouldn't incite another argument. So she motioned for Naomi to wait while she tender-footed her way out of the kitchen and scooped up the Bible from her bed, hoping she wouldn't regret her rashness.

"It's a logistical problem." She dropped the book with a smack onto the kitchen table but kept her hand on top in case Naomi had thoughts of opening it. "Mom dug this out of storage and has the crazy notion that I should return it to its owner—in Paris, of all places." It was Aglaia's idea to look for François all along—not Tina's, as she intimated—but she might as well try out the blaming technique she could be forced to use when she handed the Bible to him.

Naomi stared at the leather cover. She stammered, "Paris? Who's the owner?"

"Well, you remember that guy, François Vivier, who came as an exchange student?"

How calmly she pronounced his name and reduced him to a couple of words, *that guy*. As if anyone in Tiege could ever forget him; he was the first non-Germanic foreign student the town had ever welcomed. In fact, his reputation spread to the surrounding area, to Imperial and Holyoke, and even some girl all the way from Sterling had asked Aglaia about him months after he left. That really bugged Aglaia, the interest he aroused, and even now the thought that he had held other girls' hearts in captivity made her wonder who *she* was to him—or who she was, period.

Aglaia went on. "I guess he left this behind and it was lost in the rush of the funeral. Now I kind of promised Mom I'd try to get it to him."

Naomi's mouth hung open. "You kept in touch with him?"

"No, he never wrote." That still disturbed Aglaia, too. Sure, he had good reason, considering the way Joel treated him at the end, and it wasn't like François could send her an e-mail because no farms around Tiege had Internet access back then. Maybe he lost her phone number, her mailing address, but could he really just forget all about her like that? "Anyway, Naomi, locating him is only part of the problem. What's really getting to me is that I *want* to see him again."

Her confession sounded inane, spoken aloud like that, and she hadn't even mentioned anything about the notes François had written into the Bible. She was loath to admit the extent of her involvement with François and her deep feelings for him. Naomi would just say that all the girls had a crush on him—except she herself, of course. Everyone knew that Naomi had eyes only for Byron, her sweetheart since childhood.

"So then, it's just that you don't want to let Tina down, right?" Naomi pressed.

Under Naomi's intensity, Aglaia slipped back into evasiveness. "It'd be like searching for the proverbial needle in the haystack, I suppose."

"You'd never locate him after so many years," Naomi stated flatly, underscoring the irrationality of the whole idea.

But Aglaia didn't answer that one. Her burgeoning craving to see François again made her invincible to Naomi's dissuasion and, besides, she was becoming more convinced than ever that the way to exorcise the memories was to confront her demons. That is, she *needed* to find François and divest herself of the burden of this ruinous book and her sorrowful past if she ever hoped to regain a sense of self.

The two women cleared away the dishes and prepared for bed. Naomi, washing up in the bathroom, purred the words of another familiar hymn—"When peace like a river attendeth my way"—and it made Aglaia want to yell through the door at her that she would get her own peace, that she would find lost love and expunge herself of the confusion once and for all. But Naomi wouldn't understand. She hadn't been the one stricken, smitten, afflicted with love for someone forbidden. She hadn't been the one suppressing this secret for so long, held in its sway, unable to look any man in the eyes without seeing François Vivier.

By the time they were in bed under their own sides of Aglaia's queen-sized duvet in a grown-up parody of their old pajama-party days, the Bible was zipped back into the suitcase.

Naomi slept like a child, her mouth open and the light from the streetlamp luminescent on her teeth. But forty-five minutes later, Aglaia was still awake despite knowing she needed to get up in five hours. Her legs were jumping, restless, as though she'd had caffeine. Lou's strange baiting of Naomi tonight, Naomi's lack of awareness, Aglaia's own efforts at averting a clash between the two—to say nothing of the internal conflict aroused by her reading—hadn't amounted to a relaxing preflight day, but only riled up angst.

She could wake Naomi and talk it out, since the whole thing had its origins back when the two of them were still reading from the same page. She could explain the harassment she'd been suffering because of her mishmash of memories, could tell about her desire to make a name for herself in the arts circle, could even hint at her regret over losing something fine when she turned her face from God.

But talking about it wouldn't give substantial answers to her tenuous queries. What she needed was to find balance. Better to keep her emotions under wraps and retain the reserved exterior she projected to others. Not that she was known to be heartless; she just wasn't known. She hardly knew herself anymore. Somehow she must get rid of the burdensome Bible and, along with it, the rags of any faith that still hung from her. Perhaps by some stroke of luck she might even find François in person, peer into his eyes again, touch his cheek.

At the very least, the trip would bring blessed reprieve from all these nagging people in her life—her mother and Naomi and even Lou. She bunched the pillow up under her neck again and turned towards the corner of her bedroom where Moses' staff was propped. Dear Eb and his impulses to help her!

She willed herself to fill and empty her lungs deeply and slowly, and had the sensation of falling into a vast and dreadful desert, where she came to the bitter well called Marah and grumbled to Moses about bringing her up out of Egypt to let her die in the dry, thirsty land. And she dreamed of a man in linen with a voice like the roar of rushing waters calling to her—*Come, all you who are thirsty, come to the waters*—and she drank from a sweet, deep well that never ran dry. But she awoke in the morning to the shrieking of the radio clock, her tongue sticky and swollen.

Twelve

Two hours before her international flight on Sunday morning, Aglaia stood beside Naomi in the queue that inched towards the airline check-in counter. Even the canned recording over the terminal loudspeaker reignited her excitement, as did the din and the anonymous jostling of travelers.

During the drive over, Naomi had fretted. She warned Aglaia that the costume box was too bulky as a carry-on, and she worried about Aglaia traveling by herself with the strained ankle—perhaps she needed a wheelchair? The fussing was not merited. Aglaia supposed that Naomi had unspoken concerns on her mind.

"Thanks for the help with my bags," she told Naomi now, dismissing her.

"I'll stay with you till you get assistance with them."

"It might be a wait," Aglaia warned. "Zephyr will be lonely in the car or might decide he needs to pee. Which reminds me…" She glanced past Naomi, looking for the ladies' room for herself.

Instead she almost staggered when she spotted, against the sunshine streaming in through the elevated terminal windows, the outline of Lou Chapman striding up the wide passageway, nose high as she scrutinized the crowd.

Naomi turned to find out what had caught her eye. "Why is she here?"

"I have no idea, but she has luggage," Aglaia said.

Lou spotted them and butted past several disgruntled passengers waiting their turn.

"Surprise, you've got company," Lou said drily.

Aglaia was dumbfounded and didn't comprehend her meaning.

"I'm coming along with you to Paris, Aglaia. I've been wanting to dig out some of the resources in the excellent Sorbonne libraries for a paper I'll be presenting in San Francisco later this year, and what better reason to dip into my academic funds than for research?"

"But—"

"My travel agent had to scramble to get me a seat at the last minute," Lou said, speaking over Aglaia's weak protest, "my online agency having let me down. I don't know why you didn't book a direct flight, instead connecting through La Guardia. Money, likely. That made it all the more difficult for the girl, who finally got the ticket ready for me last night. I didn't want to tell you in case it didn't work out."

"I—"

"Then with your injury and my fluency in French, I knew you could use a tour guide on your first trip over." She paused but Aglaia was too bemused to formulate a sentence before Lou went on. "My ruse yesterday of dropping off reading material at your apartment for the flight disarmed you, I see—as I planned. It was worth waiting for the look on your face right now."

Lou dropped her Louis Vuitton suitcase on the floor with a soft plop. "Don't worry, I'll pay for half the room costs. That should free up shopping cash for you."

Naomi came to Aglaia's rescue. "We were just going to visit the restroom. Will you stay with her stuff till we get back?" She gripped Aglaia's arm and led her out of the line-up.

Uncaring that her mascara wasn't waterproof, Aglaia splashed her face at the ladies' room sink and patted it with paper towel.

She'd had three minutes to acclimatize to Lou's announcement of her travel intentions and was steadying herself already.

"The gall of that woman, prancing right in and forcing herself on you like this!" Naomi, usually charitable, was venting. Aglaia groped around in her bag for her peach gloss and smudged it over her lips with her index finger before she spoke up.

"It might not be such a bad idea, after all," she said, trying to convince herself more than Naomi.

"This was *your* adventure. She's manipulative, treating you like a puppet."

"She has a point about the finances and the language, though," Aglaia reasoned.

"I can't believe you're going along with this." Naomi's mouth was a grim line.

She wouldn't understand, Aglaia thought, since she didn't know about the university job that hung in the balance. On one level the turn of events dismayed Aglaia, her fantasies casting her as a solitary adventurer, but she was determined to make the best of it. Lou hadn't been this domineering before, but Naomi's strong reaction propelled Aglaia towards moderation. Anyway, the last thing she needed right now was a catfight, the other two women tearing her apart like some unfortunate mouse.

"What choice have I got, Naomi? If she wants to fly to France, how can I stop her?" At least, she rationalized to herself, Lou wanted to spend time with her—that was a compliment. And as a seasoned traveler, Lou knew her way around Paris. Aglaia would be giving up her cherished solitude but she could be gaining valuable assistance in her hunt for François. It was a trade-off. She might as well accept Lou's decision and get the most from it. Naomi would consider her a pushover, but being misunderstood by her was a minor price to pay for the benefits of Lou's friendship. A girl had to have her priorities straight. "Besides," Aglaia added, "you were the one stressed about me going solo to Europe for the first time."

Naomi flared her nostrils and changed the subject. "Well, I should be hitting the road. As you said, Zephyr will be yowling. Call me when you get back." She hugged Aglaia and muttered that she'd pray for her, but left without stopping to wish Lou a safe journey.

The security line was short and Aglaia passed through the frame of the metal detector as her phone in her bag on the belt rang inside the X-ray machine. She didn't get to it in time—the guards refused to be hurried—but when she flipped the cover open, she recognized the missed number and hit "send" as she and Lou walked to their gate.

"Eb, you called?"

"Lass, I wanted to see you off—at least with my voice." He laughed. "How's that ankle of yours?"

"Much better, thanks."

"I don't want you to be nervous about the delivery, now. You know that you can get hold of me if any questions come up at the museum."

"I'm not nervous, exactly," Aglaia said.

"I suppose you're out of your element already—a bit like a sheep among the wolves? You'll be fine," Eb reassured her. He must have heard the reservation in her voice—but she could hear his smile. "Just be your lovely self. And eat as much of that heavenly French food as possible."

Eb hung up the bedroom extension and saw he had enough time for a shave and a spit-bath before the Sunday morning service. He could hear Iona humming in the kitchen, brewing tea and steaming his oatcake—to which he'd add some "unhealthy" marmalade when she turned her back. Their son, Ian, had been converted to toast and packaged cereal as a schoolboy, but last time they were home the grandkids sat on Eb's lap and sampled his breakfast. Maybe they were too big for that now, he thought, and he sniffled a bit as he ran hot water into the sink. Well, anyway, he anticipated a time of blessing at kirk today. It always brought his whole perspective back into focus, and he needed that after the work week he'd just survived.

Now that Aglaia was on her way to Paris, he'd be able to give full attention to the overlapping project, which he admitted would have been less onerous with her input. The public call for bids had come across his desk just as Aglaia was getting into the meat of her museum assignment, and he'd locked himself into his own office for long hours, strategizing procedures and estimating costs. He'd have loved to include her in the process, even if only for her professional edification; the next movie contract might very well be negotiated under her guard. This current film was a major undertaking. If Eb were able to win the contract for Incognito as the on-location costumer for RoundUp Studios—and assuming Aglaia's success in Paris—headquarters would be left without any grounds for closing the Denver branch.

He was awaiting the best time to discuss the subject in full with Aglaia, when stress levels were lower. Eb had no doubt that headquarters would love to transfer her to their offices, but if that happened she'd lose all seniority and be devoured in the dog-eat-dog environment. She was just too tender yet. Worse still, it would be the death knell for her sense of artistic fulfillment, as Montreal's machine required lock-step compliance very different from the flexibility of Eb's own department. So the turf war was his to fight until he could define his own territory without further challenge, and position Aglaia more securely. Then maybe he could retire in good conscience.

Eb lathered up with his badger-hair shaving brush and began to scrape his jaw clean of whiskers, lifting one side, then the other of his moustache in turn. He'd heard through the grapevine that Incognito faced some stiff competition, but in his assessment Platte River University's theater arts department had eyes that were too big for its stomach. That was often the case with institutions of higher learning, where the academy's overweening philosophies couldn't keep up with the demand for applied knowledge in the workaday world.

Not that he was contemptuous of education! In fact, Eb esteemed scholarship, having himself earned from St. Andrews an interdisciplinary degree in arts, literature, and theology before emigrating. That was back in the day when academics still valued the record that came down through faithful writers, before the resurgence of arcane philosophies by postmodern advocates who worshipped the gods they made rather than the God who made them, who boasted of erudition but didn't know about providence and redemption.

Eb shook his head at his reflection in distress over the state of education today. Wisdom wasn't confined to the classroom and foolishness wasn't barred from it, he thought as he toweled off the pudding bits of shaving cream from his jowls.

Aglaia seemed naïve of this fact, judging by her avarice for certification. Going back to school and completing what she began would do her good, but only for the right purposes—not, for example, to impress that professor whose name she dropped into the conversation now and again. In Eb's view, education wasn't an end in itself but was only a way to an end. The pursuit of truth was disappointing without the attaining of truth.

Aglaia, now, was a picture in contrasts about the process of attaining truth. It looked as if she used her emotions, her impressions, to *feel* her way through life, but had shut down on expressing them so that Eb couldn't get a handle on what they were. He believed she was waging an interior war between the purely intellectual and the generously sensual. He saw the two flicker across her face at odd times of the day—say, when she first methodically sorted through his office shelves for a title and then subsequently lost herself in the ecstasy of its pages. But a person couldn't find truth with one and not the other. If the brain knew God, it was the heart that felt Him. Rationality and faith must walk hand in hand, as Blaise Pascal had written so long ago.

Call a truce inside her, Eb suggested to God as he made his way into the kitchen with his Bible in hand, ready for the Sabbath and for his marmalade. *Bring the factions into harmony so the lass might find her way to serenity.*

Aglaia boarded the aircraft and followed Lou down the narrow aisle and found her seat. She wedged herself in beside an obese man, but at least she was by the window. Lou's travel agent couldn't arrange for them to sit together until the second leg of the journey and that didn't displease Aglaia. After the flurry of activity these last two days, she needed some quiet time to acclimatize to the new situation.

The flight attendant served breakfast, and the man beside Aglaia was eager to engage in chitchat with her over his scrambled eggs. To forestall that possibility she retrieved the Bible, which she'd decided this morning to carry in her shoulder bag, and opened it to the beginning.

She'd been speculating over her motivation for deciding to take the book. She declared to Lou that she'd ignore her mother's request and leave the Bible behind, and intimated the same to Naomi. Yet here she was, with the Bible on her lap and the man next to her leaning away as though she were some religious nut ready to launch into a sermon.

Well, she hadn't told the whole truth to either of the other women about the writing in the margins and the memories that bound her up—hadn't even told the whole truth to herself, she admitted. Even if delivering the Bible to François might be impossible, she wanted to investigate his thoughts. How could she leave the book behind when she wanted so badly to study those enticing scribbles? How could she be free in her soul until she faced her memories once and for all? She was embarking on a new phase in her vocation and getting ahead in the social world. It was high time for a sweeping change in her life, a sweeping out of her life. It was time to open the closet doors and air the linens, and the place to start was with a thorough reading of François's notations and a fearless remembering.

She leafed through the first few pages, rereading the notes in the margins in order and turning over the corner of each marked page for future reference (as she had done with the story of Artemis in the book of Acts) till she found the first missed one. He'd scrawled *le baptême* beside the crossing of the Red Sea, where the chariots of the enemy army had been hurled into the waters, the whole brigade sinking to the depths like a millstone. The eddies of her memory drew her in.

The water in the baptismal tank is not as cold as Mary Grace expects. How is she to know? This is the kind of thing, like marriage, you do only once. The white gown clings like pond weeds to her legs as Pastor Reimer preaches to the congregation on the meaning of the ordinance—the putting to death of the natural and the birth of the spiritual.

"In the name of the Father, and of the Son, and of the Holy Spirit," he finishes, and plunges her backward and under and up again so fast it doesn't matter that she hasn't plugged her nose. Then like the others before her, she climbs dripping up the baptistery steps, clean and new and full of light. They'll all be watching closely—Mom, Dad, Joel. And François, of course. What will François think of all this?

Afterwards they eat in the church basement to celebrate—molasses cookies dipped in coffee and (though it isn't Christmas) Päpanät, the peppery, nut-sized goodies even the younger kids pop whole into their mouths. Elderly ladies with their hairnets and chin whiskers congratulate her on the testimony she gave before the whole congregation that evening, about needing forgiveness for her sin.

François doesn't mention anything about sin but tells her later, when they're alone after everyone else has gotten out of the car, that she looked like Aphrodite rising out of the ocean, born of the sea foam that boiled up out of the immortal flesh of the cast-off genitals of a castrated god, Father Sky.

François's graphic, provocative words make her stomach flip—it's too personal, too masculine for her to bear!

But then Dad, coming back out to see what's taking them so long, opens the car door and fractures the darkness.

Then here, after the disobedient children of Israel had wandered for forty years because they broke the commandments of the Lord, as Moses broke the tablets of stone upon which they were engraved, as she had been breaking that indelible law of grace written on her once-soft heart—here, where the High Priest stood with his censer of coals amidst the fragrant smoke of the incense before the blood-spattered atonement cover in the Most Holy Place—Aglaia read *branding* and remembered the day at a neighboring ranch.

"Sit tight! We'll make a man of you yet." The stringy old cowboy is wielding the metal pole with his outfit's brand still smoldering red.

"But monsieur, *the cow's moving!" François's eyes water as he squints up from the ground through the acrid smoke of seared hair, laboring to hold the animal still.*

"Of course the calf's moving, son. You'd be moving, too, if that hot iron was burning your hide, which it will be if you don't sit heavier. And this is no cow, that's for sure. A bull calf about to become a steer, in fact." Mary Grace notes the flick of a knife, the bawling of the calf, and the commiserating grimace of a city boy.

She laughs at him, satisfied that he'll have another story to take back to his homeland, another incident that ties him to her country, to her. He catches her laughter in his eyes and bounces it back at her, smudges of dirt on his cheek and cow dung on his jeans.

Where Aaron burned an offering as an aroma pleasing to the Lord, François had jotted *camp-out.*

The coyotes are just over the closest dune, yipping and lamenting to a full June moon that is brighter even than the bonfire. She and the two boys have wriggled their sleeping bags into the sand and are roasting hotdogs, the flames slapping at the dripping fat.

"You eat this with moutarde?*" François is leery but lets Mary Grace squirt it on liberally. It squishes from the bun as he bites, and she reaches out and wipes the yellow smear off his cheek. He grabs her wrist, holds it fast, and turns his mouth towards her hand to lick her fingers clean one by one.*

Joel ignores them—at least, he pretends to, though this last while he's increasingly been finding ways to interrupt. François's flirtation is becoming more brazen each day. Perhaps soon her parents will see it, too. For now, she lets François pull on her fingers like a suckling lamb orphaned by the ewe, and his adoring gaze is as intense.

In this manner, sitting in the plane on her way to Paris, Aglaia buried herself in the Scriptures—or rather in the coffin of memories made by François's words—and the time passed unnoticed.

Thirteen

Lou returned to her seat from the airplane toilet—filthy cubicle!—cursing silently that she hadn't insisted on an upgrade to first class, for herself at least. She was owed the higher quality of service, considering her frequent-flyer points. What with her recent belt-tightening, she couldn't justify paying the extra herself and, though her university research fund covered some travel costs, she doubted PRU's admin department would let her get away much longer with her refusal to itemize expenditures. She shook her head; Aglaia hadn't even thanked her for the sacrifice she was making.

The coup at the airport in Denver went off better than Lou anticipated and Aglaia, out of sight now behind the bulk of her seatmate several passengers ahead, had recovered her balance nicely. She'd be in top form by the time they landed for their connection in New York City within the hour, left alone for the whole flight while Lou gave herself over to one of Colette's novels. The girlfriend Naomi, however, had appeared disapproving about her accompanying Aglaia.

Lou was apprehensive about that Enns woman. She could be problematic, with her simplistic take on life, her either/or thinking processes. Naomi was obviously a literalist without any symbol system in place to help her nuance imaginal discourse, unlike Aglaia who always had her head in the clouds.

Naomi treated Aglaia like a younger sister, and Lou recognized the suffocation because she'd put up with her own older sister's wheedling ways for too long.

The latest e-mail Lou received from her sibling, which she deleted as usual without reply, said something about Mother starting to fail. She didn't know what Linda expected her to do with that information anyway. It wasn't as if she could change all her arrangements on a whim and fly out there every time Mother had another little health scare. One of these days it would be over, and they'd be planning a funeral.

Given Linda's shyness and her own facility as a speaker, Lou expected to be asked to say a few words. What eulogy might she give Mother? She wouldn't lie and pretend filial affection, and she couldn't very well tell the truth—that she'd been waiting for the day so that she could collect her inheritance and ease the strain of her overextended lifestyle.

Linda might challenge her claim to the estate; she was a do-gooder and, when both sisters had received a bequest upon their father's death four years ago, Linda donated hers to charity, critical of her sister's spending habits. So Lou wasn't looking forward to the details of dividing Mother's assets.

There was some mercy in death, she granted, at least for the dying one who slipped into the void of nonexistence. But it was rather more difficult for those left behind, sweeping up the ashes of a life gone by.

Lou looked down at the postcard of Pradier's carving clipped to her sheaf of papers. She was withholding it from Aglaia, saving it for the right moment, as it seemed to have some effect on her. Lou wasn't clear yet in what capacity she could employ it, but she was always on the alert for that teachable moment, using whatever educational tools were at her disposal.

Lou was curious about how her young friend was coming along with her assigned reading. She probably began with the article on mythology that first caught her eye. The subject also fascinated Lou, with its epitomization of woman as sexual goddess, and fed her theories on pluralism in the current ethos. How better to further the harmonious meshing of today's plethora of worldviews than with a unifying narrative constructed upon the polytheism of ancient oral traditions?

All myths sought to explain the origins of the universe in emblematic form, and she'd found the application of the goddess as a type helped shake loose the postulations of more orthodox scholars who saw the arts as a reflection of some greater creation by one omnipotent Creator—an outmoded idea.

Take the Three Graces, Lou thought, glancing again at the card. As a literary person, she'd known about them generally and their place in Greek literature long ago. But since Aglaia's interest in them became apparent to her, she'd undertaken some of her own research.

The Titans of antiquity, elder gods ruling the universe, were said to have been overthrown by the twelve Olympians, who took over the affairs of man and of all other creatures such as nymphs and centaurs and gorgons that resided above the earth or on the earth or in the underworld. Up in the elementary aether, the lesser gods cohabited with the twelve in a cacophony of dissonance, with the Three Graces applying their soothing ministrations as they were able.

Now, the Graces were often mistaken for the Muses, those goddesses who inspired the poets and stimulated the creative process of all the arts, written about by Homer and Chaucer and extending even to the Puritan writings. Some mistook the Graces for the Three Furies (who were daughters of Mother Earth and who took revenge on crimes against conscience) or the Three Fates (who wove the web of life, measured its length, and cut it off at the predetermined point).

In fact, Lou thought, classical literature took liberties in mixing up the roles and tales of all the divinities—gods and goddesses alike—so that the whole body of myth became one jumbled, happy, incestuous mess.

But Lou knew it was certainly the Three Graces who traveled in the retinue of Aphrodite, present at human and divine marriages to enliven the wedding feasts. It was the Three Graces who dressed the gods in the finest of clothing for their sumptuous banquets and brought luxury to the pantheon of deities, making merry their celebrations with song and dance. In art and literature, the Three Graces always appeared as a triad, a composite without individuation, and one Greek philosopher described them as standing for the three-fold aspects of generosity in the giving, receiving, and returning of gifts. Lou preferred the lustier application of the Graces as the three stages of love: beauty, arousing desire, and fulfillment. They personified splendor and festivity, as effective today at explicating metaphysical concepts as when they were first conceived for religious veneration by pre-modern humanity.

For example, a primitive history told of three meteorites that fell from the skies onto a Grecian hillside, dropped by the gods in jest to perplex poor humans about the mystery of the aeons. This initiated the building of a sanctuary for the cult of the heaven-sent stones, taken to be a visitation of the Three Graces themselves.

By the early nineteenth century, the subject had been explored by artists of many media. Lou studied the postcard again. Pradier's statues depicted the Grace on the left-hand side of his grouping as goddess of the harvest, holding a swath of blossoms, her eyes lowered towards the earth from which sprang her bounty. The middle maiden raised her face towards the skies, with her toe resting atop a jewel box overflowing with glittering gems, signifying radiant beauty. The Grace on the end, with head tilted onto her companion's shoulder, was the goddess of gaiety, of cheer. Lou theorized that the three beauties gave rise to the Christian virtues of faith, hope, and love, despite theologians' blustering about its being the Jewish God through divine revelation who first delivered the virtues world systems subsequently imitated.

It made no difference to Lou. The point was that these tales were useful to remythologize women's lives away from the tyrannical imperialism of Western monotheism. We incarnate the Graces ourselves by becoming them, she thought, becoming splendid and festive ourselves with the whole of womanhood a trinity of reciprocity, a perception in each other of our own inherent deity. For Aglaia, this was played out through her aesthetics, her needlework becoming the experience of creation itself.

Of course the girl, reading the articles right now a few seats up the airplane aisle, wouldn't have a clue about the significant contribution Lou's work made to academia. Aglaia was drawn to Lou's thesis without understanding it. How enthralling, then, that she could be so tuned in to their gifts of the arts, so artistic herself.

But what Aglaia needed was a new job, closer in proximity to Lou herself. The subject hadn't come up again since she'd mentioned, at the girl's apartment a few nights ago, that she'd been campaigning for Aglaia at the university. She'd been doing more than that, of course. Besides the deal she cut with Oliver Upton, Lou had put in motion her political connections to ensure the position of wardrobe consultant would be partly supported by arts funding boards at the county and state levels, outside the jurisdiction of the university itself. This endowment wouldn't go far—it was more honorarium than actual income—but Lou's success in obtaining it signaled the validity of her proposal as Aglaia's benefactor. And maybe it would help catch the attention of the tenure committee as well as Aglaia's trust.

That's what Lou needed to concentrate on during their short time in Paris—Aglaia's intimate trust, which could be acquired in any number of ways. She'd like to somehow milk Aglaia for information about the movie bid that she, as an employee of Incognito Costume Shop, could provide. But more importantly Lou hoped to inveigle Aglaia, to make the girl beholden to her on the social level, by convincing her that they made a good team. But, Lou reassured herself, she had Aglaia's best interests at heart as well, didn't she?

Lou unclasped her seatbelt, deciding to check up on Aglaia before they landed and maybe clarify any unfamiliar terms she'd encountered in the literature. But when she was close enough to the girl's head bent over her reading, she saw that it was not sheets of stapled paper that held Aglaia's attention but a bound book opened on her lap. So she'd brought that Bible after all! Lou held her breath and watched Aglaia's finger running along beneath the letters of a sprawling notation scribbled on a page in the book of Joshua: *Land of milk and honey—sa peau, ses lèvres.* Would the French be too difficult for Aglaia to catch its erogenous inflection—"her skin, her lips"?

Without disturbing Aglaia or awakening the fat man lolling beside her, the professor returned to her seat. Her guess about François's intentions had been correct, then. He'd been sniffing around Aglaia and she hadn't recovered from it; hence the lack of boyfriends in her life. Aglaia was not frigid, just unfulfilled. Evidently François had left behind a souvenir for her in the form of a message written into the pages of the sacred script. How ironic; it was the ultimate gloss on the biblical text, a personalized love letter! What a mundane joke—the worldly wise cosmopolitan boy trifling with the starry-eyed farmer's daughter only to forsake her and leave her pining.

The plane change in New York City was a blur, with crowds at peak density and Aglaia limping as they careened from arrival to departure gate. Only when they were strapped into their seats on the international flight after takeoff, each with a glass of hideous airline wine to celebrate, could Lou lure Aglaia into focused discussion.

"How did you like the articles?" Lou asked, not hiding her cynicism.

"Um, your articles," Aglaia stalled. "I didn't quite get to them."

"Oh?" Lou waited. It would be best if Aglaia admitted of her own accord that she'd been reading other, apparently more riveting, material.

"The titles sounded clever," Aglaia offered.

"Hmmm." Seconds passed. "Did you watch the movie?"

"It was a rerun," Aglaia said. She removed the papers from her purse and sifted past each cover page.

"Did you read the airline magazine then, perhaps order some duty-free items?" Lou enjoyed the prodding and Aglaia couldn't hold out any longer, turning on Lou eyes full of appeal and fully appealing.

"No, I was reading something else. I ended up bringing that

Bible along after all." Then, like an insincere afterthought, Aglaia added, "I couldn't very well let Mom down, could I?"

Lou fell silent for effect, relishing the control Aglaia gave her. She opened the cellophane packet and munched on a sesame cracker, arranging her face to appear engaged and evaluative as though waiting for more input. Aglaia licked her lips; she would crack any second now. Slight taciturnity on Lou's part, she found, always loosened the tightest tongue.

"It's not that I'm interested in the Bible itself," Aglaia finally said.

The tension left Lou's jaw at this, and she realized she'd been on edge after all, worried that Aglaia might be giving in to some sporadic religious inquisitiveness. It was one thing for her to seek out the memory of François, another altogether for her to seek out the presence of God.

"Go on," she said. It dribbled out then: Aglaia's decision to look for François preceding her mother's fortuitous request, the discovery that the boy had journaled in the book's margins, Aglaia's compulsion to puzzle through the meaning of his words and the recollections they evoked, and the suspense and delight of reliving, step by step, the summer's events she'd been blocking for years.

"I'm being hounded to death by the thoughts," Aglaia said.

The notion of Cerberus came to Lou—the three-headed dog defending the gates of Hades so that no being could escape. Aglaia's conscience was her Cerberus, a merciless jailer keeping her spirit backed up and locked away. Lou saw now the futility in any attempt to dam up Aglaia's onslaught of feelings brought about by reading that Bible. The sooner Aglaia worked through her obsession, the sooner Lou would be able to salvage her own aspirations for this trip.

The younger woman did not have the capacity at present to read her articles, nor was there the slightest chance that Aglaia might listen to a verbal précis of the writing. Already she was tugging at her shoulder bag for the Bible, anxious to re-enter some fantasy world from which Lou was barred. No matter; this only challenged Lou to explain her view of life to Aglaia in more concrete terms, to articulate—perhaps through the instructional tour she planned of Paris's main attractions—her understanding of reality, relativity, and women's powerful place in the world, especially as it spoke into their own relationship.

Aglaia leaned on the plane window, the glass cool against her forehead. If she focused on the reflection of the cabin interior she saw Lou, who at last slept beside her after keeping furtive watch on her page turning from the time they left La Guardia. The vigil had unnerved Aglaia; she felt Lou reading along as she sought out François's notations, one by one, in the Bible's margins. But Lou couldn't read her mind, after all, where the real action was taking place.

Aglaia turned her gaze into the night sky, even cupping her eyes against the glow inside so that the exterior gloom consumed her full view. They were flying over a sea of moon-washed mist, too high up to cast a shadow. The wing of the 767 was her point of reference, its metal the only real substance between the earth below and the stars above. She was disembodied, belonging to neither earth nor sky, hurtling through the stratosphere like Pegasus ridden by the goddess of dawn or like an archangel dispatched from heaven's throne.

Or maybe like a driblet of lukewarm spittle expelled from the mouth of God.

Aglaia closed her eyes, disoriented by the obfuscation of the black night, the throbbing of the plane's wing strobe, and the labyrinth of her thoughts. She had vertigo of the soul.

Each page of the Bible read during the past hours had taken her to another memory, and her recollections of that summer were now lining up chronologically—François's notes reminding her, chapter after chapter, of the events that surged towards a climax neither of them knew at the time of his writing. She ignored the formal English terms he'd copied from the minister's outline, not concerning herself with the theme for more than its ability to guide her understanding of François's perspective and her own responses. His words punctuated the Word of God in a sort of progressive revelation, layering meaning upon meaning in an allegory that didn't fit with a literal reading of Scripture.

In the first book of the Bible, Aglaia had found herself again in the genesis of that paradisal summer, when François first walked and talked with her and showed her the enchantment of the Three Graces and breathed into her the consciousness of her own enchanting womanhood. Her exodus from an unquestioning childhood faith into the arid wilderness of confusion was marked by his notations in the margins of the second book—*Mount Olympus* written beside Mount Sinai, *Minotaur* beside the golden calf. By the time the youth group had reached the end of the Pentateuch several weeks into François's stay, like Moses she, too, was standing on a precipice overlooking the River Jordan—or perhaps the River Styx—into a new land but not yet entering it.

When Jericho, city of the moon god, came tumbling down in the pages of the Bible, her own walls of resistance to François's charm had begun to collapse in that summer of her love.

When Samson perished in the rubble over Delilah's betrayal, she longed for François's fingers to unbraid her own hair, as Odysseus might have done to Penelope.

When David slung his fatal pebble towards Goliath's forehead, the spirit of chastity was dying within Aglaia and, although the shepherd beseeched her from his book—*Who is the Rock except our God? The Lord is my Rock, in whom I take refuge, my Rock and my Redeemer*—yet David's poetry was muted by the overriding voice of François, who'd written *Atlas* on the page and said so long ago with his mouth: "He carries the great rock of the universe on his shoulders."

The building of the Great Temple out of the cedars of Lebanon, carved with cherubim and palm trees and flowers overlaid with gold, brought to Aglaia's mind the ringing of hammers as the boys constructed new corrals behind the barn, François's arms cording up as he reached for another rough-cut slab and pounded it into place.

Then, while Manasseh bowed down to the starry hosts, she was idolizing François but still kept herself from him though the fire burned in her, the convention of decorum holding her to at least some morality.

As Job scraped his itching, running sores with pottery shards, the Lord was speaking to her out of the maelstrom of her own suffering: *Where were you when I laid the earth's foundation, when the morning stars sang together and all the angels shouted for joy?* She, too, had shouted for joy with her friends—with François—during the overnight retreat down at the lake, as the fervent youth leader urged them on and they sang unto the Lord a new song, sang of the mercies of the Lord, sang with their mouths making known His faithfulness: *Praise Him, sun and moon, praise Him, all you shining stars... The heavens declare the glory of God!* But her desire at the moment she sang His praises had not been not for the One above, the One within. Her desire was for the one who drew her apart to sit by the lake in the reflection of the midnight skies, and filled her senses with his presence and her imagination with his tales. While the other teens, studious around the campfire, read in Isaiah about the coming king of righteousness—*Wonderful Counselor, Mighty God, Everlasting Father, Prince of Peace*—François was identifying the planets for Aglaia and whispering to her about Chaos, the original dark nothingness from which all else sprang. He spoke of Gaia, the mother earth who gave birth to the starry heavens as an eternal home for the blessed and bestial gods, and then gave birth to Tartarus as the lowest level of the underworld and a wretched pit of blackness reserved for interminable punishment, and then gave birth to Eros as erotic love. Heaven, hell, and sex all born out of one womb.

In retrospect, that was the beginning of the end for her, there in the Prophets where God weighed her on the scales and found her wanting—or where she weighed God and found Him wanting. God had declared, "Let there be light," but François reawakened in her the mysteries of darkness with his convoluted theories, and she liked the danger hiding in his shadowy innuendo. By that time, her field of vision was limited to the glory of François, and there was no longer refuge in the voice of the Scriptures crying in the desert of her heart, for she was withering like sand-blasted grass and falling like overblown flowers at the end of a drought-ridden summer. There was no longer refuge even in her brother, Joel rejecting any mention of myths and chastising her for having her head turned by stories, chastising her for not reading her Bible anymore.

And now hours into their second leg of the flight, Aglaia dozed with the Bible still open on her lap.

The night sounds seep through the window screen like berry juice through a cheesecloth bag—gentle cricketsong, the humming breeze, the faraway groan of a calf calling maa-maa. Everyone else is in bed, but how can Mary Grace sleep when François is lying a room away? How can she restrain her whirling thoughts and calm the twisting in her gut and alleviate the misery? She sits alone in the unlit kitchen with her elbows on the checkered oilcloth, cheeks cupped in hands.

François finds her like this. The floorboards creak beneath his bare feet, and she's aware of him before he touches her. She feels his body heat close to her right side without looking up at him. She doesn't need to look up at him—she has his image burned into her subconscious as surely as Argos, the giant with one hundred eyes, could never shut away his visions even in sleep until he was crushed beneath a great stone and beheaded and his eyes transplanted to the tail of the peacock.

"You're crying."

"I'm sad," she says. She wants him to ask her why, but he doesn't. If he'd only ask her, she'd be forced to tell him that her fear is he'll forget her, and he'd be forced to say that would never happen.

"Sad?" is all he asks. "I'll make you happy." And he leans down to her so that a curl of his hair tangles in with her lashes as he kisses her with his sweet, moist mouth.

Aglaia woke up with a start, burning with thirst and not a flight attendant in view. The cabin lights were dim. Someone a few rows up coughed but otherwise everything was quiet. She tried to suck up some saliva to moisten her mouth but hesitated to creep across Lou and risk rousing her.

Soft light illumined Lou's patrician profile and Aglaia took some solace from its flinty angles. Lou was strong and sure-footed, even if she did march over others in her way. Following behind her was safer than pressing on ahead. Yet Lou invited Aglaia to reach out beyond self-imposed boundaries, going as far as to endorse her for the position at PRU. Maybe Lou might understand some of her torment if only Aglaia would open up, explain why she was driven to find François. It wasn't just about seeing him again, or at least Aglaia hoped that was so. It was about making an end to her fantastical story of love and death and God. Naomi wouldn't get it, even if Aglaia came clean with her. Maybe she should talk to Lou.

But she was so thirsty! Eventually she sank back into dreams about the burning, unquenchable torment of Tartarus until the captain announced their descent into Paris.

Fourteen

Aglaia's fingers wrapped around the demitasse from which she had taken two delectable sips. She hated to polish it off with a final gulp but Lou, watching her from across the table, had already finished hers. Aglaia wanted to sit here forever.

The streets of Paris fulfilled her every expectation. This moment of lounging at her first sidewalk café was a condensation of all of her long-held expectations—the pungent coffee and chocolate-drizzled pastry, the wafting perfume of passers-by, the music pulled from a violin by a gypsy-busker in the shade of the boulevard's trees. Ignoring Lou's surveillance, she dipped into her bag to hook out her sketchpad and, with a few deft strokes of her graphite, captured the swing of the violinist's skirt, the strain at the sleeve seam as the girl propelled her bow across willing strings.

She recalled her first crude drawing for Eb—of a princess in costume. It had been a cartoonish figure with each eyelash delineated, the gown outlandishly puffy and the tiara decorated with curlicues. "Don't design from some preconception of prettiness," he'd instructed. He taught her the value of copy work, how to first see the essence of what was actually there and record it with accuracy before embellishing. The original was a pattern, a type foreshadowing what it would become in its fullness, like mirroring like. "Be intentional, not fanciful," Eb had said, pointing out the drape of a gown in the textbook illustration on her table. "The bias of the fabric will dictate how this garment hangs. I see a waywardness in you, lass." He clucked. "Save the creativity for later."

"*Plus de café*," Lou called out to the waiter.

"*Oui, madame*," he answered, taking a quick swipe with his damp cloth at their table in passing.

Aglaia turned the page to draft another hasty contour of the musician. It was Tuesday morning, eighteen hours since landing, and the first time Aglaia had consciously absorbed the aura of the city. She was in a daze upon arrival at the airport yesterday and almost nodded off during the Métro ride to the Hôtel du Caillou, where she and Lou dropped off their baggage, freshened up, and set out on a walking tour of the Montmartre neighborhood stretched prostrate below the great white basilica of Sacré-Coeur. They read the grave markers of famous poets as they took a shortcut through a cemetery. They raced through a Monet show, Lou stopping long enough to instruct her on the Impressionist's conveyance of light, although she had no use for the portrait artists in the square who called to them for a sitting. They spotted the red windmill of the Moulin Rouge from a distance as they marched along the avenues till Aglaia's ankle could take no more. She didn't get a chance to practice her French, since Lou was so quick to speak—to purchase entrance tickets to a gallery or to order a bottle of *vin blanc*. And she didn't get a chance to check out a Paris phone book either, Lou yanking her past at least two booths. The day's heat was unbearable, and after an early supper at an elegant restaurant, Aglaia fell into a deep sleep on her first night in the hotel.

So now she sat beneath the red awning of a Parisian café on a sunny morning with her sketchpad, and she only half listened as Lou began to outline their sightseeing agenda without once asking for her input. For the moment, Aglaia didn't care. She was immersing herself in the whole luxurious encounter—the tastes and scents and sounds—like she might slide into her bath after a long day of work.

"Bach," Lou said.

"Pardon?" Aglaia dragged her vision back to Lou.

"The busker." Lou tipped her head towards the street. "She's playing a sonata of Bach's, as you'll know with your training in music."

"I haven't studied music," Aglaia said without thinking, then pinched her leg under the table for not having phrased it more subtly. She should have replied that she loved classical music, always a genteel put-off. But then Lou might have asked her for a favorite composer, and who might come to mind but Newton or Watts or some other name from the pages of the church hymnal?

"But you sing. I heard you on your friend's balcony," Lou said pleasantly though Aglaia listened for the sarcasm, suspecting guile. There'd been no song on her tongue for a long time; what Lou heard on the balcony was Naomi's song. "Come now, Aglaia," Lou coaxed. "Admit that you sing. You hummed in your sleep last night—unless that was a moan of desire. Were you dreaming about your boyfriend?"

The woman was too much! Stalling, Aglaia filled her mouth with the last of the croissant. For all Lou's show of elegance, she was a vulgar person. Having to share the room with her in the hotel, Aglaia was discomfited last night with Lou's unabashed disrobing, and turned away. But maybe the problem was with *her* and not Lou, who likely had a lot healthier view of the human body than the modesty she herself inherited. This morning upon awakening, she noted Lou's expensive bra and panties tossed on the floor, and a small nautical star tattooed high on the thigh of her uncovered leg. From her bed Lou caught Aglaia's glance and leered at her—actually leered!

Well, Aglaia's love life was no business of Lou's, whose prying was ruining her first taste of Paris.

"There are some things I prefer to keep to myself," she said. Was that a challenge? She added, "Not secret, you understand."

"Right."

"I don't have anything to be ashamed of," Aglaia said.

"I'm sure you don't, but that doesn't mean you live free from a misplaced sense of culpability." Lou sipped from the *demitasse*.

Was it that obvious? "I don't have a guilty conscience," she said.

"Why else do you refuse to talk about your mystery man, this François Vivier? You dread admitting your passion."

"It's not like that," Aglaia countered. Lou had it all wrong. Then, weighing her words with no intention of disclosing any more family circumstance than necessary, Aglaia decided to explain the minimum, since maintaining silence would only draw more of Lou's probing. "François is unfinished business. At a critical point in my life he took off suddenly, before he was scheduled to leave." Her eyes stung. "If only I could meet him just once more, maybe I could figure it out. Every time I look up since we've stepped off the plane, I see him crossing the street or disappearing into a shop. See that guy walking in front of the *boulangerie*? He could be François—same black curly hair, same long stride."

"You've got it bad."

Aglaia straightened up on the chair and ran her thumb over the grain of the wood on the tabletop. How could she make this sound saner than it was coming across without telling Lou the whole story?

"If I can locate him, even if it's just to give him the Bible Mom sent along, it'll help put an unfortunate string of events behind me so I can get on with living."

"And?"

"That's it."

Lou observed her through hooded eyes but Aglaia held her chin high. Likely Lou was as dissatisfied with the incomplete explanation as she was. So much for hoping she might get some respite by talking about it. Under the pretense of a dripping nose, Aglaia reached for her bag and unfurled a tissue like a flag of surrender. She was no match for Lou's steely disposition but Lou, for some reason, didn't take advantage of the opportunity to interrogate her further about François. She didn't know how close Aglaia was to confessing it all.

Paper crackling, Lou unfolded the Métro map, subway being the preferred mode of transportation around Paris for tourists and residents alike. She said, "Well, come on. Let's be intentional about our day." She had all their options for the entire stay figured out, with time set aside for her own research at the university and for Aglaia's appointment tomorrow morning at the costume museum. Relieved to be off the subject of François, Aglaia became more animated with every turn of the *Fodor's* page.

Lou went on about the parks and galleries and bridges. "We'll fly by the Opéra Garnier, make reservations for a boat trip down the Seine, and take in the Rodin museum." Lou ran her fingertip along their intended path on the map. "I'll show you Victor Hugo's setting for *The Hunchback of Notre Dame*, where the movie was filmed, and then we'll stop for some cherry sorbet from Berthillon."

But Aglaia's *joie de vivre* dissolved when she remembered her mission.

"I need to find François first." It was out before she had time to pad the words with reason.

Lou snorted. "You can't refrain from stalking your prey."

"I know locating him is a long shot. I thought if I could give it one serious attempt, maybe telephone around for any Vivier listed in Paris, I'd enjoy the rest of our vacation a lot more." She was making excuses; this trip to her was now, first and foremost, about finding François.

"If that's what it takes for you to let go of that bulky book, I promise to help you make the calls. We can't have you lugging the Bible around Paris for the rest of the week only to take it home again." Lou pushed the wrought-iron chair back from the café table and said, "There's a *tabac* on the corner where you can buy a phone card, and sometime soon we'll find an hour to do the calling. So, for the love of God, forget about the man and attend to more pressing matters."

Aglaia pitched into tourist mode for the rest of the day. She admired the architecture, nodded along to Lou's overview of French rationalism, and shuddered through a demonstration of a guillotine. She gasped at the fiendish ferocity of the 384 masks carved on the oldest bridge in the city, glaring down at her from their height like some ill-tempered gods, and she recognized another bridge—when Lou pointed it out to her—that Marlon Brando stood upon in *Last Tango in Paris*. She trudged through several cathedrals to appreciate their historic significance and even put up with a lecture on Lou's view about the socio-cultural impact of Joan of Arc upon the women of late mediaeval France.

But they didn't pause to taste the *crêpes* sizzling on a curbside griddle, drenched in butter and folded up in a cone of waxed paper but discounted by Lou as peasant fare. They didn't inspect the bolts of lace stacked up on a vendor's table in the flea market. And they dashed past the dead chickens that hung from their twine-wrapped claws beneath canopies blowing in the wind, and brown blocks of Marseillaise soap, and round goat cheeses powdered with ash.

When they did sit for a few minutes on a park bench, shaded from the burning sun, to rest Aglaia's ankle and watch a cluster of middle-aged men who played *pétanque* on the grass, Lou couldn't explain to her the rules of the game.

It was almost seven o'clock by the time they got off the Métro at the Saint-Georges stop, and the phone calls to any existing Vivier households still hadn't been made. As they walked into their hotel, Lou asked the concierge to book a table at a nearby seafood restaurant.

"It's superb, Aglaia. *Bouillabaisse* as it was meant to be supped and *Coquilles Saint-Jacques* that trumps any you've eaten at home."

Aglaia hadn't ever eaten either dish at home, and she was intimidated by her culinary ignorance—though she could bet Lou had never tasted really superb *Kjielkje* noodles rolled out, boiled, and fried in bacon drippings by an old Mennonite cook. She felt herself grin at that, and salivate just a little.

Lou continued, "Later we can tour the Latin Quarter and drop in somewhere for a nightcap."

"I shouldn't stay out too late," Aglaia said. "My appointment tomorrow morning is at ten." Tonight she still needed to see that the costume had no wrinkles and that her own outfit was pressed and smart, that her notes for the interview were in order, and that she clearly understood the subway route to the Musée de l'Histoire du Costume—no matter that Lou always bullied her way into the lead on their forays.

"You worry too much, Aglaia. It's time to kick up your heels. I promise I'll get you to your meeting on time."

Aglaia figured this promise was about as good as Lou's promise to begin calling around for François today. But she didn't disturb the other woman's mood by saying it aloud. Lou was bound to get around to the phone call tomorrow.

Lou Chapman needed a drink. It'd been a hellish day of leading Aglaia from one tourist site to another and of trying to deliver a rudimentary French history to someone constantly distracted by frivolous details. But it was a necessary procedure, Lou thought. Anyone who came to Paris the first time needed to get the basics out of the way in order to appreciate all the city had to offer. She hoped her efforts wouldn't be lost on Aglaia who, if she interpreted Lou's self-sacrifice as true friendship, would only come to depend further on her.

Huchette Street was as crowded tonight as usual, with tourists clutching souvenir bags and students milling in front of coffeehouses and well-lit storefronts. A pair of high-heeled Asian girls teetered past them on the uneven *pavé*. A *restaurateur*, who lounged against the arch beneath his sign and flirted in his apron, tempted prospective diners with sweet talk and a menu, but Lou and Aglaia had already gorged themselves on *fruits de mer*—mussels gathered from their beds in Quiberon, creamy shrimp bisque, a lobster *ragoût* in white wine sauce. Jazz floated on the night air from the open doors of cabarets and, while Lou preferred the more celebrated nightclubs such as Le Pulp, any bar here would serve as well tonight.

"Pick one," Lou said, and Aglaia chose an unobtrusive establishment near the looming silhouette of Notre Dame. The tavern's interior was paneled in oak, its chairs upholstered in maroon leather, and inverted wine goblets hung like grape clusters above an L-shaped counter. Musicians on a piano and a saxophone improvised a duet, and the barkeeper—ignoring the anti-smoking by-law—took a slow draw from his cigarette and squinted a welcome at the women as they sat. Lou ordered two glasses of sauternes, perfect as a chaser to their dinner—though she was beginning to suspect Aglaia didn't, after all, have the discerning palate for wine she displayed just the other night in her apartment.

But Aglaia seemed sated, her eyes closed and her toe moving to the beat of the music. Lou held back from smoothing out a wrinkle on the younger woman's top, bunched at the breast. Aglaia was mellower than in the café that afternoon, with her tortured attempts to explain away her turmoil, her fixation on locating François. Lou had seen her frailty and her pleading eyes ready to spill over in frustration, and she'd wanted to fold Aglaia up in her arms then and tell her to hush, that it would be all right. Her maternal instinct disarmed her. How had a trait like that survived the brutalization of her upbringing?

Lou reflected on their day of sightseeing. All in all, though she'd accomplished the educational goals she set, she was no longer convinced this trip was the best platform for acquiring Aglaia's support. She surmised that there wasn't enough time to win her over. Perhaps her spontaneous decision to accompany Aglaia for such a brief jaunt had been optimistic, even reckless.

Their return flight was departing on Saturday morning, which left only three days—hardly enough time to forge an alliance in light of Aglaia's preoccupation with sleuthing out the boyfriend. That wild goose chase could cost valuable time Lou would rather spend with Aglaia's undivided attention.

The girl was incognizant of the effect she was producing in Lou, personally as well as professionally. For one thing, Aglaia was bound up by the constriction of her religious past and needed philosophical and perhaps sexual release—both of which Lou would love to orchestrate. But more to the point, her young friend was in a position to advance Lou's standing within academia in a way that could make or break her career, if Aglaia would accept the job she'd arranged. So Lou had a two-fold appetite for Aglaia.

She finished her wine and mouthed to the bartender to bring over a couple of glasses of absinthe without asking Aglaia, who was still keeping time to the music with her eyes shut. Enough liquor—especially with the high alcohol content of the "green fairy"—might lubricate communication and, besides, any tourist coming to Paris should partake in the Bohemian ritual.

Lou had been hoping Aglaia would broach the subject of the *Buffalo Bill* prequel and Incognito's interest in it, and all day she'd tried to arouse discussion around the subject of cinema—not difficult to do in the city that was the setting for movies with stars of every era, from Humphrey Bogart to Matt Damon, Gina Lollobrigida to Nicole Kidman. In passing the George V that afternoon, Lou pointed out to Aglaia's the hotel's lobby where Meg Ryan was robbed in *French Kiss*; on a side street, she showed her the alcove where Harrison Ford declared his love in *Sabrina*; at the boarding point for the Seine River cruise, she pondered aloud upon a famous boat scene with Cary Grant and Audrey Hepburn in *Charade*—all to no avail.

Could it be that Aglaia's boss hadn't discussed with her the possibility of Incognito's part in the Denver movie, that she had no clue about what bid the company was submitting? Actual production was still a long way off, and the newspapers weren't yet making any public announcement, so it was conceivable she was unenlightened about the plans. In fact, perhaps Lou had overestimated Aglaia's rank in the costume company all along and was wasting her time in this esoteric courtship.

But then, as the musicians struck up another number, Aglaia opened her dreamy blue eyes for a second and Lou caught her breath at the innocent defenselessness in them, and her other greed—her greed to possess Aglaia—again possessed her. Whether or not Lou managed to squeeze her for details of Incognito's bid, this trip would be worth the effort if Aglaia warmed up to her enough to take the university job and be seen in the academic circles as her own little conquest. Aglaia was an asset either way.

Fifteen

The throaty saxophone lulled Aglaia as she lazed on the tavern chair, her belly full and her mind mellow. Maybe too mellow, she thought; she hadn't worried once since dinner about meeting with the curator in the morning. Lou kept plying her with alcohol and, if she were honest, she couldn't tell one wine from another.

"Madame? Mademoiselle?"

Lou's eyebrows clumped together at the bartender's words as he set a small tray on their table, maybe because of the differentiation he made between their ages when he addressed them.

Aglaia sat up grudgingly as Lou—with exaggerated ceremony—placed a sugar cube on the slotted spoon spanning the rim of each glass, through which she poured water to make a murky drink of the green liquid already in the glass. Aglaia took an obligatory sip while Lou and the waiter looked on in expectation; she faltered over its bitterness and Lou upbraided her.

"If it was good enough for Oscar Wilde, it's good enough for you."

But Aglaia didn't finish it. Instead, dizzy, she slumped down in her seat and hid again behind the veil of her lids. Hebe, she recalled, poured the nectar of immortality as a libation to slake the voraciousness of the blood-thirsty gods, with the Graces gathered around her in worship. Was Lou chasing the youth of ever-young Hebe in her mad pursuit around Paris today, as she force-fed Aglaia lessons about the Age of Enlightenment and the blood of the revolutionaries spilled on the altar of the cobblestones before the Bastille, lifeblood seeping away into the cracks between those dead stones? Aglaia's own sleepy inebriation, allowing the flow of such loosely associated thoughts, was no protection against the sharp words that so quietly cut to the very marrow of her memory: *Come to Him, the Living Stone... like living stones... offering spiritual sacrifices acceptable to God.*

Lou tipped the goblet up for the last drop of her wine and then reached for the absinthe. At least Aglaia was not locked up in the hotel room, poring over that Bible. Keeping the girl's mind in the here-and-now was becoming a chore. She'd hoped today's schedule would result in at least more vigor on Aglaia's part, but instead here she was nodding off and likely plotting how soon she'd be able to get back to her reading. Lou considered perusing the diary François left behind in the Bible's margins. Her voyeurism didn't typically include such tame entertainment and she was inclined to leave Aglaia to her own fantasies, but perhaps she'd delve into it after all.

Lou toyed with the idea of appropriating the book and then dumping it somewhere, to get it over with, but the least obtrusive action might be to just fulfill Aglaia's demand to locate François, or at least make it appear as if she were aiming for that goal. Suggesting Aglaia purchase the phone card today had been a good stalling technique. The girl would never be able to negotiate the bureaucracy of France Télécom alone to find a listing for someone she wasn't even sure lived in the city, anyway.

A couple sauntered through the door. Lou could tell they were native to Paris by their aloofness in scanning the room, their off-handedness in ordering kir. The man was tall with thick, straight hair, wearing an expensive trench coat open over designer jeans. Aglaia's age, Lou surmised. His girlfriend had narrow hips and was reaching into her Prada bag for a lighter when their eyes met— Lou's and hers. The woman held her gaze just long enough, then shifted over to Aglaia and back to Lou. Her mouth turned up slightly, a query in her eyes.

Lou motioned them over and jostled Aglaia. "Wake up. We've got company." This was the kind of excitement that would do them both good.

The room was roasting when Aglaia got back to the hotel, alone. She shuffled across the carpet to the window and fought with the heavy latch till it gave way, skinning a knuckle in the process. The late-night air floated in, clammy and close, and it wasn't much of an improvement.

Aglaia collapsed on the bed. The taxi ride back from the bar in the Latin Quarter had been difficult without Lou along to do the talking. Unable to comprehend Aglaia's accent, the driver resorted to stopping the vehicle and examining the name on a packet of matches she dug out from her purse. "*Ah, l'Hôtel du Caillou. Oui, bien sûr, mademoiselle,*" the cabbie had said courteously enough, but with a hint of exasperation as though he were tired of dealing with tourists.

On top of that, Aglaia had botched the payment and offended him with too small a tip. Now she was no longer sleepy. She surveyed a crack running alongside the molding of the ceiling, fuming over Lou's indiscreet behavior tonight.

Philippe and Emmanuelle, or whatever their names were, dominated the conversation and even Lou couldn't keep up with translating out loud. She didn't try for long, soon ignoring Aglaia completely and throwing herself into animated discussion with the couple, some of it seeming to be about her—the buffoon who couldn't speak French. But Philippe was checking Aglaia out and his girlfriend didn't care much, concentrating as she was on Lou and even, at one point, sipping from her glass—playing Worm-wood to Lou's Screwtape, Eb would have said.

"They want us to join them for cocktails in their apartment around the corner," Lou finally explained.

"I'm not comfortable with that." They were total strangers after all, and, besides, Aglaia didn't like the dynamic. "I'm tired, Lou. I need to get back to the hotel."

"Philippe would be devastated. He has a taste for blondes, he says."

"I think we should leave right now."

"Oh, loosen up," Lou said. "Your lack of libido is putting a damper on the whole night."

A blush burned Aglaia's cheeks, and she was sure that Lou's English insult could be understood without translation. "It's after midnight and I have that meeting tomorrow," she said.

"I'll have the proprietor call you a cab, then." Lou's words were clipped and snippy. She arose with the couple and left Aglaia stranded to wait for the taxi by the window like some stood-up date as the three of them walked off arm in arm down the narrow alley.

Now, sleep was not an option for Aglaia; she was too keyed up. Lou's desertion took her off guard, but Paris was the woman's second home, after all. And hadn't Aglaia been jaundiced about Lou tagging along with her in the first place? She should let Lou do what she wanted and get on with her own responsibilities. This was a business trip, after all.

Aglaia got ready for bed and then leafed through her docu-mentation again for the morning. She packed her satchel, un-wrapped and rewrapped the miniature oil painting, and opened the costume box to rearrange the tissue. But all the while she was wondering when Lou would show up.

After a couple of sleepless hours, she thought again about find-ing François's number. The bureau drawers held no Paris phone book, and it was too late to begin calling around for any Vivier that might be listed. But Aglaia slipped on her jeans and her shoes, then picked up her purse. There was a phone booth down the street and it had to have a directory. She might as well get going on her research.

The night clerk, snoozing behind the front desk, woke up enough to stretch out his hand for the gigantic brass key she held, and he placed it in the slot corresponding to her room number. She turned left outside the door of the hotel but found, when reaching the phone book, that the last pages—everything after "Trotte"—had been ripped out.

Aglaia's aggravation was replaced with her common sense. What were the odds that she'd happen upon the right number, anyway? And when she did call, she'd likely only make a fool of herself without Lou's intervention.

Now almost three o'clock in the morning, Aglaia's insomnia had set in for good. She counted backward; it was evening in Nebraska. She'd promised to call Naomi from Paris and now was as good a time as any.

The French instructions on the booth wall were unreadable, scratched out by some vandal, but Aglaia consulted her traveler's guide for directions. She inserted her phone card and punched the buttons for the Ennses' phone, and she was almost surprised to hear Naomi answer. The children were raucous in the background.

"You just caught us in from harvesting," Naomi said. "I can't hear you very well—hold on a sec." She shushed her kids and clattered some pots, and the homey sounds made Aglaia ache. She pictured Naomi in her kitchen—fertile mother, bountiful farm wife weary from her day in the field with Byron. "How's Paris?" Naomi asked. "Are you having fun?"

"It's great," she said with false gusto. She recapped the day's events, leaving out the escapades at the bar. There was a lag in the timing of the telephone transmission so that Naomi's appreciative mumbles broke into Aglaia's descriptions, and it took a while to get through her report. Then Aglaia let it slip that she'd packed the Bible along with her after all, and she heard no response.

"Naomi, are you still there?"

"Have you found François, then?" Naomi asked, her voice reedy and hesitant.

"No, but I'm sure Lou will help with that in the morning." Was she so sure?

"Because I need to tell you something first," Naomi said, their words crossing in midair. "I should've come out with it before now, but I didn't know how."

Aglaia strained to hear her. A dog yelped in the room.

Naomi was puffing, shooing the dog out the door perhaps, and she said, "Before you meet François—"

But then the line went dead. The phone card credits had expired and when Aglaia plugged in her credit card to redial, she was unsuccessful. She tried to call collect, but one attempt at speaking to the rude French operator convinced her that the ethnic barrier was insurmountable tonight. Naomi's confession—whatever it was—would have to wait.

Aglaia spent the next hour kneading her pillow into different shapes and stewing over Lou's continued absence. In all probability she'd be going to the costume museum on her own in—what was it?—five hours, and she was beginning to reassess Lou's loyalty as she sank into a short and troubled sleep.

The air in the attic smells stale to Mary Grace. Mouse droppings litter the floor between cardboard boxes full of holiday decorations and outgrown clothing, but François doesn't notice, taken up as he is with her. His lips tickle her neck.

"We're supposed to find the coffee perc," she scolds. Mom wants it in preparation for harvest time, when caffeine is needed in great quantities.

François pays her no mind but draws her in closer to push her breasts up against his chest. Something sharp makes her shrink back. "What's this?" she asks, and pulls a postcard from his shirt pocket.

The photo is just discernible in the dusky light and she sits down on a rough wooden desk to examine the Three Graces—their burnished nudity, their otherworldly air. She hasn't seen the card since the night François arrived over two months ago, though he refers often to the Graces in his storytelling.

"See how they're worn smooth with time, as you're smooth with youth," he says, stroking her face. He perches beside her, his thigh

pressed close to hers. "Three silent girls telling a story of the gods. Les Trois Grâces are lovely like you, innocent and so full of mysteries." His breath in her ear makes her stomach do gymnastics. She'll never get used to his touch or his flattery! But she elbows him, fearful that her mom, impatient for their descent into the kitchen, might pop her head up through the attic trapdoor and discover them.

"What mysteries?"

"The mysteries of a woman's beauty," he murmurs, his hand sliding around her waist under her top, sending electricity across her skin.

"No, François." She pulls his hand away and thinks that he can't have been carrying the card around for a thrill—the nudes aren't that detailed. By now he's seen her nearly naked, in her skimpy bikini. Why would he want a picture of them?

Jealousy digs at her and she reprimands herself; they're just old statues, after all.

François inclines backward on the desktop to rest on his elbows, stretching his long legs out in front of him. "You like the Graces, my little Mary Grace?"

She nods. "But why do you?"

François takes the card from her hands and examines the photo, smiling to himself. "I first saw them with my classmates when I was a boy. We studied ancient Greek poetry about them." And he looks deeply into her eyes as he recites words that she vows never to forget: " 'Then Eurynome, Ocean's fair daughter, bore to Zeus the Three Graces, all fair-cheeked, Aglaia, Euphrosyne, and shapely Thalia; their alluring eyes glance from under their brows, and from their eyelids drips desire that unstrings the limbs.' "

Her breathing has become ragged. There's a mania in the way his pupils dilate, but if it's madness that makes François so irresistible, she wants to be mad, as well.

"They're my ideal," he says to her. He grins crookedly at her, but she thinks his meditation upon the Greek goddesses is not such a stupid idea; the guys in Tiege are all talking about Sharon Stone as if she were a goddess. At least somebody wrote real poetry about the Graces. "Together they represent total happiness," François contin-

ues, *"the three of them serving the gods with their gifts. Which one of them are you?"* He points to the middle statue. *"Maybe you're like this one. Aglaia was the youngest and most beautiful of all."*

Most beautiful? Mary Grace can't help herself then; she slams her body into his and kisses him with ferocious jubilation, and he says, *"You unstring my limbs."*

The nighttime rain of Paris didn't present itself with ear-splitting acclaim. Aglaia grew aware of its presence through the shroud of her awakening, through an odor cheesy like the sourness of her brother's bedroom in the morning, clothes strewn on the floor. As a girl, she welcomed rain, even during harvest—especially during harvest, though her dad would gripe that the crops should be in the bins by now, out of the weather. Rain on a weekday after school had begun was no fun because she and Joel had to slog through the mud up the road, and the driver would be foul about their mucking up her bus. But on rainy Saturday mornings, the day they'd normally be roused by Dad's voice from the bottom of the stairs— "Kids, the chores won't get done by themselves!"—she'd be allowed to stay in bed a bit longer with nothing urgent to do but listen for a while to the music of the rain. Mom loved rainy days best for baking bread, the humidity giving the dough a wonderful elasticity, and so the household cleaning waited until after a midmorning spread of crusty *Bulkje* sliced thick with gooseberry or wild plum jam. It was like a holiday when Aglaia awoke to the rain pounding against the farmhouse window.

The rain of Paris, on the other hand, made only a soft pattering on the panes of the half-opened French window. So, after noting that the second bed in the hotel room was still vacant and that her alarm wouldn't go off for another hour, Aglaia fought back into an uneasy somnolence like the burrowing beetle in her childhood sandbox kicking the grains out from behind its rear legs into a soft pile of bedclothes.

Sixteen

Eb MacAdam steeped himself in the writings of the Reformation by such giants as Luther and Knox and Calvin. In fact, he kept a stack of their books beside his bed on the floor—piled up so that his dear wife complained whenever she vacuumed—and he would read some nights as he dipped into his stash of butterscotch candy after Iona had drifted off to sleep.

Eb was doing just that late on Tuesday night, working his way through a bag of the sweets and the pages of *Institutes of the Christian Religion*. It would be Wednesday morning in France, he thought, and Aglaia must be preparing to deliver the costume to the museum about now. Maybe that was why he couldn't sleep tonight.

His study in theology was an ongoing affair because he found such immediate application to everything he read by the great figures of the church. Take the section he was perusing right now, entitled "Scripture, to Correct All Superstition, Has Set the True God Alone Over Against All the Gods of the Heathen." Here he'd just been thinking about the swarm of gods that inhabited the chaos of imagination found in the pagan stories of ancient peoples, and which were being revived in current publications.

Not that he read much of the drivel written today.

Eb reprimanded himself for his pride. He had his own superstitions that needed correcting, he supposed. The idea that he couldn't live without sugar might be one, and at the thought Eb resolutely tied a knot in the top of the plastic bag of confectionary and hid it again under some old letters inside the drawer, where Iona never dusted.

Eb had been thinking about the subject of paganism lately because of Aglaia. Of course, he'd never heard her use the word and she likely didn't think of herself as a pagan at all—perhaps not even as a spiritual being. But Eb suspected a religious influence somewhere under her defensiveness.

Just last week, for example, using busy-ness as her excuse, she'd relegated the biblical research for costumes of the three Magi—commissioned by one of Denver's large churches—to the student volunteer, as if reading the story of the nativity might trigger dangerous emotions.

Eb recalled the days of his own youth, when he wondered whether the Bible itself was just a superstitious myth, whether its writers had simply borrowed themes from civilizations pre-existing the Jews. After all, oral folklore from every tradition included stories that sounded similar to what was written by the "people of the book"—stories of creation and of a great flood and of propitiation through a savior coming down from the skies.

Eventually, Eb found that argument weak. Mythological literature tried to explain origins using symbolism (much like costume making tried to illustrate personality using caricature). Mythological religion based its rituals on sympathetic magic—if the crops withered, the pagans believed their god was dying and so offered sacrifices to ensure their bellies would be filled—but those stories said nothing about life's spiritual, transcendent meaning or mankind's purpose on earth. Those stories expressed a *desiderium*, a longing for something lost, that only biblical truth could satisfy.

Eb believed that back in Abraham's day Jehovah called His people out from the blind worship of nature to a relationship with a living and personal and holy God. And he believed that God was still calling—calling *him*, Eb MacAdam, not to some mythic record of so-called "sacred history" that revered the mysteries of world religions, but to the supernatural events recorded in the Bible and taking place within the framework of real-life history.

That is to say, Eb believed in miracles but didn't trust in magic. He believed in a Book written by a loving Being but didn't trust books full of imaginary beings. The Bible might be a story, he thought, but it was a true story; it might be a philosophy, but it reconciled daily life with Holy Spirit. He reached down beside his bed and picked up his own worn copy of that living Word and entered it, expecting to find God in its pages.

Aglaia sat by herself in the hotel's small breakfast room, her suit already constricting because of the clamminess. Last night's rain hadn't broken the heat and the morning sky again threatened precipitation. She tore off chunks of baguette to dunk in her *chocolat chaud*, as the French couple by the fireplace was doing, then quaffed the rest of the cocoa in spite of the crumbs.

The neighborhood outside her window was rousing itself for a day of commerce. The tradesman across the street clattered wide his shutters and, one by one, the other shop windows blinked open to reveal their wares—sausages or souvenirs or cigarettes. The crumbling brick wall of the upper stories above the shops was graphed with miniscule apartment balconies, pots of scarlet blooming behind wrought iron railing.

The cab pulled up for Aglaia—using the Métro today was out of the question for her after all, she'd decided—and she gathered her purse and the costume box and documentation. The drive to the museum didn't take as long as she'd anticipated. She hardly had time to reapply her lip gloss and review the French terminology she'd underlined in preparation for the meeting: *la livraison*, delivery; *la réplique*, replica; *le jupon*, petticoat.

But when she arrived at the museum, a Neo-Renaissance palace, she found that the officials there spoke polite English after all.

The receptionist awaiting her introduced herself, with a genuine smile, as Christelle, and then ushered her through massive pillars into a conference room.

Three committee members welcomed Aglaia with a handshake; they hung the dress, offered gratifying accolades about her fine handiwork, examined the papers, and signed notification of delivery.

A long-haired journalist with a flashing camera peppered her with questions and informed her that the article would be printed in tomorrow's *Le Parisien*. The curator, on exiting with his associates, handed her his business card and advised her to call if she needed anything else.

The whirl of activity—its formality and in particular its brevity—threw Aglaia off, the whole affair taking less than an hour. It wasn't that she liked to be in the limelight, but she'd expected more ostentation somehow, more hoopla, perhaps even a luncheon. The meeting hardly justified the expense of the trip over to France, she thought as she picked up her handbag and glanced around the emptied room, wondering what to do next. But the receptionist stood by a tray of pastries behind her, and held out a steaming cup as if she read Aglaia's mind.

Christelle shrugged. "They are industrious businessmen, *non*?"

"It's the same at home." Aglaia laughed, relieved that she hadn't been left totally on her own. She deliberated over an *éclair* dusted with chocolate and a caramelized *palmier*, and chose the former. Christelle didn't take a pastry until Aglaia urged her to help herself and said she didn't want to eat alone, and then the woman picked out a buttery *brioche*.

"*Bon appétit*," Christelle said.

While Aglaia finished her coffee, the receptionist explained that arrangements had been made for her to view a segment of the museum's archived costumes. She led her through the stately halls of buff-colored stone, over intricate mosaic floors, beneath arched windows tinted gold, and alongside an exterior colonnade through which Aglaia spotted the Eiffel Tower in the distance, poking like a thick darning needle up into the fabric of the sky.

The exhibition they skimmed along the way showed manne-
quins dressed in suede fringes and miniskirts, celebrating the attire of the 1960s. Although the facility housed tens of thousands of
garments and fashion accessories, only a small section of the palace was dedicated to the rotating showcase of costumes. Aglaia's
expectation of spectacular variety was a bit blighted, but at the end
of a long hall they entered a chamber with high ceilings and carved
columns where the next show was being organized for the floor.
No one else was among the racks now, and Christelle left Aglaia
unaccompanied to view the eighteenth-century clothing at her lei-
sure.

The light was muted to protect the outfits but still allowed
Aglaia to make out the tidy stitching around the cuff of a lace-
ruffled blouse and the worked buttonholes in a striped jacket. She
was enthralled with the protective cloak and headgear donned by
a physician to protect himself from the miasmas of the Plague,
and stockings worn by the Montgolfier brothers when their inven-
tion—the hot air balloon—first ascended to the skies above Paris.
But the dresses were what captivated her most.

Aglaia was tempted to dash off a few sketches for future
reproduction in her own studio but was afraid she'd be breaking
some code and be embarrassed if anyone walked in. She gave
herself over to the clothing, and her sensual enjoyment went
beyond sight. Not spying any security cameras, and even though
she wasn't wearing cotton curatorial gloves, she allowed herself
to stroke the rich textures of satin jacquard and felted wool and
hand-loomed linen worn thin at the seams, and she picked up a
lawn handkerchief and inhaled the mellowness of three hundred
years.

She wished Eb could be here with her; he'd find such joy in the
workmanship.

At the mental picture of Eb, Aglaia pulled herself away from
examining a pair of hunting breeches—maybe sported by some
aristocrat chasing a fox through the royal forests of the king. Perhaps "joy" wasn't at all the word Eb would use in this situation,
particular as he was about his vocabulary.

She recalled, years ago, admitting to him how happy she was at Incognito, what *joy* the job gave her. Eb took that as an invitation to discuss her inner life, and he made a point of distinguishing between joy and aesthetic pleasure. Artistic endeavor would never fill her void, he prophesied, quoting another of his author-heroes who'd said that joy must have "the stab, the pang, the inconsolable longing" mere happiness didn't bring.

She comprehended his meaning on the spot, though she didn't admit it to Eb, and the phrase had embedded itself. She knew only one source for that stab, pang, and longing—and it didn't have anything to do with sewing or even with François Vivier.

Aglaia abolished those thoughts and concentrated on a flounced *panier* and *robe volante*—a hoop skirt beneath a "flying gown" that had graced a lady-in-waiting attending a duchess in the royal courts. Her hour with the costumes passed swiftly into noon.

"*Excusez-moi.*"

At the sound of Christelle's voice, Aglaia looked up from a shelf of footwear—beribboned dancing slippers and crude wooden *sabots* and embroidered cloth mules with silver buckles. The receptionist was at the open door and standing behind her was Lou, appearing miffed.

"Why didn't you wait for me this morning?" she barked. "I got back to the hotel to find you gone, and I was worried about you. Come along, the *maitre d'* down the street is holding a spot for us." Lou ignored Christelle's farewell and hustled Aglaia past the curator's closed office door without giving her the chance to thank him.

"You say you were worried about me?" Aglaia picked up the challenge when they were seated at the bistro. "That wasn't evident when you ditched last night, leaving me to wait for a ride until even the musicians were gone. And as far as worrying goes, what in the world you were you thinking by going off with total strangers like that?" She marveled at her own offensive; it had been a while in coming.

"You have abandonment issues, Aglaia."

That was just like Lou—deflecting the point to her advantage.

"This has nothing to do with my feeling abandoned." Had it?

"Don't raise your voice," Lou instructed. She shook her napkin open on her lap and addressed the waitress: "*Une bouteille d'eau.*" Lou's insistence on using French was becoming supercilious. She couldn't even ask for a bottle of water without sounding as though she were instructing Aglaia.

"But why didn't you come back to the hotel last night?" Aglaia pressed her complaint. "What would keep you from at least calling and letting me know you weren't dead or something?"

Lou cocked her head and asked in a snide tone, "You're serious? You want the lurid details of my nighttime activities with Philippe and Emmanuelle?"

Aglaia turned her face away, mortification dousing her anger.

"I thought not," Lou said. "Let's get on with our day then, shall we?"

And that was that. Repelled by Lou's reference to her lasciviousness, Aglaia didn't know what else to do but ignore it and resign herself for the afternoon to the pace the other woman set.

Lou escorted her along the grand avenues—Saint Germain, Haussman, and Montaigne—pointing out the *haute couture* houses and even stopping in at one to actually purchase a gown for herself at extravagant cost. It was made of deep magenta organza and *peau de soie*, the bodice encrusted with crystals. She said it was for the university function next weekend and suggested Aglaia try on an outfit that would have been completely out of range for her pocketbook, though it was on sale. Her own little black dress Naomi so admired couldn't approach Lou's in pizzazz, even if it did show off her *décolletage*, but it would have to do for the society dinner.

Lou led the way back to the street with the Givenchy bag in her hand to advertise her good taste to other wealthy shoppers. Despite Aglaia's objections, and maybe as an apology for her hideous behavior of the preceding night, Lou insisted on buying her some *eau de toilette* in a Belle Époque boutique along the way, paying an exorbitant amount for the miniscule bottle.

Aglaia willed herself to forget her misgivings about her travel partner, especially when Lou vowed that tonight, on returning from their shopping spree, she'd track down François by telephone. Aglaia didn't doubt Lou's ability to do that—just her will.

Later that evening, with a cup of *tisane* in hand, Aglaia curled up in an armchair beside Lou's in the hotel's quiet lobby. She was worn out from the afternoon of shopping but excitement knotted her throat; she expected to speak with François at any moment. Their corner was a private place to sit, all the more because the other occupants of the hotel weren't lined up tonight to check their e-mail on the courtesy computer, which was out of order according to the sticky note pasted to the screen: *hors service*. Lou's laptop was useless as well because wireless was unavailable in the budget hotel—a disagreeable fact Lou blamed on Aglaia's prepaid choice of lodgings. The shabby-chic establishment didn't allow for outgoing telephone calls from the rooms, either, but guests were permitted to use the phone in the lobby for local calls—for a fee, of course. The two-star circumstances had an obvious effect on Lou, whose mood deteriorated with each call she placed.

Lou had already spoken in smooth French to the occupants of five residences listed in the phone book borrowed from the front desk, solicitous in her tone and taking enough time with each household to explain why she was calling. With apparent ease, Lou connected with numbers in several different *arrondissements* of the city, and Aglaia was glad not to be bearing the burden alone beneath a street lamp in a public booth. But each failed call brought Lou's eyebrows closer together and produced a tightening in Aglaia's own chest.

"Run up to the room and see that you have the spelling of your boyfriend's name correct," Lou ordered.

"I know I have the spelling right," Aglaia said, bristling. As if she could make a mistake like that.

"I think 'Vivier' may have an 's' at the end, like the city name. It will speed up the calling."

Aglaia didn't want to toy with Lou's ferocity tonight. She acquiesced to the demand and, by the time she returned with proof of correct spelling, Lou was replacing the receiver with a pat of finality.

"Done."

"What do you mean?" It was a stutter, and Aglaia picked up her pace across the lobby towards Lou.

"I located him. The number was right here all along, the first call I made after you left. Everything's set, then." Lou gave a brisk nod. "You're to meet at the Louvre in front of the Three Graces at two o'clock on Friday—the day after tomorrow."

Aglaia stopped dead on the area carpet that covered the grey masonry floor. At first, sheer delight flooded her, and then skepticism set in. How could Lou have introduced herself, explained to François all the details, and made the arrangements in the short time she was absent?

"Well, close your mouth and quit gawking," Lou said. "You look like an imbecile and I hear somebody coming down the stairs—probably those gloomy crones from London." She was organizing her research now, spreading papers out on the low table and slipping a pen from her briefcase. "This exercise of calling half of Paris took long enough and I need to review my notes for my stint at the Sorbonne, so if you'll excuse me… ?"

Lou held out the telephone book and Aglaia automatically reached for it to return it the clerk, disparaging herself at the same time for being so subservient.

"But Lou," she blurted as if her physical motion reactivated her speech, "what did he sound like? Was he surprised? Shouldn't I have spoken with him?"

Lou peered over spectacles perched on the end of her nose, and her eyebrows twitched disagreeably. "He was going out and didn't have time for pleasantries."

"But isn't Friday awfully late for me to meet him? I mean, it's our last day here." She was flustered. Lou was making changes she couldn't keep straight in her head. "I thought we were spending tomorrow at the Louvre and then taking in Versailles on Friday."

"I've reconsidered our schedule, Aglaia. Versailles is only a forty-minute train trip, perfect for Friday afternoon as soon as we're finished at the Louvre." She sorted through the papers laid out before her. "Tomorrow I'll have enough to do here in the city with my research at the university."

"But you're allowing only a few hours for the Louvre," Aglaia said. She knew from her reading that the museum held an immense treasury of works that would require at least a day for even a cursory exploration. But, more to the point, the meeting Lou had coordinated with François would be very brief if they hoped to squeeze in an excursion to the *château* of the Sun King as well.

Lou's lips pinched together. "As far as I'm concerned, you've caused this time-constraint issue yourself. You should have planned a longer stay in Paris to begin with. And your decision to book such an early morning flight home necessitates our last night's stay in that generic airport hotel, though it'll be an improvement on this dump."

Aglaia glanced up at the clerk, but he didn't react to the insult. Lou disregarded the feelings of others, Aglaia thought—hers in particular. Lou was right about her mistake in the timing of the return flight on Saturday; it meant they'd have to check out of the Caillou on Friday and drag their bags along with them for the day—first to the Louvre and then all the way out to Versailles and back to the airport. But that didn't mean Lou had to be so offensive. Whose trip was this, anyway?

"That doesn't leave a lot of time for a proper reunion with François," Aglaia persisted.

"Listen," Lou said, "if my provisions are unsatisfactory to you, I'll dial François up again right now and you can speak to him yourself."

"No, I wouldn't know what to say." Aglaia prickled at the other woman's condescension and her own lack of confidence.

"I thought not. Now, if you don't want to grovel before me in appreciation, at least let me get my preparatory work done. There's nothing more I can do for you tonight," Lou said in dismissal.

"Well, thanks for phoning," Aglaia muttered, out of habit rather than gratitude. She was uneasy as she left the lobby with her cup of herbal tea and headed again for their room. As tired and agitated as she was tonight, she wanted to spend some time in bed with the Bible notes, making her own final preparation before delivering the book.

Seventeen

Once she was under the covers, Aglaia paged through François's notations again to make sense of his thoughts and recapture the progression of memories. The last turned-down corner took her to Hosea, the story of the whore, where François had underlined a few words here and there—*sin* and *kiss* and *lovers*. But the words of the text itself pummeled her: *I will make her like a desert, turn her into a parched land, and slay her with thirst. I will wall her in so that she cannot find her way.* Aglaia didn't welcome the rebuke to her own parched and walled-in soul, and she turned the pages quickly.

A four-hundred-year silence separated the Old Testament from the New, she remembered—four centuries where no voice rang from the prophets to the people of Israel, though they sought their Messiah through ceremony and ritual. They didn't recognize him when he appeared because they hadn't harkened to that final voice crying in the desert—*Prepare the way for the Lord*—for their hearts were calloused and their eyes were closed.

Lou would return to the room shortly, so Aglaia sped up her reading. She skimmed another page to find herself at the birth of Christ, where François circled the words *angel* and *virgin*, and wrote in the margin the words *Les Trois Rois*.

How could she have forgotten the night of the stars, the night he had called *her* an angel for touching him?

Mary Grace is thirsty. That'll be her excuse, anyway, if her parents catch her creeping by François's door at three in the morning in her skimpy nightwear. She finds him sleepless, as well—the air is too hot. So they tiptoe out to the dewy grass, closing the screen door gingerly behind them.

"It's called the Big Dipper in English," she answers him, "and that one's Orion's Belt."

"We say Les Trois Rois—*the Three Kings."*

"Oh, like the Christmas story," she says. "The Wise Men saw the star in the east and followed it to the place where Jesus was born, and worshipped Him there."

"I worship you," he says, and she's thankful the darkness hides from him the naked pleasure that must be glowing on her face. "But I prefer your English name of Orion's Belt."

Then he tells her the tale of Orion, the giant huntsmen of the heavens born near Boeotia in Greece, the son of Poseidon who imparted to him the power to walk on water.

Orion met the nymph Merope and fell in love. He couldn't do otherwise, for she was attired in the raiment of the Graces—gossamer threads, diaphanous and flowing so that not a curve, not a dimple, was hidden from his lustful sight.

But Orion was refused consent to marry her and so, in his passion and frustration, he raped her. The hunter, rendered blind in revenge by Merope's protector, was cured by the wonder-working rays of the sun to continue his amorous pursuits until he was punished again, this time stung to death and then placed in the heavens opposite his nemesis, Scorpius in the east, from whom he still perpetually flees beyond the western horizon.

And so Orion remains among the stars forever—a twinkling, cold, dead monument that bears witness to the wrath of the gods of Olympus.

She'd come so close to giving herself to François there on the dewy grass, but they heard someone open a window in the house and snuck back to their rooms unfulfilled. She couldn't fall asleep for hours on that long-ago night, shivering with the dark, divine sensations that threatened to snuff out the light of truth that had, till recently, so warmed her soul.

Aglaia shivered now beneath her sheets in the French hotel bed. She was sleepy but licked her finger and turned another page. She must be very near the end of François's notations, she thought. The youth group had been outlining the Gospels about the time the crops had ripened in the fields that summer—about the time François was forced to leave.

Yes, there it was in the margins of Matthew, where John the Baptist preached by the Jordan River. François had written a string of names—*Abraham, John, Jesus,* and then *Amphion*—with an arrow pointing to a line of text: *Out of these stones God can raise up children.* Aglaia stared at the names, trying to make sense of the quartet.

She strained to remember who Amphion might be—what god François might have inserted into this mix. She closed her eyes in concentration and finally it came to her: Amphion was the king of Thebes, who fortified the walls of his citadel without bodily exertion by charming the stones with music from his magical lyre, raising the stones up into place under the melodic direction of the Three Graces, those conductors of all charm.

Was François comparing Amphion's construction with Jesus' declaration that He would raise the stones of the temple—the flesh of His own body? And with God's promise to Abraham of progeny, numerous as grains of sand on the seashore?

The images were muddled in Aglaia's mind: sand on a beach; cobble on the Jordan's banks; the mighty walls of Thebes, long ago crumbled; the quarried bricks of Solomon's Temple, not remaining one on top of the other. And the broken and resurrected and instituted body of Christ, more lasting than fragile earth.

She knew her speculations tonight went beyond anything François could have intended. It was as though her thoughts were being directed by something outside of herself. She was curious in spite of her resolution not to be drawn into the Bible, and told herself it was the mystery of Amphion alone that held her spellbound.

She closed her eyes to focus her deliberations but, try as she might, she couldn't take her thoughts captive and make them obedient to her memories of François.

Aglaia shook herself awake. Lou could enter the room at any moment and Aglaia wanted to finish her overview. She wasn't sure there was anything left to discover, but then she came to François's last handwritten note scribbled into that big, black Bible on the day before he fled home to France, next to the story of Jesus' temptation in the stony wilderness—the final Wednesday study he'd attended. She wasn't prepared for it: *Aglaia, quelle belle diablesse!*

The words staggered her. François saw her as a "beautiful devil?" She was his *angel*, he'd said. And except for a hint or two that she hadn't even picked up at the time, François never directly referred to her as Aglaia; that hyperbole had been her own choice, a secret and subconscious conception given birth at Joel's funeral. But had she originated this name for herself, after all, or had it in reality been chosen by François without her acknowledgment? She'd been devilish all right, she recalled as she was pitched back to the youth group in the basement of the church that fated August evening a decade and a half ago.

"Flee youthful lust," Pastor Reimer admonishes them. Mary Grace peeks from under her lowered lids at François, whose hand rests high on her upper leg, hidden beneath the open Bible.

"Read how Jesus dealt with temptation," the minister goes on. " 'It is written' is what He said. When Satan told Him, 'Turn these stones into bread,' Jesus replied with Scripture. When He stood on the highest pinnacle of the temple, tempted to leap off and prove the angels would stop Him from even bruising his toe on a stone, He had a ready answer. When Satan ordered Him to bow his head to the stony ground in worship, Jesus again quoted the words of the Bible. And so should you."

She's never felt so convicted in her entire life, and she has no intention of repenting.

That very evening before the meeting, when François was changing from his work clothes, she crept into his room and wrapped her arms around him from behind, thinking of his kisses and his roam-

*ing hands. She couldn't look him in the eye; she was too scandalized
at her own deliberate transgression of God's commands.*

*"Soon," she promised, standing on her tiptoes and wanting to lick
his neck to taste his saltiness. "As soon as we can get alone again."*

*So when the youth meeting is over, she and François slip out
through the cloakroom door of the church. Her brother catches a ride
with someone else, as if by answered prayer or luck of the gods, leaving her alone with François to take the pickup home.*

*They drive the back road over the fields and they park, half hid-
den in the standing grain beside the swather still toasty from the
sun's rays, grasshoppers bouncing off the truck's chassis. One springs
into the cab through the open window and she stomps it, the crunch
beneath her sneaker making her queasy.*

*"Poor Tithonos," François exclaims with a laugh, and launches
into the tale of the mortal son of a water nymph, loved by the goddess
Eos who asked Zeus to make the boy immortal but forgot to ask for
his eternal youth.*

*So Tithonos aged into everlasting senility, wizening until he
turned into a cicada dressed by the goddess Aglaia in a suit of vibrant green, and danced with by her sister Euphrosyne, and sumptu-
ously fed by generous Thalia—a pet for the Three Graces.*

*Mary Grace shudders at his story, so François opens the glove
box and removes a brown paper bag. "This will help," he says. He
unscrews the top from the bottle of gin and gives her the first swig,
the unfamiliar liquid burning as it goes down.*

*He slides her over to him, dust puffing up from the seat fabric.
A magpie scoffs at them from its cache of road kill as the evening
wind dies down. François turns on the radio and kisses her, gently
for a while and then with increasing urgency. She trembles as he un-
does the buttons of her shirt one by one, exposing her bra and then
removing it. He doesn't say anything and doesn't meet her eyes as he
caresses her.*

*He's working on her zipper when they hear the whinny of Joel's
horse.*

In her hotel bed in Paris, Aglaia was immobilized with exhilaration or exhaustion—or maybe exhumation. Yes, that was it; she

was being dug up by the spade of her memory and subjected to an autopsy that should have been performed years ago. She opened her eyes; she tried to put the recollections out of her mind, but they were coming to her in real time now and she couldn't prettify this one.

Joel had been enraged that night, and he wrestled François from the truck onto the ground, yelling at him to get the hell off their farm while she fumbled for her top to cover up.

"Not with this girl, you don't!" Joel shouted, and she heard the thump of flesh on flesh, and a French curse. They tumbled in the tall grain, grunting, while she cried and begged Joel not to hurt him, damned Joel for being mean, promised Joel anything if only François could stay.

But François was gone the next morning without a word of good-bye, stolen away in the night by her brother, she assumed, and likely dropped at the Greyhound stop on the highway, with his guitar and his airline ticket and maybe enough of Joel's cash to get him to the airport in Denver.

At breakfast time, Mom took the biscuits out of the oven and asked, "Is François still sleeping? Can't he smell the *Schnetje* baking?"

Joel shot a hollow-eyed glance at Dad, who gave a slight shake to his head to silence him.

"Mary Grace," her mom said, "are you sick this morning?" She placed a hand on her forehead but Aglaia shied away. "Well then, please get the butter from the fridge. Henry, where's that boy?"

Harvest was in full swing and Mom would have expected François to do his fair share.

Her dad cleared his throat. "Tina, Joel tells me he's gone back to France." Dad looked right at Aglaia then—right through her—and she was ashamed. He said, "I guess that's what happens when we invite a city kid to the country." Her mother began to fret but Dad shushed her. "Don't worry about it, Tina. It's all taken care of."

The despicable subject was never addressed from that day forward although, sitting at the kitchen table that morning, Aglaia knew in her heart that her father fully comprehended her indiscretion, and she wanted to kill Joel for telling what she and François had been up to.

She waited in vain for Dad to bring it up but he never did, and their relationship changed for good at that moment.

Then again, that was the day Joel died and everyone else forgot about François.

Lou finished up her paperwork well after midnight, the clerk having long since shut off the lobby's main lights and, shooting her a reproving frown, gone to his own bed. Aglaia was sleeping as Lou entered the room but breathed erratically, mumbling a few indiscernible words as she rolled towards the wall. The Bible was open on her blankets and slid to the floor with a thud. Lou shook her head in disgust. What did Aglaia hope to find in its pages?

The thing seemed almost to have a life of its own, at least as far as Aglaia was involved, and it had been working its way between them from the beginning. Lou caught the girl reading it at every turn and she resented the interference while at the same time acknowledging that, if not for the Bible's emergence from Tina's basement, she may not have had the excuse to come along to Paris as an intermediary in locating its owner.

Lou retrieved a cleansing wipe from her cosmetic bag and began to remove the day's residue from her face. Her fabricated excuse to help Aglaia find François had been handy, but not something she ever intended to fulfill. The girl's badgering had gotten to her this evening; she couldn't put Aglaia off any longer. Hopefully her action tonight would keep the peace between them in the interim and they could enjoy their last couple of days together in Paris—as long as her plan didn't backfire on her.

The Bible lay on the floor between their two beds. In light of all the time Aglaia spent reading the literature, one would think she'd have something to say about it. But she withheld her perspective and, even with a couple of drinks in her, she wouldn't open up. Lou didn't care to hear any moralizing or a reiteration of the Jesus

myth; she got enough of that on the rare occasions she returned
her sister's phone calls. But Lou was running out of ideas on how
to stimulate meaningful discussion with Aglaia—that is, discussion that would earn her the girl's intimacy. Lou needed leverage,
but it didn't appear as though the Bible would afford that after all.
Unless, she thought in the middle of applying paste to her toothbrush, the Bible itself held the secret to her quandary.

Lou stooped to pick the book up. Aglaia was out like a light;
now was the time to read for herself what the elusive François had
to say that so commandeered Aglaia's concentration. Lou sat on
her bed and opened to the first turned-down page and read, *In the
beginning, the gods created.* That was innocent enough, if a bas-
tardization of the original writing. The second page was inscribed
with the words, *Naked and we felt no shame,* and that, along with
a couple of sexually charged remarks and François's attribution of
devilishness to Aglaia, looked promising. But overall the words
and phrases held no significance for her except to suggest that
François hadn't been too interested in the biblical content itself.
His comments relating to Greek mythological figures were erratic
and disjointed, and leafing through the book left her unenlightened about what fascination the notes held for Aglaia, as scant as
they were. But it seemed François and Aglaia shared an interest in
the gods of yore.

Lou came to the last creased corner in the book of Acts, where
the name of Artemis was circled without any attendant notation.
Apparently that was as far as Aglaia had gotten in her reading, and
as Lou paged through the following books, she understood why.
The remaining margins were clear of any writing—until, that is,
she came to Revelation at the end of the Bible. Possibly François
had started into the book on a whim and grown discouraged at
the confusing language, or perhaps he'd been browsing and this
passage caught his eye. But here Lou read an arresting message not
yet discovered by Aglaia, if her folding of the corners indicated the
extent of her reading.

François had underlined a verse that referred to the writer giving someone a white stone with a new name written on it. The allu-

sion was lost on Lou; she was uninformed about the much-disput-
ed apocalyptic writing and couldn't fathom why this specific verse
might attract François, until she read his words scribbled up the
left-hand margin and across the top of the page: *Idée de génie! Des
biblots, des joyaux, y graver "Kallistei," en combler mes Grâces, et
leur donner la pomme!*

For the first and only time throughout Lou's perusal of the
Bible, François had dropped his terse note-taking style and written a complete thought, perhaps working out some spontaneous
inspiration that had just come to him.

His salacious remark made it clear that he was a bit of a knave
when it came to girlfriends, what her students nowadays called
a "player." The whole thing smacked of licentiousness, but Lou
was unfamiliar with one word in the message. She knew Latin, of
course, and several Romance languages, but *Kallistei* was almost
certainly Greek. She postulated that it related to a particular myth
with historical implications, something she'd have to think about.

In the meanwhile, Lou might make some mileage out of her
discovery. Aglaia would doubtless find the French too advanced to
translate on her own when she came to this section in her reading.
When and not *if* she came to this section, Lou emphasized to herself; she knew the Bible wouldn't be going home with François on
Friday despite Aglaia's plans. Positioning the book firmly on her
knee, Lou snatched a pen from the night table and wrote in capital
letters in bright blue ink below the pale penciled French scrawl:
SEE ME. LOU.

That would grab Aglaia's attention, she thought. Then, satisfied
that she'd yet have the final word over François Vivier, Lou went
to sleep.

She was awakened an hour later by Aglaia's sobbing. She turned
the lamp on. The young woman—hair mussed, eyes running—was
contemplating the tears wetting her hands with the glazed gaze of
a sleepwalker. Lou moved to her side in a show of comfort.

"Blood everywhere," Aglaia mumbled.

"There's no blood," Lou said. Was she visualizing some tor-
mented nightmare—perhaps her first sexual encounter?

"He begged me," Aglaia whimpered, staring straight at her with wide, blind eyes. "He begged me, 'Don't go, Mary Grace.' "

"Who begged you?" Her guess was accurate, then—François in an ardent moment wouldn't be dissuaded. Lou hoped to get Aglaia talking. "What did he want?"

But Aglaia just jabbered incoherent phrases about fallen stones and stones raised to life, about Orion and the Graces and shining like stars in the universe. Her agitation increased and she kicked away the covers and shrank to the far side of the bed, her expression horrified by some imagined scene. "Get up! Oh, Joel!"

Lou reached for her and pulled her into the restraint of her arms, the terror making Aglaia rigid. Wasn't her dead brother named Joel? Maybe this had nothing to do with the French boyfriend after all.

"Hush, Aglaia."

"All alone, all alone." She was doubled over with the labor of crying, her fingers clawing with the desolation of a supplicant begging for absolution.

"You're not alone now," Lou said, patting Aglaia and nuzzling her sweet-smelling hair. The girl's distress was pitiable but Lou's tranquil words didn't issue from the motivation of compassion; rather, the heat of Aglaia's bed linens on her own naked thighs aroused her. But she denied the urge to kiss Aglaia on the lips and instead hummed a line from a lullaby.

"Hush, little baby, don't say a word," she sang out of tune, not remembering when or where she'd learned the ditty. The girl's body relaxed and her breathing evened out, and Lou tucked her back under the duvet with some regret, not even stroking the luscious curve of Aglaia's waist. Though the girl was unlikely to remember the whole incident in the morning, it was better to move slowly. She needed to gain more of Aglaia's trust for the benefit of her own career, even at the expense of her personal gratification.

So Lou began to have second thoughts about her newly devised agenda for Aglaia at the Louvre. The phone episode earlier this evening had been a knee-jerk reaction on her part, maybe a strategic error, born from Aglaia's insistence that she contact François.

But she couldn't undo her action now and she might as well make the best of it. At any rate, Aglaia needed to wake up to reality. The imminent lesson would serve her right for her high-and-mighty show of morals, turning her nose up last night at the bar over the arrangements Lou had made with Philippe and Emmanuelle.

Tonight Lou had glimpsed beneath Aglaia's daytime costume of propriety. At last she might be getting to the heart of the matter. The girl was unbalanced. Aglaia had been madly in love and she hadn't recovered from her brother's death, both traumatic enough events for a teen. But how did they relate to one another? It had to do with Aglaia's current insistence on delivering that Bible back to François, Lou deduced, but she couldn't see desire to connect with an old flame as motivation enough to pack a Bible around Paris. Maybe there was a religious element, Aglaia wanting expiation for past sins by tying up the loose ends of this romance. How would she react when she discovered she couldn't offload the Bible on François after all? Watching the struggle made up for some of Lou's impatience in waiting for Aglaia to respond to her own supplications.

Lou glanced sideways from her bed at the girl, who wore a faint smile now under the influence of some new reverie. "Hush, little baby," Lou whispered again as she clicked off the lamp. "Enjoy your sweet dreams while you still have them."

Eighteen

Aglaia awoke Thursday morning with bones aching and mouth fuzzy, recalling vague nightmares and a fleeting, bizarre impression of Lou singing to her. The disquietude clung to her as they rushed to catch the Métro to Île de la Cité for a hurried tour of Marie Antoinette's cell and the torture chamber in the Conciergerie.

Having given Aglaia explicit instructions on when and where to meet up again, Lou took her leave for the Sorbonne library. "You'll be fine on your own while I get my research done," she said, as though Aglaia were reliant on her, incapable of enjoying an afternoon unchaperoned in Paris. And she did enjoy the rest of her day, resisting her impulse to head over to the Louvre on her own in sheer rebellion against Lou's directive. She stuck close to the river so as not to lose her way and followed narrow streets of gabled buildings, passing shops and galleries, throwing herself into the frenzied colors and aromas of a flower market. Peckish, she bought a *croque-monsieur* at an outdoor stand, the *gruyère* melting into the ham, and she ate it as she sat in a leafy alcove of a park watching children at play.

Thus nourished, she spent several hours strolling along the quay bordering the Seine, counting the bridges that laced together the Right and Left Banks like the ribbon on a corset—Pont Neuf, Pont Saint-Michel, Pont Saint-Louis. The foundations of Paris itself rose up from the river, its ancient limestone footings exposed at the waterline beneath an arch or at the base of a pier. She had a sense of wandering back in time, of the insignificance of one young woman whose forebears had not even broken sod on the North American plains when most of these blocks were set in place.

Sometime during her pensive expedition into the heart of Paris, she thought about phoning Naomi again. Their last call had ended oddly with Naomi about to make a statement that Aglaia suspected involved François in some way. She looked for a *tabac* to buy another phone card but was instead waylaid by a newsstand. The article on her costume delivery was to be printed today, she recalled. She found the short piece buried in a back section, accompanied by a grainy photo of her standing beside the acquisitions committee. The journalist had quoted her in French but she bought another six papers anyway for the clippings, forgetting all about the call to Naomi.

Late in the afternoon, Aglaia stood in front of a must-see she'd starred in her guidebook back when she plotted her trip—it seemed years rather than weeks ago. She paid her fee and entered the main floor of Saint-Chapelle, following behind a couple of nuns in dark habits who crossed themselves repeatedly. It was a low-ceilinged, Gothic space, devoid of notable ornamentation, that cast no prediction of the celestial splendor she'd find upon climbing the dank stairwell. But upstairs, multi-colored sunlight fractured the air above her head, the stained-glass kaleidoscope surrounding her like a halo of rubies and sapphires and emeralds. She rotated in a slow circle, head tipped upwards. Fifty-foot windows soared around her within a framework of marble arches extending into the vaulted ceiling like the ribs of an overturned ship, a thousand glass pictures she couldn't at first interpret for their sheer profusion.

A uniformed man with thinning hair was delivering by rote a monologue in wooden English, likely intoned with the same accent a hundred times before, to a group clustered near Aglaia within the larger crowd. She lowered her lids and listened to give her eyes and neck a rest.

"Sainte-Chapelle was constructed by Louis IX and consecrated in 1248 to showcase the relics purchased from the emperor of Constantinople. The devout in the Middle Ages called it the 'gateway to heaven' since the windows tell the story of the Bible in pictures." He jabbed his thumb towards the entrance. "Begin with the Creation in Genesis portrayed on the left-hand lower panel and follow clockwise through to the Crucifixion and then, behind you, to the apocalypse crafted in the eighty-six panels of the Rose Window."

The lesson faded out. It couldn't compete with the exquisite blaze of color singing to her—azure and gold and crimson—the whole radiant work a visual orchestra with each pane trilling in its own voice within the grand cantata. She swore she could hear it: *Oh, tell of His might; oh, sing of His grace; whose robe is the light, whose canopy space.* Aglaia shook her head to jar free the lyrics and music that had invaded unasked.

As she focused on the individual scenes, the diorama became clearer piece by piece. The sun—that flaming rock—was throwing itself through the windows, separating the blur of bright pigment into meaning, forming order out of the chaos. The colored glass, itself just processed sand, became a mediator illuminating the story, a conduit between heaven and earth. Light was shining through the darkness, the translucent delivering the transcendent in a depiction of Incarnation.

She first made out the Garden of Eden where God, having scooped man from the red soil, brought forth life. From years past, she again heard the swelling harmony of her church choir, Joel's tenor behind her blending with her alto: *Breathe on me, breath of God, fill me with life anew.*

In the next scene Isaac was on the altar, about to be slaughtered by Father Abraham, whose blind faith was counted as righteousness: *Be thou my vision, O Lord of my heart.* Her memory surged in song, pictures bringing forth hymns unbidden. Moses stood before the burning bush, here leading his people through forty years in the desert—*He hideth my soul in the cleft of the rock, that shad-*

ows a dry, thirsty land—and then, grizzled, descending from the mountaintop with his face glowing from the presence of the Lord as he carried the Commandments written by the very finger of Jehovah: *Thy Word is a lamp unto my feet and a light unto my path.*

The noise was so bright! Aglaia longed to extinguish it by diving back down the stairs to the cool dimness below, as Jonah, running from God, was hurled through the deep to the roots of the mountains and swallowed up by the fish that regurgitated him at the gates of the great, walled Nineveh. The crescendo swelled as image upon image burned into her consciousness: Mary borne by a donkey, her belly swollen with her own cargo, bearing God Himself. The babe in the manger. The boy in the temple. The man in the crowded streets healing the paralytic and the leper and the blind, calling into the grave, "Lazarus, come out!" while the grieving sisters wept. His own empty tomb, His resurrection, His ascension, and the River of Life flowing through the Eternal City, clear as crystal from the throne of God: *Like a river glorious is God's perfect peace.*

Aglaia's interior choir wouldn't be hushed: *Crown Him with many crowns, the lamb upon His throne… Praise Him! Praise Him! Jesus, our blessed redeemer.* She knew no one around her could hear it. She covered her ears with her hands and wasn't noticed in the crowd, but still the words came at her—now holy words from the Bible itself calling out beyond even the hymns that were tormenting her and the mythology that had been twisting her: *Come! Whoever is thirsty, let him come; and whoever wishes, let him take the free gift of the water of life… Come to me, all you who are weary and burdened, and I will give you rest… Come to me and drink.* Aglaia was penetrated and permeated with sight and song and spirit.

She couldn't take anymore! She scuttled out of the cathedral to arrive at the *brasserie* around the corner an hour ahead of time, and ordered water—in French, after all her criticism of Lou. What had come over her in Sainte-Chapelle? The Sunday school lessons of her childhood had replayed in fast forward and hijacked her senses, the visual stimulation of the biblical overview portrayed by the windows sending her into some kind of auditory hallucination. She'd never before undergone such an unwitting cantata, and she was still quivering when she saw Lou arrive in the doorway.

Lou's mouth watered as she entered the restaurant. Re-energized by her research at the library and an invigorating conversation with an established French professor whose work she admired, she thought again about how good she was at her job and how badly she needed tenure. Aglaia was slumped over a menu, disheveled, and Lou took charge. She ordered an epicurean platter of *charcuterie* to share: tongue rolled with truffles, Leberwurst, veal and *foie gras*. Aglaia only sampled the regional specialties and took just a few sips of her wine before pushing the glass away. She was ready to call it a day but Lou wasn't so inclined.

"This is the life," Lou said, and sat back with her coffee. "The dining, the shopping—it's what I work so hard to afford. Isn't it what we all want—the perks that come with career advancement?"

"I guess so," Aglaia said. "I mean, I suppose I never thought of that as my main motivation to do a good job."

"And what would your motivation be, if not money?" Lou presented her credit card to the waiter and waved away Aglaia's attempt to pay for her half. "Recognition, I suppose."

Aglaia frowned in thought. "It's true," she admitted. "It's not that I want to be famous or anything, I'd just like my abilities to be acknowledged."

"And rid yourself of the hayseed persona, is that it?"

Aglaia felt another blush creeping up and tried to change the topic, saying, "My main motivation right now is to meet François and hand off the Bible." But Lou ignored the dodge.

"Employment at PRU would give you status and job security, Aglaia. I've ensured you'll receive a tidy benefits package as soon as you sign on." She was stretching the truth, but it was time to apply pressure. She couldn't wait much longer to wrest a commitment from Aglaia.

"I haven't thought that far ahead yet, Lou."

"Then you'd better begin. The theater department is getting anxious to fill the position." The girl's hesitation spurred Lou to push harder. "I've heard that several contenders are lining up for the job," she lied outright. "It's a once-in-a-lifetime opportunity, Aglaia. It could signal the zenith of your career and is nothing to sniff at."

"Don't get me wrong. I know it's an amazing break for me and I'm really grateful to you. But," Aglaia bit her lip, "I don't want to leave my boss in the lurch."

"You've got to start thinking about your own career goals. At the university you'd be recognized as a real artist." Aglaia nodded at that, so Lou carried on in the same vein. "I'm told you'll have great artistic liberty and a research budget of your own. Who knows, you might even expect more artsy trips like this one—maybe for London's theater season." The dishonesty took less effort with every sentence and the girl was swallowing it whole. "And imagine your name coming up on the screen as the assistant costume designer at the end of the movie."

"What movie?" Aglaia straightened her back.

Lou cursed herself for the slip. She didn't want Aglaia twigging yet to the connection between the wardrobe consultant job offer by the theater department and PRU's involvement in submitting a bid for *Buffalo Bill*. Any inkling that Lou was actively recruiting her away from Incognito as bait for RoundUp Studios might spook Aglaia, with her well-developed sense of morality.

"I'm talking about the next PRU theatrical project, of course, whatever it is they're putting together—stage play, film study. Come on," she said, changing the subject, "we should be getting back to the hotel."

The next morning Aglaia lived through centuries in a matter of hours as she and Lou toured the Louvre museum. Upon their arrival, Lou plunged her beneath the modern glass pyramid entrance and swept her through the halls of time, past an Egyptian mummy and busts of Roman orators and seventeenth-century Dutch paintings—ignoring Aglaia's appeal to follow the plan she'd mapped out online at home. Instead, they climbed a staircase to this pavilion and doubled back to that wing, and all the while Lou carried on a didactic commentary that Aglaia, chasing along behind, strained to hear within the throng of tourists. She labored beneath the weight of history and the burden of art.

The tour book photographs punched into 3-D around her with dizzying speed while Lou fulfilled her self-assigned duty as guide, pointing to examples of Greek deities in every salon as though she'd at last caught on to Aglaia's intoxication with the mythology and were rubbing her nose in it. Lou stopped in front of a picture of Pygmalion and recounted his tale: The Greek sculptor fell in love with his own ivory creation of a faultless woman and married her after an empathetic goddess filled her lungs with divine breath. Then Lou pontificated on a painting of Eve as Pandora, inflicting misery upon all humanity forever with her witless act of opening the jar of evils held in one hand or biting into the flesh of the forbidden fruit held in the other—the artist left the viewers to decide which. Before a bronze statuette of a young man in traveling boots, Lou related how the death of his mother during pregnancy caused the would-be father, the god Zeus, to tear the fetus from her still-warm body and stitch it into his own thigh from which, upon gestational completion, the child was *born again.*

At that, Lou's eyes glinted with silent laughter. She was ridiculing Aglaia's faith background, but Aglaia didn't share Lou's humor or appreciate her rendition of the myths that had such an impact when Aglaia first heard them from François or discovered them on a library shelf or sanctified them in her daydreams. Lou's accounts were dispassionate, told to make some philosophical or sacrilegious point rather than stir a feeling. The lessons diminished the romance for Aglaia, ruining her pleasure in them through Lou's bleak reduction.

"Slow down," she complained.

"François will be waiting for you in front of the Three Graces at two o'clock," Lou reminded her, but Aglaia wasn't stalling. She just wanted to look fresh when they met. An hour now separated her from him, a sliver of time and a few steps instead of what used to be an eternity and an ocean. She couldn't wait! She hardly believed François chose the Graces as their meeting place, and she wanted to ask Lou if she'd planted the idea in his head. But there was no chance to quiz her about it as they ricocheted through the crowded museum. They stopped one last time in front of a statue of an armless woman.

"Venus de Milo, one of the Louvre's most prized possessions," Lou said, although of course the carving was familiar to Aglaia and she knew its Grecian name: Aphrodite, goddess of love. Lou went on, "Experts say her posture indicates that, in her completeness before she was damaged, she would have been studying an item in her upraised left hand—an apple perhaps."

Lou gasped as soon as she'd said the words.

"What is it?" Aglaia asked

"Oh, never mind. I just solved a riddle that's been bothering me for a day or two." Lou smiled at her own secret. "Let me fill you in on some of Aphrodite's exploits."

Aglaia had a moderate store of knowledge regarding Aphrodite, but most of it related to the goddess's entourage of the Three Graces, her royal handmaidens with the high calling of serving her every demand. Anything to do with the Graces drew Aglaia. But she hadn't made an organized study of the complex body of Greek mythology in which one story intersected another in a baffling maze of versions. So she made no claim to know Aphrodite's every role.

"You've heard about the Trojan War?" Lou asked. She wouldn't be dissuaded from her narration, and Aglaia steeled herself to submit to the tutorial.

"The one where soldiers hid inside a giant wooden horse as a ploy to get inside the city walls, you mean."

"Yes, that was what the imaginative Homer wrote," Lou agreed. "But Troy was an existent city, its ruins excavated by a nineteenth-century German archaeologist. The authenticity of the fall of Troy is wreathed in myths, none so intriguing as the part played by this very Aphrodite before whom we stand."

Aglaia was mistrustful about Lou's emphasis on mythology, especially the stress she was placing on the tales during this museum tour of hers ostensibly for Aglaia's welfare. She chafed under the professor's long-windedness, glancing yet again at her left wrist. It was ten minutes to the hour. Was Lou trying to make her late for the rendezvous?

"The story tells of a wedding feast to which our Aphrodite was invited along with several other major goddesses who, true to form, were very jealous of one another."

Aglaia tried to listen politely but couldn't concentrate when so many people were standing near them or walking by. What if François were passing them in the same hall, making his way to the Three Graces right now?

"Dissent erupted among them under the direction of the goddess of strife," Lou said, "who wrote the word *Kallistei* on the surface of—"

"Can you finish this later? We're going to be late." Aglaia's interruption was beyond rude and she heard the peevishness of her own voice, but she couldn't stand to wait a minute longer. So Lou finally led her at last to the French sculptures in the Sully wing with a promise she'd be in the terrace coffee shop when the meeting was over.

Aglaia dug through her small bag between ticket and passport for a compact to check her makeup. She gave the people around her a quick once-over as well. A couple dressed in matching khakis brushed by her, and several art students slouched against the wall or crouched on the floor as they sketched—but she saw no lone Frenchman in his thirties with, say, with a magazine folded in the crook of his arm and ardor, or kindness, or even simple recognition lighting up his charcoal eyes.

She walked towards the statue grouping Lou had pointed out, transferring from her left to her right hand the Bible she'd carried around the museum since the women traded their baggage for numbered tokens upon entry. The officious guard there had flipped through its pages, questioning Aglaia's feeble reasons for taking it into the palace.

Would François be as incredulous as the guard when she tried to explain the Bible to him? Would he even remember he'd left it behind, or care that her mother had rediscovered it in the moldering trunk? He couldn't guess the effect of his long-forgotten notes on her these past few days, or that she was suddenly reluctant to let the book go. He himself had been so eager to leave it behind—to leave *her* behind—never once in fifteen years phoning or writing. Aglaia should have left well enough alone and never reacted to her mother's suggestion, should have disregarded her own compulsion to find him. Yet here she was in this predicament, hoping François might buy her excuse to look him up, hoping the reunion might ignite something in him. Would he even recall the significance of the Three Graces?

Aglaia approached the statues of the three marble nudes. François had predicted, "I will take you to the Three Graces when you come to Paris, *ma petite.*" And now here she was, the gods having engineered fate in her favor.

Lou had no intention of isolating herself in the museum café, and stood obscured from Aglaia's view behind another of the many nineteenth-century sculptures celebrating the revival of classical antiquity. The irony tickled her: Aglaia, examining the Three Graces, was unconsciously assuming the poses of the statues—shifting her weight, tipping her head—as the Graces in their turn emulated those before Pradier. Lou was tickled as well by Aglaia's abrupt shut-down when she'd told the story of Aphrodite in front of Venus de Milo. Too bad for her, Lou thought; there was more to the Trojan myth than Aglaia allowed herself to hear. But Lou didn't mind having time to read up on details. She'd be able to unburden herself of the story when Aglaia came to her office asking for the translation of François's last Bible note. And certainly she would come.

In fact, the translation might be Lou's last card, as she'd played her hand out to no avail during this trip, the purpose of which from the beginning had been to show Aglaia how useful Lou could be to her career. Aglaia hadn't responded to her overtures of intimacy, her generous expenditure of time and money, or her subtle encouragement to talk about the movie. Even her promotion of the consulting job with PRU's theater department seemed to be falling on deaf ears. What an asinine girl! Lou offered Aglaia a significant leg up and she was being rebuffed. The scene unfolding before Aglaia now was likely to incur her anger, but any emotion was preferable to the blank wall the girl usually projected.

She watched Aglaia fidget, put on lip gloss, even turn a few pages of her French phrasebook—maybe nervous that François would not understand her. Lou hugged herself in sly glee. It was pathetic how Aglaia lingered for him as the hour wore on. Steady, Lou advised herself; let Aglaia have her fill of waiting before breaking in on her. But she acknowledged a twinge of anxiety because her off-the-cuff scheme for the lovers' meeting didn't have a plotted end. All Lou knew for sure was that Aglaia, in ignoring her advances and refusing to take her into confidence, was systematically crushing her dreams and deserved some of her own medicine back.

While Lou waited in the shadows, she reached into her purse for her cell phone and, using the international prefix for calling home, tapped in a text message for Oliver Upton, as ambiguous as possible to protect herself should it be intercepted:

> *Still in Paris. Trust nomination is proceeding. No leaks for you—sorry. Must depend on your pitch at the gala. Make it good.*

Lou had to concede that Aglaia was ignorant of any quote Incognito might be submitting in the bidding process. She'd pushed the issue almost too far when she blundered by referring to the movie in conjunction with the job at PRU, but Aglaia didn't make the connection. Lou's best bet now—perhaps her only option—for attracting the favor of the tenure committee was to hire Aglaia on as theater consultant and keep a close eye on her, so that when credit for the costumes was being given out, she herself would be available and noteworthy. The rules she was forced to bend! And Aglaia was completely oblivious to her unfolding future.

Since she had her phone in her hand, Lou reviewed her electronic calendar for the coming week—her lectures, a meeting to facilitate communication between the sociology and arts departments. Then, of course, she was acting as master of ceremonies for next weekend's function just mentioned in the text message. It was an exclusive dinner of fewer than a hundred guests, arranged jointly with Oliver under the auspices of PRU—though the institution, if asked directly, might officially deem the project outside their educational mandate. They'd be wining and dining a complement of members from the film studio, development team, and investors. Perhaps a screen celebrity or two might even make an appearance. Certainly Dayna Yates was invited; Lou wanted her there to witness the influence she as a tenure candidate brought to the sociology department—to the whole university, for that matter. Aglaia as well had agreed when asked to accompany Lou to the gala, but Lou doubted the girl understood the cruciality of the event, if her attitude towards their shopping this week was any indication.

She wouldn't even try on the gown Lou had picked out for her at the Givenchy shop. It was a perfect choice for the *soirée* at the Oxford Hotel in Denver, since Aglaia was to sit at the head table with Lou. But the girl insisted she couldn't afford it because it was worth four months' salary. Imagine living on that pittance! Instead Aglaia said she'd wear the same dress she'd put on for their dinner the first night in Paris, a little black, low-cut number. So Lou had bought a gown herself, crossing her fingers that Aglaia's homemade frock might be mistaken as a Lacroix or at least a Gaultier.

Her chance to ingratiate herself with the proper people right now rested to a great degree upon Aglaia's ability to impress these same people. After all, Lou was presenting her as a sort of debutante, but Aglaia might not have the will to carry it off. Perhaps Lou needed a back-up plan so as not to be caught off-guard at the gala. On that note, she verified that she did, indeed, have young Whitney Wadsworth's number, then sent her a brief text message inviting her to the affair as well. The university chancellor's granddaughter would make a nice addition to the head table, as though the old fellow himself were attending.

Lou craned her neck around the statue that hid her in order to see Aglaia before the Three Graces, still gawking about for her knight in shining armor. She'd better accelerate her seduction of the girl if she hoped to get any use out of her, Lou thought, but her patience was wearing thin.

Nineteen

The life-sized Graces stood on a marble base so that Aglaia had to look up into them like a fourth party, a child approaching a trio of grown-ups who were companions of each other in an intimate alliance. They didn't condemn or condone her intrusion; she was to them a specter, unseen and unheeded while their communion continued. The personification of grace, they were poised as if asking, "May I throw my spell around you, beautify you as I clothed the very gods?" Aglaia could sense their infinite waiting, triplets frozen in marble for all time, three persons chiseled from one substance. They were a tri-unity of personhood.

Aglaia wanted to lose herself in their lifelikeness, to wish them into reality. The pearly grey skin, bellies rounded and buttocks dimpled, dented under their mutual caresses. Did she see the throb of a vein in a neck, or a breast rise and fall? She almost smelled the heat of flesh. Could *their* noses smell, *their* tongues taste? She was nearly persuaded, but their eyes gave them away—sightless, flat, no markings of iris or pupil. Now that she studied them in the flesh, so to speak, she couldn't differentiate them except by their props and their postures. The three faces could be one; there was little to set each goddess apart, and it perturbed her.

The Grace on the left peered downwards as if in expectation that a plant would sprout at any moment from the soil. She held a swag of flowers draped across her thigh and behind her *derrière* to wrap around one sister and up in an encompassing bond over the shoulder of the other, who stared out at eye level across the distance, the back of her hand pressed against the breast of the center figure, wrist softly bent.

But the middle Grace was the one that claimed Aglaia attention. The middle Grace stepped lightly on a jewelry box, like a victor claiming possession or a child at the beach sinking her toe in the sand. She held her chin high, gaze cast heavenward seeking the radiance of the sun or of her father, Zeus.

Aglaia knew her name—knew all their names, read many times since she first saw that postcard, murmured to herself on lonely nights. Thalia, on the left, was the goddess of the garden and all that flourished in nature's abundance; she was given domain over the harvest and brought hearty nourishment to her sisters and all the gods. Euphrosyne, on the right, was the pleasure-giver, goddess of mirth and dance, the life of the party. But the middle Grace, Aglaia, was known as the most beautiful, the brightly shining one, the keeper of treasures.

Aglaia, her self-approved namesake and her idol.

Golden light flowed through the courtyard windows, bathing the Three Graces, coating their surface without breaking the barrier of their solidity or solidarity. Pradier had carved life *onto* them, told a story out of the marble and it was an enchanting story but incomplete, for he couldn't breathe life *into* them. They were an unfinished covenant, a memorial. They were a tombstone like Lot's wife, a pillar of salt languishing for the cities of destruction, blinded by the gods of their age as, perhaps, Mary Grace had been blinded.

For the first time since she was a teen, Aglaia began to second-guess her decision to change her name, her identity. She found herself inexplicably irritated by the marble statues, as lifeless as Pygmalion's carving before its vivification, as Eve before hers. What had Aglaia, after all, expected from them throughout these years? Seeing the Three Graces in person, Aglaia felt the wind go out of herself.

At that moment, a breath on her neck brought her back to the present and sent a rush of heat to her loins. She stiffened without turning around—François had arrived! She must compose herself, relax her face as she'd practiced in the bathroom vanity before leaving the hotel this morning. She moistened her lips and fixed them in what she meant to be an alluring, Mona Lisa smile, and then she turned at the touch on her arm.

"So he didn't show after all, did he? That's men for you—fickle." Lou, not François, stood before her. Aglaia surveyed the gallery, bewildered, and Lou continued, "Haven't you waited long enough? We don't want to miss our train to Versailles."

"He's only twenty minutes late." Aglaia rubbernecked past Lou but the other woman moved to block her vision.

"He's not coming, Aglaia."

"He promised," she said, then stooped to pick up her bag and the Bible resting on it, scanning the room again. Nonplussed, her own voice sounded naïve to her, even puerile. "He likely got caught in traffic."

"Your Adonis isn't coming." It was a sneer this time.

Aglaia's stomach lurched and she said, "What do you mean?" Involuntarily she recalled that myth: Adonis was conceived in passionate incest and died in the arms of his lover, Aphrodite, who sprinkled his blood on the ground so that wherever the drops fell, anemones grew. Wherever Aglaia's thoughts of François fell, memories grew.

"You must get over this imbecilic obsession," Lou said, rolling her eyes. "You can't actually believe I managed to locate François in a city of ten million people with a few phone calls." Aglaia's cheeks burned and Lou added with a snort, "François's coming here was a joke, you idiot. Honestly, your gullibility knows no bounds. You've been so fixated on him that it's been ruining your vacation—and mine—so I attempted to distract you, for your own good."

"A *joke*? You mean you never even spoke to him?" Aglaia asked, incredulous. "You lied when you knew how important this was to me?"

"You've had your nose stuck in that storybook," Lou said, poking her index finger towards the Bible and then into Aglaia's face, "while the culture of Paris is passing you by. It's beyond me why you would choose some fantasy of romance over what's right in front of you. You have a problem with dealing in real-life issues, Aglaia."

Aglaia's astonishment gave way to a fury she was only now admitting, though it had been simmering in her mind for days. "I have a problem with believing anything you say!"

"Don't bellow at me, young lady. Show some respect—you owe me at least that."

"I owe you *nothing*," Aglaia said, her words chips of glass. "You monopolize my personal life, criticize my friends and family, bully your way into my trip to Paris, and now lie to me about talking to François. I've had enough of you!" Aglaia didn't wait for a reaction but tramped away, tearing open the Louvre pamphlet to get oriented.

"Where do you think you're going?" Lou snatched at her arm but Aglaia shrugged out of her grasp and picked up her pace, heading towards the baggage check to retrieve her suitcase. She had to get away from that woman.

But Lou followed her to the exit and outside of the museum, nattering at Aglaia about her lack of gratitude, about how Aglaia was beholden to her, and then—as though giving up—Lou said to her in a controlled sneer, "I suppose you think you can find your own way to Versailles? Good luck with that."

Aglaia, still bold, asserted over her shoulder, "I won't be following your agenda any longer, Lou."

"Is that right? The fledgling is taking wing, making a break for freedom, is she?" Lou's next words impaled Aglaia. "I suppose you're rejecting my 'agenda' to get you a decent job, too? Watch yourself, girl, or you'll find yourself pounding the pavement for any job at all. You're nothing to Incognito but a glorified shop girl, yet you'd disregard the one break I'm offering you for significance in life."

Aglaia almost stumbled. She hadn't been thinking straight; she was messing up the deal with PRU. But she regained her equilibrium immediately. She wouldn't be held ransom any longer.

"Don't expect to see me any time soon," Aglaia said, but she doubted she was heard. She knew Lou wouldn't follow—was counting on it, in fact—but somehow the thought didn't give her much relief.

Aglaia got lost in Paris. She rampaged off the Louvre grounds in a fit like none she'd thrown since her teens, and tromped directionless down this street and that in a temper of a workout. Why would Lou deceive her about meeting François? If she'd put her foot down and refused Lou's accompaniment in the first place, her prospects for finding François on her own would have been better. Now, with her plane leaving in the morning, her chance was gone forever.

Furthermore, she was still laden with the Bible, which was jammed back into the suitcase that throughout her tirade had bounced along behind her and even rolled over the toes of a stylish office girl on her way home from work. That Bible had become symbolic to her of all the baggage she carried around. She'd hoped off-loading it on François would be a finish to things—an end to her memories of him and to the scraps of faith still clinging to the edge of her consciousness like lint from the dryer. But most of all she'd wanted to look him in the face again, to search his eyes for traces of that summer.

Aglaia stood at a crossroads nonexistent on her street map. She'd passed the Picasso museum a while back and the Pompidou Center long ago, but now not one of the fancy *art nouveau* Métro signs was in sight. The sun was getting low in the sky and she didn't want to be left in some seedy neighborhood alone on a Friday night.

By the time she found her way beneath the sidewalk to the Chemin Vert station, her feet and her frenzy were worn out. She pressed her back into the sloping tile wall in front of the tracks and waited till the hollow hum proclaimed the train's arrival, its doors opening with a sigh to exhale and inhale its passengers. A kind man slid over to make room for her, and she wedged her bag between her sneakers and gripped it with her jean-clad knees.

Aglaia drooped on the burgundy vinyl seat, her adrenaline depleted. Listless, she beheld the passing scenery through the window: the blackened walls lined with wires and graffiti, the flashes of waning daylight, the bright bustle at each momentary stop. Anaesthetized by the rhythmic rocking and clatter, she watched the station names pass by: Liberté, Maisons-Alfort-Stade, Créteil-L'Échat.

She was jerked alert by the laughter of a couple of rowdy teens and took note of the *plan du Métro* posted above their heads. She was almost at the end of the line and should return to a larger station near the center of the city to make her transfer out to the airport, she thought. Maybe she'd catch a few hours of sleep on one of the benches there before heading through security; she had no intention of checking in at the nearby hotel even though she'd lose her deposit for the last night's room. She wasn't ready to see Lou again and hoped to forestall facing the professor until boarding time.

République was an onslaught of activity when Aglaia disembarked. She minced past an Algerian beggar huddled at the foot of a column and stopped before a flautist, case open for change as he piped a cheery tune. Aglaia fished out a Euro and dropped it in, then turned back to the poor bundle of rags and gave him a few coins as well before she entered the stream of connecting passengers flowing through the tunnels and up stairways.

At last she broke through to the surface of the station, where shops were open for business. Aglaia grabbed a fast-food *crêpe*, as buttery and sweet as she'd imagined it would be, and then spotted an adjacent Internet café.

She should collect her e-mails at least once while in Paris, she thought, and waited her turn in line at the busy depot. It took her most of her prepaid ten minutes just to negotiate the foreign keyboard before she got to her inbox. A few messages hid amongst the junk mail but she clicked on the one with a startling subject line: *Aglaia or Mary Grace?*

Dear Ms. Klassen, it ran,

> *I read an article in* Le Parisien *about your meeting at the Musée de l'Histoire du Costume here in Paris. The photo was unclear, but your surname is the same as an old girlfriend's of mine, also from the U.S. You must be Mary Grace Klassen, Joel's sister.*

Aglaia stopped breathing, her icy fingers inept on the mouse, all thumbs as she scrolled to the bottom of the message. Stunned, she read the closing line typed above the automatic signature and street address of the Tedious Beatnik Taverne:

> *Love, François Vivier.*

This couldn't be true! Was Lou up to her old tricks again, now e-mailing her under François's name to mock her further? The English was excellent and the timing too coincidental. But returning to the body of the message, she became convinced that the author was no prank writer but her own François. She resumed reading.

> *I found your e-mail address linked to the Incognito site. You're still sewing, I see! I still sing. In fact, I perform most nights at the cabaret I co-own. I'm sorry to have missed you while you were here. I could have bought you a drink, at least. I like your new name, Aglaia. It unstrings my limbs.*

Flabbergasted that he'd remembered the poetry first quoted to her on the farm—that he'd written at all—Aglaia gaped at the monitor until the proprietor of the café walked by and tapped his watch in forewarning. Other clients were waiting. Aglaia scribbled the street name of the bar on the back of her hand before her screen blanked out.

Eb combed the crumbs out of his moustache with the fork Iona always thoughtfully packed in with his lunch. Tea at the office was never quite as refreshing as drinking it at his own table at home, but it helped his digestion and put a nice end to his break—taken later today than usual. As he was draining his first cup, his receptionist patched a telephone call through to his office.

"Mr. MacAdam? This is Naomi Enns." He didn't know the voice or the name. "I'm calling to locate Mary Grace Klassen—I mean, Aglaia. There's been an emergency. I wonder if you know how to get hold of her in Paris?" She relayed to him the details of the family crisis.

"Leave it with me and I'll tell her to phone home if I find her," Eb said. He scrambled for the name and number of Aglaia's hotel and placed the international call, but a sleepy front desk clerk informed him that both Aglaia and her companion had departed early that morning.

Her companion? Eb was disturbed that Aglaia shared her room with someone unknown to him while on her business trip, though she wasn't breaking any company rules, strictly speaking. He'd never taken her for the sort that would pick up a stranger, but loneliness did odd things to a person. There was much that the lass kept from him, and why shouldn't she? He wasn't her father, after all, despite his paternal mindset towards her.

Eb dialed Naomi back and she answered on the first ring, breathless.

"It seems we'll not talk to her till she's back on American soil," Eb said, dispatching the hotel clerk's news but not, of course, mentioning his concern over the sleeping arrangements.

"Why would she check out a full day before she was supposed to leave for home?" the friend asked Eb. Then, in an aside apparently to one of her children, she rasped, "Sebastian, don't let that dog in!"

"Aglaia should be boarding the plane in a matter of ten or so hours," Eb said, hoping to soothe her.

"I suppose you're right." The woman sounded doubtful, the way Eb felt. "Do you have her arrival information?" Eb gave it to her and ended the conversation by wishing her luck, though he didn't believe luck played any part in life.

Aglaia would be coming home to an emotional storm, unprepared. Concerned as he was, there was no use fashing about the situation—it was out of his hands. But he raised a silent prayer on Aglaia's behalf as he replaced the receiver and settled back into his chair.

He lifted the teacup to his lips again, casting his gaze over the surfeit of books peopling his office, teetering on the shelves, cavorting on the floor—Bunyan and Chaucer, Bacon and Galileo, Hawthorne and Herodotus and Gerard Manley Hopkins.

He loved them all, every one of the "truths wrapped in fables," as Pascal described human writings. But when it came to needing guidance—when Eb was troubled about something outside of his control—only one book allowed pure contemplation of the mind of God.

He opened his right-hand desk drawer and withdrew a copy now.

Twenty

A neon sign pulsated above the bar as Aglaia, across the boulevard, steeled herself to enter. It was ten o'clock and a few customers
straggled through the door—a middle-aged couple both sporting
grey ponytails, a group of students already noisy with inebriation.
She could tell this was no tourist attraction; only French words
floated to her on the night air.

Finding the place had been time consuming—not that she was
in a rush. After all, she had the whole night to kill before her plane
left. But she'd already wasted time on the Métro and another half
an hour finding a street-side pay toilet, which was dimly lit and
cramped. It sufficed for her purposes—to change into her lace
camisole, sheer over-blouse, and strappy heels, and to reapply her
eyeliner in the heavy fashion she noticed on some of the younger
Parisian women. She'd removed her pins and shaken out her hair,
too, so that it fell in long, soft waves.

Now that she stood before the tavern, her intestines twisted
in anguish. She grappled with her memory for some vision, some
recollection of a story of François's that might boost her bravado.
The tale that came to her mind was of Cephalus and Procris, lovers reconciled after unfaithfulness, but that myth ended badly in

the death of the woman by the arrow of the man. And the Three Graces didn't even figure into it at all. She found no courage in her imagination. Then, from a different direction in an inaudible voice, she heard the words, *Come to me,* but she ignored them, too. She couldn't turn back now. She was committed; this was her destiny.

Aglaia opened the door, not wide to announce herself with a gust of fresh air but enough to let her slide in, a stealthy shadow. She sat at the booth closest to the exit. Let the server find her in the corner—she wasn't about to stand at the bar to place her order. Meanwhile she took stock of her surroundings. Andy Warhol prints were fixed to the walls, and antique bongos and retro lamps decorated the tables. Half the stools pulled up to the bar's counter were occupied and she was safe in her anonymity for the moment, as the focus of the room rested on the languid poet at the mike executing some tragic verse to the background of canned blues and a smattering of applause.

But then the lights came up a bit and there was François taking his perch on the chrome stool with his guitar on his knee. Aglaia gasped so that the girl who appeared beside her with pad and pencil, wearing dead-white lipstick, said, "You okay, Miss?" with British enunciation.

Aglaia muttered, "*Café crème*, please," ignoring the question. She didn't want alcohol fogging her mind tonight and wished the girl would get out of her way so she could inspect François again.

It was impossible that fifteen years had passed. His silhouette was a bit fuller, perhaps, and his hair slightly shorter, though as thick and wavy as she remembered. He wore his jeans the same way—low on his hips and tight, faded at the knees. His long fingers curled over the strings with the same dexterity as when he'd strummed in the church basement or out on the hay-bale stacks. He closed his eyes to sing his French melody, the unfamiliar words breaking her heart with familiarity, and then he made a few comments, maybe in introduction to his next number.

That's when he saw her. His scrutiny was inquisitive at first, as though he were uncertain about this lone female tourist ducking into the gloom at the back of the room with a suitcase by her feet. She averted her face but their glances crossed again and then recognition lit up his countenance.

His eyes danced as he cajoled his audience, calling them *mes amis*—my friends—but tipping his head towards her. He finished his routine—another three songs that she couldn't understand but knew were meant for her because of his smoldering inflection every time he sang the word *amour*. And then he left his guitar propped against his stool and headed across the floor, stopping by the bar to pick up a bottle and two wine glasses. Aglaia's legs were shaky even though she was sitting.

"Mary Grace Klassen! You got my e-mail, then?"

"François, is it really you?"

They spoke over one another and laughed; he stooped to smack her right cheek, left cheek.

"I thought you'd gone from Paris days ago," he said, pulling a corkscrew from his back pocket. "You look fantastic!"

"And your English is perfect," she said. "You've been practicing."

"I did my time in university, spent a couple of years pubbing around London," he said as he slid into place across the table from her and lifted his goblet in a silent toast. "You know how it goes."

She didn't, but she nodded and the small talk went on for several moments, giving Aglaia's heartbeat time to stabilize. His charming accent was discernible despite his fluent, even colloquial, English as he asked about her job, her travels, whether she still sang in a choir. He refilled his glass but she'd hardly touched hers. According to the bottle's label, it was some complicated blend from the Rhône Valley and likely expensive, but if so, Aglaia thought, it was wasted on her. She couldn't tell the difference and, besides, tonight she wanted to keep her head about her.

She answered François's questions but there was only one she wanted to ask him—about why he'd never called, never sent her even a card of condolence. He brought it up himself, in a roundabout way.

"So, is Joel still pissed off with me?"

Aglaia became very still. He didn't know, then, about the death—and how could he?

"Joel was killed the morning after you left," she said.

"Killed? How?"

"Agricultural accident. He was standing in the wrong place at the wrong time." She caught her bottom lip between her teeth, the stinging starting again at the corner of her eyes.

He took her hand in his and she was going to explain more, but he cut through her mood. "What a fight we had! I thought he was going to tear me apart that night."

"That night," she stuttered involuntarily, heat rushing to her face.

His features softened and he held his tongue for a moment, letting his eyes flit over her hair, her lacy top. He ran his tongue over his lips.

"It was a pity Joel interrupted us that night, don't you agree?" François asked, but any words she might have thought got stuck in her throat. He reminisced. "After the fight, we were both beat up, bleeding. You might not remember because you were pretty hysterical."

She remembered that part, all right. The three of them had snuck back into the house, jumpy as cats, and she immediately went to her room and covered her ears with a pillow, willing herself to sleep—only to wake up in the morning to the new nightmare of him missing.

"I think your mom was already sleeping, but your dad saw our condition and came into the bedroom. Joel told him, well, *his* version of what happened." François turned his face away but not in embarrassment over their tussle, she thought; his mouth curved up a bit. "Henry agreed that Joel should take me to the airport right then."

That surprised her. "What? In Denver?"

"Yeah. It was a long, silent ride, I'll tell you. He dropped me off at two in the morning with my duffle bag and told me he'd break my neck if I ever contacted you again. Then he turned right around for home. Lucky I had an open-ended ticket."

How dare Joel threaten François—scare him off like some gangster might in protecting his turf! Before she could express her dismay, François carried on with a different topic.

"And what about the others in Tiege, in that youth group?" he asked. "What about your best friend?"

"You mean Naomi?" She didn't want to waste their time talking about Naomi.

"Yeah, the motherly one."

"She's got six kids now," Aglaia confirmed, thinking it odd that François would describe a teen girl in that way, though it was true that Naomi had always been rather nurturing.

François whistled. "Fertile."

"I guess," Aglaia said. Why would that matter to him? His interest in Naomi rubbed her the wrong way, but she put it out of her mind when he arose from the table and spoke again.

"Hey, want to take a walk? It's not private enough in here." He touched Aglaia's elbow to help her up, and he kept his hand there as he motioned the waitress over. She'd been watching the two of them from the counter, retaining distance from her boss out of respect, Aglaia had assumed. But now the waitress glowered at François's request: "Abbey, love, take my friend's suitcase out to the back. We'll return for it later." Then to Aglaia he said, smirking, "It's great to have staff to order around. I picked Abbey up on one of my most recent trips across the Channel." Aglaia wondered what he meant by "picked up," but for the moment she gave him the benefit of the doubt.

"Tell me about this," she said, patting the wall of the bar. "How long have you been in the business?" They stepped into the cool night air and moved down the street, Aglaia still dazed that she was actually with him.

"A good eight years," he replied. "I think the name's a bit weird but it was the co-owner's idea."

"What would you have called it?" Aglaia asked.

"Sisyphus," he answered promptly. So, then, he was still into mythology. "At least my partner went along with my concept for the sign design," François said, pointing back towards the building they'd just left. Aglaia studied the multicolored neon animation incorporating the name of the Tedious Beatnik Taverne. Through an illusion created by lighting sequence, a muscular figure rolled a large and shapeless object forward and upwards; it then rolled back down and the figure pushed it up again, the action repeating itself perpetually. "Sisyphus symbolizes tedium," François said.

"I don't know his story," she fibbed. She'd read most of them by now in bits and pieces, but she wanted his adaptation, smooth and sensuous. How she'd missed that! He seemed pleased, and paused to light a cigarette. They watched the movement of the sign as François launched into the tale with his characteristic narrative style heightened by his increased facility in the language and, if it were possible, with even more self-assurance then he'd had as a teen, as though he'd practiced the telling many times.

"Sisyphus was a clever mortal, a prince charged with promoting travel and commerce in his father's kingdom. But he was greedy and abused the gift of hospitality received at his birth from the Three Graces." François took a drag, then winked down at Aglaia as if they shared private knowledge of the goddesses. She melted inside, just as she had when she was seventeen. "The prince killed and robbed wayfarers. This violated the laws of generosity demanded by the gods, and angered them. But it was only his first trespass as he aspired for domination."

François talked around the cigarette in his mouth so that the glowing end bobbed in the dark. "You're chilled?" he asked, when she rubbed her arms through the flimsy silk of her blouse. "Here, take my jacket." He drew it around her, the smell of him encapsulating her, and kept his arm over her shoulders as they turned and walked.

"Now, Sisyphus stole not only goods from earthly travelers but also secrets from Olympus. He was crafty and fancied himself to be more cunning than Zeus, god of gods, who was always defiling young virgins.

"One day while prowling in the woods, Sisyphus came upon the Graces preparing a chaste island nymph for her assignation with Zeus. From his hiding place, Sisyphus watched them bathe her in fragrant spices and adorn her with wildflowers—violets and blood-red poppies and delicate almond blossoms. They wove a robe of mist to shield the maiden's modesty. Suddenly and with great commotion Zeus rode in on the back of a thundercloud, and the Three Graces scattered. But Prince Sisyphus stayed just long enough to watch Zeus blow his tempestuous breath under the drapery of the nymph's gown to expose her lovely form."

François dropped his voice and Aglaia pressed closer, carried on the cloud of his fantasizing as she closed her eyes and breathed in his earthy, heavenly breath. François's arm tightened around her and he went on, "In a spirit of treachery, Sisyphus peddled his knowledge to the nymph's protective father—the god of the river— telling him that his daughter was at that moment being ravished by Zeus.

"This infuriated her father, but not as much as it enraged Zeus when he learned of the betrayal. For Sisyphus's treason, he was damned to Tartarus with an everlasting punishment, charged with the repetitive task of pushing uphill a huge boulder that, upon reaching the apex, rolled back to the valley so that Sisyphus must begin again, over and over for eternity."

When Aglaia blinked open her lids, François's grey-black eyes were intense and his head was inclining towards her, but in re- flex she pulled back. So many years had passed since the last time they'd kissed, so many rhapsodies had been dreamed, that the real thing incurred some trepidation for her.

"Don't you like my stories any more, Mary Grace?" he asked, slipping his arm around her waist now as they walked on. "Or should I say, *Aglaia*?"

"They're as riveting as always," she answered, although in fact the story disturbed her, with its violence and its dismal end. Fran- çois's delivery—slick as a sales pitch—disturbed her as well. She said, "But you have to admit that the fate of Sisyphus is depressing, maybe even best forgotten."

"Not so!" He stopped on the sidewalk and dropped the butt of his smoke onto the cobblestones, swiping at it with his boot. "Our own French philosopher Albert Camus used the story of Sisyphus to make some very good points. He referred to him as the proletarian of the gods, powerless and rebellious, a perfect illustration of the plight of the workingman and the boring absurdity of life. Camus said, 'A face that toils so close to stones is already stone itself.' What we do, over and over again, we become. Life beats us up, and we're at the mercy of our circumstances.'"

Aglaia always thought it was the other way around—that actions arose out of attitude, that the heart dictated the deeds and overcame circumstances. Still, the conversation stimulated her, though its implications were disheartening. "So you're saying there's no point to life at all but bitter futility?"

"I'm saying that life itself is absurd. I imagine Sisyphus as a bloke of today, stumbling under the weight of society's conventions that threaten to crush him, dodging the boulder of morality, stubbing his toe on it. But my goal is to break the boulder of Sisyphus," François bragged. He lit another Gitane, cupping the flame of his match against the breeze. "I refuse to be sentenced to an existence of boredom, stuck in a meaningless repetition of unthinking tradition."

"That's easier said than done."

"But you've broken out of the rut, haven't you? You've become Aglaia."

She said nothing. François could never know the depth of the ruts she'd worn going up and down the hill of her life. Her boulder wasn't conventional morality but rather family, farm, and faith— and she'd been trying to smash that boulder and escape her Tartarus for years. She might have told him that next, but they came to a cluster of activity under a light standard—a vendor about to close up his stall as a few browsers moved away from his jewelry.

The man sitting at the booth hailed him, "*Bonsoir, François.*"

"*Salut, Rémy.*" François turned to Aglaia. "I want to buy you something." He took her to the stand and fingered a few pendants hanging on a dowel. "This one! It's very bobo," he said. He slipped off an alabaster disc hanging from a leather thong and gave it to Rémy with a twenty-Euro note. "*Écrivez ceci en Anglais, je vous prie,*" he said, writing something for the man on a scrap of paper.

"*Un autre collier—une autre conquête?*" Rémy bantered with an impudent grin.

François answered with mock sternness, "*Ça suffit, Rémy. Écrivez.*"

Aglaia's French was too basic for her to understand the interaction between the two men, but she picked up the intonation of Rémy's teasing and François's reprimand.

They watched as the craftsman engraved upon the white stone with his fine drill, then blew the dust away. When it was done, François slipped it into his jeans pocket and said to her, "Not yet. It's too bright here." So they returned down the alley towards the bar and soon were alone again in the night, holding hands as they walked. When they reached the back entrance, François halted and leaned against the age-stained wall, facing her. He withdrew the necklace from his pocket.

"I've looked a long time for the perfect woman and now you've come back to me," he said. François couldn't be sincere about this, Aglaia thought, but he quelled her objection by placing his fingertips on her mouth. She tasted them, opened her lips and let her tongue touch the ridges on them.

"When I first met you as a teen," he continued, "I saw right past your outward resistance to your open heart and vowed right then that you'd let me in." He turned her hand up and placed the pendant in it for her to examine.

The thin, polished stone lay in her palm, cool and white, with a decorative design on one side and, when she turned it over, a tribute inscribed in her honor on the other: *To my fairest Aglaia*. Elation swelled in her breast while skepticism cautioned that she'd better not read too much into the gift.

"Let me put it on for you," he said, and fastened the clasp from behind as she held up her hair. "It's only a trinket but it symbolizes a great deal."

"Does it?" she asked. He stroked the nape of her neck and she tensed against the pleasure.

He turned her around to face him, keeping his hands on her waist. "Yes, a great deal. Your name is Aglaia—I thought you understood." She didn't, and it must have shown. "Aglaia was the youngest and most beautiful of the three," he explained, "like you. Back there in Nebraska I told you how beautiful you were as Mary Grace—now as Aglaia herself. Didn't you believe me then?" He gave her no time to answer, and that was just as well because she might have replied that she wasn't sure she believed him even now. But—oh!—she wanted to. He gathered her close to him and burrowed his lips into her hair so that her cheek was pressed against his sweater. "I love your femininity, Aglaia. I love the feminine essence of women."

She stepped back at his choice of his last word. "The feminine essence of *women*?"

She didn't know, after all, about his romantic life, but judging from the way that waitress Abbey drooled over him, he was no saint. He hadn't offered information on his marital status, either, but then she hadn't asked. She didn't really want to know—hadn't ever really wanted to know that she wasn't his only love. So now, couldn't she finally just give in to him without burdening herself with the thought of consequences? Hadn't she waited long enough?

She was scandalized by her own desires even as she asked herself the questions.

"Don't take me wrong," he pacified, and he drew her back in to kiss the tip of her nose. "There's only one of you—only one Mary Grace. But like all women, you're complex, made up of many layers. What are the elements of your personhood?"

"What do you mean?" she asked. She was body, soul, and spirit—three parts, one entity.

"I've considered the mystery of women over the years," François said, taking his time though she was impatient now. He wrapped his arms around her again so that she felt snug in his embrace—almost safe.

Almost, but not quite.

François continued, "I figure every guy wants that ideal woman who will satisfy all his needs. But it's not realistic. No one's perfect enough to satisfy another completely."

"Well, my parents seem happy," she began. But her voice was

lost in the soft knit of his sweater and he went on talking, which was just as well because, at the bottom of it, he was right. She had to accept his logic that people needed something more than humanity offered. She'd always known that.

"This is where the Three Graces have been most useful to me," he said. "Together they represent the fullness of womanhood, each aspect of the stone girls corresponding to a characteristic in human girls."

"Really?" Aglaia tipped her chin up to him. So this was the source of his interest in the Graces all along; they were a pattern to him, a prototype.

"Oh yes. You know, in spite of our sexual experimentation, what men really want is one woman who embodies the attributes of all three. We want Thalia, the girl we can take home to meet the parents and have babies with, but only when we're ready to settle down after we've had some fun and 'sown our wild oats,' as the saying goes. Partying is Euphrosyne's job, and I see plenty of her kind coming into the bar, always ready for a good time. But Aglaia," he said, pulling her torso hard against his, "Aglaia is the one who gets to us in the first place. Dazzling goddess, a jewel herself, she's so spectacular to look at that she calls us away from our boyish oblivion and the drudgery of labor. She turns the stony face of Sisyphus away from the earth and up towards the heavens. Aglaia is what all men idolize."

François's spiel fascinated Aglaia, as much for its poetic whimsy as its self-interest. Her cynicism gained a toehold and she asked herself how many women he'd scored this way. But in spite of his whopping pick-up line, her intellect took second place to her emotions and all she wanted to do was kiss him.

But his lips were in her hair again, one hand running up and down her back, the other unlocking the bar's alley door. She caught sight of her suitcase just inside the room.

"Stay the night with me, Aglaia. Share some of your treasure." His words thrilled her, and then to sweeten the invitation he covered her mouth with his, parted her lips with his tongue, and she could have thrown herself into him then, could have drowned in him. But the picture of Joel with lacerated fists popped uninvited into her mind—her brother who was willing to shed his own blood for her teenaged virtue.

"I thought you lived clear across town," she said, but the mild protest was muffled by his lips and her resolve all but dissolved.

"I keep a room here for when I work past Métro hours." He was easing her over the threshold but she balked at his words, wrenching away in sudden panic.

"Métro hours? You mean the subway *closes*?"

"Of course," he answered. "It opens daily at five-thirty and the last train comes through here around midnight." He bent for her again, grabbing both wrists and pinning her against the doorframe in one smooth move. His action was playful but his eyes were flint.

"I have to be at the airport before five to catch my plane!" She struggled to free herself, twisting under his tightening grip.

"I'll call you a cab later," he insisted. "Come on, Aglaia—let's finish what we started." She was writhing but he thrust himself up against her, his mouth hard against hers again.

"No, I have to go *now*!"

François jerked his head back and clamped his teeth together, his jaw flexing and nostrils flaring for a split second (so that Aglaia wondered if she imagined it) before he recovered his mask of suave composure—almost indifference.

"Fate is against us," he said, and he loosened his hold. She yanked her bag from inside his room then grazed her cheek across his so that he smiled. "I'll e-mail you," he called after her as she ran in the direction of the subway.

She realized as she passed under the flickering light of the neon sign that she'd forgotten altogether about giving François the Bible.

Twenty-one

Seat 27B was empty in the airplane the next morning when Aglaia took her place in 27A. Maybe Lou was stuck in the security line, but Aglaia harbored some hope that she'd miss the flight altogether.

Making her way to Charles de Gaulle Airport on public transit in the dead of night, with a heavy suitcase, had been a bad idea after all, Aglaia admitted now. For the sake of timeliness, she should have taken a taxi as François suggested, but she wasn't thinking straight at that moment and was still struggling to get her psychological bearings.

Once past the airport security gate, she lost all hope of finding a quiet seat, what with the cranky babies in strollers and the keyed-up high-school kids bound for cross-cultural exchange. So she meandered through the duty-free shops instead, her emotions a maelstrom as she stroked the souvenir François had given her, the pendant hanging around her neck. In no time she found herself boarding with the other passengers.

Now that she was buckled in, she calmed the flurry by sorting out the experiences of the past eighteen hours. The intensity of her disillusionment about Lou's treachery in the Louvre was overridden by the magic of meeting François, the flattery of his attentions resulting in her flustered reaction, and her culpability in neglecting to leave the Bible with him. It was a grocery list of feelings and she crossed off the simplest one first: She could always rectify the predicament of the Bible by mailing it to the Tedious Beatnik Taverne for François to open in front of his staff and clientele. The thought made her giggle aloud, giddy as she was with sleep deprivation. The last thing he'd want was that Bible.

Next she considered François's come-on and her own responsiveness. In the harsh light of day, she was relieved the situation hadn't progressed any further last night. The whole thing in retrospect was tawdry, she argued. But François had wanted her—there was no denying that!—and she still tingled at the thought of being so desired. He promised to write, and regular flights connected Denver to Paris. It was a small world and possibilities, however slim, existed for a future with him. In the meanwhile, she could spend many hours reliving that kiss and his lusty proposition and her own hot-blooded response.

However, there was the issue of his hedonistic philosophy regarding women. Honesty now forced her to concede that, even as a love-struck farm girl, she suspected François all along of infidelity. Wasn't that part of his attraction? It was never his *loyalty* that drew Aglaia to him, certainly, but rather his dangerous knowledge of what she wanted when she didn't even know herself. Back then, as a teen, she hadn't entertained curiosity about rival girlfriends' identities, and even now she didn't see the point. As François had told her, Aglaia was the fairest after all.

She tucked her chin into her chest to study the upside-down inscription on her necklace and its gold-etched design—a stylized circlet with an angled slash through the top like the stem of a fruit. It was very pretty; she already cherished it.

The flight attendant locked the cabin doors and still the place next to her was empty. Lou would not be on the flight, then, and Aglaia was free of her muzzling encumbrance! Besides not having to deal with Lou's bossiness, the extra seat would make the long flight home more bearable.

She squeezed a blanket in behind her lower back and covered

herself with the second one. As the plane taxied to the runway, she reviewed her trip as a whole.

The past five days in Paris were a whirlwind, and not all bad, she granted. The main point of going in the first place was to deliver the costume as a representative of Incognito, and she'd been successful in that—Eb would be pleased.

In Paris, she saw many famous sites, and she shopped and feasted and learned some new French words. She stood within the splendid light of stained glass windows and in front of her precious Three Graces. She could take satisfaction that a life-long aspiration had been fulfilled. Maybe the time had come to put memories and questions of faith and even romance (that blessed kiss!) behind her and to get on with living in the present, she thought.

But the appraisal of her trip brought up the question of her vocation and of Lou's pestering her to consider the PRU offer. She might soon have a choice to make between Incognito and the university. On the one hand, Eb MacAdam had taught her everything she knew about garment design and construction, and she almost certainly had a future in management there. Besides, even if he was a bit extreme in the religion department, Eb cared about her—Aglaia even suspected he prayed for her. On the other hand, prestige could be hers in the echelon of the arts world if she ended up employed by the university—if in fact what Lou promised her was true. And if she could ever stand being in the company of that woman again.

Aglaia yawned even as the force of the plane broke gravity and pitched itself upwards against the hand of God, pressing her into the seat with its force. Perhaps it was the combination of dead tiredness and the exhilaration of flying that reminded her of Eb reading Milton aloud in his study last week as she sewed with her office door ajar—reading in a somber voice the story of Beelzebub hurled headlong and flaming from the never-ending sky, with hideous ruin and combustion, down to endless perdition.

"Naomi, what in the world are you doing here?"

Aglaia was confused. It was early morning; she'd just picked up her luggage from the carousal and passed through border control to find the other woman in the crowd on the arrivals level. Naomi should have been home in Tiege, not at the Denver International Airport a state away. Aglaia squeezed her eyelids together to wring some moisture into them; they were gravelly after the flight despite the rainclouds the plane dodged on descent. She noticed the bluish smudges under Naomi's eyes as she rushed over and hugged Aglaia soberly.

"Don't get upset, but I have some bad news." Naomi let her digest this statement before going on. "It's your dad. He's had a heart attack."

Aglaia's own heart thumped hollowly and she sucked in air.

"It's okay. He's stable for now," Naomi said, reaching out for Aglaia's hand. "It happened yesterday—Friday. We called your boss and he tried to catch you at the hotel in Paris, but you'd left already. Meeting you at the airport was the best thing for me to do."

"But you came here all the way from Tiege just to tell me? That's almost four hours away." Aglaia was disoriented. She should ask more about Dad—she was sick for the details—but for some reason her head got stuck on the logistics of transportation. It wasn't surprising, really; the distances between major towns and the shortage of rural medical services made every countryside dweller conscious of geography.

"No, I spent last night at the hospital with your parents in Sterling," Naomi explained. Aglaia was sorting it out now; it made sense for Naomi to continue driving on into the city this morning to catch her at the airport.

"But how did it happen—the heart attack?"

"Henry was working in his shop fixing the combine," Naomi said, "and Tina saw that he was wobbly when he crossed the yard to the house. She phoned us when he admitted he was having chest pains and Byron rushed right over. He tried to load Henry into the truck, but your dad wouldn't agree till Byron sweetened the deal by suggesting that they attend the calf sale at the auction mart after finishing up at the hospital. As if there was any chance of that!"

"Classic," Aglaia said, shaking her head. Dad was a typical farmer—proud, self-reliant, and hating the spotlight. He'd need that empty promise to justify the cost of the gasoline to town.

A smile softened the corners of Naomi's mouth. "Anyway, that convinced him. Your dad is one tough guy. The pain was much worse than Henry let on and the doctors said he barely made it."

Aglaia didn't know what else to say, but they were walking fast now and words weren't expected. They strode out the exit towards the adjacent parking lot. The back bench seat of Naomi's old Ford truck was taken up with children's toys, a baby blanket, and a toddler's seat.

"Sorry it smells like a wet dog," Naomi said, "but it'll still get us back to Sterling by early afternoon. Then I need to head home. Byron's stressed out with harvest and the baby's coming down with something."

Naomi drove for the first twenty minutes and reported on the status of Tiege's crops—that the late seeding and then the searing heat had stunted the growth of the grain, and now the rains were playing havoc with the swaths lying in the field—and how Henry probably worried himself into this heart attack in the first place. Aglaia didn't break in until they stopped for gas and some fast food.

"Let me take the wheel. You're exhausted," she offered, though she wasn't perky herself after the transatlantic flight. But driving the beater would be easier than remaining a passive passenger.

Naomi had been rambling, overloading her with the minutiae of life in Tiege—about the roads being cut up because of the rains, and that the local grocery store ran out of coffee three days ago so that everyone was loading up on cola to keep awake. The way she went on, Aglaia thought, it was as if she expected the government to declare a national disaster. Yet somehow Naomi's outpouring was calming. The rhetoric of the farmer at harvest was the same every year, when the annual income for massive operations and small family ventures alike was at the mercy of the weather. Naomi didn't quiz her about the trip to Paris, even when Aglaia handed over the box of fine French *bonbons*—a thank-you gift for taking Zephyr out to Mom and Dad's while she was gone. Aglaia didn't need to use the excuse she'd gotten ready to deflect any possible questions about François, either, because Naomi wasn't asking and, in fact, was maybe avoiding the subject.

And so, by noon Naomi was hunched up against the passenger door and Aglaia, in the driver's seat, was cruising northeastward on the interstate, listening to the radio, her fingers dialing through the available stations and getting nothing but static because of the atmospheric conditions. She eventually made do with a cassette already in the tape deck—churchy, but at least it was peaceful—as she finished off her drive-through burger and bunched the foil bag into a slot beside the ashtray, promising herself she'd throw it out later.

So much for her plan to get right back into her routine of work and the solitude of her city apartment, Aglaia thought. She was being selfish—perhaps she was still in shock over the news about the heart attack. But things were changing in a direction she didn't like. She didn't like the thought that, given her dad's hospitalization, she might be expected to act like a normal and loving daughter—whatever that was.

She hated hospitals with their antiseptic reek of death, but her reticence to see her father was more than that. What did she plan to say to him, all hooked up with tubes and lying inert under the sheets? They hadn't spoken much in the years since she left home, father and daughter. She evaded discussion during her rare trips back to the farm, always restricted to a couple of days during which she occupied herself with wrapping gifts to put under the tree or helping Mom bake hot cross buns while Dad kept busy with chores—plowing snow or fencing. Somehow her bond with her mother had never been totally severed, but with Dad it was different. There'd been a more complete break, with no sharing of cookbook recipes to smooth over the rough spots. When Dad had something to say, he always came straight to the point. What would he say to her today? Words of his from the past streamed into her mind.

"Saw you out at the burning barrel this morning, Mary Grace,"
her father says on the day after graduation. It's suppertime. She
hasn't told them yet that she's leaving.

"Just getting rid of stuff I don't need," she mumbles around her
mouthful of smoky ham. Then, to put off further conversation, she
stuffs in some more Varenikje. It's her favorite dish—doughy boiled
pockets filled with cottage cheese and smothered in cream gravy.
She'll miss Mom's cooking.

"You took the old suitcase out. Going somewhere?" Dad asks.

There's no use trying to hide it. Mom starts to sniffle.

"I've got to leave, Dad. I can't stick around here anymore."

There's no talk at the table for a good ten minutes after that,
while they sop up their plates with heavy brown bread and finish
with rice pudding, sweet with raisins.

"I need you," Dad blurts. "With Joel gone, well... I don't know if
I can do it without you." He's looking at her with his bleary, sad eyes.

It's the only time he's ever asked her for help, maybe the only time
he's ever asked anyone for help. Sure, she's had her chores, has taken
part in operating the place since she was a kid. Now he's asking for
something else. He needs an heir.

But she just gets up from the table and goes to her room to finish
packing.

The highway wasn't as congested as it might be, at the end
of summer like this. With Naomi asleep and nothing to distract
Aglaia but the background music and crackles of lightning high on
the horizon, she thought again about her mad midnight dash from
the grasp of François Vivier. Had it really happened? She touched
the pendant that still hung around her neck, the stone now warm
as skin. She glanced at herself in the visor and saw the same flush
on her cheeks that he must have seen when she fled, the besotted
virgin befuddled.

Steering with her knee, Aglaia unlatched the necklace hook
and rolled the leather cord around the disc for protection before
she tucked it into the outside pocket of her purse. She didn't need
anyone else's curiosity making the situation even trickier than it
currently was. Navigating whatever rough waters she'd find at the

hospital would be difficult enough. So she fixed her eyes on what was seen rather than what was unseen—wires linking one telephone pole to the next along the miles of highway, round hay bales dotting the golden fields. It didn't work: the poles became crucifixes and the bales bits of a giant's breakfast cereal spilled into the basement of heaven.

Naomi didn't stir despite an ambulance that sped by them near Fort Morgan, and she slept through a cloudburst that left the pavement slick for miles. At last Aglaia picked up a financial talk show and drove the rest of the way half listening to advice on how to build a stock portfolio. It shut up the other voices.

Naomi woke up as they rolled into Sterling, drowsy and apologetic over having missed the opportunity for a good visit on the drive down, over neglecting to ask Aglaia about Paris and now there was no time for that. She gave directions into the hospital parking lot.

In the elevator, Aglaia controlled her gag reflex by swallowing a few times and breathing through her mouth until they reached the cardiac ward and entered the room, its blinds drawn against the light.

"Tina, are you awake?" Naomi said softly as she bent like a daughter to the aging woman in the visitors' chair.

Aglaia hung back and studied her father, long and slim in the bed, his thinning hair now grey. His eyes were closed and his complexion was ruddy, at least below the cap line where the skin had been exposed for decades to the elements. His upper arms—and his shoulders under the hospital gown too, she knew—were stark white in contrast to the leathered hands, the sinewy forearms. She used to watch him strip off his shirt and wash his two-toned skin in the enameled basin Mom always set out on the porch at lunchtime, leaving behind him a filmy pool.

Now Tina spotted Aglaia in the dim corner of the hospital room, and she fumbled for the hanky tucked in her sweater sleeve to mop at her eyes.

Aglaia moved towards her and said, "It's okay, Mom. I'm here." She didn't know what that was supposed to mean, but Tina seemed heartened, or heartening, as she patted Aglaia in a frail embrace.

"Is he… ?"

"He'll be fine," Tina said. "The doctors got the drugs into him fast and they say now it's just a matter of time." She gave her simplistic version of the medical goings-on before Henry opened his eyes, a jolt of blue like a field of blossoming flax.

"Mary Grace," he uttered, and held up his creased palm to her. "Daddy."

Don't cry, she commanded herself, but she let him close his fingers around her hand, wishing for his arms to encompass her like they had when she was a small girl with night terrors.

Suddenly she recalled being held like a child by Lou in her bed in Paris, and with clarity the nightmare of Joel's death—the reality of Joel's death. The horror of Joel's death hit her like a boulder in the chest. She pulled away from her dad at that and stood before the window overlooking a stand of pine trees and an empty picnic bench. At her withdrawal, conversation ceased.

Then Naomi piped up in a conversational tone, "So Henry, Byron and the boys are all set to finish off that eighty-acre field you have left."

"No," he said. "You have your own crop to take care of."

"We can manage yours, too. You'd do the same for us. In fact, you often have. It's our turn, Henry. As for you, Tina," she said, "don't even think of leaving his side."

"*Danke*," Tina said. "Mary Grace will help, won't you, dear?"

Help with the harvest? Her mother's request was astounding, but all three of them stared at Aglaia.

"What a great idea," Naomi said. She beamed as though Aglaia had already agreed to come. "If the rain holds off and we don't have any more breakdowns, it should only take us three days. Byron, Sebastian, and Silas can operate the two combines and our International grain truck"—she counted off the vehicles on the fingers of one hand and matched them with the family members on the other—"if you can handle Henry's two-ton Chev. You still know how to shift gears on that dinosaur? No offense, Henry." He grinned weakly and Naomi continued. "I'd offer to do the hauling,

Aglaia, but that would leave you in charge of taking all the meals to the fields while tending the three girls and the baby. That would be too much for you."

The whole thing was too much for her! But Tina, working the soggy tissue over in her hands, regarded her daughter with welling eyes. Even Dad was watching her. It was no use bringing up her work schedule—she'd already told Naomi that she wasn't expected back at Incognito on Monday.

"I suppose I can spare a few days," she said.

Twenty-two

By Aglaia's watch, it was eleven o'clock on Sunday morning and already sheets of heat undulated over the standing grain. The wind swept the crop like a hand brushing velvet, swatted the clouds and a flock of skittering sparrows across the sky. Aglaia squinted through all the rushing movement and the truck's dusty windshield to see if the combine at the far end of the field was ready for her to pick up another load. The wheat wasn't spilling over the lip of the hopper yet; maybe she had a few more minutes to nap.

She was still travel weary. The drive from the hospital yesterday ended when she and Naomi pulled into the Enns yard just before supper. Byron served them a casserole from the freezer, part of Naomi's emergency supply, and went back out to work till sundown with the boys while the younger kids helped with the dishes. Naomi sent Aglaia to the top bunk in the girls' room when she caught her yawning, and warned the kids not to giggle late into the night even though they'd be skipping Sunday school in the morning.

Aglaia came to in the middle of night, wide awake, but forced herself to stay in bed until she dropped off again. Then she slept until eight, when Naomi awakened her to say that the crop's mois-

ture content finally allowed the beginning of the day's harvest. She
fed Aglaia what was left of a huge pan of rhubarb *Plauts* and filled
her with coffee while Byron finished greasing and fuelling up the
machinery. Naomi explained their plan for the day: While the boys
finished swathing the Ennses' northwest quarter, Byron and Aglaia
would work together on the Klassen farmland.

And here she was, waiting in the cab of the two-ton to haul
another load, wearing jeans and t-shirt borrowed from Sebastian. She'd only caught sight of Naomi's eldest child as he swung
his slender frame up onto his tractor and drove off, his tow-head-
ed brother Silas trailing behind in his truck. Nothing in her bag
packed for Paris was suitable for fieldwork, and Naomi's clothes
were too big for her.

"Just shift the stick into first gear and let the clutch out as you
slowly step on the gas," Byron had instructed this morning when
she climbed behind the wheel of Dad's Chev, parked in the Enns
yard. It sounded simple enough but she stalled it several times before getting through the gate, and her ears were ringing and her
hand was numb with the vibration of the gearshift before they
made the few miles of gravel to the turn-off for her childhood
home. But she was getting the hang of it by now, after hauling her
first three loads. It was coming back to her.

She saw Byron on his self-propelled combine at the other end
of the field, waving for all he was worth. So she stomped down hard
on the clutch and turned the key, and the truck engine hacked like
an old smoker and she was off, bouncing across the stubble, the
seat springs creaking. Byron motioned her into place alongside the
moving combine until its spout was centered over her truck box,
and she concentrated on keeping pace with his speed amidst the
swirling grain dust and the roar of machinery.

Aglaia trundled off to her parents' yard then, and backed up
close to one of the unpainted wooden granaries, tilting up the
truck box. She was sweaty and itchy as she climbed down out of
the cab, and she wiped her forehead with the back of the clumsy
work glove. She fired up the clattering augur and forced open the
trap door on the back of the truck box to allow the wheat to pour

out onto the ground; the augur drew it up and dropped it in a torrent through the granary roof.

Aglaia thought about how she'd climbed that roof when she was nine, wanting to touch the clouds. Her father thrashed her for the foolishness of it, and then clasped her close to his oil-stained shirt in a hug.

Aglaia shrugged away the pain—not at Dad's long-ago discipline but at her lack of self-discipline in keeping the memory at bay. There were too many memories here. Reluctantly she turned towards the farmhouse, overshadowed by the gnarled elm tree with a loop of sun-bleached rope still tied to its largest limb. The white lace curtains in the kitchen windows drooped like eyelids and the porch railing sagged, likely rotting. The house wore a morose expression now.

But Aglaia's childhood had been dominated by the pleasure of home, more at this time of the year than any other season, when the plentitude in the grain bins and her parents' euphoria made her feel rich. Every autumn in the trustworthy rhythm of the seasons, when spring's sowing had produced fall's reaping, she celebrated with the family, and with the whole community, as they gathered in the church for the annual *Schmeckfest,* bringing platters of roast duck and pots of jellied pigs' feet, tubs of cracklings and fried potatoes, and basins of pickled melon rind and steamed cabbage and two-layer buns baked with butter and milk.

Now as she looked back at harvest through the lens of the Greek myths that had given her new perspective, she saw a pattern not evident to her more youthful eyes. Then, her father prayed thanks to the Lord for His kindness in giving rain from heaven and crops in their seasons and peace to fill their hearts. But now the cornucopia of her imagination brimmed with stories that repeated over and again themes of the power, the chaos, the caprice of the gods who ruled the heavens and earth in a non-ending cycle of self-serving sovereignty. They gave to humanity based on humanity's sacrifice, with no kindness or grace in their begrudging, tyrannical provision.

The augur had finished its work and Aglaia shut it down. It

was a dangerous machine and she never operated it as a girl, busy enough with running the truck and taking meals out to the fields. Of course, in her teens she'd rather have worked at the local store stocking shelves or bagging groceries, but the village kids always got first dibs on those jobs.

However, that summer—the summer Joel had spontaneously arranged for the student exchange without thinking ahead about how busy he'd be with Dad—she didn't mind being at home to act as hostess for François. It fell to her to occupy him when the chores around the place were too complicated for his city skills. Dad said he was lazy, the way he sat around after meals sipping coffee or, propped on the tire swing with his heels dug into the sandy soil, picked on his guitar in the shade of the same elm still growing in the yard. She couldn't have foreseen how that summer and that student would separate her from Joel.

She determined right then to spend the night in her childhood bedroom with her memories, whether of François or Joel, rather than with the Enns family. The phantoms that drifted through an empty house were preferable to a baby crying half the night and the incessant queries of the girls during breakfast: Does the Eiffel Tower sway in the wind? Is it true that French children drink hot chocolate at breakfast? Only Naomi had been too busy to talk this morning, her hands in a batch of bread dough. But it was a long while yet before Aglaia's first day of harvest would be done and she could sleep.

At noon Naomi dropped off covered plates of cabbage rolls at the field for Aglaia and Byron, bringing news that Henry was responding well to the treatment and that Tina managed to get some rest in the hospital lounge. The day wore on for Aglaia in dust and chaff and coughing until another break at suppertime, when the complete Enns family converged upon her.

She sat with them on a blanket laid out on the prickly stubble, the field itself a laid-out blanket of golden corduroy with its even rows of swath in parallel lines stretching as far as she could see. Five rambunctious kids laughed and rough-housed around her, the baby was crying, and Naomi was unruffled by it all as she served out stewed beef, and cucumbers in sour cream, and bowls of simmered fruits.

If Aglaia had been missing the gourmet cuisine of Paris, she still found herself stuffing her belly with all Naomi's home cooking. Mennonite food wasn't subtle, Aglaia thought in comparison— none of the *fine herbs de Provence* or the *gruyère soufflé* scented with a *soupçon* of cayenne. The ambience was all wrong, too, but somehow it didn't matter at the moment.

Aglaia's farm relationships had always revolved around food— its production, preparation, consumption. This had been true through the generations of her family, true of her agricultural heritage that stretched back to Europe. Mothers taught daughters to cook and sons flattered wives for their efforts, so that the same recipes were passed around households bearing surnames like Friesen and Harder, Neufeld and Loewen, Unger and Toews and Dueck—names that branded families Mennonite like the name Vivier branded François French. Funny she hadn't changed her last name too, Aglaia thought.

The grueling work of the day so far left her grubby and wind burned. She was gulping another glass of whole milk when a young voice spat into her ear.

"She's cracking."

"Don't talk with food in your mouth, Suzannah," Naomi reprimanded.

The ten year old said, "But she is. Look at her," and little Sarah paddled up closer to eyeball her as well. Aglaia understood what the girl meant; her skin was peeling, flaky and dry, and Aglaia could just imagine the condition of her face. She didn't have on a lick of makeup, and her hair was hidden under the bandana she retrieved from her Dad's handkerchief drawer that morning.

"Yep," Byron agreed. "She's had some sun."

"If your snooty friend from the city could lay her eyes on you right now," Naomi laughed, "she wouldn't recognize you."

All three girls studied her, one even rubbing her dehydrated arm, and Aglaia shied away from them so that Naomi scolded them for rudeness. It wasn't that Aglaia minded their fawning—

they were sweet things—but their plump cheeks and rosebud mouths reminded her of the girlhood she long ago suppressed.

Being near them all like this stirred up something in her gut. It was more than that her skin was cracking; she was a slumbering volcano coming to life, the molten lava beginning to churn deep within. She swallowed the last bite of her dessert with effort and compressed her lips to keep everything inside in its place.

Byron yelled over to the two boys tumbling like a pair of puppies in a mock fight beside the truck and told them to settle down. They might be best friends, considering how they continued to joke and poke at each other. Silas at thirteen was the younger and looked exactly like his sisters, blonde with a freckled pug nose and a grin that reminded her of Joel. Why shouldn't there be a family resemblance? After all, Byron's great-grandpa was hers and Joel's as well. The older son, Sebastian, favored his mom with dimples that dented his cheeks every few minutes, but his hair was darker and tousled, thick and heavy across his swarthy forehead.

As Sebastian and Silas wrestled together on the ground, Aglaia was caught up in a sort of *déjà vu* and she almost said something, but one of the little girls asked her a question and broke the spell.

"Can you talk French? Mommy says 'mercy' means *danke*. Did you talk to any children in Paris?"

The boys, interest piqued, ambled closer and contributed to the conversation.

"Yeah, you just got back from France, didn't you?" Silas asked.

"What were you doing over there? We knew someone from France, right Mom?" Sebastian caught his mother's eye then, as if unsure he should be asking the question, and Aglaia couldn't pinpoint the emotion behind the look on Naomi's face. Byron rushed to her rescue.

"Kids, save that for later. We need to get back to work before this heat brews up a squall. We haven't had such a hot, wet harvest for at least ten years. But first, since we missed church today, let's read."

He tugged a paperback New Testament from his hip pocket and Aglaia thought of the Bible still packed in her bag at the Enns house and those last, terrible words jotted in the margin of the Gospels: *Aglaia, what a beautiful devil!*

Byron began the devotional in a formal voice that sounded like her father's when the Bible was open in his hands, and read something morbid about the crucifixion. Aglaia wished he wouldn't talk about death. Didn't he have any sense of propriety, considering Dad's close call? More to the point, didn't he recall that Joel died just one field over from where the nine of them were sitting now, alive and well?

When they were finished their family prayer and Aglaia opened her eyes, she saw Naomi scrutinizing her and then inhale as though steeling herself to make an urgent statement. Aglaia almost heard the drum roll.

But at that moment Byron's cell phone beeped a text message alert. He read it and then said, "Oh, Aglaia, you wanted to borrow my phone to check in with your boss?" She'd left hers in her suitcase, its battery drained with no way to recharge it. "Better do it now, before we get back to work."

She hated to phone Eb at home on a Sunday evening, but she grabbed the cell for a break from the intensity and walked a little away from the family bustle into the field. Aglaia had a terrible premonition that Naomi was trying to tell her something about François that she wouldn't want to hear. Eb answered on the first ring. He indicated relief at hearing her voice and concern over her dad's medical situation, and then fell into a comforting confirmation.

"Ah, the slings and arrows. You take as much time off as you need, lass. Staring death in the face is a wondrous and a fearsome thing—there's the rub. It seems as though the Maker isn't ready yet to let your father shuffle off the mortal coil."

Eb's empathy, embroidered as usual with words from another era, soothed Aglaia. Eb was so sincere that he could be a funeral director, if it wasn't for his sprinkling of humor. He was a droll blend of the solemn and the sanguine.

"Head office was ecstatic with the results of your costume delivery," Eb said. "Montreal faxed over a note of receipt from the

French museum along with the newspaper article and that photo
of you handing off the costume to the curator. You're famous!"

In spite of his assurances, Aglaia knew he must be swamped at
Incognito, just waiting for her return.

"The harvesting should be done in a couple of days," she said,
ignoring the thunderclouds building in the west. "Then my friends
will drive me home, so I'll be in to work on Thursday morning."
She was sorry now that she'd left her car in the city and had to wait
for Byron to take her back.

"There's no rush. Your family is more important than your occupation. Take the whole week off—you've earned it."

"I don't know if I can stay away for another whole week, but I'll
need a day or two to catch up on my sleep after this harvest."

"I want you rested," Eb said. "I have news for you concerning
that movie being shot in the area—I mentioned it to you a while
ago." He told her Incognito was in the process of placing a bid on
a contract to provide costuming. "It's likely we'll win the competition, lass. No other shop in the city has our reputation or the weight
Montreal is throwing behind us. I think headquarters wants to be
connected to a box office hit." He snorted. "I hadn't made a fuss
about it to you earlier because I didn't want to get your hopes up
or take you away from the museum assignment. Our winning this
film job, on top of your performance in Paris, should lock in that
promotion I promised you."

Aglaia thanked him for watching her back, but her attention
had been caught by Eb's talk of the movie project. She recalled that
Lou, also, had mentioned movies on a couple of occasions during
the trip, and she'd thought it odd at the time because the comments
were out of context and the woman had paused as if to give her
time to react. What were Lou's motives, and did Eb's movie have
anything to do with Lou's offer of employment at PRU? The timing
was fishy.

She felt justified in her new wariness of Lou who, after all, had
told a bald-faced lie about François meeting her in the Louvre.
Aglaia gritted her teeth just thinking about it again. Lou promoted
herself and her own purposes at every turn, with no thought of the

consequences for others. Eb, on the other hand, was concerned for her family, wellbeing, and personal success. How could Aglaia even think of leaving Incognito for a job under Lou? Guilt pricked her conscience.

She and Eb said goodbye and, since Aglaia had the phone anyway, she retrieved her messages left over the past week. There were a few from friends, and one from Tina calling from the hospital to ask about the crop yield because Henry was making a racket, wanting to know how many bushels to the acre they were getting. She also said that the doctor planned to send Henry over to Denver for some specialized tests unavailable in Sterling. Aglaia could hear the worry behind her mother's words but there was no time to return the call because Byron fired up the combine again.

Aglaia was bone tired by the time Byron shut down that first night, after the sun had set and the dew came on and the tough crop started plugging the combine. They stood together in the Klassen farmyard under the light of the great orange moon, Byron's face streaked with the day's labor.

"I'll be staying here at Mom and Dad's for the night," she told him. "You go on back to your family and I'll be ready for you in the morning. I don't need my suitcase. There's got to be a spare toothbrush somewhere."

Byron rubbed the blonde stubble on his chin. "Naomi must have a cake or something in the oven for us."

"She's been feeding us all day. Besides, I'm beat," Aglaia answered to excuse her lack of sociability. "I'll just fall into bed anyway."

She found the door unlocked. Zephyr streaked over from the barn and mewled around her feet on the veranda. She picked him up to stroke his fur and pat his round belly; apparently he'd been eating well, too. He was a natural predator. Had he tangled with a rat yet? They used to lurk beneath the coop, dilapidated now with its roof caving in and the chickens long gone. Gathering eggs had been her first after-school chore, delegated at age six when she'd grown tall enough to reach the nesting boxes and Joel had graduated to milking.

"Let's line this wicker basket with a clean tea towel so the eggs won't break," her mother says as she folds under the ends of the striped muslin cloth. "Now Mary Grace, be quiet with those Heena and don't excite them."

So she pulls on her sweater and trots across the grass, crunchy underfoot with new frost, and steps down over the sunken sill of the door into the closeness, the smell of ammonia making her eyes water. Trying not to upset the roosting hens, she sneaks her hand under each downy breast so she doesn't get pecked and brings out brown speckled eggs, fragile and warm with the life still growing in them.

"Mary Grace!" It's Joel calling to her from the barn. "The mama cat's had her kittens, five of them. Come see!"

Aglaia put Zephyr back down and closed the house door behind her, leaving him outside in his natural element; she'd pour milk for him in the morning. She reached for the switch but stopped herself. She hated the fluorescent ceiling light as much for the buzz as for the moths it always attracted. The homey aroma that rose from a bucket of ripening tomatoes on the counter took her back to the garden, where she used to meet her father just after dawn to help him hoe before the mosquitoes started to bite, or to fill a battered tin basin with new potatoes, the loam making wrinkle patterns on her knuckles.

Aglaia groped through the kitchen and up the creaking wooden staircase of the house. The moonlight shone through the windows. She trailed her hand along the banister and her arm bumped the frame of the cross-stitch she'd made two decades ago in kids' club: "I am the light of the world." Even before she was old enough for youth group, the family always went together to church midweek, her parents for prayer meeting and Joel to play floor hockey in the basement with the boys. The girls' group met in the choir loft around a long table set up for their crafts, and they memorized Scripture to earn badges. They started with all the "I am" and "Blessed are" verses, and tested each other to see who could rattle them off the fastest: *I am the good shepherd... Blessed are those who mourn ... I am the bread of life... Blessed are those who hunger and thirst after righteousness, for they will be filled.*

Well, she'd left her shepherd behind years ago, and worked hard at not thinking about light or righteousness, and had been ignoring her pangs for something more than the creativity that fed and watered her memories of François—something like manna.

Now, in the darkened house, Aglaia continued upwards, gripping the smooth staircase railing with resolution against the invasion of memories, against her weariness that was allowing such thoughts to bleed into her mind again.

Aglaia's bed was made up with the floral sheets Tina ordered from the Sears catalogue for her sixteenth birthday. They hadn't had much wear. It was well over a year since she'd last slept here, and she hadn't been home during harvest since moving to Colorado.

Aglaia unfolded the quilt that Tina had pieced together with scraps from sewing projects. She fingered the worn binding and assessed its cotton content. Was that striped patch from the Sunday shirt Mom made Joel? She found another square from her Easter dress the year she first partook of the Lord's Supper.

She slipped between the covers and into sleep without another conscious thought but that the full moon glowed on her through the old elm's branches and that the forlorn wind called her, tapping on the glass. She dreamed about the first-ever costume she made in kids' club for the Easter play— a flowered tablecloth fashioned into a cloak and a batch of willow suckers cut from the banks of the coulee.

Mary Grace and the other children wait for the pianist to give them their cue but not patiently—rather, tittering and scuffling behind the door to the stage, jostling one another, the boys teasing the girls with leafy fronds. Then they burst forth in all their childish enthusiasm and spill down the platform steps into the church aisle to meet the make-believe donkey and its rider, spreading their garments and palm branches before him as they shout, "Hosanna! Blessed is he who comes in the name of the Lord!" And no one in the congregation rebukes them for their jubilant cries in the sanctuary because, if they dared, the creation itself would testify—the prairie wind, the endless sky, the very stones of the earth would surely take up the children's silenced chorus of praise.

Aglaia awoke momentarily in the tumult of a thunderstorm rattling the windows of the farmhouse, blazing neon bright and branding her vision with black tree branches against the burnished sky. How many childhood pot-bangers like this had sent her flying into her parents' bed in fright? She fell in and out of another distressing dream.

The echoing crescendos rage like a beast, howling and reverberating through the skies like Leviathan thrashing his tail from the Abyss. Mary Grace is thirteen now and hasn't cowered like this since she was a kid at the demonic fury of the wind's screams unleashed in wrath from their restraints.

"Mary Grace," Dad reminds her when she's tucked between them in the fortress of their presence, "it is the Lord's voice speaking out of the whirlwind from His throne, the Bible says. He's robed in majesty and armed with strength. The world is firmly established; it cannot be moved."

They spy a twister backlit by flashes forming in the roiling clouds, and Joel, who's slept through the onset of the din, joins them on the porch as they watch in awe a funnel dipping and lifting, a dark finger stirring the blacker fields before closing up into the fist of the sky. Then Mom mixes up cocoa in the aluminum pan on the stove and they dunk ammonia cookies like Grandma used to bake.

Tonight there was no tornado, no cocoa prepared by a motherly hand, no Bible-quoting daddy to calm a frightened, storm-tossed girl. And now she was no longer dreaming but half-sleepwalking, barely aware of the chill in the soles of her feet. She didn't have the ability to stop her movement over the basement floor towards the trunk of cast-off clothes beneath the stairs, the will to resist bending her knees onto the cement as she gathered up a sweater and pressed her nose into it and smelled it for François—or was it for Joel? And the mildew, or maybe the grief, made her eyes water, so she rubbed them with that raw wool, but still she was torpid, peering more deeply into the recesses of the cellar, seeking but not finding.

Her delirium and the incessant hounding of the still, small voice followed her as she padded back up the steps, and up the steps, head raised now to the bedroom window and the elm branches full of the bright harvest moon. And even then, in her sad state of half-awake sleep, verses from the Bible invoked her: *You who dwell in the dust, wake up and shout for joy!... Wake up, O sleeper, rise from the dead, and Christ will shine on you.* The next thing she knew, it was Monday morning and Byron was honking outside and she had a sweater of Dad's balled up in her fists, using it for a pillow.

Twenty-three

Harvest was completed on Tuesday night, the mania over. Aglaia awoke in the dark at four-thirty on Wednesday morning, her internal clock still topsy-turvy from the disruption of travel and the pace set by Byron, Sebastian, and Silas as they pushed to finish off the work. She swung her legs out from between the floral bedsheets of her maidenhood, her whole body stiff and sore, then propped her elbows on her knees and bent her head to her palms till the fog lifted.

Aglaia reached for the drinking glass by her bedside but it was empty, so she took it downstairs to the kitchen and turned on the tap. Well water, full of iron and tinted yellow, had a flavor Dad relished. Since her childhood he'd refused to put in a softener despite Tina's entreaties. Aglaia never wore true white until she moved to the city and found out how sudsy water could be. But she craved the taste and gulped down two glasses, letting the frigid overflow dribble onto her top.

Aglaia was wide awake for the first time in three days. The Enns family would still be asleep, no breakfast cooking at their place down the road, but she was famished now. Mom's refrigerator held a bowl of eggs and a sealer of sweet cream, so Aglaia mixed up an *omelette mousseline* and brewed coffee for dunking her toasted *Zwieback*—a truly multicultural breakfast. She sat at the table in Dad's chair and contemplated the nightscape out of the window as she ate.

The tempest had passed while she slept, the thunder cell moving westward and leaving a puddle shimmering on the grass outside like a shard of mirror blinking back up at the sky. Dawn wouldn't break for a while yet. She might as well resign herself to getting dressed, but somehow she dreaded the day ahead. Her thought life had been so occupied with physical labor that the free time might be hard to take, with the whole day to kill. The plan was for Byron to drive her to the city tomorrow morning, stopping along the way to pick up her parents at the hospital in Sterling to save them the cost of an ambulance ride to Henry's appointment with the specialist in Denver.

Aglaia's suitcase lay unzipped on the floor near the table. She'd brought it from Naomi's Monday after supper and hadn't bothered to take it upstairs to the bedroom, just digging through it for her shampoo and clean underwear as needed. The Bible had slipped out sometime during the night and sprawled open, face down on the linoleum. She prodded it with her toe.

It was abhorrent to her, an indictment of her failure on so many levels. Yet she couldn't despise it—either the particular volume heaped at her feet or the timeless composition of the Bible itself that was more than leather and paper and ink. It held too much meaning that went beyond her attempts to either deliver this copy to François or decipher his memoirs. Be honest, she told herself: They were her memoirs as well, and not restricted to that summer fifteen years ago. Her life had been written between the lines of that book long before François ever inserted his thoughts into the margins.

Aglaia withstood the urge to pick it up; it had served its purposes and she was done with it. But the Bible wasn't so easily dismissed. Her subconscious was soaked in the words of the text, and they taunted her now while she sat at the table with the starlight twinkling through the lace of the window curtain, bright specks of creation reminding her of heaven. She might try to ignore the Bible, but a far-off roll of thunder still boomed out praises to all who would listen. *Come, all you who are thirsty, come to the waters,* her memory echoed. *As the rain and the snow come down from heaven, and do not return to it without watering the earth and making it bud and flourish... so is my word that goes out from my mouth: It will not return to me empty, but will accomplish what I desire and achieve the purpose for which I sent it.*

The words antagonized her. She stood up and kicked that book once, and then again and again with rising fury, panting with the exertion, its pages tearing between her toes, until the Bible rested crumpled near the hot air vent by the cupboard and torn bits with lay scattered around. She turned her back on the mess.

She put on Tina's rubber boots encrusted with last week's mud and trudged away from the house and the ravaged Bible into the candy-floss sunrise, all pink and blue, and kept her head down to shun the celestial splendor. She must stretch her legs and air out her mind but, though it wasn't even seven o'clock, she wouldn't risk walking the road in the direction of Naomi's home in case she was spotted and called in for coffee.

She'd seen enough of Naomi these past few days, though never alone—a silent but mutual decision. So far Aglaia had withheld the fact of having met François in Paris and she didn't want to be quizzed about it. But Naomi was deflecting something, too, for all her culinary hospitality. At first, Aglaia chalked up Naomi's preoccupation to the taxing harvest tasks rather than out-and-out avoidance. But since Aglaia's arrival, Naomi never entered a room without a child on her hip or a teen within earshot, almost as if she were as wary in sidestepping some subject as Aglaia was in resisting reference to her romance in Paris. For just a while longer Aglaia wanted to hug the secret of François to herself till she grew tired of fondling it and was ready to admit its cheapness. Two sides of her character contended within her, one beatifying her passion for François and the other denouncing her gullibility.

Aglaia was dubious that he'd write—he hadn't yet, when she'd logged in to her account on the Enns computer yesterday afternoon. She considered sending off a quick message to him but had only his commercial address from the tavern and didn't know who else might access it. Anyway, if something were to come of the interaction in Paris, she wanted François to be the one to make the next move, to woo her as he'd done that summer. But she was no shy teen after all and, to be honest, she wasn't serious about going back to him in France. The exotic setting made her too vulnerable. Her stomach leapt again at the thought of his kiss in the doorway of his room before she ran off to catch the subway to the airport. But her heart's desire was to stay in her dream as long as possible.

Aglaia filled her lungs with the fresh morning air. The farmyard never changed except for the trees—the maples and elders and the windbreak of lilac bushes twice her height. Less than a foot tall at planting twenty years ago, the four hundred seedling bushes had required hours of hoeing by Aglaia and Joel. Weeds still thrive during drought, she thought. Ah, how they fought that prairie drought! Every week throughout the growing season, Dad hooked the tank up to the tractor and crept along the periphery of the yard, water draining from the half-opened valve in the back for the kids to catch in their one-gallon plastic ice cream pails and fling at the thirsty roots. They'd fill and empty, fill and empty, jogging to keep up, sweating and cheerful because Mom always poured them fruit punch as a reward and, more, because they splashed one another every couple of bucketsful. Who needed air conditioning when you had a brother with good aim?

She passed the sandbox overgrown now with quackgrass, and the bunkhouse her grandfather constructed for his hired hands before her father was even born, and the old smokehouse where her great-grandmother hung up the *Worscht* to cure. A flock of partridges took her by surprise, rising from the grass with a noisy flutter and a flash of white bellies. She passed the machine shop where she and Joel watched their father weld or work his circular saw while they squatted on the oily concrete, discussing together how the corroded blacksmith tools might have worked in the olden days—the bellows, the tongs—imaging they could hear the ring of the hammer on steel glowing orange from the forge.

And the barn! If anything defined this farmyard, Aglaia thought as she stepped onto the cement pad at its entrance, it was the weathered, red-and-white barn with the cedar shingles, the sliding door that always stuck. Did it still? She butted her shoulder up against the door's edge and leaned into it until it gave way with a grating squeal and moved, bit by bit, to expose the cavernous interior with its cobwebs and rough-hewn beams and hay-strewn floor. Joel's tack was still there in its place, the scruffy blanket she crocheted for his birthday still hanging askew over the saddle. The milking stool lay broken nearby.

She counts seven days since the funeral—that's 168 hours or 10,080 minutes or 604,800 seconds. Today the charitable neighbors finally let the family resume daily tasks, no longer leaving pots of sweet Plümemooss *or casseroles of smoked sausage in batter bread, and now she's taking over Joel's chores.*

Dad brings the Holstein in through the back door of the barn for Aglaia—she's calling herself by her new name now, even if Dad and Mom won't. Belle's hoofs clop and her full bag swings beneath her as she plods to the chop in the manger. Aglaia removes the stool from its peg on the wall and positions the stainless steel bucket. She presses her forehead against Belle's coarse flank and grasps the teats distending from the bag heavy with milk. As Joel taught her, she curls her fingers from the top down—left, right, left, right—and beats out the zinging tempo of the milk as it froths upward and changes tone. Joel always emptied the udder in much less than the forty minutes she spends, even counting the time he took to shoot a stream, now and again, into the mouth of a waiting cat. Joel never let the cow's flicking tail get on his nerves. Joel wouldn't have cried, either, she thinks when Belle kicks the pail over and the milk runs out onto the planks of the stall.

Aglaia moved away from the barn and the haunting thoughts of that summer. She stepped through the gate and lined her vision up with the barbed wire fence stretching northward. A couple of miles ahead, a massive, lone boulder jutted above the horizon. It was the fragment of a mountain deposited at the end of the last ice age, the glacial remains like a giant's skull signaling the beginning of the dunes—the Nebraska Sand Hills—themselves vestiges of the vast inland sea that was now dried and gone.

The Klassen farm bordered the southwestern-most tongue of the hills, down in the corner of the state where Tiege's founding Mennonites had tenaciously preserved their seclusion.

With her eye on the boulder, she began to run in her mother's unwieldy boots—to run like a flustered goose, flailing, her neck stuck out as she strained away from the ghosts of the yard. If she'd been pursuing memories of François, she hadn't found him here on the farmyard. He was confined to the margins of that bruised Bible lying on the kitchen floor.

By the time she was winded, she reached the grove of choke-cherry bushes marking the boundary of the field.

Mary Grace is ten, and the sand flies are driving her crazy, but Joel just encourages her to keep on picking. Mom's promised to simmer up a jug of syrup for their supper pancakes.

It's good they had their first frost last night, he says, because it brings out the sweetness of the berries. As if she doesn't know that. As if he has to tell her again how the settlers bootlegged wine from the fruit, how the nomadic Plains Cree pounded them into their bison pemmican to keep them nourished on their wanderings. But his stories distract her and the picking is done before she realizes the flies have quit biting.

The field had lain fallow this past season, and it was brown and dead looking. The harvest she'd been trying to forget took place late that year as well, and the last time she was in this field the air was heavy with the dusty-mellow perfume of freshly cut wheat. She didn't want to be here. She hadn't meant to come here today, had she?

This sacred field was where she'd read her Bible on spring mornings in her early teens, sitting on the periphery atop the pile of stones she and Joel had picked over many seasons to earn spending money. And this profaned field was where she and François parked the truck on his very last night, right here in the presence of that altar of stones where she'd spent so many hours in prayer. And this field of reclamation was where Joel declared her untouchable and put the run on François, removing him from her young life with the threat of further violence.

Aglaia's heart was pounding, but now not from the physical exertion of her run. She forced herself to face the field against her revulsion, and turned towards it with intensity, almost expecting to see the blood. Not François's blood from the fistfight. He didn't figure at all in her final memory of this field—the most appalling memory—because he was already gone by then.

Her dreams for years had been leading her to this very spot, and she'd been running the other way for too long. She steeled herself and took a step into the brown field, the ground denting underfoot. It had taken place near the center—she recognized the dip, where the saline soil was white.

It's the morning after her night of shameless lust, just a few hours since Mary Grace discovered François to be gone, and she's drying the dishes as her mom takes a coffeecake, fragrant with cinnamon, out of the oven.

"You're very quiet, dear," Mom says. "I suppose it has something to do with the French Jung leaving?" Mary Grace almost drops a bowl as her temper and the temperature of her skin both flare. Did Joel blabber to Mom, too, about the compromising position he found her in last night? It's bad enough that Dad knows.

But Mom can't know, after all; she continues talking brightly. "Well, take your mind off your troubles and run this cake out to the field for Joel. He must be hungry."

Dad's gone to the village for repairs while her brother finishes up swathing the canola crop. He didn't touch the biscuits when the family sat down at daybreak four hours ago, instead getting up to fill a thermos with coffee and snagging a banana from the bowl as he headed out the door.

But she isn't sorry for him at all. She isn't sorry about his bloodshot eyes; she didn't sleep well, either. If he'd just kept his nose out of her business last night, François would still be helping him with the day's work.

The cake pan cools on the seat beside her as she drives the trail along the fence towards the giant's skull and turns west at the choke-

cherry bushes. She can see the tractor stopped in the field, Joel's truck half-parked behind its front end. As she bounces closer, she sees the tractor must have stalled; she can make out the booster cables tying the two vehicles together, but no Joel. He's not sitting in the cab of the tractor trying to restart the engine, and he's not under the open hood of the truck removing the cables.

Something doesn't look right. She rams her truck door open, adrenaline rushing, and catapults across the mounds of fallen stalks.

"Joel, are you okay? Joel!"

She doesn't spot him until she runs around the far side of the tractor, and knows in an instant that he neglected to put it into park when he got out to boost the battery. The tractor had pitched forward, its tires crushing Joel into the furrows of the ground between the swaths, pinning him from the waist down. His eyes are closed, his face blanched. His blood is making mud beneath him.

"No!" she screams as she falls on her knees beside him, grabbing his hand. Childhood horror stories screech through her mind—the neighbor who was rolled up alive by the baler, another who slipped into the chop grinder. This can't be happening to her brother. "Joel, talk to me!"

He opens his eyes then as if he's been waiting for her. Opens them wide this last time—clear and blue like the heavens above them—and he smiles at her.

"Sis," he bleats faintly.

"I'll get Mom!" She's shouting. "Wait. Hold on, Joel!"

But he doesn't let go of her hand and he says to her, in a voice full of peace and awe, "It's okay, Mary Grace. François left for Paris last night and you'll be safe now."

Then, with a final breath, his awareness of this life drains away through his eyes and she is left all alone under that wide blue sky.

Aglaia, in that same sacred, profaned, reclaimed field of sorrow fifteen years later, now buckled onto the earth where Joel gave up his life, his last words an unconsummated benediction: "You'll be safe now."

She hadn't been safe after all. She prostrated herself on the ground before that burning bush of her worst memory and didn't arise for perhaps an hour—until the dampness of the soil seeped through her clothing and chilled her to the soul.

In the outer reception area of Incognito first thing Wednesday morning, Eb MacAdam shook the hands of two evaluators from Hollywood's RoundUp Studios. They were wearing business suits and introduced themselves as Jerry and John. Eb hid his amusement; denim would be more suited than Italian cashmere for representatives of a western movie. Had Aglaia been present, she'd likely have worn her bonny pink riding boots.

Eb led them into the conference room to avoid the clutter in his office.

"Please, sit down," he encouraged them. "I'll have some tea—or coffee?—brought in." He asked his young work-program volunteer from the local high school to brew a pot of Arabica and then returned to his chair. "Now gentlemen, what can I do for you?"

"We were impressed with the timely submission of your bid for the costuming contract, since the deadline isn't up for another few weeks," the tall one, Jerry, said as he adjusted his tie.

"Incognito likes to keep on top of things." Eb had sent the movie company an e-mail expressing interest as soon as the call for local companies was publicized, and had subsequently been invited to submit a bid on the costume package proposed by RoundUp's design professionals. In consultation with Incognito's parent office in Montreal, Eb spent long hours putting together the preliminary documentation and sent it off to California.

"If the quality indicated by your paperwork plays out in your workshop, you have an excellent chance at being awarded our contract." John had hair close to Eb's in color, and creases around his eyes as though he laughed with his family.

"We just wanted to make your acquaintance and do an initial inspection," Jerry said. "It's fortunate that we happened to be in town for a few days for preproduction exploration and could meet with you."

Hardly fortunate, Eb thought. He knew from the society page blathering that PRU was throwing a dinner in honor of the Hollywood bigwigs this weekend, ostensibly as a gesture of civic hospitality but in unmitigated conflict of interest, as far as he was concerned.

"You're the first bidder we're reviewing, since yours is the only submission we've received so far, but we'll catch the others on our return to the area after the closing date," John explained. "You're a strong candidate and we thought some dialogue was in order at this juncture."

"I'd have loved to introduce you to our head designer, who's away on compassionate leave right now," Eb said.

"Oh yes, that would be"—John flipped up a page of his dossier—"Aglaia Klassen?"

"That's right."

In Eb's estimation, Aglaia was Incognito's greatest asset, and all the more so if they won this bid. Her artistic vision and her expertise in period fashions, her skill with all aspects of garment design and construction, and her stamina in working for long hours in a high-pressure environment—to say nothing of her brilliant native creativity, that finely honed, intuitive response of craft Eb so admired—equipped her to spearhead the operations.

He said as much to the men now and added, "Aglaia's practical experience includes membership in professional associations, extensive participation in stage costuming at the national level, and reception of several prestigious awards."

"Yes, she's got some notches on her belt," Jerry said, taking the file from his partner. "I see her work is even internationally represented—in Paris, at that. However our background checks show a real gap in her credentials. We want to be honest with you, Eb. Your company's up against some pretty well-educated competitors."

"You're talking about Platte River University, I suppose," Eb said. The older gent protested but Eb wasn't probing. "This isn't Hollywood. Our fishbowl is small enough that everyone here knows who's in the game. As far as Aglaia goes, she's got a concrete record of success that far outweighs theoretical learning. Her natural aptitude is highly regarded and we can provide recommendations from several organizations she's served."

"With luck we'll be around again to meet her," John said. "At any rate, your financials look solid but, as I'm sure you'll appreciate, our contracts aren't awarded on the basis of price alone. We like to get a good feel for our prospective suppliers on a project of this magnitude, where local, unknown companies like yours work in tandem with our own crews."

Eb's familiarity in bidding for projects his branch had brokered thus far had been significantly less rigorous than RoundUp's demands, but then a lot of money was in play with this contract. He glanced over the list of evaluation criteria the visitors offered, and when the student brought in the coffee, Eb poured both men a cup. He passed sugar and cream to them and longed for a sip of Darjeeling or Ceylon, but contented himself with java. He answered their questions frankly and supported his claims with verifying records, hoping to convince them of Incognito's technical merit, flexibility in fulfilling on-the-job requirements, and sustainability of service objectives. They asked to view Aglaia's full portfolio, and after a short tour of the facility, they took their leave. Eb begged his student volunteer to make him a spot of tea and retreated to his office to put his feet up.

He'd done his best but there was no guarantee about the outcome of the bid Incognito had submitted. Headquarters, insisting that Eb pass all the applicatory information through them for vetting before submission, would criticize him for not introducing their Canadian point man through teleconference as requested— unless Eb won the contract. Then all would be forgotten on that front, and he and Aglaia could get down to work.

And work was what Eb prized—not for the way it occupied so much of his time but for the way costumes communicated meaning deeper than the physics of fabric and thread. Throughout history clothing spun a story; from the earliest record it wove its own plotline. Take the biblical record of Joseph, Eb thought as he tested the heat of the tea with the edge of his lip. Joseph was a dreamer like Aglaia whose dreams got him into trouble, too. His robe paralleled his life story: Given to him by his father as a mark of favored status, it was stripped away and used to fabricate his death, but Joseph was eventually adorned again with robes of royalty when he rose to great power as a political leader in Egypt.

The story encouraged Eb in his everyday work, even in this bidding process with RoundUp he was undergoing for the sake of Incognito and, particularly, for the sake of Aglaia. *You've stuck with humanity through thick and thin*, he said silently now to God, *in our affluence and our misery. You saw Adam and Eve shivering naked and wretched beneath fig leaves; you watched as Esau allowed his brother to swindle their father by putting on the hairy hide of a goat. If you exemplified your grace through costume in the days of Abraham, Isaac, and Jacob, then surely your grace extends to a couple of costume makers in twenty-first-century America.*

Twenty-four

$\mathbf{D}$r. Lou Chapman clicked away on her keyboard, sitting in front of her computer on the upper level of her immaculate condominium in downtown Denver on Wednesday morning. It was good to be home, much as she loved Paris. The flight delivered her refreshed on Sunday evening, almost two days later than the originally scheduled return, but she was in fine form for her lectures at the beginning of the week. She made time to meet with young Whitney for an invigorating discussion on Greek poetry, eliciting bits of personal information about her grandfather, the chancellor, for future reference. And then she took care of final details with the Oxford Hotel regarding the Friday night film-related festivities at the university. It was a satisfying beginning to her week and she could afford a day off.

Lou hit the print button for a hard copy of online map directions just acquired with some effort on her part. She'd leave on her road trip as soon as she got hold of Aglaia, who wasn't answering her apartment or cell phone although Lou had tried several times since returning home. She resorted to calling Incognito late yesterday and duped the receptionist into disclosing the information she needed, learning about the family health crisis and enough specifics regarding the farm's location to start her Internet search. She must ensure Aglaia's presence at the formal dinner; her non-attendance would be disastrous in light of this new honor Oliver managed to procure.

Lou had set aside her initial irritation over Aglaia's tantrum at the Louvre. True, the girl did leave her standing at the palace entry like a jilted lover. But Lou considered the bind her own impetuous joke had put her in—that is, the possibility Aglaia might run away from her offer of a job as resolutely as she was running from intimacy. Lou shouldn't have lied about finding François, shouldn't have set Aglaia up in front of the Three Graces. That was where she lost control of the situation. Her tactic had backfired, allowing the invisible François to succeed after all in coming between them by his very absence. He was a trickster bringing conflict to her as certainly as the deity of strife had caused the Trojan War—to use the story that François himself referred to in his last biblical commentary—and she hated him forcing her into a vanity-fuelled contest where the stakes were much higher than in some fabled battle.

But maybe all hope was not yet gone. A broken heart invited consolation, and Lou might yet catch Aglaia on the rebound. Since François was out of the picture for good, maybe the girl would take seriously the opportunity PRU presented. Lou dialed the telephone number of one Henry Klassen of Tiege, Nebraska. The phone rang eight or nine times before Aglaia answered, panting.

"Did I catch you exercising?" Lou kept her tone pleasant.

"Who's calling, please?"

"You don't recognize me? I'm hurt."

Aglaia hesitated. "Lou. So you made it back home then."

"Did I give you a scare?" That had partly been Lou's intention with her detained departure from France. She didn't make it a habit to miss flights; that got too costly for her salary, even augmented as it was by her credit cards. But she wasn't finished with Paris anyway—with Emmanuelle—by the time Aglaia left. Conveniently her new friend was a physician, albeit a pediatrician, who'd penned a convincing enough medical slip to guarantee Lou's seat in business class for her return trip. Reimbursement of her original fare would

be almost automatic, thanks to the insurance policy she carried
for just such emergencies. But missing the flight worked well into
Lou's strategy to secure Aglaia's attention—if only to shake her up.
A little respect was in order, Lou felt.

"I heard about your father. He's recovering well, I trust."

"He'll live," Aglaia said.

"I drove past your apartment complex last night and noticed
your car was still in its stall, so I assume you'll need a ride home."

"It's taken care of."

Aglaia's unresponsiveness nettled Lou, so she got to the point
before her own voice gave her away. "Listen, about that tiff over
meeting François in the Louvre, I want to make amends for pulling
the wool over your eyes." Aglaia remained stoic. Lou swallowed,
then persisted. "It was churlish of me. I shouldn't have taken the
joke that far, I suppose. So I'm coming to fetch you back to the
city."

"No," Aglaia said. "I told you I've made arrangements for a
ride."

"Nonsense. I have a map to both the Klassen and Enns places,
thanks to satellite technology. I'll be there for you after lunch."

Lou hung up her cordless before Aglaia could contradict her
further. Today might be her last chance to promote the university
job and ultimately influence the decision of the tenure committee.
Her relationship with the girl needed restoration, and if that meant
physically driving out to the sticks to haul Aglaia back to civilization, so be it. Whatever it would take, she was willing to do.

Lou folded the printout and slid it into her bag alongside the
picture postcard of the Three Graces. That card was no longer
blank on the backside; she'd used it as a notepad to record her English translation of the difficult French phrase she discovered in the
book of Revelation when leafing through the Bible in Paris. Had
Aglaia come upon the passage yet, annotated by François and now
by Lou as well? The corner of the page had not been dog-eared like
the others. Eventually Aglaia would find it and beg her for help in
understanding it, and then Lou would give back the card. So she
kept it at hand in her purse.

There was almost a metaphorical aspect to returning to Aglaia the postcard fallen from between the pages of that ridiculous Bible in her apartment only two weeks ago—the pagan Graces fallen from the prophetic Word like Lucifer cast down through the heavens from the very presence of the Lord, or Icarus with his wax feathers melting from flying too close to the sun. Well, it was time for her angel to flutter back to reality, Lou thought as she locked the condo door behind her as she left, and she was just the wind to blow Aglaia in the right direction.

Aglaia stood in Tina's kitchen holding the telephone receiver in her hand, the line dead. She'd heard the phone ringing through the open window as she sprinted the last few yards to the house in the oversized rubber boots, but now she was annoyed she'd bothered to answer, with the pain of Joel's death so newly re-enacted in her mind. Lou always had to have the last word.

They hadn't spoken since Aglaia's embarrassment in front of the Three Graces, when Lou scoffed at her credulity that François was coming at any moment, and taunted her with the threat of joblessness. Well, she wouldn't take the contempt any longer! She punched the buttons corresponding to the call display but Lou didn't pick up, and Aglaia didn't lower herself to leave an angry message. By the time she thought to root out her address book for Lou's cell number, she'd cooled off enough to reconsider her indignation.

Lou would be speeding along the I-76 towards her by now. Offending the professor by refusing the ride would be unwise, what with the career prospect Lou was brandishing and the impression Aglaia hoped to make at the upcoming university dinner. She mustn't be too hasty in slamming that door, though she wished for more time to mull over the pros and cons of the job offer.

Of course, Lou's apology for her atrocious behavior at the Louvre was insufficient. She was haughty and didn't know how to say she was sorry. Not that Aglaia cared much; she'd found François on her own anyway, a fact Lou didn't need to learn. But Aglaia wasn't interested in hanging around the farm longer than necessary, anyway, and a ride home by Lou might be her grey cloud's silver lining. She'd better not relinquish Lou's friendship altogether just yet.

Aglaia left the house again in search of Zephyr. Hunting that hunter could take a while, and she called his name into the hayloft and the chicken coop, the tall grass beneath the trees and the smokehouse—maybe he'd caught a residual meaty whiff embedded in walls of the hut generations ago. Finally she found him sunning himself out by the spring. She gathered him up, digging her nose into his warm fur as she carried him back to the house, but decided before entering to let him stay outside in his element. Lou wouldn't look favorably on a feline passenger, she was sure, and Zephyr could take care of himself for a while longer. The cat streaked off towards the barn, and she spent the next couple of hours washing sheets and the clothing borrowed from Sebastian.

Noon was approaching by the time Aglaia climbed into the shower and stood beneath the pulverizing stream, washing the sweat and sorrow from her skin. The hour spent mourning at the scene of Joel's demise had offered a partial cleansing of its own, though little solace. The blame she'd been placing on Joel for François's departure dissipated when she replayed his valor in the face of death, his selflessness in thinking his last thought of her. Holding a grudge against him was juvenile and she let it go today, there in the field. But it was only the first of many emotional matters that needed her consideration, not all of them concerning Joel.

For example, how was she to deal with the idea of François once again being a living, breathing entity in her life, no longer a memory for her to tailor according to her moods? She projected what their future communication might entail—perhaps pillow talk or more discussion on his view about the futility of existence. Somehow neither appealed to Aglaia, though she admitted her own life had her in a rut of Sisyphean proportions.

François argued he could shatter the boulder of traditions distasteful to him—moral virtues such as celibate self-restraint. If *she* had a boulder that needed smashing, it was her identification with this farm, which had given rise to her past faith and resulted in her present malaise. Aglaia's overriding aspiration to find success in the arts world had not as yet been an effective sledge hammer.

That brought her back to the subject of Lou, Aglaia thought as the hot water beat on her back and filled the room with a cloud. If she took the job as wardrobe consultant at Platte River University, maybe she'd finally feel on the inside as polished and urbane as Lou looked on the outside. Her job at Incognito lacked the prestige of the academic scene, and although Eb was an authentic friend who didn't play mind games, ingratiating herself to Lou could clinch the position at PRU. It came down to a question of Aglaia's values.

She swept aside the curtain to see her melting reflection in the mirror, her blurred visage a mask of tragedy as tears of condensation rolled down its shiny surface. She couldn't tell whether she felt dread, despondency, or simple discontent. She'd been jumping through hoops ever since Lou showed up unannounced at the airport. No, ever since Naomi demanded they get together for their first coffee. Or maybe it was since that summer fifteen years ago, when her affiliation with everyone in her life changed so drastically.

Come to think of it, when had she last been transparent with anyone, or even conscious of her own feelings—not just the sensations of the body like smell and taste, but the very sentiments of her spirit?

She toweled off and smeared buttery lotion onto her legs and arms, regarding her reflection. She smoothed the cream over her full breasts and the silky skin of her thighs, and defied François's Thalia or Euphrosyne to live up to her. For all her vacillation, she still wanted him to think her the most beautiful.

Aglaia turned off the bathroom fan and heard a banging at the porch door. She answered it wrapped in a bath sheet, cracking the door open while leaving the chain fastened (a city habit now entrenched) and blocking Naomi's view of the kitchen floor and the Bible.

"I didn't know your parents even had a lock on their door." Aglaia heard a tremor behind Naomi's words but saw the set of her jaw, the steel in her eye. "I must have called you five times in the last hour. Come on, get dressed. Soup's on, Byron's busy in the shop, the kids are in school, and the baby and Sarah are napping. I think we need a heart-to-heart chat."

Aglaia sighed. There'd be no putting off Naomi's compulsion to talk, she could tell. "I'll be right out—I've got to pack up my things." In particular, she thought of the Bible she'd kicked around the kitchen earlier. She didn't want Naomi going on at her about that. She wiggled into her clothes and, during the short jaunt over to Naomi's house, told her that Lou was coming from the city to drive her home.

Naomi frowned. "I'm glad we have a chance to talk before you leave, then. It's important."

In the Enns house Aglaia dipped into her bowl of *Rintsupp*, beef broth scented with star anise and loaded with dumplings. She faced the window that opened onto the gravel driveway, expecting Lou's car within the hour. Aglaia wasn't ready for whatever Naomi wanted to discuss, though she could venture a guess about where it was heading.

"I thought we'd have another day together to talk about this," Naomi said. "I tried to warn you when you called from Paris. It's hard to know how to bring the subject up with you, but I can't hold off any longer." The apprehension in Naomi's eyes was unfamiliar. What scared her into such solemnity? "You know I care about you. I admire what you've done with your life—your career and living in the city and traveling all the way to France like that."

The topic of religion would come up now, Aglaia conjectured. Naomi had that earnestness usually preceding exhortation. She'd criticize her for lack of church attendance or some other short-coming Tina might have shared. Aglaia stirred her soup as if it were still too hot and eluded eye contact.

But Naomi took her off guard. "In fact, it's Paris I need to talk to you about."

"Paris?" Aglaia asked. This had nothing to do with religion, then? Only one option remained—the subject of François Vivier—and that made Aglaia even more leery. Come to think of it, Naomi, too, became jittery every time they talked about François in any capacity—even as early as when Naomi first heard Tina's request about the Bible delivery. But Naomi had no way of knowing about Aglaia's tryst with François, unless she could read it in her eyes or smell it on her. Maybe Naomi had guessed.

"Did you manage to track down François and give him that Bible, like your mom asked?"

"No, it was… unfeasible." Aglaia didn't elaborate.

"So you didn't see him then?"

"Did you actually think it was possible?" Aglaia hoped Naomi wouldn't detect her evasion. "Paris is a city of over ten million people," she said, mimicking Lou's statistic—and arrogance—to cover her own lapse of truthfulness. She sounded more like Lou every day. For many years she'd spoken just like François, she realized with a start—telling his stories to herself, using his voice. When had she lost her own?

Naomi mushed up a dumpling. "You've been standoffish ever since we got back together in Denver. Not the old Mary Grace, that's for sure."

"Aglaia," she corrected automatically, and was smacked back into a long-forgotten conversation two nights before the accident, when Joel came into her bedroom without knocking, and caught her kissing François, who made a quick escape.

"You're not the old Mary Grace, that's for sure," Joel says.

"I'm more like Aglaia now," she answers, not caring that she's changed. It's for a good cause. It's for love.

"What's with the weird names—Euphrosyne, Thalia? François is full of them." He shakes his head. "He's using you, Sis." Joel puts his hand out to her but she veers away from his touch, so different in intent from François's, and flings herself across the bed.

"Mind your own business."

"You don't really know him." Joel picks up her brush from the dresser and absently pulls out a strand of her hair as though it were a thread of gold he might use to sew a stitch. He's pensive. "People are talking. Girls are saying things about him."

"They're jealous," she says, but she's heard the slander, too.

"And Byron talked to me."

"You're a gossip." She wants her hiss to cover the truth.

"Before he left this summer, Byron said something about Naomi and François—"

"You're both stupid, gossiping old women!"

"Mary Grace—"

She gets up from her bed to open the door for him. "Get out. I'm going to sleep."

Naomi was talking. "It's just that we used to share our burdens with one another, you know?"

Did Naomi really expect they'd be buddies again? Aglaia said, "It's no wonder I'm guarded after what you did."

"What do you mean? I was the one who took the risk in getting this friendship back on track again."

"You were the one who derailed it in the first place."

"Me?" Naomi cleared her throat. "Look, I want to take responsibility for my part, but you've been so indifferent to me. With this scare Henry's given us all, I'd hoped we might lean on each other. You know, talk about things that matter."

"Okay then." It was time to take the bull by the horns. "Why did you leave me that summer, Naomi? You never even said good-bye." She tried to keep her voice tight. This was the crux of the problem with Naomi that had bothered her from the time she was seventeen. Naomi had just up and left when she needed her most.

"Leave you? What are you talking about?"

"You knew I was devastated about Joel's death. Best friends don't jump ship when the water gets rough. You weren't even there for the funeral." Her words came out ragged, misery tearing at her throat.

To top it off, besides her pain over Joel, the whole affair with François that summer was the kind of trauma teen friends were supposed to help each other through. But what would her boyfriend troubles, back then or even now, mean to Naomi anyway? If she couldn't empathize with her best friend's suffering when it came to a brother's death, how would she understand lost love or Aglaia's attempt at reinstating it again?

But Joel's words resounded in her mind: "Byron said something about Naomi and François." If he'd been right, if her boyfriend and her best friend had been romantically involved, that would change the whole scenario. Was there any truth to it?

"Oh Aglaia, I'm so sorry. Joel's death must have been awful for you." Naomi's eyes glistened. "I cared for Joel, too, and there's no excuse for my having moved away without so much as a word to you. I guess I was caught up in my own problems."

"What was terrible enough to justify skipping his funeral and dropping from my sight altogether?"

A glow pinkened Naomi's face. "That's what I wanted to talk to you about, what I tried to tell you when you called from Paris and what I should have said to you long ago. Maybe we could've avoided a lot of hurt if I'd just come clean then."

Aglaia had heard the rumors that circulated around the community when Byron followed Naomi up to the city after they graduated, the year she herself moped through twelfth grade. Everyone in the youth group knew how *close* Naomi and Byron got that year, even before they moved away, despite the purity pledge they all took under Pastor Reimer's direction. Everyone found out how fast a wedding could be planned. Were those the problems she referred to?

Naomi confirmed her suspicion. "I got pregnant early that summer and I didn't want anyone to know." Her chin quivered.

"For Pete's sake, Naomi, it's not that big a deal these days. Byron did the right thing in the end, if that's what's concerning you."

But even as Aglaia said these words, and as though she'd been insensible to the possibilities before, she saw afresh Naomi among the girls of Tiege pining for a wink from the exotic French student, heard again François's offhand inquiry about Naomi last week in the Tedious Beatnik Taverne: "What about your best friend... the motherly one?" Aglaia felt sick in the pit of her belly, but the discussion had gone too far for either of them to turn back now.

"Byron had nothing to do with this," Naomi muttered. "Byron never slept with me till after we were married."

Blood pounded in Aglaia's eardrums, knowing now why the

oldest Enns boy looked so familiar. She pictured Sebastian's profile, his hair, the way he rolled on the ground of the field roughhousing with his younger, blonde brother. How had she not admitted the truth to herself before this? She didn't want to hear Naomi's next sentence but the words came at her in a rush anyway.

"Aglaia, Sebastian is François's son."

Twenty-five

Aglaia recoiled from the table with such force that she knocked her chair over. She ran out, almost tripping on the dog's bowl, and reached the cottonwood grove before the nausea stopped her.

Naomi gave birth to François's baby! Despite all his proclamations of love for Aglaia, François chose Naomi first!

Denial, like bile, choked her. She dropped onto her hands and knees and vomited in the grass, as she had vomited by the tractor the day she watched Joel die and vomited the day she left the farm by the side of the burning barrel.

Naomi ran out after her but Aglaia pushed away her disloyal hands.

As a youth François swore his love for Aglaia—for *her*, not for some backstabbing hypocrite who called her friend. And while François had been clawing at Aglaia in the truck on his last night in America, his child was already growing in Naomi's body. All the years Aglaia dreamed about him, François's own son was living next door to Henry and Tina. All the hours Aglaia spent reading his words in the Bible margins, the existence of François's progeny under Naomi's roof proved the lie. And during every moment she was with François last week on the streets of Paris, he and Naomi were still bound in a mutual embrace that neither time nor distance untied.

For years Aglaia had blamed Joel for chasing François away and blamed herself for Joel's death, overcome with guilt that she chose a lover over a brother, losing them both. Just when she reclaimed François again, she found Naomi to be at the heart of the blame and guilt.

Naomi pressed a tissue into Aglaia's hand and held her hair out of the way as she bent over the grass, until she composed herself and marched back to the house to rinse her mouth and sit again, rigid in her acrimony.

Naomi, standing before her, looked perplexed. "I guess you must be angry that I didn't tell you, since we were so close."

She didn't know the half of it, Aglaia thought. Naomi's unwelcome explanation came at her in a barrage.

"It started in May at a party, the first week François was here, when everyone was gaga over him. You remember? He got in with the wrong crowd. Byron and I'd had a fight, and out of spite I offered François a ride to the party. I stayed and I guess I drank too much, but after that first time, um, *with* François, I couldn't stop. For the next few weeks, every time we got together"—her voice broke—"there was this unspoken threat that he'd tell Byron, and I think Joel had a hunch all along."

Naomi squatted on her haunches and stuck her face up into Aglaia's, beseeching.

"I have no excuse for being loose. I knew better. I've cleared my conscience before God and Byron, but I've been so afraid to tell you. I was like an older sister, and I should've been a better example."

"You should have kept your hands to yourself!" Aglaia spat it out.

"But you can't imagine how convincing he was, Aglaia, how he made me feel, the way he looked at me."

She understood it only too well. Naomi was the one under an illusion, apologizing for her brief lapse of morality without tweaking to Aglaia's enduring obsession with François. Naomi seemed to think Aglaia's response was righteous indignation—not self-reproach, not humiliated disgrace.

Naomi kept talking. "When I missed my first period, I climbed our windmill and almost jumped, but Byron got to me first. He was so mad he wanted to kill François, but I convinced Byron to leave Tiege, like I was doing. When I was almost three months along, I told François but he said I couldn't prove it was his child and that he didn't want anything more to do with me or it." Naomi pulled up a chair and her voice grew husky. "Byron eventually forgave me and said he'd raise Sebastian as his own, that he'd take the blame rather than see me suffer alone. And he helped me forgive myself. By the time we got married François was long gone. Sebastian knows the truth now. We told him last year."

"So you got away with cheating, then," Aglaia said.

"What do you mean? I told you Byron knows everything."

"I don't mean your cheating on Byron. I mean your cheating on me."

Naomi's head snapped up. The wind battered against the window, rattling the glass, and the baby in the next room made fussing sounds. Naomi opened her mouth as if to ask a question she couldn't quite articulate.

"Don't you get it, Naomi? I was in love with him—François was *mine!*"

"All the girls had a crush on him."

"But I was the one he wanted, or so I thought." Aglaia coughed up a rough laugh. "I was still such a good girl in the beginning, probably reading my Bible while you two were making out in the back seat of some car. Or did François drive Dad's half-ton the back road out to your place for your little orgies?" That'd be the icing on the cake, François and Naomi in the cab as a trial run for her own planned deflowering in the same vehicle weeks later. Had there been other girls in the truck?

"It wasn't like that," Naomi protested.

But now they heard the whine of a high-performance engine; Lou was tearing up the drive. Aglaia tugged her suitcase out the door without a backward glance, stepping away from the mugginess of the kitchen and into the grit of gravel dust swirling around the BMW. She swallowed the effluence of her emotions and took a deep, arid breath before climbing into the car.

Lou's calves were cramping. Her legs needed a stretch after the long drive but she'd barely applied the brakes in front of the bungalow before Aglaia jumped in and locked the car door against Naomi's exclamations.

"Let's go," Aglaia said.

But Naomi was pawing at Aglaia's handle and so Lou turned off the engine and lowered her own window. She was curious.

Naomi trundled over to the driver's side of the car, disregarding Lou. "Aglaia, don't leave like this. We need to talk about him."

"There's nothing left to say."

"I'm sorry. You were my best friend. I should've guessed."

"What's done is done." Aglaia's icy outrage amused Lou, but then she noted a tear forming in Aglaia's eye. What was this about?

"Please stay another night. Byron will drive you back."

Aglaia didn't answer immediately and Lou thought her resolve to get away might be weakening, so she decided to add another ingredient to the bubbling cauldron. Apparently Naomi had some stake in the whole François affair; she should find the information interesting.

"I have a message for you two from the home of François Vivier," Lou announced. Both women gaped at her. "I tracked him down through the Sorbonne alumni registry, attained his residential address, and placed a call to his estranged wife."

"His *wife?*" both women shrilled in unison.

Lou found it gratifying to be the bearer of such news. "The French woman didn't want to talk to me when she learned I was inquiring after François, likely presuming I was one of his *paramours*. Her *patois* was difficult to understand and she hung up when I explained your attempt, Aglaia, to return a prized possession to François." Lou hadn't told the wife it was a Bible—better to let her think it was something valuable. "No matter," Lou continued, noting that, in addition to Aglaia, Naomi was hanging on every word as though the story involved her—and maybe it did. "I have the phone number here for you, if you'd like it." But neither of them made any move for the slip of paper she held up. Lou was aggrieved, after all her effort and the time she took away from Emmanuelle to accomplish her mission for Aglaia.

"Leave," Aglaia insisted again. So Lou put her Beamer into gear and tore out of the yard, headed for home.

Aglaia's head throbbed with information overload—about Naomi's disclosure and Byron's decency, about François's wife in Paris and the depths of his philandering, about her own willful blindness. Lou plied her with questions until she wanted to scream: What was the cause of Aglaia's argument with Naomi? Did she know if Dayna Yates, their mutual friend, planned on gracing the sociology-arts affair on Friday? Had she ever gotten through her reading—all the way to the *end*, Lou stressed—of that Bible?

Aglaia put off the queries by turning up the volume on her iPod, the most insistent questions arising from her own mind, questions she resolved to ask herself another time. It didn't take her long to retrieve reading material from her bag in the back seat as an excuse for not engaging with Lou—anything to escape the monsoon hitting her from without and within.

The Bible was worse for wear, pages ripped and a few torn completely free, so that Leviticus interjected into Hebrews, a page of the Psalms was stuck in with Romans. Aglaia ignored the pencil marks and flipped past the last down-turned page. The red words caught her eye, and she skipped through the sayings of Jesus, here and there. *You are the salt of the earth... Don't be afraid; just believe... Follow me.*

That was easier said than done, she thought. How could she be tasty for others when life itself was so bitter? How could she follow what wasn't in her sights? She herself was as desiccated as salt crystals, as blind as the man with the mudpack on his eyes before he washed in the Pool of Siloam.

Out of the overflow of the heart the mouth speaks, she read. *This people's heart has become calloused.* Her own heart was hard, her dry tongue stilled. *Everyone who drinks this water will be thirsty again, but whoever drinks the water I give him will never thirst.* What? Never thirst again? *Indeed the water I give him will become in him a spring of water welling up to eternal life... If anyone is thirsty, let him come to me and drink... Streams of living water will flow from within him.*

But her reading wasn't helping her headache, and she couldn't clarify the meaning behind the words, now that she wasn't heeding François's interpretations. These verses were familiar from her childhood but she didn't know what to do with them anymore, staring into the mirror of them and seeing the dirt of her own blameworthiness but unable to wipe herself clean.

Lou slowed up for speed traps as they neared Sterling and said something she couldn't hear. She pulled out one earphone and asked Lou to repeat herself.

"I said I hope you aren't expecting me to stop at the hospital on the way through."

"No, Dad and Mom will be in Denver tomorrow, anyway." Aglaia started to replace her earpiece.

"Shall we discuss the reception Friday?" Lou tried again.

"What's to discuss? I'll meet you at the hotel at six, as we agreed." Aglaia used a civil tone of voice as she reached for a button to recline her seat and plugged her music in again, though she turned the volume off. She was fighting tears of exhaustion but wouldn't give Lou the satisfaction of witnessing them and, so, turned her back to the driver's side and read for a while, then feigned sleep with her finger in the Bible. She didn't trust Lou— or Naomi either. She'd been putting faith in the wrong people for quite a while. Whom could she trust?

Through the slits of her lids, Aglaia watched the Great Plains fly by, the mountains appear in the distance, and (though her iPod was silent) she could swear she heard someone singing the words of the king and of the prophet and of the apostle: *Trust in the Lord with all your heart... Trust in the Lord forever, for the Lord, the Lord is the Rock eternal... See, I lay a stone in Zion, a tested stone, a precious cornerstone... See, I lay in Zion a stone that causes men to stumble and a rock that makes them fall, and the one who trusts in Him will never be put to shame.*

That night Aglaia slept late in her own bed, and she decompressed all Thursday morning, wishing she had a farm rooster to stew up *coq au vin* and fill the apartment with the smells of poultry and fresh thyme. She didn't answer the phone when Lou called twice, and was glad after all that Eb had given her the whole week off, and didn't even miss Zephyr left behind at the farm.

She stuffed her laundry into the washing machine and watched the foam rise, the agitator chew and swish. If only purging herself of the grime ground into the fabric of her being were so easy.

Since downloading her photos from the Paris trip last night, especially the ones taken in the Louvre, she'd been thinking a lot about the Three Graces. The statue grouping she'd examined up close in the museum was carved from the stone of the earth—the essence of grime, really—and came from the same dust she'd return to someday, as Joel had done. In Pradier's rendition of the Greek goddesses, her namesake Aglaia stood with sightless eyes raised to the heavens—albeit to the god Zeus—as flesh-and-blood Aglaia used to worship the God of the Bible. But for a long time now, Aglaia's own eyes had focused not on the heavens but on François who, like some thwarted King Midas, had turned her to common stone through and through, and her eyes had been fixed on him for what seemed an eternity.

Aglaia sifted through her mental store of myths for some escape from her doldrums, but only Niobe came to mind, the tragic figure of mourning who cried inconsolably over the loss of her children so that Zeus turned her into a statue that wept forever. And Echo, the mountain nymph rejected in love, who pined away till just her voice remained. Hollow consolation they were—two more sad goddesses who offered no hope but only admonished her for her inability to shed her own tears, to raise her own song in praise. All her daydreams had deteriorated since meeting François again. All her myths had lost their luster.

When the washing machine splashed Aglaia in its agitation, she came back to herself and closed the lid. The jet lag must still be getting to her. The telephone rang, but the number was blocked on the call display. She'd better pick up.

"I know you don't want to talk to me yet, but I need to update you on Henry's situation." It was Naomi, and remorse stabbed Aglaia; *she* should be the one doing the calling about her dad. "Byron will be at the hospital with your parents by two-thirty. He'll book Tina into the nearby facility for visiting relatives. I hope you don't mind our making the arrangements."

"That's fine, thanks." She didn't sound grateful.

"I suppose you'll be meeting Tina and Henry for the appointment with the specialist, then? Because someone should be there for them when Byron leaves."

"I'll make sure they're taken care of." Aglaia wanted to brush her off, but that'd be the height of discourtesy in light of Naomi's altruism.

"Well, since I have you on the line, let's talk for a couple of minutes," Naomi said, pressing her advantage. "I mean, you left in such a state yesterday."

Aglaia might as well get it over with, tell Naomi straight out that she wasn't interested in trying to patch things up. How could Naomi expect friendship when she didn't even deserve forgiveness? Aglaia plopped down on her couch in the living room to tell her so, but caught the Bible as it bounced open to the book of Revelation, and from that point on she didn't hear another word Naomi said. Her full attention was taken up by handwritten words she hadn't seen before, recorded in two distinct scripts.

First, François's pencil had written in extensive and complicated French: *Idée de génie! Des biblots, des joyaux, y graver "Kallistei," en combler mes Grâces, et leur donner la pomme!*

Then beside it, a bold blue ink command read: SEE ME. LOU.

"I've got to go," she blurted to Naomi, and slapped the telephone receiver onto its cradle. When had Lou snooped into the

Bible, and how much had she read of François's notes throughout? How dare she write her own dictum into the margins, like some divine commandment—"Come unto me, all you who are unable to read the language"—assuming that Aglaia was helpless without her?

But maybe she was. Aglaia comprehended a few of his French words: "idea" and "apple" and, of course, "Graces." But try as she might using her phrase book, her dictionary, and even an online translation tool, she couldn't decipher his meaning as a whole, and it was time to leave for the hospital if she didn't want to be late. She despised François Vivier now and wanted to put an end to the whole, humiliating debacle. The quickest way to see it through was to ask Lou what the phrases meant; evidently she had some knowledge after all that Aglaia needed. It galled her to be at Lou's mercy, but she'd better make nice to the professor before tomorrow night's function anyway. Calling on her to ask for translation of the passage was as good an excuse as any.

Aglaia fitted the Bible into her purse, first taking out her travel documents and the incidentals she'd carried on the plane. She determined to stop by the university as soon as she was done with her parents and ask Lou what the writing in the Bible was all about. She wanted to tie up the loose ends, maybe even throw the cursed book into the trash on her way home, as she'd done with her own Bible when a teen. It would be symbolic of her renunciation of François, and even of God.

Twenty-six

"**D**ad, you can't just discharge yourself." Aglaia stood beside the bed and looked towards Tina and the cardiac specialist for support, but her father's chafing was nothing new to her. "Besides, Byron's left for home and can't come to fetch you until Monday."

"The doctor said my color is better." Henry elbowed himself up on the bed. "Didn't you say that, Doc?"

The specialist, a petite redhead wearing heels, paused from scratching on her clipboard. "I said we want to observe you through the weekend," she corrected Henry. "The beta-blockers seem to be doing the trick, and the test results should confirm your status. But you need to get your energy back before we discharge you. You're a lucky man to have lived through that heart attack, Mr. Klassen."

Tina thanked the doctor as though her husband had been given a stay of execution. When she was alone with her family again, Tina said, "Don't think about escaping this time, Henry. Let's celebrate with take-out from some fancy restaurant—maybe pizza."

"I don't think he's up to it," Aglaia said. For all his bluster, he was pale and nodded in agreement.

"Tomorrow then?" Tina asked Aglaia. "You have the day off from work, don't you?"

"Tomorrow I'm busy. I won't be back till Saturday." The disappointment in her parents' eyes prompted Aglaia to explain further. "I have a formal engagement and I can't get out of it." The dinner wouldn't occupy her earlier in the day, but she didn't mention that.

"A date?" Tina asked.

"Don't pry," Henry said.

Aglaia laughed in spite of herself. "No, I'm going with an associate to a business dinner at the Oxford, downtown. You know, it's that expensive historic hotel right across from Union Station." Aglaia might have gone on to say something about the professional connection with the university and the likelihood of a new job, but Henry had something else on his mind.

"Sit down, Mary Grace," he said. "We want to talk to you."

Henry motioned for his wife to bring out a ledger from the bag by the window. The sight of the slim journal evoked in Aglaia's mind the many evenings she worked on math homework beside her dad at the kitchen table while he transferred numbers from sales receipts into an identical book.

He opened it now and traced a column with his finger.

"What is it?" Was her dad worried about finances? That'd be the predictable response to his brush with death. Was he wondering how Tina would manage someday without him? Aglaia didn't have time for this now. It was already late afternoon and she wanted to catch Lou before she left her office. "If this is about your will," she began, but he shook his head.

"No, that's all taken care of." He turned the ledger towards her. "But the farm's not doing too well," he said. "Right now the price of wheat is going up, but ever since Joel died..."

Aglaia hadn't heard her father speak Joel's name since the day she left home.

Tina filled in the rest of his sentence. "We miss him so much."

They were both watching her, waiting for her to say something—to offer them her verbal denouement of Joel's death. If Dad had withheld Joel's name from her, she'd withheld her feelings from them.

"Don't you?" her mother asked.

"Don't I what?" Aglaia lamented their timing; she had to run. And why did they have to bring up the subject after all these years anyway, just when she was struggling through it herself?

"Miss him. Don't you miss Joel, Mary Grace?"

Now both of her parents were openly weeping so that she crossed the room for a box of tissues.

"We know how close you were as kids," Dad said. "I always thought, since he was dead and gone, there was no sense in talking about it, digging up old pain."

Aglaia agreed; they should all shut up about it now. This emotionalism of theirs must be coming from Dad's health scare, but knowing that didn't alleviate its effect on her. It was difficult to observe her parents' sorrow.

Tina chimed in. "You know, when you were just a *Bäbe*, he loved you already."

"The youngster said he wanted to marry you when you grew up." Henry chortled, then swiped at his dripping nose. Aglaia remembered promising Joel that they'd be best friends forever, and yet—the thought ripped at her heart—she had discounted the value of such brotherly love in allowing François to turn her head away with his own faithless version.

"My doctor told me I need to get some stuff off my chest." Henry rubbed at the front of his hospital gown and grinned wanly at his own joke.

Then he began to talk as Aglaia hadn't ever heard him talk before. He admitted he shut his daughter off for a long time because it was so hard to see her leave after Joel was killed. He told her of his loneliness out in the fields as he worked the land without his children beside him. Tina made damp noises of agreement as he explained his love for working the soil, his grief over dashed plans for the family farm, and, mostly, his regret over losing both his kids.

"Won't you come back home to us?" Tina interrupted, cutting to the chase.

Henry nodded. "That's what I'm saying, Mary Grace. Won't you come back?"

She was rendered speechless by the outlandish request and only stared at them.

Henry clarified the question. "We don't mean you should *move* back to the place or anything like that. I need your help to run the place during harvest and seeding for a couple of weeks, like you helped this year."

"We'd never have done it without you," Tina added. "Byron said so."

"I need you to become a partner, Mary Grace, so when Mom and I get too old to run things anymore, you can manage it for us from your home in the city. When we die—" Aglaia's hands shot out, palms open, in reflex, but Henry started again. "When we die, you can rent it out for income, maybe to Byron. There'll be good money in it someday. It's all we've got to leave to you, girl. It's your inheritance."

Overcome by the deluge of their generosity and the sodden load of their expectations and the buoyancy of her own unanticipated joy, Aglaia fled.

Lou heard the tentative knock and almost ignored it, taken up as she was in drafting her remarks for her stint before the microphone tomorrow night. But her office door creaked open and Aglaia peeked in with something like contrition written on her face. She hoped the girl wasn't planning to renege on their engagement and had come instead to collect the item Lou was retaining for her. Her advantage might yet garner the cooperation of the seamstress regarding the plan she and Oliver had concocted.

"Come in, sit. Nice to see you again so soon," Lou said, generous despite Aglaia's cold shoulder during their long drive back to the city yesterday. "I thought I wouldn't have the pleasure until tomorrow."

"I'm not interrupting you?"

"Not at all." Lou put aside her speech notes and clasped her hands in front of her. "What can I do for you?"

Aglaia blushed. "I have a problem." She pulled the black leather Bible out of the bag on her lap and deftly turned to the back, to the page on which Lou had penned her summons that night in their Paris hotel room.

Now Lou was certain the girl was not in her office to break their date but had finally read far enough in the book to discover Lou's own message written beside the lover's script. She suppressed a smile of triumph.

Since first reading François's French notation in the margin, Lou had put some time into research. She investigated the context of the Bible passage using commentaries in the religion section of PRU's library, and brushed up on the myth referred to by François—the myth she tried in vain to tell Aglaia in front of the statue of Venus de Milo in the Louvre nearly a week ago. Lou found her study uplifting; it suggested that François possessed some literary intelligence and understood the rudiments of cultural analysis in Greek mythopoeic literature, current French linguistics, and biblical hermeneutics. Perhaps she was crediting him with too much acumen, but she felt an affinity with this faceless François Vivier.

Aglaia was showing her the familiar notation now, which began *Idée de genie* (though Lou had already transcribed its translation from memory—she wouldn't easily forget his words). Beside it, the underlined biblical passage read: *He who has an ear, let him hear what the Spirit says to the churches. To him who overcomes, I will give some of the hidden manna. I will also give him a white stone with a new name written on it, known only to him who receives it.* The girl was running on, explaining how she tried to figure out the French for herself, and Lou nodded absently as she mentally reviewed her own findings.

In her research, Lou had first considered the textual passage of the Bible, in which allegedly the author was writing to the early Christ-followers living in Pergamum. The city still stood in modern-day Turkey near Troy's ten-level ruins and, as the birthplace of parchment, it was an ancient center of learning with a library of two hundred thousand books. Theologians, she read to her amusement, designated Pergamum as the "throne of Satan" because of its temples dedicated to Zeus, Asclepius, Dionysus, and Athena. The Christian acolytes under discussion in the passage were being taken to task for tolerating the immorality and idolatry surrounding them, and for compromising on their own doctrines. Those who held fast to the purity of the church's teaching and resisted assimilation into the world systems, the author promised, would be rewarded by God. The "hidden manna" spoken of was Jesus Christ, Bread of heaven sent down like desert food to the church today, she read, while the "white stone" stood as a pledge of Christ's affiliation with them. Lou supposed this was a reference to the white stone given at the ancient games of Olympia as a token of honor, or the pebble of acquittal awarded by the Greek courts to declare the accused "not guilty."

The quality of scholarship existing at the theological level surprised and impressed her.

After understanding the milieu of the apocalyptic passage, Lou then reviewed the details of the Greek myth only hinted at in François's writing in the margin. That story began with a great wedding feast to which all the deities but Eris, the goddess of strife, were invited. Eris was the daughter of the primordial goddess of the night, and bore her own shadowy children—the personifications of toil and trouble, quarrels and lies, concealment, ruin, and folly. As retribution for being left off the guest list, the troublemaker Eris lobbed a golden apple—engraved with the word *Kallistei*—into the nuptial celebrations, proclaiming that the one who possessed it would be named the most desirable in all the heavens.

Hera, Athena, and Aphrodite converged upon the apple and claimed it as their own, arguing among themselves in what Lou thought must have been a magnificent catfight. A tie-breaker was called and the prince of Troy chosen as the judge of the three deities who convened before him.

Each goddess offered the prince a bribe. Hera promised political power, and Athena military prowess. But Aphrodite, goddess of love, knew the weakness of the prince and the potency of sexuality. With the charms of the Three Graces to heighten her own allure, Aphrodite bribed the prince with the love of Helen, the world's most beautiful woman. Helen was already married to the mighty king of Sparta. The prince's lust perverted his judicial wisdom, and he chose beauty over skills of battle. He gave Aphrodite the apple in exchange for Helen, stealing her away from Sparta and triggering the Trojan War.

With her biblical and pagan research in order, Lou understood much better François's meaning in his impulsive message, his idea inspired by the fancy of Scripture. Now Aglaia was finishing up her own explanation of how she'd come upon his writing herself and wondered if Lou would, indeed, be of assistance as promised.

"So, you're asking me to… what, exactly?" Lou knew why Aglaia had come to her, but she wanted her pound of flesh.

"Well, I hoped you'd give me the translation."

"You're unable to read it? But Aglaia, your grasp of French was excellent in Paris," Lou said, toying with her. Aglaia wasn't oblivious to the sarcasm; she frowned. Lou knew she was treading on thin ice. Now was the time to court Aglaia's favor in preparation for the job offer Oliver would formalize at the banquet. It was an opportunity to show Aglaia that she'd walk alongside her. But Lou continued her baiting. "You really couldn't decipher it?"

"You wrote in the margin to come see you." A muscle in Aglaia's jaw flexed.

"Don't panic. I have the translation already written out for you on your picture of the Three Graces I borrowed for my class lecture. Remember this?"

Lou withdrew the well-traveled postcard from her purse, keeping it an inch or two from Aglaia's reach and in no hurry to hand it over. Lou read it to herself, again parsing and analyzing each French phrase in her mind: *Idée de génie! Des biblots, des joyaux, y graver "Kallistei," en combler mes Grâces, et leur donner la pomme!* François's opening remark conveyed youthful confidence, and his following choice of nouns implied his motivation to give satisfaction in the affairs of love—very sexy. His use of the Greek word was masterful, particularly in combination with his reference to Eve's temptation of Adam.

"May I have it, Lou?" Aglaia was straining across the desk towards her now for the card, but Lou leaned back on her ergonomic office chair.

"What's it worth to you, Aglaia?" She was pushing her luck, dangling the translation like some fruit from the tree of knowledge. "Can I sell it to you for the promise that you'll accept the position of wardrobe consultant here?"

Even as she spoke the words, Lou knew she'd overstepped her bounds; Aglaia pulled back her hand, her lips tightened, and recrimination flashed from her eyes.

Lou dropped the card hastily, written side up. "I'm jesting, Aglaia," she said, then read her English translation aloud: "A marvelous idea! Trinkets, precious stones, engraved with '*Kallistei*,' to please my Graces, and to give them the apple."

Aglaia picked the card up and read it again to herself, and Lou pitched into a summary of her research regarding Pergamum and Troy. Then she explicated François's complex French, and Aglaia was all ears.

"The first phrase gives the sense of François being sure this idea that had just come to him was foolproof," she began. "His use of the words 'trinkets' and 'precious stones' indicates the spectrum of the gifts he intended to bestow, the value lying not so much in the items given as in his motivation to 'please' his recipients in a sexual sense." Aglaia's demeanor was guarded and, if she'd ever received such a gift or such satisfaction, she wasn't letting on. Lou continued, " 'To give them the apple' is an interesting French expression. In a reversal of Eve's gesture in the Garden of Eden, François here asserts it's now his turn to do the tempting."

"But what is *Kallistei?*"

Lou saw Aglaia's eye twitch; the tension was ratcheting up. "Well, it's not French," she said. "It's the Greek word written by Eris upon the apple of discord tossed in among the goddesses to cause their jealous squabbling."

Lou was still unclear about what a golden apple had to do with Aglaia. Of course, she'd picked up on the girl's affinity for the Three Graces, first when Aglaia reacted to the postcard brought to her apartment by Tina, and then by Aglaia's stated intention to see the statues in the Louvre and her absorption in them as she waited there for her truant lover to appear.

And Lou also understood by her reading of François's margin notes that he shared—or perhaps initially ignited—Aglaia's passion for Greek mythology. But the relationship between Aglaia and the legend of Troy was foggy. Lou guessed that the Greek word was the key to Aglaia's enlightenment, though it shed no light for her.

"But what does *Kallistei* mean?" Aglaia repeated.

"It means, 'To the fairest.' "

The offending syllables were hardly out of Lou's mouth before Aglaia leapt up from her chair, her eyes popping, her mouth wide.

But just then, Dr. Dayna Yates tapped on the half-opened door and entered with an envelope, coming up behind Aglaia.

"You're back from France! What are you doing here at the university?"

Dayna didn't wait for the answer but—not catching the look on Aglaia's face—placed her hand on the girl's arm. "Hold that thought for a moment," she said, then addressed Lou as she deposited her envelope on the desk. "This is from the tenure committee regarding your examination as a candidate. We have some concerns about your preparedness. You might want to review it so you can address the issues in your defense."

Alarm buzzed in the back of Lou's mind like the drone of faraway bees, but she was focused on Aglaia's complexion, now white. The girl's lips trembled.

" 'To the fairest'?" Aglaia's voice must have risen an octave.

"What's the matter? Are you all right?" Dayna asked Aglaia, then glared at Lou as though she were the offender.

Lou was put off by the hostility aimed at her. She didn't understand Aglaia's distress and only knew she must placate Dayna or the professional situation could become even stickier. She still hoped to gain social status in her supervisor's eyes through their mutual friendship with Aglaia.

Though she opened the envelope Dayna had just brought in, she didn't glance at it yet, instead reasserting her position as Aglaia's mentor when she addressed the girl.

"I must say, it's a good thing after all that I didn't let you meet your boyfriend while you were under my charge in Paris, and that I got you home safe and sound. And as far as what he wrote," she said, with self-control disintegrating as Dayna's squint narrowed, "his recording mythology into the margins of the Bible is an excellent illustration of intertextuality. The Greek apple of discord resonates with themes occurring as well in the tale of Sarah and Hagar quibbling over Abraham's favors, and with themes in 'Sleeping Beauty' or 'Snow White.' " She was spouting whatever came into her mind, and Dayna gawked at her as if critiquing an idiot's lecture for performance assessment.

But now Aglaia's color changed again. She jerked the Bible off the desk and made a growling sound in the back of her throat, but Lou couldn't make herself stop talking: "And don't forget to factor in the archaeologically substantiated facts behind the legend of Troy. Where history and myth intersect, who can tell what's true? And does it matter, anyway?"

"What are you rattling on about?" Dayna asked her. "Can't you see Aglaia's upset?"

"Oh, yes, certainly," Lou said, kowtowing to Dayna. "Sit down, Aglaia. Can I get you some water?" But the girl ran from the office with as much chutzpah as when she'd stormed out of the Louvre, and Dayna was close behind. Lou hated her own wretched voice as she called after her superior, "Won't you reconsider and sit with Aglaia and me at the head table tomorrow night?"

Dayna didn't answer.

But Lou had bigger problems, she saw as she glanced down at the paper in her hand, printed on formal Platte River University letterhead and signed by the dean of the faculty of social sciences.

Dr. Chapman,

Last month our Committee met to discuss your case for promotion with tenure to the rank of associate professor at PRU. The Committee requests additional information as summarized in the attached list of questions. Please submit a written response within

*two weeks, following which the Committee will meet
again to deliberate before your appearance. Should
you have any questions about this request or the
process of promotion and tenure, please contact my
office.*

Lou's stomach constricted; this was not good news. She'd prepared and submitted her tenure package in late spring, confident
that all was in order. But confidence hadn't been enough seven
years ago to secure her tenure at the eastern institution where she
was then teaching. There she'd received just such a letter, to which
she responded with a six-page defense arguing her case. But she
was denied promotion on the grounds of an inadequate research
record, and she left immediately for her new posting here—her last
kick at the can. If she didn't meet with success this time, her name
would be worthless throughout the university system.

Twenty-seven

All the way down the corridor Aglaia's teeth ached from clench-
ing them, and she smoldered in a paroxysm of ire, hardly knowing
where Dayna steered her. Once behind the door labeled "Associate
Dean of Sociology," she let loose.

"To the fairest! To my fairest Aglaia! I can't believe that lying
creep had it planned all along!"

Dayna said, "What has Lou done now?"

"No, not Lou." There was no use shooting the messenger. But
she couldn't answer Dayna more explicitly; she was seething and
had to organize her thoughts. She'd been blindsided by the translation of François's message and the connotations were coming clear
only now. The rancor churning her stomach was not unrelated to
other recent events—Dad's business proposal, the revelation of Sebastian's parentage and François's marriage, her evolving ambiva-
lence regarding the Bible she clutched to her chest right now. Her
hands were full, not just metaphorically but also physically, so that
her bag slipped off her arm and landed upside down on the floor,
spilling its contents from the outside pocket.

"What's this?" Dayna asked, picking up the pendant François
had given Aglaia. She turned it over to examine one side, then the

other. Aglaia glimpsed the stylized circlet design on the front and now saw clearly that it was meant to be an apple all along.

"That's part of the problem." Aglaia gulped for air like a swimmer with a cramp. "And this," she said, waving the postcard at Dayna, who was leaning against the edge of her desk with her ankles crossed. "And this." Aglaia held up the Bible, which might be her biggest problem of all. She chided herself aloud as she paced back and forth, from the window to the potted fig tree to the window.

"He used to call me Mary Grace like everyone else, but then he gave me a new name without my even realizing what was happening. He impregnated my best friend and was working on me—and, stupidly, I wouldn't have stopped him." She strode, unaware of anything else in her vehemence. "And then in Paris, when he told me his convoluted view of women as three types, I was willing to play along and accept his definition of me just because he said Aglaia was the fairest—as though I were one of his make-believe goddesses that would do his bidding for the honor of his approval. Was I just a contestant in some self-absorbed mind game of his?" It should have unsettled her right from the beginning—the implication of a competition, of Aglaia being judged against Thalia and Euphrosyne, of Mary Grace against the other women in François's life. What would Joel have said to that?

"Breathe, Aglaia." Dayna rubbed the pendant between her thumb and forefinger, then handed it over. "Start with this necklace. It's strangely familiar."

Aglaia breathed deeply and blew out slowly. Where should she begin? "An old boyfriend gave this to me while I was in Paris." She couldn't believe she'd let François use the magic of the myths to capture her, like some fly, in the web of his stories—used the Bible, in fact, to do the same to her. "That was years ago. Come to think of it," she said, "you might have met him the summer you stayed in Tiege with your uncle and aunt."

"Don't tell me you got tied up with that exchange student!"

"You do remember him, then?"

"No one forgets François Vivier." Dayna crossed her arms. "He was a regular at my parties and always brought a bag of weed along—high-quality stuff he scored in Amsterdam. He was a bad influence all around. And he came on to me right away."

"Really?" She should have expected that—first Naomi, now Dayna.

"Oh, yeah. In fact, I admit that I was interested when we started making out." She paused. "It doesn't bother you that I talk about him like this?"

Aglaia shook her head. It did bother her, but not in the way it might have a week ago. Her rage against him was cooling to a low, steady burn, and Dayna was only substantiating her suspicions that François sweet-talked his way around girls even back then, comparing them, playing one against the other like some rutting satyr. "Go on, please."

"Well, he couldn't keep his pants on, that boy, and he got pretty pushy—and not just with me, either. At my first party, François—shall we say—found his satisfaction but left me wanting. I wouldn't let him touch me after that, but it's funny," Dayna said, motioning to the jewelry in Aglaia's hand, "he sent me a keychain something like your necklace when he got home."

"Is that so?"

"It was gaudy and cheaper, the charm shaped like an apple. He explained in the accompanying note that he got the idea for the gift from something he read somewhere. The back was inscribed as yours is, with an odd word like 'Euphrates' or something. "

"Euphrosyne?" That took the cake, Aglaia thought. François had a real system going.

"That was it—'To my fairest Euphrosyne.' How did you know?"

"Party girl Dayna, Miss Fertility Naomi, and me," Aglaia muttered, more to herself than in answer to Dayna. "Euphrosyne, Thalia, and Aglaia."

"I tossed the thing—I didn't want payment for services rendered," Dayna said, but immediately put her hand to her mouth. "Oh, I didn't mean to imply that you—"

"No, it's fine," she said, not correcting Dayna's misapprehension that she and François had consummated their feelings, but livid all over again at the man's arrogant presumptuousness. Dayna wasn't a close enough friend yet for her to go into the whole history, and Aglaia wasn't even sure she'd ask Naomi about ever receiving a similar item from François—his symbol of conquest. It would be redundant. She just said, "The guy was a sleaze. Let's leave it at that for now."

"I should run—got to get supper on for the family," Dayna said. But she paused before opening the office door. "I heard Lou mention something about you coming to the gala tomorrow night. I don't have anything against her idea of building bridges between departments, but I think she's going overboard with her amalgamation plans. What's your interest in her hare-brained scheme to integrate social sciences, theater, and the movie industry?"

"I don't know anything about that," Aglaia said, puzzled. This wasn't the first time a movie had been mentioned in conjunction with Lou, but Aglaia had believed the gala was just another generic arts function, the likes of which Lou was fond of taking her to. She understood that Lou had recommended her for the position with the performing arts department, but nothing had been brought up about amalgamation or a movie, either—other than the one Eb had mentioned Incognito was bidding on.

"This shindig will be attended by a bunch of Hollywood types preparing for the filming of a prequel to that *Buffalo Bill* blockbuster that came out last year," Dayna said. "I bet Lou's involvement is another of her attempts at academic brownnosing."

Aglaia, in turn, bet this was the very movie Incognito was chasing for the costuming contract. After all, lots of movies were filmed in Denver, but she thought it unlikely for two big-name companies from Hollywood to be seeking trades in the area at exactly the same time.

"Actually, Lou is introducing me to the head of PRU's theater department tomorrow night," Aglaia said. "I'm expecting to be offered a position as the new wardrobe consultant. Not that sewing costumes for the university's stage productions has anything to do with a Hollywood movie." Or did it?

Dayna chewed her lip and silently regarded Aglaia for a moment, as though trying to guess what Lou had up her sleeve. "I'll give you some advice about that," she said. "I love to work for PRU but I suggest that, in dealing with Lou Chapman, you be very shrewd and intentional about your goals, and don't get embroiled in the political goings-on here. Watch your back. Lou might not be exactly the person she projects. Even I have to take care that my reputation doesn't get sullied through my professional association with her."

As Aglaia made her way to the main exit of the university, she passed the janitor's cart in the hallway, then turned back to it. She dumped the pendant into the deep, bag-lined trash bin, followed by the postcard of the Three Graces, torn into pieces. Now was her chance to dump the Bible once and for all, as well, but on second thought she pushed it back down into her shoulder bag instead. To a dying nomad, even a mirage is better than no hope at all.

Aglaia drove to the supermarket. The produce section was sterile and expansive after the bustling markets of Paris still fresh in her mind. She added items to her cart one by one, palpating a golden peach, sniffing a pineapple, sampling a grape. Maybe occupying her five senses would leave no room for the pain at the back of her brain, she thought, but then she wheeled past a stand of browning bananas and the odor of decay brought thoughts of death.

The past two days had been overwhelming, starting with Naomi's confession yesterday. Aglaia had been hostile to her but now, in light of Lou's translation and the full disclosure of François's character, she had to admit that Naomi's acknowledging and repenting and getting on with life was much healthier than her own approach.

Then there was her parents' unforeseen request at the hospital that she take a more active part in the farming. It didn't altogether displease her; it had been a long time coming and the strings attached to it were pulling at her heart. Her dad admitted the distance between them and took responsibility for more of it than she should allow. Becoming a business partner with them could be a wise investment, better than waiting for the farm, run down and no longer productive, to be handed to her in the will. But the thought of associating herself again with the farm—with them—scared her silly.

Aglaia picked up a vine loaded with field-ripened tomatoes and passed it beneath her nostrils before bagging and setting it into the cart. But they were missing the smell of the sun on the tomatoes in the bucket in her parents' kitchen.

Henry and Tina might expect more time from her than her job allowed. What would her job even be, in the near future? Lou's juggling to get her into PRU gave her the brass ring she'd been waiting for, whatever the woman's ulterior motives for her own advancement might be and despite Dayna's warnings. True, Aglaia would be walking away from a possible promotion and increase in salary at Incognito, and taking the university job might be seen as disloyal to Eb after all the investment he'd made in her apprenticeship over the years. But Eb would understand in the end.

Suddenly she missed him. In fact, she'd go see him tomorrow, before the university reception. But even as Aglaia resolved this, she admitted her own duplicity; if she couldn't come right out and ask for Eb's blessing on pursuing the theater job, she might at least be able to learn details about the movie deal—if it were indeed the same one—and put herself in a more informed position for the evening's event.

Aglaia bagged a handful of green beans, then pinched off a sprig of cilantro to stain her fingers and inhale its perfume. She knocked on a rock melon and hefted it in her hand.

Maybe this was her chance to fully shed the clothes of the farm girl and gain an exalted reputation as a university-employed costumer and lecturer, replete with job security and all the benefits. If she'd failed in her attempt to find true love, at least she could break out of the bonds that imprisoned her in her awkward self-esteem and ensure a future within the hallowed halls of academia.

But by the time Aglaia reached the checkout line, tears unbidden stung in her eyes as though she'd cut up a bowl of onions. By the time her food was loaded into the trunk of her car, tears were rolling down her cheeks, blurring her vision as she drove to her apartment, dripping off her chin while she unpacked her purchases in the kitchen. She didn't know where it came from, this well springing up, this torrent from without, this melting of snows. She folded her laundry and wept without abandon over each article worn in Paris, over the loss of her dreams, over the infidelity of François Vivier. All evening she wiped at her salty tears, her running nose, and then cried herself to sleep wrapped up in the smell of wet goose down.

Friday morning Aglaia lay in bed for a long time after she awoke, studying Botticelli's poster of the Three Graces on her wall, until she threw aside the covers and stood up on her mattress. She loosened the fixative holding the picture, rolled it into a cylinder, and snapped a rubber band around it.

It was time to clean house.

She gathered up all the paraphernalia in her collection—the art book she'd justified in her budget as a business expense, the antique tin decorated with the three ethereal figures, the brass sisters dancing on her dresser. She searched through her apartment for every visible sign, and packed them all away at the back of her top shelf in the hall closet to ponder in the cold light of some other day. They were, in the end, only an illusion conjured up when she first forgot who she really was. They didn't point her to reality.

Aglaia walked through the doors of Incognito and was swarmed by her workmates asking questions about the trip and squealing as she handed out Eiffel Tower fridge magnets. During the commotion, Eb MacAdam lumbered through his office door.

"What are you doing out and about when I told you to catch up on your rest?" he asked, engulfing Aglaia in a bear hug. She squeezed back, maybe for the first time ever. It was just a reflex, she told herself.

"I came to return Moses' staff." She could have waited till Monday, but it was a handy excuse for driving all the way downtown when she might have been pressing her dress and choosing her shoes for tonight. "Besides, I wanted to bring you something from

Paris." The box of *Punitions* cookies was sealed with a foil sticker
bearing the name *Poilâne*. It was the last of her souvenirs to dis-
pense; she'd left an apron printed with cheese wedges on the kitch-
en counter for her mom and a calendar with French agricultural
landscapes for her dad.

"Sit yourself right here and I'll brew something to wash these
biscuits down. I'd love to hear all about the costume delivery, but
let's save that for next week, after you've written up a report for
me." Eb grinned; he knew she hated word processing. "But tell me
how your father's doing."

"I've probably got enough time." She checked his office wall
clock and determined to keep the interaction as neutral as possible, though Eb's cozy confidentiality invited secrets. She filled him
in on the heart attack and the harvest, but the mistiness of his eyes
took her off guard and, though she managed to avoid reference to
more personal problems, she slipped up and mentioned the business offer made by Henry and Tina.

"I can't see myself doing farm work as a weekend habit," she
said to exonerate herself.

"I can," Eb said and then, as though he were quoting directly
from the Bible, "God sets the lonely in families, and only the rebellious live in the sun-scorched land." Was he calling her rebellious?
She began to refute the point but Eb kept talking. "As the wise Solomon said, a father's instruction and a mother's teaching are like a
garland to grace the head and a chain to adorn the neck."

"I'm in my thirties, for Pete's sake!" Aglaia laughed, but the
biblical injunction rubbed her the wrong way. She thought she was
done with garlands and necklaces.

"One never outgrows the great truths of literature, don't you
agree?" Eb had a wily way of weaving her into the tapestry of his
conversation.

"Solomon lived back where myth and history intersected," she
said, reiterating Lou's last comment to her though she hardly remembered hearing it. "Who can tell whether the writer's words are
true or not, and does it matter anyway?"

Aglaia spoke in an off-hand way but she knew it mattered, so she didn't let Eb say anything when she saw his wisdom gathering in a crease between his bushy, silvered brows. Instead, she stood up, ready with an excuse to dodge more of his words that might hit home.

"I've got to go," she said. "I need to pick up a couple of things at the drugstore and have enough time to wash and style my hair for tonight." Maybe she'd pin it up in loose curls, since Dayna had clued her in that the formal function would be attended by Hollywood dignitaries. It was a once-in-a-blue-moon chance to capitalize on Lou's connections and convince Platte River University about her suitability. She finished explaining to Eb, "I've been asked to some swanky university dinner tonight and I'm pulling out all the stops."

Eb's teacup clattered onto his saucer. "Do you mean the black-tie affair over at the Oxford?"

Her assumption had been right then. "I take it that the mysterious deal you've been working on so hard is for the same film after all, Eb—the *Buffalo Bill* prequel? It just dawned on me recently that there was a correlation between our project and the gala tonight."

Eb looked shaken. "I suppose I should have told you a wee bit more detail regarding the contract we've been courting, but I didn't want to break your concentration on the Paris assignment," he said. "In fact, I had a surprise visit from the Hollywood film company this week."

Aglaia sat down again. Anything Eb could tell her might help her chances tonight with Oliver Upton—possibly her future boss. She suffered a pang of remorse over her intention to fleece Eb for information to her own advantage. He'd never hold her back from professional growth, but he'd also never condone any underhandedness. And she was being underhanded. However, Aglaia was increasingly convinced that PRU could give her what she needed, and this was the way the world operated, after all.

Eb asked, "How did you as an Incognito employee wrangle an invitation to the university affair? I hear it's a tightly closed event." Aglaia read between the lines: He disapproved and wouldn't have gone himself, even if begged.

"A friend asked me to escort her ages ago. I thought it was just another run-of-the-mill arts mixer, but now it appears as though I'll be in enemy territory tonight." She framed her next words craftily. "Would you rather I not attend?" Aglaia held her breath over her bluff, not meeting Eb's eyes but picking at the stitching on her purse handle. To her relief, he answered in the negative.

"No, by all means go. After all, it's not as though Incognito were the one currying the favor of the studio. You understand that PRU is shamelessly trying to get the costuming account, don't you?"

"Oh, I hadn't realized..." Aglaia let her voice falter despite the guilt she felt over her deceit.

"In fact," he said, selecting a folder from his filing drawer, "you should be armed before entering their camp." He held out the thick report labeled *RoundUp Bid Tender*. "You may as well have a look at it now. I think you'll be as excited as I am about the project possibilities."

Aglaia couldn't believe her luck, Eb handing her the sensitive data like this. She paged through the file, noting the scale of the job and the challenge it would present for Incognito—or whoever would win the contract bid. She was sincere in her approving comments about Eb's marketing skills: his selection of costume sketches from her own portfolio, his division of labor that depended heavily on her input as head designer, the record of Incognito's past successes—many of them her own creations.

That's when she spotted what she hadn't allowed herself to admit she was looking for—the bottom-line figure Eb had submitted for the bid to win the *Buffalo Bill* wardrobing contract. She almost gasped. Little wonder the university wanted this account and that Lou was meddling in it!

At that moment the penny dropped for Aglaia. As clear as day, she understood that Lou was using her and that, if her services were procured as the consultant for Oliver Upton's arts department, Eb would be left handicapped, without a chance at winning the movie contract, which—as Eb's tender proposal made clear—rested greatly upon her own skills. Aglaia would then be working for the competitor on the most lucrative deal Incognito Denver had ever had a shot at. She stood at a fork in her road, knowing she faced a decision of much greater magnitude than whatever job she'd have in a week from now. She stood at a moral crossroads, cursed without a compass if she continued to reject the guidance of morality offered by the biblical convictions of her forebears.

Twenty-eight

"**A**re you ill, Aglaia?" Eb, waiting to refile the folder, had seen the lass's eyes widen and the color leave her cheeks. She shook her head, but she'd seemed edgy since entering his office half an hour ago and, for all her pother about getting home to change for the evening, she didn't look as though she'd be going anywhere just yet. He topped up her china teacup and poked it towards her. "Take a sip."

It was good to have Aglaia back safe and sound. There was always some danger in travel these days, and he didn't know what the business would do if it lost her. But of course travel wasn't the most likely way to lose Aglaia. He wasn't blind; he was aware of the risk that his training and her proficiency could result in her defection to another company. Perhaps that was even the reason for her attendance at the festivities this evening; perhaps she was trolling for a new job. He'd known it before he handed her the classified RoundUp file, but true freedom of will was predicated upon knowledge of one's options, Eb believed, and at the end of the day he had confidence in Aglaia's ethics and discretion. If he couldn't trust her with sensitive information, then he'd misjudged her as management material for Incognito.

But the poor thing looked miserable at the moment, so Eb took Aglaia's hand in his own. She didn't pull it away as at other times he'd chanced such an unprofessional, fatherly touch.

"What's troubling you, lass?"

She bit her bottom lip, she shifted in her chair. "I'm petrified," she finally blurted.

"I suspected as much. Your eyes are stormy." He waited; there was more, he was sure.

"I've been reading the Bible," she said with effort, as though admitting to pornography. Eb was gratified to hear it; the Bible seemed to be the last book most people picked up these days.

"Ah. That would do it."

"What are you saying? The Bible is supposed to bring comfort, first of all."

"Where did you get that daft idea?"

"I used to be comforted when I read it long ago," she said, and he knew then that the inscrutable Aglaia had a past of faith, after all. "But all the comfort dried up," Aglaia said. "The words keep haunting me but they mean nothing, as though I'm reading Greek."

"Perhaps it's just seemed that way to you for a period—your soul's dark night." Eb had discovered that when one lost faith in the literature, one lost faith in the writer—no matter the book. "You feel as though God has let you down?"

Eb moved the tissue box a bit closer to Aglaia, just in case. She sniffled but didn't respond. "The Bible's not some fabrication like this," he said, pointing to *Alice's Adventures in Wonderland*, "or this." He nudged the copy of *Theogony* still sitting where Aglaia had put it down before her trip to Paris. "In these the reader is invited to gain immortality through the nectar of the gods, or be saved from a crisis by emptying a glass fortuitously labeled 'Drink me.' But I've found the Bible is no quick fix for the psyche, nor is it some vague commentary about the inclination we all have towards the supernatural."

"It sure isn't a quick fix. I'd just as soon read either of those," she said bitterly, pointing to the books Eb indicated, "as trust in something that promises hope and doesn't deliver." Eb discerned a wailing in her heart, like a little girl missing home, and breathed unspoken words to God: *Lord, hear her prayer!*

Aglaia pulled a tissue. "I don't know why I'm crying," she apologized. Eb had never seen her weep. He patted her hand again.

"I've always said a few tears are cleansing, lass. We were born from the waters of our mother's womb, after all—a river meant from eternity to sweep us into the glassy sea, into the presence of the Lord. Longing for heaven but made of the earth, we all climb out onto dry land to save ourselves and end up wandering in circles in the desert, noses to the ground, lost in the middle until the voice of the Living Waters calls us on."

Aglaia had a mushy clump of tissues in her hand, and Eb lifted his trash basket from behind the desk for her convenience.

"If you love the Bible so much, why surround yourself with all these other books? How do you know they're not just as real, just as true, as *that*?" Aglaia pointed her chin towards Eb's hand resting now on the large-print, illustrated version of the Bible he kept at work for when he needed a little pick-me-up.

"You keep reading your Bible and you'll know the difference," Eb said. His words weren't the ones that would confirm truth to her heart—it would take the Scripture itself to convince her, he knew. "A wiser man than I once said that the Bible fulfills all the longings aroused by fairy tales passed down through the ages and tells us what they really mean. Look into the Word and it will look right back at you; it will see you and change you. It's a living text. You can read every other book in the world, lass, but the Bible is the only book that reads you."

The uniformed doorman at the hotel directed Aglaia through the Victorian lobby to the Sage Room. She entered to the strains of a Latin soul band and the flux of the elegant masses milling between tables set with linen and silver—definitely not in the cowboy theme one might expect for celebrating a western movie, she thought. The chandeliers hanging from the high ceiling cast a glow that bounced off sparkling earrings and sequined gowns. Her own little black dress wasn't floor length, and the retro Japanese buttons scavenged at a garage sale—a few of which she'd worked into a simple bracelet—weren't even cut glass. Perhaps her style might pass as "understated," but she already felt out of place.

"There you are." Lou moved away from her surrounding group and greeted Aglaia by kissing the air near her ears, French style. She was wearing the flamboyant magenta designer dress purchased in Paris. "Come and meet my associates."

They were turning heads, she and Lou. Someone placed a flute of champagne in her hand and Lou led her regally into the throng by the elbow, introducing her as a chef might present his *pièce de résistance*, alternatively as one of America's top costume designers and as a world traveler just returned from an international business trip to meet leading curators in Paris. Aglaia didn't know how to put the lid on Lou's exaggeration, and her sputtered disavowals withered beneath their praise—praise Lou seemed to take as complimentary to herself, the way she puffed up and beamed. She once even said, "She's sitting with me up front tonight. Perhaps she'll have a word to say to us all then."

A word to say? Aglaia hoped Lou was kidding. She gulped at the thought of speaking publicly and eyed the head table set on a dais above the multitude. But she'd better get used to the limelight if she intended to work in this circle. *Since* she intended to work in this circle, she corrected herself. Her decision to go for the PRU position was all but sealed, and if it took dropping the sum of Incognito's bid into the right ear, she might be willing to do even that. The realization of her own avarice threatened to sadden her.

Throughout the cocktail hour Lou and Aglaia flitted from one cluster to another, here meeting a colleague from the sociology department, there a scriptwriter. The words came more easily to Aglaia with each introduction, the flattery of being recognized grew more pleasant. It was good that Eb wasn't present tonight because his down-to-earth honesty would be embarrassed for her, especially after their talk this afternoon that she was trying to banish from her mind.

"You're perfect arts world material," Lou said *sotto voce* as the university's president raised a glass in their direction over coiffed and dandied heads. Aglaia was at last succeeding at her long-held desire to rub the bumpkin off herself. Lou disappeared to consult with hotel management, leaving Aglaia to stand solitary in the crush. Behind her two women gossiped, speculating on who was who.

"Is that Brad Pitt over there by the *hors d'oeuvres* table? There's a rumor he owns a home in the area."

"I don't think so—get a load of the ugly escort. Speaking of which, did you see Chapman's new girl? She's a pretty decoration, but not Lou's usual sort."

Jolted, Aglaia listened more closely.

"I heard she's grooming a new *protégé*. But what's Lou doing here anyway? I thought this dinner was an arts event."

"I heard about an alliance between arts and sociology, something to do with this movie—it's been kept very hush-hush."

"Well, she sure loves to show off. Take a gander at that gown! I suppose she thinks she can get away with it because she's from New York."

Their voices faded as they moved away, but Aglaia continued to eavesdrop wherever possible. She sidled up to a rookery of scholarly types who were arguing the shortcomings of blind peer review. Boring, she thought as she moved towards the champagne fountain, a hot spot in the room, and listened in as a tall fellow in Armani raved with a couple of associates in a Californian accent about some designer's portfolio. Just then, Lou caught up to her with a stout, bearded man in tow.

"Aglaia Klassen, I'd like you to meet Dr. Oliver Upton, head of the university theater department," Lou said. Aglaia's belly jumped with nervousness. This was the man responsible for hiring the new wardrobe consultant!

"Pleased to meet you, Dr. Upton," Aglaia said.

"Call me Oliver." He pumped her hand. "So you're the genius Lou's been bragging about. I've kept an eye out for your work ever since she recommended you to me. You're a busy gal."

Aglaia made a polite objection but Lou broke in. "You'll soon learn that creativity is greatly admired in this crowd, Aglaia. Get used to it."

"Talent like yours shouldn't be wasted in the private sector," Oliver said. "The university has funding to encourage *real* arts development." He laughed heartily, but it sounded fake to Aglaia.

"Excuse me for interrupting," the Armani-clad stranger broke in. "I couldn't help overhearing. I don't think we've met formally yet." He introduced himself as Jerry from RoundUp Studios, along with his coworkers, then turned to Aglaia and began conversationally, "I hear you're the city's up-and-comer for costume design." Aglaia read something more beneath his off-hand manner, and both Lou and Oliver were listening intently. "I understood you worked for a private firm, not the university."

"Well, at the moment I do." How had he known her employment history?

"I met your boss earlier this week," Jerry said, reading her mind. He was likely curious about why she was at the university function—the competitor's territory—to begin with, but he didn't ask. Aglaia's face heated up; it looked bad for Incognito that she was here and, besides, Eb's words from earlier today still echoed in her mind as though he were standing next to her.

"Her *current* boss," Oliver interjected in the discussion. "We hope to remedy that soon—don't we, Lou?" A knowing glance passed between the two.

"On that note, Oliver, why don't you and Aglaia find a quiet spot somewhere while I squire these gentlemen around?" Lou asked. She took Jerry by the arm.

"Yes, let's move out into the lobby and have a chat about the advantages of working for Platte River University," Oliver suggested. Aglaia saw him hand Lou a royal blue cloth folder, nodding meaningfully at it, as though Lou should take care of the item for him.

During the next few minutes, as Aglaia stood by a marble column, Oliver Upton pitched the consulting position to her, outlining the salary scale and the benefits she might expect to receive if she accepted his offer.

His tone indicated he expected her to accept. When he alluded to the possibility that she might have information from Incognito useful to PRU, Aglaia didn't contradict him though she didn't tell him yet the figure she'd read in Eb's office, either. He smiled smugly as though they had a deal, then, and Aglaia felt powerful and very desired.

"We'd be delighted to have you join our team, Aglaia. Submit your *resumé* directly to my office—don't go through human resources, now—and we'll set up an interview for early next week. Just a formality," Oliver said as they re-entered the ballroom. He gave the thumbs-up to Lou, who rejoined Aglaia now.

"You made an excellent impression," Lou said.

"How can Oliver tell anything about me with that short an interview? I hardly said anything."

"He values my referral of you, and he made the job offer, didn't he? Besides, I meant you impressed the movie VIPs, too." Then, almost inaudible as though speaking to herself, Lou added, "This is going better than planned." She checked her Gucci watch and frowned over towards the entrance as though awaiting someone who was late.

Lou went back to working the crowd until the band wound down and she took the mike to direct everyone to their seats. Food service began and white-gloved wait staff poured wine—though Aglaia declined, placing her hand over the mouth of the glass. A scattered young woman joined her and Lou at the head table wearing a strapless sundress made of cheap stretch polyester.

"Dr. Chapman! Sorry I'm so late, but I couldn't find a parking spot."

"And the dog ate your homework, I suppose," Lou said in a voice she also used on Aglaia sometimes. "Whitney, meet Aglaia."

"Are you one of her students, too?" she asked Aglaia, but she didn't pause for an answer before leaning forward to talk around her to Lou. "I'm so excited to be at the head table with you, Dr. Chapman. It's cool that you think I'm, like, worthy. Do I look okay?"

"Why not drape yourself in my pashmina? That's better," Lou

said as she reached across Aglaia and hid some of Whitney's overly exposed cleavage. Then, handing her a napkin, she added, "And maybe blot down some of that lipstick?"

Lou's insolent re-dressing of the newly arrived dinner guest annoyed Aglaia, stuck between them as she was. In addition to that, she thought she was to be Lou's sole companion this evening.

Apparently Whitney didn't get that the point of dialogue was for two people to take turns speaking to each other, because she didn't pause in her exuberant rambling aimed exclusively at Aglaia now that Lou was taking the microphone.

"Isn't this cool? I mean, all the glitz and everything? Somebody said Brad Pitt was supposed to be here, but I can't see him. When are you graduating? I'm out next spring with a double major, sociology and creative writing. In fact, I'm researching a special paper for Dr. Chapman right now. She's, like, *amazing*!"

Her prattle was slowed only by Lou's opening words of welcome to various representatives from the city council, the university, and two arts funding bodies, as well as members of the L.A. film studio and local affiliates, RoundUp's development team, and potential investors. She introduced the head table but Aglaia, alluded to as a "sensational emerging artist," didn't see how she fit in. Even Whitney had a better excuse; Lou said she represented her absent grandfather, the chancellor of PRU. Aglaia spotted Dayna Yates at a back table and nodded at her friendly wave, relieved to see someone familiar in the crowd.

The appetizer was served: *fois gras terrine* with wild cherry preserves, cashew butter, and toasted crostinis. The band provided background music, but Whitney kept up her chatter throughout the dinner, hacking big chunks off the rare beef served with a port-wine-and-chocolate reduction, and stuffing asparagus into her mouth without, Aglaia was sure, even appreciating the flavor of the Hollandaise. Aglaia was picking at her cream-filled *éclair* when Lou stood in front of the mike again, putting a merciful end to Whitney's babbling.

Lou made a joke about academics—"We all know God never received tenure at any university because He had only one major publication"—and another about actors. Both were received with genteel laughter, so she went on to flatter the crowd and punctuate her speech with several other discriminatory pokes. It wasn't dignified, Aglaia thought.

The body of Lou's talk focused on the role Denver had played in RoundUp's original filming of *The Life and Times of Buffalo Bill* and described the studio's production-in-progress, *Buffalo Bill's Birthday.* She gave a short biography of main character William F. Cody—Pony Express rider, buffalo hunter, and army scout who first came to Colorado for the gold rush and who now lay buried on Lookout Mountain with a fine view of the Rockies and the Great Plains, making Denver an ideal filming location. Expressing regrets for boring any aficionados, she briefly explained the process of generating a movie and said that the script for the prequel was already drafted, the production office had been established in the city, and the cast, crew, and trades were being "rounded up." The location manager, she reminded her audience, was present at the dinner and was scouting the lay of the land for outdoor and out-of-studio sequences—hadn't one scene in the first movie been filmed in the very parlor they were occupying now?—and Lou suggested that perhaps he'd consider a few shots on the campus of PRU. Whitney preened at this, as though she were devising a walk-on role for herself.

At the close of her talk, Lou begged pardon that her final announcement might be of little interest to the filming company— here she glanced over at Jerry and his team as if they'd dispute her statement—but it was of special interest to the educators gathered tonight. Aglaia noticed Lou picking up the royal blue cloth folder before she asked Dr. Oliver Upton to join her at the rostrum.

"This evening, on behalf of Platte River University," Lou said, "we'd like to bestow a special tribute upon a female member of our community who has already made a significant impact on the artistic and sociological climate of our city. We anticipate more of the same."

Lou glanced to her left and Whitney giggled. "Does she mean *me*? I won a poetry contest last week." Aglaia almost shushed the student, but held her tongue. She felt a quaking uneasiness as Oliver took a turn at the mike.

"As head of the theater department and familiar with Denver's wider performing arts scene, I concur with my esteemed sociology colleague's choice of candidates." Aglaia saw his lowered lashes flicker towards her. "I was able to speed up the nomination process, persuading the committee to grant exemption from the statutory requirements, and learned only today of the university's formal approval to present this award, the honorary Master of Fine Arts degree."

Aglaia's skin tingled.

"Our successful nominee," Lou said, "has had her work displayed in theater and film and even in a museum in Paris, France! You may have seen one of her costumes on our own mayor's wife at the last New Year's Eve masquerade ball. And so"—Lou motioned towards Aglaia to arise—"for her outstanding contribution to costuming on the national and international stage, please salute Aglaia Klassen as the latest PRU graduate!" The crowd applauded and a camera flash blinded Aglaia as she stood up in confusion.

Oliver now asked into the mike, "Sorry for the short notice, Aglaia, but perhaps you have a few words to say?" Since she was already on her feet, Aglaia had no choice but to step over to the podium where Lou beckoned her with the certificate of her honorary MFA degree.

Aglaia Klassen, a fine arts graduate? She stared down in disbelief at the diploma folder open in her hands and tried to think fast about what to say to the expectant audience, all waiting for a word.

Just then a commotion interrupted her. The eyes of everyone turned to the door, where an official was attempting to deny access to some agitated newcomers. An ashen-faced man wearing a tattered plaid jacket was leaning on the arm of an elderly woman, who fairly shouted in her guttural accent tinged with panic, "We need to talk to Mary Grace for a minute, that's all!"

Appalled silence filled the room and Aglaia's wanted to slither beneath the platform. But now all of them—including Henry and Tina Klassen—were staring at her, waiting for her to speak.

The tension was broken instead by Lou's facile tongue. "I know you Hollywood film types stick together, but I didn't expect you'd bring the Beverly Hillbillies!" The room erupted in relieved laughter. Lou winked at Aglaia and tilted her head towards her chair. She hissed with her lips hardly moving, "If you have nothing to say, at least sit back down!" But that would mean letting her parents suffer the humiliation alone, and Aglaia's indecision froze her to the spot like a tongue-tied preacher in a pulpit. The moment was drawn out, the laughter died down, and Lou was beginning to scowl at her standing there.

The lull became sepulchral.

Then Aglaia set down the diploma she held in her hands, stepped away from her place of honor at the podium, and descended to the floor, walking all the way across the Sage Room as Lou mumbled back into speech to cover Aglaia's social blunder.

Aglaia lifted her dad's bulk off the slight frame of her mom and linked arms with them both. Dayna Yates, sitting by the exit, arose and opened the door for the family, following them out to the lobby.

Twenty-nine

That idiotic girl! Lou was furious as she scrambled to redeem the desperate situation Aglaia placed her in by walking out, even leaving behind her diploma. What would the studio representatives think of the goings-on? Aglaia's inexplicable indiscretion towards the homeless couple—or had that been her mother, Tina, whom she'd met in Aglaia's apartment?—surely snuffed out any chances Lou still had at tenure, judging by the scornful glare Dayna Yates leveled at her upon exiting. That was twice in two days Yates literally and physically turned her back to chase after Aglaia.

Lou told the audience another canned joke she had on hand for awkward moments, and invited them to continue mingling at the close of the evening. But she could see that Oliver was apoplectic despite his polite words of farewell at the microphone.

Lou would suffer his vituperation as soon as they were alone, and she wished she'd never arranged for him to consider Aglaia for the position of theater wardrobe consultant in the first place. She'd perceived Aglaia's lack of malleability in Paris, but Lou's earlier boasting of the girl's stellar reputation had already convinced Oliver of her worth, and he just had to have her. His resulting praise for Lou's commendable introduction of Aglaia into the university

arts world would bring shame on his head now—and, consequent-
ly, on Lou's. If he did hire Aglaia, Lou would get no credit. She
prayed that any damage from the girl's gauche deportment could
somehow be alleviated or Lou might find herself without a job at
all.

She caught Whitney's arm as the student was leaving in her
hideous outfit. She just didn't shine up like Aglaia, but one took
what one got, Lou supposed.

"Oh, Dr. Chapman, that was a fabulous evening! You're so
good at public speaking." The girl was a moron, but Lou pasted a
smile on her face.

"Don't rush off," she said. "Maybe after our guests leave you'd
like to have a drink with me in the lounge?"

Whitney was the chancellor's granddaughter, after all.

Aglaia turned into the parking lot of her apartment block. "No,
Mom, it was good that you came to find me at the hotel," Aglaia
said, meaning it. "But I can't believe the hospital let you check
yourself out like that, Dad. You're not strong. Why didn't you at
least call me instead of taking a cab?" It was a rhetorical question;
her cell was shut off during the banquet anyway.

Aglaia's choice tonight to stand beside her parents in their
neediness had been a defining moment for her. She appreciated
Dayna's support—her friend had waited with Henry and Tina in
the lobby while Aglaia fetched her car—but the mechanics of getting her parents back to the apartment and even the bolstering
Dayna offered were only secondary in importance to the internal
change that took place when she saw sick old Dad leaning on frail
little Mom in the presence of all those eminent movers and shak-
ers.

Something broke in her then, she thought—or maybe mended
in her.

The thrill of holding the MFA diploma in her hands lasted
about as long as the heartbeat it took for her to recognize that she

hadn't earned it. It was worth only the paper it was printed on. Someday she'd get a professional degree the honorable way and complete her schooling, knowing now that it didn't complete her.

The drive home to Aglaia's apartment had been quick, Tina talking all the way to her place about how *nietlijch* Aglaia was dressed and how *sheen* the hotel was. Henry tried to coerce her into driving him back to the farm right away, but she put her foot down and called Byron, and they arranged to meet halfway in the morning. Dad was in no shape to travel farther tonight.

Aglaia made up the couch for herself. After her parents were quiet in the bedroom, sleep still eluded her. She got up and heated some milk, wincing when the microwave timer went off. As she feared, it awakened Tina, who padded out to the kitchen with her hair straggling around her shoulders.

"Making cocoa? I'll have *en Bätje* too."

The coziness of sipping hot chocolate at bedtime with her mom reminded Aglaia of all she'd left behind. How could she even begin to tell the truth to her mother, who'd suffered so much in this life because of her children? How could Aglaia start to explain the sorrow in her own life—the loss of face tonight, the bereavement over a brother in childhood and over François just days ago, even her own repeated rejections of Naomi's friendship? But she had to start somewhere.

She followed her mom back into the bedroom and sat down on the mattress so that her father opened his eyes.

"Dad, I'm sorry." Her tears started up again. "I've been so angry at you for so long. At you and at Joel."

He nodded as if he knew what she was talking about.

"It was my fault," he said, pushing up into a sitting position. "I should have taught him better to always leave the tractor in park and not in gear when he boosted the battery. I should have made sure he knew not to stand where the tractor could run over him."

"But if Joel had gotten more sleep, if he hadn't had to, you know, drive so late in the night on my account..."

Tina looked befuddled. "Joel was driving late the night before he died?"

Mom never did get it about François, Aglaia thought, and it was just as well. But Dad understood, and he drew her into his wonderful fatherly arms and he hugged her and rocked her. "We have a lot to catch up on, Mary Grace."

When her parents were settled again and the mugs were rinsed, Aglaia made another decision. Despite her implicit agreement at the gala tonight that she'd submit her *resumé* and set up an interview, she changed her mind. She booted up her computer and typed in the e-mail address from Oliver Upton's business card, followed by a terse message:

> *Oliver, thank you for your tribute tonight. However, I hereupon withdraw my name from consideration for the position of theater wardrobe consultant in your department. My loyalty lies with my current boss and my real calling.*

On a Saturday afternoon several weeks later, Aglaia stood in front of the farmhouse stove, transferring a batch of *Rollküake* from the pot of hot fat to an antique platter. Kneading up a bowlful of the rich dough from Great-Grandma's recipe all the way from southern Russia had been Aglaia's idea, the craving strong. Tina stood beside her dusting the crullers with powdered sugar, and Henry sat at the table munching celery.

"You have chokecherry syrup, right?" she asked Mom, since the usual accompaniment of watermelon was out of season.

"*Na jo*," Tina affirmed, taking a jar out of the fridge. "I always have *Soppsel* for dipping, dear." She spooned a taste into her daughter's open mouth.

Today marked Aglaia's third visit from the city since the night of the university dinner. This morning she'd helped Dad inspect the combine parked in the shop for the winter, Henry instructing her on loose bearings and cracks in the belts.

He asked her now, "So when are you going to tell us about this

movie you're making costumes for?" Aglaia almost dropped her
ladle.

"How did you know about that?" She herself had just learned
last week about RoundUp's awarding the contract to Incognito,
and she hadn't told her parents about it yet, sensitive to their bias
against the cinema. "And since when have you been interested in
movies or in costumes?"

He grinned at her. "I've been reading the weekend arts section
of the *Denver Post* for years, watching for your name."

He hadn't been the only one congratulating her. Dayna tele-
phoned the day after Incognito's win was publicized and mentioned by-the-by that she was holding Aglaia's diploma at her
university office, rescued from Lou's maniacal plan to have it re-
scinded. Aglaia picked it up, more to see her new friend than for
the item itself, and stored the royal blue folder on the top shelf of
her bedroom closet along with other deferred memories.

Lou's office had been cleared out by then, Aglaia saw when she
passed its door, and the buzz around campus was that she'd been
let go a day or two after she found out her aged mother died in New
York. Dayna didn't offer particulars about her associate's dismissal
other than mentioning how, out of revenge, Lou took a young arts
student with her to the funeral and that her grandfather, Chancellor Wadsworth, was fuming over the impropriety.

Of course, Aglaia had heard directly from Lou herself sometime after the formal affair but before Incognito's status as bid win-
ner became public. Lou had called her at work.

"Oliver just let me know he's found a new wardrobe consultant," Lou said, her voice full of wrath. "What about our agreement?"

"I guess you could say I rejected the terms."

"Oh my God, what were you thinking?" Lou demanded.

Oh my, what was I thinking, God? she asked silently. *Where has
my head been all this time?* She said aloud to Lou, "It's not a good
time for me to talk right now." Or ever, she thought.

"So that's your *modus operandi*. You suck up to a prominent
person to bask in her glory and then run when the heat's turned

up." Lou's voice rasped. "Well, you've missed your chance, Aglaia. If I can help it, there won't ever be employment for you at the university—or for Incognito as a subcontractor, either—once PRU wins the tender for *Buffalo Bill's Birthday*."

The threat didn't faze Aglaia and she answered as graciously as she could, "I don't believe the boss will mind. He's received encouraging news on that front."

Before Lou slammed the receiver in Aglaia's ear, she shouted, "You've burned your bridges behind you, girl. That was your first big mistake!"

No, Aglaia thought now in her parent's kitchen, her first big mistake had been entering her name incorrectly at the vital statistics office all those years ago.

The Enns family arrived en masse, stamping the first snow of the season off their boots and crowding into the kitchen. Henry and Tina didn't have enough chairs, but kids doubled up on adult laps and the older boys—typical teens—hoisted themselves onto the countertop, one of them holding a very fat Zephyr who now made his home on the farm.

Aglaia still couldn't get over how much Silas looked like his shirt-tail relative, Joel, and how closely Sebastian resembled his birth father, François.

Aglaia was able to think about François without a visceral reaction, now that she understood she'd only been in love by proxy anyway. She'd used François Vivier as much as he'd used her, with a second-hand love having the wrong object in view, and ended up twisting her view of herself.

Across the room, Naomi beamed at Aglaia as she bounced her baby on her knee. Their first conversation after discussing François's true identity had been difficult for Aglaia as she asked forgiveness from someone who, she felt, had wronged her in the first place. Aglaia called her own wrongdoing "naïveté," but Naomi wouldn't let her get away with that. "Nobody's innocent," Naomi had said, and the truth cut deep.

Aglaia turned off the stove element and took her place at the table. Tina's kitchen was a vortex of all that Aglaia had once known and knew at this moment and would know in the future. Her brittle loneliness was being assuaged.

And as if her pleasure was to be without limits, she heard her cell phone ring. It was Eb.

"Sounds as though you're in the middle of a party, lass," he said. "Here's something else to celebrate—put me on speakerphone." He announced that, as reward for the U.S. branch's performance of late, Incognito headquarters had promoted Aglaia to managerial status as the new creative director, coordinating and executing all Denver projects and having artistic veto over anything leaving the workshop. "They've taken my advice to streamline," Eb said. "I'll stay beside you as a part-time consultant until my full retirement. And in the meanwhile, I'm taking Iona to Hawaii for Christmas."

"I propose a toast," Byron said when Aglaia hung up. He lifted his coffee cup; Naomi and the kids followed suit with their glasses of juice, and Tina and Henry *could* have been drinking wine, they were so jovial. "To Mary Grace, traveler to Paris and beyond!" Everyone cheered and she raised her mug to them—the cup of communion—and slaked her own thirst.

"Speaking of Paris," her mother said to her, "did you ever deliver that Bible?"

It was the question Aglaia dreaded from the moment she took on the challenge from her mother over a month ago, the question that marked the end of her roving down dusty, dark paths of daydreams.

The dry old bones of lost love and death were finally being put to rest. Now every morning, in the pool of light cast by her bedside lamp, like a parched wayfarer coming home to the well, Aglaia opened that Bible and soaked in its message.

Just yesterday she'd taped up the torn pages, carefully lining up the edges as she hummed in practice for her upcoming duet with Naomi: *He hideth my soul in the cleft of the rock, where rivers of pleasure I see.*

She'd clipped out and thrown away the message Lou had so imperiously penned: *SEE ME. LOU.* The three words had served their purpose; she'd seen Lou, all right—seen her for what she really was. And then Aglaia had kneaded her art eraser, warming up the grey putty and shaping it into a pointed tip so that she could lift all the penciled words off the paper and take François out of the book, leaving only the indelible ink behind.

"Deliver the Bible?" she asked. "No, Mom—at least not to François."

About the Author

Deb Elkink lived the life of a cattle-rancher's wife in the Great Sand Hills of Saskatchewan, Canada, before she began writing novel-length fiction. She cooked for branding crews of a hundred, earned her private pilot's license, helped round up a thousand-head cattle herd, homeschooled three children through the ninth grade, and professionally sewed theatrical costumes (not unlike the heroine of *The Third Grace*).

This was a surprising transition for a woman raised in cosmo-politan Winnipeg, Manitoba—someone who had earned a B.A. in communications from Bethel University (in St. Paul, Minnesota).

Today, her three kids grown, Deb lives with her husband, Gerrit, on the banks of a creek in the rolling hills of southern Alberta near the city of Medicine Hat, a stone's throw from the Montana border. The Elkinks offer hospitality to a great assortment of wildlife and one, lone, eighteen-year-old Texas Longhorn steer.

Deb also holds an M.A. in historical theology from Briercrest Seminary (Saskatchewan). She loves to travel and, so far, has visited five continents. Deb says, "My smattering of foreign phrases delivered with gusto has offended the ears of Japanese, French, and Spanish alike."

The Third Grace is her first novel.

Visit Deb's website: *www.debelkink.com*

CPSIA information can be obtained at www.ICGtesting.com
Printed in the USA
BVOW08s0636300913

332411BV00002B/4/P